A SIME~GEN® NOVEL

A SHIFT OF MEANS

CLEAR SPRINGS CHRONICLES #2

THE SIME~GEN® SERIES

1. *House of Zeor*, by Jacqueline Lichtenberg
2. *Unto Zeor, Forever*, by Jacqueline Lichtenberg
3. *First Channel*, by Jean Lorrah and Jacqueline Lichtenberg
4. *Mahogany Trinrose*, by Jacqueline Lichtenberg
5. *Channel's Destiny*, by Jean Lorrah and Jacqueline Lichtenberg
6. *RenSime*, by Jacqueline Lichtenberg
7. *Ambrov Keon*, by Jean Lorrah
8. *Zelerod's Doom*, by Jacqueline Lichtenberg and Jean Lorrah
9. *Personal Recognizance*, by Jacqueline Lichtenberg
10. *The Story Untold and Other Stories*, by Jean Lorrah
11. *To Kiss or to Kill*, by Jean Lorrah
12. *The Farris Channel*, by Jacqueline Lichtenberg
13. *Fear And Courage: Fourteen Writers Explore Sime~Gen*, edited by Zoe Farris and Karen L. MacLeod
14. *A Change of Tactics*, by Mary Lou Mendum, Jacqueline Lichtenberg, and Jean Lorrah

OTHER BOOKS BY JACQUELINE LICHTENBERG

Molt Brother
City of a Million Legends
Science Is Magic Spelled Backwards and Other Stories: Jacqueline Lichtenberg Collected Book One
Through The Moon Gate and Other Stories of Vampirism: Jacqueline Lichtenberg Collected Book Two

OTHER BOOKS BY JEAN LORRAH

Jean Lorrah Collected
Savage Empire
Dragon Lord of the Savage Empire
Captives of the Savage Empire

BOOKS BY JEAN LORRAH & LOIS WICKSTROM

Nessie and the Living Stone
Nessie and the Viking Gold
Nessie and the Celtic Maze

Order of the Virgin Mothers and Other Plays

A SIME~GEN® NOVEL

A SHIFT OF MEANS

CLEAR SPRINGS CHRONICLES #2

MARY LOU MENDUM,
JACQUELINE LICHTENBERG,
AND JEAN LORRAH

WILDSIDE PRESS

CONTENTS

DEDICATIONS

MARY LOU MENDUM

My work on this novel is dedicated to the people who taught me to write: Phyllis Cates, who taught me not to be afraid of a blank page; Jacqueline Lichtenberg, who taught me how to work through a plot; and Judith McKibbon, who taught me how to edit.

JACQUELINE LICHTENBERG

I want to dedicate my work on the Clear Springs Chronicles to Karen MacLeod and Zoe Farris, and all the friends and supporters of the Sime~Gen universe stories.

JEAN LORRAH

All my work in the Sime~Gen universe is of course dedicated to Jacqueline Lichtenberg, whose imagination produced the original concept. I will be forever grateful for being allowed to help the universe grow.

ACKNOWLEDGEMENTS

I want to thank Karen MacLeod for copyediting, and everyone who has been so patient with us as we work through the details blending these characters into the main historical line of Sime~Gen, in a three-author collaboration. Every word has had all three of us sifting and sorting it.

—Jacqueline Lichtenberg

Thanks to Mary Lou Mendum for coming up with the first stories set entirely within Gen culture, the Clear Springs Chronicles. Mary Lou brings a welcome comic touch that neither Jacqueline nor I have in our repertoire.

—Jean Lorrah

FOREWORD

The second book in a trilogy is always the hardest to write, because it not only must continue the story arc that spans the three novels, but it must have its own separate plot as well. The neat thing about Mary Lou's Den and Rital stories is that they combine a family story with a career story. The two men work at the top of their game as one of the channel/Donor pairs who make Unity possible between Simes and Gens. Hence they are always living a new story.

CHAPTER 1

AN EXCHANGE OF WORDS

"Clear Springs isn't a decent place to raise children anymore!" the Reverend Jermiah Sinth's resonant voice proclaimed. "Not when a Sime-kissing traitor can bring his slimy friend into what *used* to be a respectable school!" The preacher's bushy eyebrows lowered like thunderclouds on the horizon of his domed forehead and the sleeves of his black cassock fluttered as he pointed an accusing finger.

Sosu Den Milnan controlled his temper with difficulty. He had hoped to slip his cousin, Hajene Rital Madz, into the Southside Upper School without a confrontation. Reverend Sinth's goal was to prevent local Gens from donating selyn, the energy of life that only Gens produced. Harassing parents in front of the school was a new development.

Sinth had finished a jail sentence for blocking access to the Sime Center less than three weeks ago, but the preacher's anti-Sime group, Save Our Kids, was out in force, passing out copies of Sinth's latest pamphlet, "**The Tecton Conspiracy**" and waving signs saying, "**STOP THE CLASSES**" and "**Parents for Sime-Free Schools.**"

Rital moved into Den's selyn field to block the hate-filled emotions of Sinth's people. In response, Den placed a protective hand on his cousin's arm, just above the retainer that enclosed his tentacles. The channel spoke with quiet dignity. "We are attending this *public* hearing at the invitation of Principal Buchan and the Curriculum Committee. They have requested *accurate* information on the proposed changeover classes."

The anti-Sime activists muttered angrily. When the channel asked, "Please step aside," the mutter became a collective growl.

Sinth's eyes took on a manic gleam and sweat poured down his face. The crushed-tomato-leaf scent alerted Den: *He's chewing melic again.* If drug-induced delusions inspired the man to do something stupid, such as order an attack on Den and Rital, his flock might obey.

Fortunately, Sinth's demonstrators weren't the only activists present. A contingent of pro-Tecton counterdemonstrators lurked under the black walnut trees lining the pavement, ignoring the slurry of dropped walnut fruits underfoot. They moved in to distribute "KNOWLEDGE IS NECESSARY" buttons and "**Changeover Classes: the Facts in Brief**" pamphlets to any parent who would accept them.

Most of the counterdemonstrators were Clear Springs University students, members of the Organization for Legal Disruption of Save Our Kids' Strategies, or OLD SOKS. They taunted Save Our Kids with obscene off-key ballads, while incorporating well-used hosiery into their attire. Without their help to escort Gens past Sinth's demonstrations, the Clear Springs Sime Center would have attracted few, if any, general-class selyn donors.

Reverend Sinth ignored Rital, lifted one arm and declaimed, "Scripture teaches: the touch of a Sime's tentacles is death, the agonizing death of a parent whose corrupt child turns Sime and *Kills* them."

"A tragedy we seek to end," Rital broke the preacher's practiced rhythm. "An adolescent who recognizes the symptoms of changeover into a Sime, and seeks help at the Sime Center, will never Kill a Gen, neither at changeover nor for the rest of a long life. We offer to teach changeover classes here, just as we teach our own children in Sime Territory. It saves lives."

Sinth rebutted, "Your help, Hajene Madz, commands a steep price. Those who let you strip their selyn away die a spiritual death: a moral decay that, unchecked, could destroy human civilization."

Behind Sinth's back his niece, Bethany, curled her lip in disgust. A pretty Gen of fifteen with long, dark hair, she was dressed modestly as her uncle demanded. Bethany knew what donating selyn was like: she'd done it once, much to her uncle's horror.

Den caught the eye of OLD SOKS member Annie Lifton. She grinned, puckering the thin white scar on her left cheek, then tightened her pink knee-sock armband and whispered to law student Silva Vornast. Silva waved to Den, adjusted the fishnet stocking tied around her waist, and tugged at the lime-green leg warmer securing the ponytail of her fellow law student and fiancé, Tohm Seegrin.

OLD SOKS members lined the entrance walk. Tohm sent Annie down one side of the walk, her older brother Rob down the other, while he, himself, went after those sluggards in the shade under the trees. Den returned his attention to the immediate confrontation.

Sinth was proclaiming, "You seduce us with new technology, tempt us to destroy the sacred purity of Gen civilization—"

"I don't know about you," Den interjected irreverently, "but I rather like trains and streetlights and telephones. Someday, we'll even soar into the sky on flying machines!"

"All to distract us from God's teachings!" the preacher retorted. "Expel the demon Sime and all his influence!"

"Reverend," Den said scornfully, "go peddle your hatred somewhere else. We are here to offer life and peace."

Sinth gasped in disbelief and again lost the thread of his sermon.

Den didn't wait for him to find it. "Your lies won't convince anyone of a Sime plot to undermine Gen society. These parents have come to learn of a better life for their children."

Freed of the hypnotic rhythm of Sinth's resonant voice, the incipient mob dissolved into a collection of confused individuals. Some glanced at Sinth for direction, but the clergyman was too outraged by Den's open defiance to provide it.

A mustachioed young man with hair the orange-red of turmeric shook a "**No Simes in Skool**" sign and growled, "I'll tan your Sime-lovin' hide!"

Rital tensed at the threat to his Donor, but the man backed down when his friends failed to support him.

That was when OLD SOKS struck.

A flying wedge of students swooped in, husky athletes forming the point. They surrounded Den and Rital and reversed their wedge, shoving back through the path they'd made.

Once free of Sinth's followers, the OLD SOKS members opened their wedge, depositing Den and his cousin safely on the school's entrance walk. Several anti-Sime demonstrators were left flat on the sidewalk. OLD SOKS taunted them: "Beating you is such a treat; you can't even keep your feet!"

Sinth's followers had their own slogan: "We'll fight to see that Heaven rules; there'll be no Simes in Clear Springs schools!"

As Den and Rital made their way up the path, the students chanted, "Hear Sinth and his braying asses claim a school's no place for classes!"

"Den, what were you thinking of, baiting Reverend Sinth?" Rital hissed furiously. "Were you *trying* to get us lynched?"

"Your sweet reason was getting us nowhere," the Donor argued.

"So, you decided to make him angry?" The channel looked down and advised, "Watch your step; this sidewalk is overdue for cleaning."

The warning was an instant too late. Den's foot landed on a recently-fallen walnut fruit. The husk split with a squelching sound, the nut skidded on the slick sidewalk, and the Donor's foot went with it.

Rital grabbed his arm, metabolizing extra selyn to augment speed and strength. As the Gen regained his balance, the channel went on, "If the Tecton finds out you insulted a religious leader, even *you* won't talk them into leaving you here in Clear Springs."

The Donor shrugged. "Is the Tecton likely to find out?"

Rital sighed and tried again, "In Clear Springs, you and I *are* the Tecton authorities. Will you please act the part?"

"Oh, all right," Den agreed, as they arrived at the entrance. Rital reached for the handle on the heavy fire door.

"I'll get that," the Donor said sharply. Retainers made any task requiring wrist rotation dangerous for a Sime, and treating a pinched lateral was not on Den's agenda. He pulled the door open and stepped through first so his selyn field would moderate the nageric chaos beyond.

The lobby was crowded with milling parents, children, and curious citizens, waiting for the gymnasium doors to open. The hollow boom of unfolding bleachers explained the delay.

Hank Fredricks, owner and editor of the *Clear Springs Clarion,* was interviewing anyone with an opinion. His young photographer was trying hard not to appear bored.

The lobby fell silent as one group, then another, saw Rital. Some people backed nervously away, while others pushed forward for a better look. The channel shifted nervously under the attention of untrained Gens until Den let his stronger selyn field block the others.

Their entrance attracted the attention of the school's principal, Ed Buchan. It was Buchan's job to 'dispose' of any student who started changeover, the metamorphosis into an adult Sime. Usually this meant locking the child in a reinforced room and contacting the school's extermination officer, Coach Farrow, or the Sime Center, as the child's parents preferred. If Farrow could not respond in time, it was Buchan's responsibility to shoot the child himself and risk being Killed in the process.

Buchan's Simephobia was obvious in the distance he maintained from the channel despite his support for their proposal. He'd never donated selyn, but his daughter, Jain, was the only student to attend every session of the changeover class Den and Rital had offered at the public library.

Jain trailed behind her father. A slender adolescent on the verge of womanhood, she moved with an athlete's grace. She had grown since Den had last seen her, but looked frail beside her father's adult Gen bulk.

"Sosu Milnan, it's good to see you again," Buchan said loudly, stepping into the open space around the Sime. The principal smiled broadly and held out a hand to Den. Den had lived out-Territory long enough to shake hands smoothly, murmuring an appropriate response.

Buchan turned to the channel and continued, "And Hi-jane Madz, I'm glad you were able to come tonight. Your insights will be invaluable." Forcing a smile, he swallowed and offered his hand again.

Shen, Den swore silently. *Why'd the man have to pick tonight to get brave?* Rital was already stressed from wearing retainers. He shouldn't have to endure contact with a well-intentioned Simephobe.

Before the Donor could intervene, Jain spoke up.

"It's pronounced 'Ha*jene*,' Daddy," she announced, twisting a lock of long, pale hair around one finger. "And they don't shake hands in Sime Territory."

Her father's smile broadened with ill-disguised relief at the excuse to avoid touching the Sime. Unfortunately, Rital had other ideas.

"This isn't Sime Territory, Jain," the channel pointed out. "We should follow Gen customs." Rital reached for the hand the principal had not yet withdrawn.

Shen you, Rital! Den swore silently, turning the full force of his attention on his cousin.

Rital gave the principal's hand one firm shake and let go before the man realized what was happening. The photographer's reflexes were better: her camera flashed, preserving the event for posterity.

The principal stared at his hand for a moment, then, "Umm, yes," he stammered. "I think the bleachers are ready. Let me show you to your places."

"That would be very kind of you," Rital responded politely.

The gym was a cavernous room with a ceiling two stories tall. The lingering odor revealed the gleaming bleachers were freshly painted. The central floor was covered with an odd assortment of mats, tarps, and swaths of turquoise carpeting.

In the center of the gym was a long table. Four microphones were spaced along its length with a half dozen chairs behind them, backed by a long chalkboard outlining practice schedules for more than a dozen teams. Above the chalkboard hung a marquee that listed the outcome of recent contests. The Clear Springs teams had earned a string of wins in a variety of sports over the summer, but lost the gymnastics tournament.

The janitor was testing a fifth microphone on a tall stand.

"Our gymnasium was completely refurbished two years ago," Buchan said proudly, "and your Sime Center made it possible."

Den lifted an eyebrow and the principal elaborated. "There's a five percent property tax on cities that have a sliderail train station, but no Sime Center. Your Tecton says it covers transport for the selyn batteries that power the trains." The principal gave Den a skeptical look. "I don't see how 'transport costs' could equal ten times the cost of the local product, myself."

"Selyn batteries are very large and heavy," Den explained. "You'd burn through several batteries to transport just one from Valzor to Clear Springs."

Buchan was unconvinced. "Personally, I think the Tecton's blackmailing our cities into opening Sime Centers."

"Of course it is," Den agreed. "The Tecton's first priority is to prevent the Kill by supplying selyn to Simes. Excess selyn fuels utilities and industry. Importing selyn to Clear Springs, a city inhabited only by Gens and children, makes as much economic sense as importing your water supply from the Moav desert instead of using the local river."

Buchan appeared unsettled by the new perspective, but continued. "When your Sime Center was approved, we lowered property taxes by four percent and earmarked the extra for the schools. Last year, we rebuilt the gym and purchased a new bus. This year, we added exercise equipment and had money left to carpet the library. Next year, we'll increase the school librarian's hours to three-quarters time."

"Watch your step," Buchan warned as they crossed the open space. "There weren't enough mats to protect the floor, but we found paint cloths and carpet that hasn't been installed yet. Coach Farrow says nonathletic shoes will scuff the floor and we've only just refinished it."

"They're refinishing the floor in a two-year-old gym, but they can't afford a full-time librarian?" Rital muttered softly in Simelan. "How the blazing shen can they educate children for the future, if all they teach is games?"

"Children who become Sime here don't *have* a future. We're fighting a centuries-old cultural imperative. Their parents say, if sports distract them from the fear of changeover, that's more than you can say for geography or spelling."

"Den, how…" Rital was so scandalized that he forgot to keep his voice down. Den urgently shushed him and the channel asked more quietly, "How can you say such a thing?"

"Many people here still think murdering new Simes before they complete changeover is the only way to keep them from Killing."

Rital drew breath to respond, then paused to point out a hazardous junction between a tumbling mat and a loose piece of carpeting.

It's a channel's nightmare in here, Den thought as he stepped carefully over the obstacle.

"Drinking beer with OLD SOKS is giving you weird ideas," Rital complained when his Donor was safely past.

"How can we change their bloodthirsty traditions, if we're not aware of them?"

"Please find a seat, gentlemen," Buchan said as they reached the table. "Now, if you'll excuse me…" He backed away, arms behind his body to discourage the channel from shaking hands in farewell.

Den chose a chair between Rital and the seats reserved for the Curriculum Committee.

"I'm fine, Den," Rital said softly. "You don't have to hover."

"If you look tense, these people will worry you'll rip off your retainers and Kill someone."

Rital sighed and nodded. The Clear Springs parents outside had seen too many people Killed by their own Sime children. Den and Rital hoped to get past that justified fear and persuade them to add changeover training as an after-school activity.

With the exception of Cessly Lornstadt, whose husband, Ephriam, was Reverend Sinth's devoted lieutenant, the committee members saw some value to the classes. Den hoped their open-mindedness would survive their first meeting with a real, live channel.

The committee members began arriving. Thaddus Webber, the Chair of the meeting, was the leader of the Church of Rational Deism. The white-haired theologian was, as usual, discussing some esoteric concept with bearded young sociology professor, Willum Ildun.

County Librarian Ada Dilson bustled in, calling a cheerful greeting. She had been feuding with Reverend Sinth since the preacher tried to censor her book collection. To retaliate, she had allowed Den and Rital to teach changeover classes in her library's conference room.

Miz Dilson sat down beside Den and announced, "I can't find accurate books on changeover and Establishment, particularly any written for children."

Den said, "I'll see what I can find in the Sime Center library."

Rital leaned around the Donor to add, "Or I can order suitable books from Valzor."

Just then a mob of Gens swept into the gym. Rital tensed as they reached the obstacle course protecting the sacred gymnasium floor.

A red-headed boy of about nine tripped and thudded face-first into the padding, shrieked with laughter, then repeated the misadventure. Den recognized him with some apprehension.

Sure enough, "Raymond Ildun, stop that this instant and get over here!" Professor Ildun ordered. The miscreant was swiftly seated under the marquee, under strict orders to "Stay right here and draw until the meeting is over!"

"The Ilduns are between babysitters again, I see," Rital observed with some amusement.

"Would *you* take responsibility for that child?" Den asked. "I pity his parents. And his younger sisters."

Along with the audience came the fourth committee member, biology teacher Nat Ulman. An **"Educate for Excellence"** sticker was glued to the cover of her notebook. She brought University Vice Chancellor Gillum Mathison, to whom the committee would report.

Den and Rital scanned the milling audience. The channel observed, "I zlin a scattering of general-class selyn donors out there, but except for Jain Buchan, none of our changeover class students are here."

"Their parents are." The Donor nodded toward the right-hand bleachers. "That's Sheely's mother on the third tier, in the blue dress, and Gavvin's parents are on the other side."

The OLD SOKS and Save Our Kids members arrived last. When the two groups tried to enter at once, Bethany Sinth used the opportunity to exchange a few words with Rob Lifton.

"So, those two are still interested in each other," Rital observed, lips twitching in amusement.

Den grinned. "And won't *that* make her uncle happy!" Rob Lifton was a regular selyn donor, like his sister, Annie.

With Sinth's group came the last member of the Curriculum Committee, Cessly Lornstadt. Her frizzy hairstyle and heavy makeup made her look strangely artificial and her mechanically sweet smile was never so evident as when she was dissecting someone else's character.

Her fellow committee members were too open-minded about Simes for her taste, so she moved her chair to place more distance between herself and Rital, yet remain close to a microphone.

Ribald hoots erupted from OLD SOKS: "That's right, Miz Lornstadt, stay away! Wouldn't want Hajene Madz to catch your lice."

Thaddus Webber frowned at the section where the counterdemonstrators sat, then picked up a microphone. "If you will quiet down, we can get started."

When something approaching quiet was reached, Webber opened the meeting and began, "Sosu Milnan from our Sime Center—"

"Not *my* Sime Center," the turmeric-haired man objected.

"—Sosu Milnan from *our city's* Sime Center has presented detailed information regarding what the changeover classes teach," the theologian continued. "We have consulted educational experts about whether they would be a sound addition to our curriculum."

"What do those so-called 'experts' know?" yelled a woman with a sculpted hairdo rivaling Cessly Lornstadt's. "They're *our* kids!"

"Tonight's meeting," Webber persevered, "is to address your concerns. Wild rumors have circulated about changeover training." Webber glanced pointedly at Reverend Sinth. "Rather than spend all evening on objections to material *not* in the curriculum, let's ask Sosu Milnan what it *does* cover."

Den interjected his carefully crafted argument before Rital could speak. "Last year, almost a hundred children went into changeover here in Clear Springs. Of the fifteen who survived it, all but the three who sought help at the Sime Center Killed the nearest Gen. In the same year, over two hundred children went through changeover in Valzor City. All but two survived, but there were no Kills. Not one."

Den waited for the murmurs of surprise to end, then continued. "Changeover classes are the reason young Simes in Valzor don't Kill, while those here in Clear Springs do. Parents often confuse early symptoms of changeover with other illnesses and either wait too long or shoot a child who isn't in changeover. Children who do think they're in changeover are reluctant to be murdered and so they hide it. Changeover classes teach children how to recognize changeover, where to get help, and how to survive becoming Sime without endangering friends and family."

Den next introduced Rital, hoping more open-minded parents would respond to the human being behind the dreaded tentacles. His expectations appeared to be met until the channel said, "Above all, the classes will teach children that if they go into changeover, they can seek help at the Sime Center. Instead of Killing, they will receive selyn collected by our channeling staff from volunteer donors."

Rital then compounded his error by adding, "When the Sime Center becomes familiar, children are more likely to come to us for help."

"That's the problem, ya slimy snake!" the turmeric-haired man heckled.

"I wouldn't phrase it so crudely, but I agree," commented a middle-aged, careworn woman. "I lost two sons to changeover before you came here, and I've got three younger daughters. I've got nothing against you folks taking over children who turn Sime," she assured the in-Territory pair. "However, there are other things the Sime Center does that I'd rather my girls *didn't* know about, if you know what I mean."

Den knew. Her objection was to the compensation offered to Gens who donated selyn. Easy money—and an irresistible temptation to cash-poor adolescents. Deliberately so, because the Tecton had to have that selyn to supply the Simes who depended on it.

That was not going to change. Sime Centers were legally Sime Territory and Sime law prevailed on their premises. Thus, anyone already either Sime or Gen was legally an adult. The Tecton could take selyn donations from any Gens who volunteered at a Sime Center, regardless of the opinions of their families.

Still, no sense reinforcing parental fears. "Because the proposed course has so few sessions, the focus must be on how to identify changeover, what to expect if it happens, and how and where to get assistance. We can't cover the full spectrum of Sime Center services."

The next speaker was a stylishly dressed young woman who introduced herself as "the mother of two future Cougars."

"They have so little time to enjoy the innocence of childhood," she pleaded. "Let them have that freedom, instead of burdening them with a future of death, pain, and loss."

Rital flinched under the cathartic wave of grief the speaker's words evoked. Den leaned closer, partially blocking it. "Children aren't stupid," he pointed out. "They notice that one-third of their older schoolmates and siblings disappear. The truth is less scary—and in this case, much safer—than what they imagine. Educate your children and changeover will not be a death sentence, for them or anyone else."

The young mother nodded thoughtfully, then surrendered the microphone to a man in a Cougars jacket and hat: Mr. Sigs, the psychology teacher. "This truth of yours," he said, "seems rather flexible. You say the lessons are limited to how to get help for a changeover victim. Yet you take the students to visit the Sime Center."

Rital said, "That's right. The source of help."

"I've been on the Valzor Sime Center tour," the man complained, wringing his hands in distress. "They show visitors a selyn donation—live! Even the children. It's not fitting. They might think it's acceptable to donate selyn against their parents' wishes! Correct me if I'm wrong, Controller Madz, but aren't Gens paid a substantial sum for doing that?"

I shouldn't have tried to prevaricate, Den realized—as Rital acted on the same thought. The channel admitted readily, "The money varies with the amount of selyn donated, but there are students whose donations make it possible for them to afford college."

As the assembled parents gasped in shock, Den whispered, "Did you have to say it that way?"

"It's true, and the young Gens have the right to know."

"You just rubbed their *parents'* noses in it," the Donor hissed, while maintaining the appearance of solidarity for the Gen audience.

"That's fine for college students," the man said, "but I can't approve of letting adolescents have so much money. They might spend it on fancy clothes, strange music, wild parties. Some might even buy drugs!"

Den appropriated the microphone before Rital could make the situation worse.

"Mr. Sigs," he said, "while I can't guarantee that young selyn donors won't spend money on clothing or entertainment, a channel easily detects if a Gen is sick, drunk, or on drugs. While we offer treatment to such individuals, they cannot donate selyn. Furthermore, our Sime Center doesn't have a collecting room with insulated windows that allow visitors to watch donations. So, no observation here."

The next three speakers, all Save Our Kids members, predicted lurid debauchery among young Gens seduced into donating selyn, as if repeating the baseless accusation gave it merit.

They were followed by the childless owner of a real estate company, who asked "How does an active Sime Center in general, and changeover classes in particular, help the business community?"

Professor Ildun, who had almost dozed off, started awake. "If Gens of any age donate selyn, it helps the Clear Springs economy. The cost per ton of cargo shipped by train depends on the number of local Gens who donate. Towns with more selyn donors become transportation hubs, providing an expanding economy, better employment opportunities, and other advantages to the community."

The young professor replaced his microphone, convinced that he had won his point. Thaddus Webber provided a translation. "So, Professor Ildun, a Sime Center is good for business because it lowers freight costs?"

"Yes, indeed," the sociologist agreed.

Webber then asked, "Sosu Milnan, Hajene Madz, have you anything to add?"

Despite his Donor's nageric "shut up" signal, the channel admitted, "Yes. Clear Springs has almost enough donors right now to qualify for an even lower shipping rate. As few as twenty more donors per month would lower Clear Springs' freight costs by five percent."

"My associates at the Chamber of Commerce will be glad to hear that," the real estate agent remarked. He shuddered, then added, "Although I'm not volunteering to be one of your new selyn donors."

A gawky adolescent boy stepped up next. "My name is Jerree Bolin and I'm thirteen. I want to take the class just in case and it would be interesting to learn about changeover and see what the Sime Center is like and…" He paused, and ended, "…and that's all I have to say."

Rital chuckled as the youngster replaced his microphone. "I'd be happy to show you around the Sime Center, Jerree," he offered, "but we'll have to limit attendance at our changeover classes to students who *haven't* already Established."

"I'm Gen?" Jerree squawked, hitting three octaves in two syllables.

The channel smiled. "You're Gen," he confirmed good-naturedly. "Congratulations."

The good will sparked by this announcement was fleeting. As ill-informed complaints and speculations continued to fly, Rital's expression became increasingly grim.

Den was glad when Webber acknowledged Joziah Duncan, Rob and Annie Lifton's grandfather. "I've been sitting here listening to 'what if's' and 'might be's,'" the elderly man began, "everyone assuming the worst possible intent from the Sime Center. Well, I'm personally acquainted with our friends from across the border."

Reverend Sinth turned purple. The preacher had expelled Mr. Duncan from his congregation for the sin of donating selyn. Instead of begging forgiveness, Duncan had promptly joined Thaddus Webber's Rational Deists.

"The Sime Center's been open over a year and they haven't harmed a single child," the old man continued. "However, they've sure *helped* a lot—and not just ones who turned Sime. Many families are mighty glad to *know,* beyond doubt, that their children are Gen."

Duncan's accusing glare elicited whispers of shamed agreement. The old man nodded. "It's hard to trust a stranger with your child. Even so, you'd best have a 'for instance' before you accuse your neighbors of undermining children's morals, even if those neighbors have tentacles!"

An indignant bellow erupted from the front row. "I'll give you a 'for instance.'" said Coach Farrow, the school's athletic director and extermination officer. He was heavily muscled, with light brown hair cut military style. Crossing the gym floor with deliberate grace, he glared down at the frail old man with the raw aggression of a drill sergeant.

Duncan raised a skeptical eyebrow and waited.

Farrow began. "For centuries, we Gens worked together against our common enemy. We fought the Simes, kept the territory border intact, and stayed alive and free! Teamwork made us great. We put the welfare of the group before...individual convenience." Farrow's voice dripped with scorn. "The Sime Wars ended over a century ago, but not Gen values. I teach children of the most dangerous age. The Tecton's proposed classes won't prevent a single changeover, but they *will* teach our children to put self-interest ahead of the common good!"

Mr. Duncan shook his head. "I've read the proposed curriculum closely," he objected mildly, "but I don't recall such a lesson. Unless by common good you mean the antiquated notion that the only good Sime is a dead Sime?"

While it was clear that Farrow did believe that, he knew better than to say it before parents who had lost their Sime children to his gun.

"The lesson's right there!" Farrow barked, pointing at the principal's daughter. "Young Jain Buchan used to be a model student, working with her teammates in gymnastics." The girl shrank back against her father. "But she wasn't content to be a Gen. She wanted to learn how to be a Sime, too. She spent three weeks in changeover classes, missing so many gymnastics practices that I had to cut her from the team. The Clear Springs Cougars lost the Tri County Gymnastics Tournament, because the Oak Ridge Alligators didn't have teammates who abandoned them!"

Farrow turned back to Mr. Duncan. "What's the point of teaching our children how to survive turning Sime, if they forget how to live as Gens? How can our students take pride in their heritage if their classmates—and teammates—put learning about Simes above being a Clear Springs Cougar?"

To Den and Rital's horror, several students began chanting, "Cou-*gars*! Cou-*gars*! Cou-*gars*!" Others joined in. With a proud smile, Coach Farrow held up both hands, fingers bent into claws. The chanters responded with similar gestures and a loud, "Rrroooowll, TEAM!"

Jain flinched. Her father gave her a hug, then commandeered the microphone. "Coach, I'm as proud of the Cougars as anyone, but having Jain take changeover classes was *my* idea. She was being an obedient daughter...and if that's not a value our school is supposed to teach, I don't know what is!"

Farrow glared at his principal, unconvinced.

Buchan added, "Jain wasn't the only gymnast who missed the tournament. Two days before, Hanna Mullen went through changeover, hid, and killed her teammate Larra Resher before you could shoot her. With two teammates missing, the Cougars would have lost, Jain or no Jain."

"Maybe so," Coach Farrow admitted reluctantly, "but with her wasting time on changeover classes, we didn't stand a chance."

"If Hanna had 'wasted time' taking the classes," Buchan retorted crisply, "*Larra* would have been alive to compete. The classes would not prevent a single changeover—but they *would* prevent *Kills!* Too many children fail the Test through fear or ignorance. Others are shot by mistake or Killed by their teammates, as Larra was. I'm proud that my daughter will never be one of them. If she shows any of the Signs, I will take her to the Sime Center and we will discover whether she is in changeover long before she is a danger to anyone."

Scandalized gasps rang around the room and Jain stared at her father in astonishment. No parent in Clear Springs had ever made such a declaration in public. Until the Sime Center opened, none could have.

Jain threw herself into her father's arms and OLD SOKS broke into cheers. A scattered handful of parents dared to applaud...but were quickly silenced by disapproving glares.

Coach Farrow backed down, grumbling, "I still think it's wrong."

"How dare you!" a woman accused, from Reverend Sinth's side of the gymnasium. Choked with anger and grief, she wailed, "How dare you dishonor my daughter by making her a martyr to your cause!"

Rital practically hid behind his Donor to escape the force of the woman's wrath. With her face twisted in grief and her hair disheveled in mourning instead of styled in the complex coifs of Church of the Purity women, it took Den a moment to recognize her.

"Oh, no!" he whispered to Rital. "That's Nancy Resher—Larra's mother!"

"My Larra died because her teammate, Hanna, failed the Test," Nancy continued. This statement collected a good many nods of agreement, even from those who didn't belong to Sinth's church. "Hanna didn't tell Coach Farrow when she developed the Signs, so that he could preserve the safety of her teammates. She ignored her duty—and died a murderer of her best friend—because she had been led to believe that perhaps Simes don't have to die, after all." She glared across the gymnasium at a tall woman Den didn't recognize.

"I never told Hanna it was all right to endanger her teammates!" The woman, who must be Hanna's mother, looked around the bleachers for support from her neighbors, then shrank back under the weight of their collective disapproval.

"Perhaps you didn't," Nancy Resher admitted reluctantly, then turned back to the table where the Curriculum Committee sat. "But by even considering these classes, we are sending our children the message that the Test is optional. Can you imagine the deaths that would result if most children faced with the Test chose not to die? How many Killer Simes would we have roaming our back alleys?"

Faces paled around the gymnasium. Den leaned forward and in a gentle voice said, "Miz Resher, I grew up in Valzor, where every child takes classes of the sort we propose to teach in Clear Springs. No child must volunteer to be murdered. As a result, you can stroll down any back alley you choose, knowing that you won't be attacked by a berserk Sime." He saw their disbelief and shrugged. "It's true. Valzor isn't a paradise: you might get mugged or offered questionable goods. But you wouldn't get Killed."

A murmur of interest spread through the bleachers and for a moment, Den let himself hope.

Then Reverend Sinth sprang to his feet.

CHAPTER 2

AN EXCHANGE OF WALNUTS

In a voice that filled the gymnasium without amplification, the preacher pointed at Nancy Resher and demanded, "Principal Buchan, hear that blessed woman! Scripture tells us that if a child has faith and is good and obedient, God will grant that child the mercy of becoming Gen. You claim to love your daughter, then destroy the faith that would make her Gen. What did you give her in return? Lessons on how to be Sime."

Sinth's theatrical gesture of pained disbelief was a poor imitation of the true grief everyone had just witnessed. "You have doomed your own daughter to become a Sime!"

There was a collective gasp. Jain cried out in horror, her face as wheat-pale as her hair.

Appalled at the man's sheer cruelty, Rital started to reach for the microphone, but Den stopped his cousin with a touch.

"We can't help Jain," he murmured, knowing that the channel zlinned his frustration. "If we defend her just after Sinth accused us of subverting her, it will be seen as an admission of guilt. Unless she's conveniently Established selyn production?"

Rital shook his head, lips pressed tight.

Den and Rital weren't the only ones offended by Sinth's abuse of a child to make a political point. A scandalized murmur spread through the audience, even including a few of his followers.

"Reverend Sinth," Thaddus Webber began, "I will not challenge your beliefs. However, schools must accommodate students of *all* faiths, and even those with none. To attack Jain Buchan for violating the doctrines of *your* sect, not hers, crosses the line."

"There *is* only one true faith!" Sinth hissed.

"Could be you're right," Webber agreed. "We just don't agree on *which* faith it is. We can debate that some other time, but tonight we are here to discuss changeover classes. Does anyone else wish to speak?"

"What if the classes *do* turn children into Simes?" a woman asked.

This time, Den didn't try to deter his cousin from reaching the microphone. "The answer," Rital promised, "is in your own town records: one-third of children who live to adolescence turn Sime.

"The chances of a child going through changeover are two in three if both parents are Sime, one in two if one parent is Gen and the other Sime, and one in three if both parents are Gen. Children are Sime or Gen from conception, just as they are male or female, although larity isn't detectable until adolescence. Nothing after conception affects the larity of a child."

Some people still looked confused, so Den claimed the microphone and elaborated. "Changeover classes don't make Gen children turn Sime, nor have prayer, obedience, or ignorance ever made a Sime child Establish. However, Sime children who can't recognize changeover are less likely to get help and more likely to kill someone." Den couldn't resist adding, "Reverend Sinth, you know that prayer doesn't stop changeover. Your nephew, Zakry, was a model of piety, but he went through changeover and almost killed you."

Rital removed the microphone from his cousin's grasp, frowning in disapproval. However, Den spoke truth. Reverend Sinth had survived his nephew's berserk Need only through prompt treatment, dumb luck, and a generous dose of melic weed.

The preacher, though, had a different outlook. "My nephew was a model child, devout and obedient. Zakry would have been Gen if you hadn't lured his sister to donate selyn. As Scripture promises, one week later, God's just wrath fell upon her family!"

Trust Sinth to come up with a new interpretation on the spot! We ought to challenge him to show us those so-called Scriptures.

He glanced sympathetically at Bethany, who kept her face blank, hands clasped in a show of modesty. But her knuckles whitened and her lips firmed.

Sinth continued. "With God's displeasure plain to see, you and this *Sime* spread poison in our schools!" He turned to the bleachers. "What decent parent would let them near their children? For what? The security of knowing that the child you doom to life as a Sime won't kill you? *If* he reaches the Sime Center in time?"

Annie Lifton marched up to the microphone. "Reverend Sinth," she said angrily, "you are no expert on changeover. *My* Gen brother also donated selyn, we both read about Simes, then a week later, *I* turned *Gen*. Not that *you* know a Gen when you try to murder one."

She traced the thin scar that crossed her left cheek, a reminder of the night Reverend Sinth had misdiagnosed her upset stomach as changeover. Only her brother Rob's intervention had saved her.

"By Reverend Sinth's 'reasoning,'" Annie continued, "it follows that children who learn about Simes are immunized against the changeover-inducing effects of having a member of their family donate selyn. By his own logic, he should support the changeover classes!"

Cheers and whistles emanated from her fellow OLD SOKS members and even Thaddus Webber chuckled at the red-faced preacher.

Then a tall, white-haired woman stalked up to the microphone. "I'm Flora Mills, from Berrysville," she introduced herself. "I'm sick of listening to you folks snipe. The Sime Center hasn't hurt anyone. Donating selyn provides cash for those who want it, and the rest have a better economy and fewer berserkers. I wish Berrysville could say that."

"So, move the Sime Center out there!" someone called.

"I would if I could. *You* certainly don't deserve it. Those two have contributed to your city's economy," she pointed a stern finger at Den and Rital. "They offer to help your children survive changeover without killing—saving both Gen and Sime lives—and won't charge you a penny for the privilege.

"You should be singing your gratitude, not accusing them of corrupting children," the finger indicated the hapless Mr. Sigs, "or whining about conflicts with the sacred athletic schedule." Coach Farrow squirmed under her disdain. "The Sime Center has brought nothing but good! Treat it like the blessing it is." She stalked back to her seat.

The light coming through the eastern-facing windows was gradually fading. The janitor turned on the lights as a balding man with a sagging belly took the microphone to say, "I agree with Coach Farrow."

Groans rose, but the man persisted. "If we allow changeover classes into our schools, we might never again see a proud record of success such as—" he pointed dramatically up at the scoreboard just as the helpful janitor flipped the last light switch. Three spotlights illuminated the celebration of the Cougars' athletic prowess and the speaker's voice broke off.

Heads turned to follow his shaking finger and a gasp swept through the room. Den turned to see what was wrong.

The Ildun boy had followed his father's orders to stay quiet, remain close to the scoreboard, and draw. Alas, those orders were insufficiently specific. Raymond perched on the top rung of a stepladder, with an assortment of paint cans. He was putting the finishing touches on a mural covering most of the scoreboard. The central image was a blood-red Sime arm with six lime-green tentacles outlined in yellow. Bold letters proclaimed the sacrilege, "TENTACULS ARE WEIRD, BUT SPORTS ARE BORING!"

"Raymond Ildun!" his father screamed.

The boy lost his balance and grabbed for the ladder. Paint cans flew, then bounced and rolled, flinging red, yellow, and lime paint over the floor's protective coverings and into the gaps between.

"The floor!" Coach Farrow yelped.

The audience moved as one to save the sacred gymnasium floor. Carpets, mats, and paint cloths were rolled to contain the mess. Towels from the shower room wiped up splatters. A graduate student with silk stocking armbands discussed solvents with the janitor, a dedicated member of Save Our Kids. As the young vandal was led away by his humiliated father, another team lowered the scoreboard.

* * * *

"But nothing was settled," Rital complained as he and Den waited for the crowd to thin.

"I know," the Donor said. "That wasn't the purpose of this meeting."

The channel blinked. "It wasn't?"

Den laughed. "Of course not. There were far too many people with different viewpoints to agree on anything. Since they were all Gens, they couldn't reach a consensus by zlinning to determine whose solutions are most acceptable, as we would in-Territory."

"So why hold a meeting at all?"

Den shrugged. "Gen tradition. Everyone is allowed to present their position. They have to do it out loud, because they can't count on anyone zlinning their sincerity."

"I suppose so."

When the gymnasium was almost empty, Den and Rital picked their way across the well-scrubbed floor. Hank Fredricks and his photographer were talking to Thaddus Webber in the lobby. Den was relieved to hear the newsman tell Webber, "I promised Professor Ildun not to publish any more stories about young Raymond's pranks."

Outside, a cool evening breeze carried conflicting chants. "Oh, shen," Den said in disgust. "After all that, couldn't they just go home?"

Their brief cooperation in paint-cleaning forgotten, Save Our Kids and OLD SOKS had turned the path into a gauntlet of waving signs and forcefully offered pamphlets. Save Our Kids chanted loudly, "Don't do as the Tecton bids! Keep our city safe for kids!"

To which OLD SOKS responded at full volume, "'We love your kids!' the morons cry. 'Especially when they bleed and die!'"

The dueling groups ignored the in-Territory pair. They had almost reached the sidewalk when a voice from the Save Our Kids side yelled, "Keep goin' right outta town, you stinkin' Gen-runner! And take yer slimy friend with you!"

It was the muscular, turmeric-haired man. "Sime-lovin' traitor!" he bellowed even louder, when he saw Den looking at him. "How's it feel to look inna mirror every morning and see a Sime-kisser?"

"Better than seeing someone who insults strangers," Den retorted.

"You filthy scum!" Too angry to find words, the turmeric-haired man picked a crushed walnut fruit off the sidewalk and hurled it at Den. The missile caught him on the left cheek, stinging sharply. Rital yelped and stepped between his Donor and the attacker.

Annie Lifton scooped up her own ammunition and returned fire, but her aim was off and the fruit hit the janitor standing next to him, adding a brown blotch to the red, yellow, and lime-green stains on his coverall.

Annie's brother, Rob, and three other OLD SOKS members, also peppered Save Our Kids members with noxious projectiles.

Victims of collateral damage fired off broadsides of their own. Brown stains appeared on signs, clothes, and hands.

Den and Rital watched from the neutral territory of the sidewalk. "We've got to stop this," Rital said in dismay.

"How?" Den asked, wiping half-fermented walnut juice off his cheek. "They built up some strong emotions in there. Better this than real weapons," he added, then ducked as a nut ricocheted off a **"SCHOOLS ARE FOR EDUCATION"** sign.

"But the ambient might provoke…" Rital began, then stopped.

"We don't have to worry about *nearby renSimes,* cousin, although there will be consequences." Den nodded toward Hank Fredricks and his photographer documenting the riot.

"Let's go before we end up on the front page," Rital counseled.

The two made a hasty retreat, just as a police siren began to wail.

CHAPTER 3
A CHANCE TO HEAL

The next morning's *Clarion* featured a double-column photo of the riot under the banner headline, "**Words, Walnuts Exchanged at Curriculum Meeting.**"

"Congratulations on ensuring that our classes won't get approved, cousin," Rital drawled as he joined Den for breakfast in the cafeteria. Since the channel's hands were occupied with his tray, one of his two dorsal handling tentacles tapped the headline for emphasis.

The dark brown stain on the tip of that tentacle matched the stains on Den's cheek and fingers.

It serves him right, the Donor thought. *He was in such a hurry to heal the bruise that he wouldn't let me wash my face first. There's a reason they use walnut juice as a dye!*

"Now people will blame us for the riot," Rital scolded. "All because you insulted an out-Territory citizen!" The channel set his tray down with more force than necessary, almost slopping his small portion of oatmeal over the rim of its bowl. One of the two ventral tentacles of his other arm darted from under his hand to catch his spoon before it jumped off the tray.

"I just hope you're satisfied," the channel finished, dropping into the chair across from Den, who occupied his attention with a bite of toast as Rital zlinned Den's selyn field to determine whether his cousin was suitably contrite.

Rital refused to be ignored. "Starting a riot won't convince the school board that our changeover classes are harmless," the channel lectured. "Someone could have been badly injured if the police hadn't broken up the fight."

Den rolled his eyes in exasperation. "One: we didn't start it. Two: being hit by a walnut isn't fatal, even if it doesn't help one's personal appearance." The Donor ran a self-conscious hand across his cheek. The coin-sized brown stain almost covered the angry red mark where Rital had healed the bruise left by the impact. "Last night's scuffle was pretty modest. Neither Save Our Kids nor OLD SOKS intended real injury and if the paper's right, I was the worst casualty."

Although Den meant what he said, the incident underscored the fierce competition between the Sime Center's advocates and detractors. To distract his cousin, he pulled a letter from his pocket. "This just came from Eddina. She's designing wings for this year's test flight contest from that composite material I sent her. She wants to consult the Clear Springs University library's section on Ancient aeronautics for the optimum shape."

Rital's eyes widened in ill-concealed horror. "Eddina, here?! She'll start designing, forget she's in Gen Territory, and wander into Reverend Sinth's church to ask directions to the nearest tea shop."

"She's not *that* absent-minded. She'll follow the Escort rules."

"And remember to stay out of the Collectorium?" Rital asked skeptically. "Some of our selyn donors can barely face a channel and none of them know how to act around a renSime."

"I'll bet she could fix the power problems in that fancy greenhouse we can't use," the Donor wheedled. "We could have fresh vegetables all winter."

Rital hesitated, visibly tempted. "Now is not the time," he objected, but less strongly than before.

"I won't tempt fate," Den assured his cousin. "I'll invite her after the changeover class issue is settled." If he didn't linger over breakfast, he could get his reply into the day's mail. He hoped Eddina had not already made a formal application to visit Gen Territory.

Outside, Reverend Sinth and his followers had arrived and were arming themselves with signs, pamphlets, and hymnals. "Right on schedule and none the worse for wear," Den told Rital.

The leaded glass didn't provide enough nageric shielding for Rital's sensitivity and the channel squirmed at the hatred generated by the Gens outside. Den blocked it by turning his attention on his cousin, and Rital relaxed.

The demonstrators stayed on the sidewalk, out of Sime Territory jurisdiction. New Washington Territory recognized no legal right of access to Sime Centers, and Police Chief Tains was a Save Our Kids member, so Sinth's group could misbehave there with impunity.

However, a dozen OLD SOKS members soon arrived, ready to escort prospective selyn donors through Sinth's demonstration while taunting their opponents with chants and songs.

"Those two groups hate each other," the channel complained, stirring his cereal. "What would have happened last night if they'd thrown something more substantial than rotting fruit?" He caught Den's admonitory look and realized that he'd been caught playing with his food. He took a hasty bite of oatmeal, then put the spoon down.

"Come on, Rital," the Donor said reasonably, "I couldn't know that red-haired fellow would overreact so badly. Those demonstrators yell worse things at each other all the time."

As if to prove his point, Annie Lifton strutted over to Reverend Sinth. The angry swish of her ponytail, adorned with fluorescent purple sequined anklets, matched the flapping of the preacher's cassock as his arms windmilled. The turmeric-haired man cheered, waving his "**Onlee DEAD Simes Can't Kill**" sign like a weapon.

Rital shuddered. "That man zlins psychotic."

"Don't waste time on him," the Donor said, starting on his eggs. "Reverend Sinth let him attack Marcy Ingleston and got OLD SOKS in return. Save Our Kids is pretty disciplined. I don't think they'll allow any more unauthorized outbursts."

The channel looked at his cousin oddly. "Den, that man is a furnace of uncontrolled rage," he explained as if to a particularly dense child. "One of these days he'll explode and hurt someone."

"I believe you," Den assured his cousin. "However, unless he explodes on the Sime Center's grounds, we have no authority to deal with him. Now eat your breakfast."

As the channel reluctantly consumed another bite of oatmeal, Den looked out the window again. The shouting match between Annie and Reverend Sinth continued, with neither accomplishing anything.

Or maybe not, the Donor thought. Five college students walked unopposed around the confrontation. When they reached the Sime Center side of the sidewalk, they headed straight for the Collectorium's entrance with students' anarchistic disregard for paved pathways. The Donor winced as a careless foot crushed a lush trin plant Alyce, the groundskeeper, had planted to supply the Center with really good tea.

One young man looked back, caught the preacher's eye, and made an obscene gesture before he followed his friends into the Collectorium. Like the Sime Center's staff, the selyn donors had enjoyed the six months of Sinth's incarceration, which let them walk into the Sime Center without opposition. Their resentment at having to force their way through a mob stressed the channels and, unlike fear of donating selyn, that stress worsened with repeated exposure.

"Den, your judgment on out-Territory culture is slipping," Rital observed, pushing his half-finished bowl of cereal aside. "That Gen might have thrown the first walnut even if you hadn't insulted him, but you did the same thing to Reverend Sinth. Personally attacking a community leader is not a recommended strategy for avoiding trouble."

"It worked, didn't it? When Sinth lost control of himself, he also lost control of his followers. I'd rather cope with furious individuals than a mob, any day."

Rital waved Den's objection away. "You can't tell the difference because you can't zlin them. I'm the channel. You should have waited for me to call it."

"Rital, I hate to disillusion you, but zlinning doesn't make you infallible in emotional situations." He turned the *Clarion's* front page around and pointed at a photo of Rital shaking hands with Principal Buchan.

"That picture shows the friendship and cooperation we, as representatives of the Tecton, are building with the Clear Springs leaders," the channel said stubbornly.

"Really?" the Donor asked skeptically. "Buchan doesn't look friendly or cooperative to me."

The channel examined the picture more closely. It captured the out-Territory Gen's alarm quite clearly. "Well…" he waffled, then stared out the window at the action on the sidewalk.

Reverend Sinth broke off his shouting match with Annie Lifton and directed his followers to spread out, so they could intercept any Gen seeking to enter the Sime Center. The OLD SOKS members also prepared for battle. Scouts wearing hosiery armbands went down the block in either direction to meet prospective donors. The rest of the counterdemonstrators scattered, trusting the greater speed of youth to let them beat Sinth's older, slower followers to their prey.

Sinth started his followers on a hymn. Veterans of many church services, they managed the four-part harmony with practiced authority:

> *"To make the world be as it should,*
> *Lord Father, help us to be good.*
> *When you declare that it is time,*
> *We'll overcome the demon Sime!"*

Not to be outdone, OLD SOKS chimed in:

> *"Reverend Sinth does as he should:*
> *Murders kids to keep them good,*
> *Stabs them when he's got the time*
> *Even when they're not a Sime!"*

The same free spirit that showed in the OLD SOKS dress code was also expressed in their eclectic choices of melody and key. Den winced, and was glad when his cousin turned back to him.

"Den, I know you're studying out-Territory culture and politics, but that's not why we're here. Our job is to provide services to the citizens of Clear Springs. Last night, you provided superficial platitudes, instead of explaining changeover training so they could make an informed decision."

"Weren't you zlinning their reactions? Last night was no time for lectures, or hot-button topics that anger people. Did you have to tell them Gens can make money donating selyn?"

"More than a few young Gens wanted to know," the channel insisted self-righteously.

"Their parents would rather they *didn't* know." Den kept his voice calm. The Sime Center's Gen chef, Ref, was clearing the tables for lunch and it was unprofessional for Firsts to argue in public. "On this side of the border, Gens are legally children until they reach sixteen natal years. Offend their parents, and we'll get nowhere."

Rital shook his head. "Being caught in a lie does more harm than unpalatable truths. Nothing infuriates people more than learning they've been tricked."

"I'm not asking you to lie," the Donor assured his cousin, "but could you please choose truths that won't lose us the battle before it begins?"

"If winning battles is more important to you than the honesty demanded by your oath to the Tecton," the channel snapped, "perhaps you should go join the New Washington Army!"

Den stared at his cousin in shock, unable to believe that a channel would say such a thing to his own Donor. Rital looked equally appalled, but also defiant.

"Are you going into Turnover a day early?" Den asked in a venomous tone too soft to reach Ref's ears. "Because if not…"

The exchange of musical taunts outside took on a darker tone. Over that background, Reverend Sinth's voice boomed, "Stop that truck!"

A horn blared, followed by a shrill scream. A van with the logo CLEAR SPRINGS PUBLIC SCHOOLS was attempting to reach the Sime Center. Anti-Sime demonstrators yelled with rage as they beat it with their signs, trying to force open the doors. As Den watched in horror, the turmeric-haired man used his sign handle, a heavy fence post, to smash the windshield and two other demonstrators tried to pull the driver out.

"Ease off, Den," Rital commanded, zlinning the situation.

The Donor obediently withdrew his support.

Rital flinched at the raw hatred. Den quelled the urge to block it and let the channel assess the situation.

OLD SOKS counterdemonstrators dragged Sinth's people away, clearing the front of the vehicle. Horn blaring, the truck lurched through the gap, leaving two attackers sprawled in the dust. Unable to reach the parking lot, the driver steered the machine over the curb. Trin plants went flying as it wove toward the main entrance.

Rital muttered, "I can't quite… Yes, it's got to be a changeover." He ran for the stairs with augmented speed.

"Ref, get a team out front with a stretcher!" Den ordered and followed his cousin as quickly as Gen feet could manage. Clattering down the main staircase, he ran across the lobby and plunged through the front door just as the battered vehicle screeched to a halt.

The channel eyed the protestors, but Sinth had not forgotten the last time he took his mischief into Sime Territory. The preacher shook an angry fist at them, then directed his people to wave their signs and chant, "Simes will kill and Simes will lie, Scripture says all Simes must die!"

"Bloodthirsty lorshes," Den growled, expecting the channel to assess the condition of the injured driver. Instead, Rital headed for the rear of the vehicle. Den followed in a show of calm competence intended to convince everyone that the situation was under control.

Rital tried the handles, then "Locked," he said shortly. He focused to zlin whoever was in there. "Not far along." He backtracked to deal with the Gen slumped over the steering wheel.

The driver roused when Den opened the door. A shard of glass had gashed the man's pale forehead, sending blood flowing down his face. It took a moment for Den to identify the battered visage as that of Principal Ed Buchan.

Still dazed, Buchan muttered, "They tried to murder me!"

"They did," Den agreed. "You're safe now, though. Can you unlock the back door for us?"

Buchan blinked uncomprehendingly at the Donor, then fumbled with some buttons on the dashboard. "If you'll give me the keys," Den suggested gently, "we can look after your passenger."

It took the principal two tries to get the heavy key chain free, but at last he held it out with a shaking hand. "Jainy made me lock her in back, " he explained weakly. "They'd have beaten her to death."

"You're both safe now," Den repeated, tossing the keys to Rital.

Ref and the emergency team arrived with a gurney. Hot on their heels came Zir Asthan, one of the Sime Center's Third Order channels, and his Donor, Hammil ambrov Keon. The two were nominally off duty, and Hammil's dripping hair and non-regulation outfit proclaimed that he, at least, had been otherwise occupied.

Rital tossed the keys to Zir and waved the young channel toward the back of the truck. At his Donor's raised eyebrow, Rital explained, "The changeover's not far advanced and Jain met Zir during her training. We'll look after her father. Buchan's badly shaken and his nager's strong enough to give a Third trouble."

Den moved aside to give his cousin access to their patient. It was a measure of the principal's state of shock that he didn't react to Nancy Resher and Florence Grieves calling, "Traitor!" from the sidewalk, or even to Rital's tentacles as the channel conducted a brief but thorough examination.

"You'll live," Rital pronounced. "Still, that's a nasty cut. Let's get you inside so we can take care of it. Den, you take his other arm."

Buchan let them lead him slowly toward the door, but after three steps, he shuddered, stopped and looked around, once more aware of his surroundings. "I'm fine," he insisted, shrugging off their hands. In the process, he glimpsed the channel's bare arms. Even though Rital's tentacles were retracted into their sheaths, his eyes widened and he shied away, bumping into Den. As the Donor steadied Buchan—and the fields—Rital stepped back.

Zir stopped at the nageric commotion and the stretcher crew stopped, too. A thin hand emerged from under the blanket and an equally thin face framed by long, pale hair turned toward Den.

"Daddy!" Jain wailed as she saw the blood on her father's face. She struggled to sit up, fighting off Zir's attempt to restrain her.

"Your father's going to be fine, Jain," Rital said quickly, moving to the side of the gurney. "Lie still, or you'll hurt yourself."

Jain glared at Rital. "He's bleeding," she accused.

"I know," Rital agreed, capturing her hand and giving it a reassuring squeeze. "It's a shallow wound, though. He isn't in danger."

Den could see swollen, red streaks on Jain's arm, but no visible lumps. It would be hours before her new tentacles were ready to emerge.

We've never had a changeover brought in this early, Den thought with satisfaction. *If we can train more children, it might become routine!*

Jain nodded provisional acceptance of Rital's assurance. Then her gaze went to his tentacle sheaths and her face twisted in disgust. She pulled her hand free, whimpering when she saw her own forearms.

Not for the first time, Den regretted that Rital had worn retainers while teaching. Jain would be less traumatized if she'd gotten used to Rital's tentacles before she began growing her own. However, while Miz Dilson was sympathetic, their classroom was publicly accessible, so the retainers had remained on.

The channel smiled at Jain. "It'll be hours yet before anything exciting happens, so you might as well rest. Hajene Asthan will look after you while I care for your father, but Sosu Milnan and I will come by soon. In the meantime, practice your breathing exercises. All right?"

Jain nodded. Rital turned toward the girl's father, who stepped back in alarm at the Sime's focused attention.

Den warned his cousin off with a gesture, then beckoned to Ref. "Would you give me a hand here?" he requested, drawing one of Buchan's arms over his shoulder. With the chef's assistance, he got Buchan moving again. Rital trailed behind, out of Buchan's view.

"Watch your feet," the Donor warned as they reached the door.

The principal stepped over the doorjamb with exaggerated care, then blinked in surprise. Because Clear Springs was eight hours by train from the territory border, the Sime Center was a consulate in addition to a medical and selyn collection facility. While most of the building's design was dictated by function, the lobby showcased in-Territory architecture. The space stretched two stories tall, with a balcony on the second floor leading to the grand staircase. Murals, comfortable couches, and potted plants provided a restful atmosphere and a stained-glass window filled the area with colored light. The effect was light and airy, in stark contrast to the fortress-like designs of out-Territory public edifices.

Since the citizens of Clear Springs rarely asked the Sime Center for medical assistance, the infirmary was a small room at the back of the building. It had a waiting area with comfortable chairs and a well-stocked treatment alcove.

The principal took three steps into the room, then balked. "I'm fine," he insisted, shrugging off their hands. As Rital disappeared into the treatment alcove and Ref bustled over to make tea, Buchan said, "It's Jainy who's sick. Woke up this morning feeling queasy. I told her it was nerves after last night, but she wanted to make sure it wasn't changeover."

Mindful of the man's precarious condition, the Donor decided not to enlighten him just yet.

"After what Reverend Sinth said, I saw no harm in indulging her," Buchan continued. "But his people wouldn't let us through." He made it to a padded armchair, leaned back, and closed his eyes. "Sorry to be such a bother," he apologized. "But after I made Jainy attend your class, I had to help her follow your instructions, didn't I?"

With a trembling hand, the principal caught a drop of blood before it could drip off his chin. He opened his eyes, saw the stain on his hand and looked around for something on which to wipe it. After a moment, he used his shirt.

"It's no bother at all," Den reassured him, inspecting the wound. It was as long as his finger and quite shallow, but like any scalp wound it bled copiously.

It'll do Rital good to heal a real injury, the Donor reflected. He pressed a sterile pad against the cut, then guided the injured man's hand to hold it in place. "Hold this until Hajene Madz gets back, then I'll get him over here to apply a backfield."

"To do what?"

Den mentally repeated his last sentence, which had seemed clear to *him*, and realized that he had lapsed into Simelan. He vainly sought a translation, noticing Buchan's growing apprehension.

"To stop the bleeding," the Donor equivocated. What the out-Territory Simephobe didn't know wouldn't scare him...yet.

Buchan staggered to his feet as Rital emerged from the treatment alcove with warm water, disinfectant, and a stack of sterile swabs. "Thank you for your assistance, Controller Madz," the principal said courteously, eyes focused firmly on the channel's face. "As soon as that mob outside calms down, we'll be on our way. Jainy belongs back in her own bed." He got unsteadily to his feet.

"I'm afraid that isn't possible," Rital said kindly. "She really *is* in changeover."

Buchan collapsed in a dead faint. "Shen you, Rital!" the Donor swore, as he guided Buchan's fall back into the armchair with dexterity born of desperation. "Did you have to tell him *that*?" Den picked up one limp wrist to check for a pulse. It was rapid but strong, and Rital looked more offended than alarmed, so Buchan wasn't in shock. At least Rital hadn't tried to catch the man himself.

"He has the right to know," the channel said indignantly. "It's not a secret, after all. Why didn't you tell him?"

"Because I thought the shock might be too much for him," Den said. "And it was," he added, letting his indignation show. "Providing full information is fine, but pick an appropriate time and place."

"Let's discuss our philosophical differences when we don't have a patient requiring help."

Den blushed at the reprimand. However, even when conscious, Buchan only understood tone of voice in Simelan, while Ref studiously ignored them. Den calmed and offered his usual support.

Rital took advantage of their patient's temporary inability to object to let his laterals touch the skin near the wound. His eyes went blank as he zlinned the wound's effect on Buchan's selyn field.

"There's no embedded glass," he reported when his eyes focused again. "It's a simple cut with no tearing or bruising. Easy to close."

The channel moved his laterals to the back of Buchan's neck, probing for the nerves that controlled the autonomic nervous system. He concentrated, restoring normal tension to the muscles surrounding the larger abdominal arteries to stabilize Buchan's blood pressure. When the out-Territory Gen stirred with returning consciousness, Rital prudently relinquished lateral contact and sheathed the delicate tentacles.

Nevertheless, the first things Buchan saw when he opened his eyes were Rital's handling tentacles in front of his nose. He screamed and lunged backward in the chair.

Not expecting such panic, Den was slow damping the surge in the ambient. Rital yelped, then complained, "Den!"

The Donor put an arm around his cousin, blocking the other Gen's nager. He concentrated on soothing thoughts. Rital shuddered.

The principal's movement had pushed the chair back against the wall. The bump jolted him out of his blind panic. He realized that Rital had not been attacking him, then noticed the channel shaking in Den's arms. "What's the matter with the Sime?"

"Because you're high field, your sudden fear felt to him…" the Donor groped for a suitable comparison, "…well, as if you'd punched him in the stomach."

"Oh." Buchan forced his eyes back to Rital. "I apologize for hurting you, Ha-jene." He said the word slowly, struggling with the proper pronunciation.

"That's quite all right," the channel said graciously. "It was an accident," he glanced pointedly at Den, "and I'm not injured."

"I'm glad." The principal sounded a bit surprised by his own sincerity. "You weren't joking when you said Jainy's in changeover?"

Rital shook his head. "I'm afraid not," he apologized.

"But…" Buchan shook his head in stunned disbelief, "you said Reverend Sinth was wrong. That your classes didn't affect a child's chances of becoming Sime. But Jain's in changeover, less than a day after Reverend Sinth predicted it!" It wasn't *quite* an accusation.

"Reverend Sinth didn't foresee anything," Den assured him. "This is just one of those coincidences that the universe throws our way from time to time." He watched Buchan's innate good sense war with his cultural traditions and sighed in relief when the man nodded reluctantly.

"I suppose you're right," the principal admitted. "But why did the universe pick on my little girl? She's the only family I have left. I'm grateful that I won't have to shoot her," he assured them. "But my baby, exiled to a foreign land…"

A tear escaped. He wiped it away, smearing blood across his cheek. A second tear followed the first and then a third. With a muffled sob, the principal buried his face in his hands.

There was nothing they could do to soften Buchan's loss except give him space to accept the changes in his life. Ref moistened a clean towel at the sink and handed it to Den.

Eventually, the principal's shoulders stopped shaking and he straightened. "I'm sorry," he apologized dully. "I shouldn't have…"

Out-Territory, Den knew, it was bad manners for a man to cry, no matter the circumstances. That cultural rule made even less sense to him than their educational priorities.

"You don't have to apologize for loving your daughter," Rital assured Buchan.

The principal looked down, embarrassed, and saw the blood on his hands. When Den offered him the towel, he scrubbed each finger as if to wash away the morning's events.

Buchan, hands now clean, looked up at Rital and asked, "If Jainy's in changeover, shouldn't you be looking after her?"

"She's in the care of one of our best," the channel reassured him. "Everything's proceeding normally. Like childbirth, changeover takes time. We can take care of you before we check on her."

Buchan's apprehension increased when Den explained, "Once I've cleaned that cut, Rital will convince the damaged cells to repair themselves."

"How?" the principal asked. "You can't argue with cells."

While Rital searched for a way to explain selyn field mechanics in a language that lacked the vocabulary, Den offered a less upsetting explanation. "Healing requires extra selyn. When there's a Sime nearby, Gens produce more selyn, because there is, uh, somewhere for it to go. Channels can focus that natural response so the injury responds with maximum healing."

Buchan cast a nervous glance at Rital's sheathed tentacles. "I wouldn't want to bother you with a simple cut. Just let me say…" His voice broke and he swallowed. "…say good-bye to Jainy, then I'll be on my way. I promise, I'll go to my own doctor."

"It's no trouble at all," Rital said, with unfeigned sincerity. "It'll only take a moment, and then the cut won't get infected or leave a scar."

Den saw his cousin's sheathed laterals quiver. While it was true that injured Gen tissues produced extra selyn as they healed, the wasted selyn that leaked from injuries evoked subconscious fears of Attrition in nearby Simes. It was tremendously satisfying for a channel to zlin a selyn-leaking injury heal under his tentacles; even better, if the patient was Gen, since it gratified the Sime urge to protect the source of selyn.

There were few opportunities for channels to heal Gens in Simephobic Clear Springs. Like the other Sime Center staff, Den was tired of having every stubbed toe and paper cut become a medical emergency. *If a real emergency escapes untreated, Rital will be impossible to live with.*

"You can't drive across town like that, Principal Buchan," the Donor pointed out. "Blood is dripping in your eyes."

"I don't suppose it would do any harm to stop the bleeding, but…" Buchan began uncertainly.

This was as close to legal consent as they were likely to get. "There's nothing to it, really," Den promised, moistening a swab before their patient could reconsider. "I'll start by cleaning the cut so it doesn't get infected. You'd better close your eyes. The disinfectant will sting worse than onions if it gets in them."

Buchan cast a last nervous glance in Rital's direction, but the principal was a fundamentally reasonable man. He closed his eyes and slumped back in the padded chair.

Den washed the blood away, keeping part of his attention focused on blocking Rital's perception of Buchan's pain. As he worked, he murmured reassurance in a soothing monotone.

Gritting his teeth at the sting of the disinfectant, Buchan didn't notice the hovering channel cautiously extending two handling tentacles to lift sticky hair out of Den's workspace. The Donor let disinfectant dribble down the Gen's face to encourage him to keep his eyes closed, but with the pain distracting him, it was unlikely that Buchan would notice a few extra "fingers" touching him.

Still, he tensed when Rital handed the Donor a fresh swab. It didn't take an expert in psychology to guess that the Gen would refuse channel's healing, if given a choice.

So, we won't give him one.

CHAPTER 4

SIMEPHOBE

Den exchanged his swab for a damp towel. Without altering his reassuring monologue, he cleaned the blood off Buchan's forehead, draped the towel over his patient's eyes, then signaled Rital to start healing.

Rital's eyes widened at his cousin's deception, but swallowed his objections as Den savagely mouthed, "Shut up!"

Treating a conscious adult patient without that patient's knowledge and consent was both ethically dubious and legally a form of assault. However, since Buchan's reluctance stemmed from Simephobia, not a moral objection, he'd probably accept a *fait accompli*. Besides, the out-Territory Gen knew nothing of Tecton regulations or how to report a violation.

As if to conquer his nervousness, the principal interrupted Den's soothing monologue to ask, "How long before Jain...?"

"She should reach breakout by dinnertime tomorrow," Den said. "Then we'll throw her a changeover party."

"A party?"

Rital's laterals extended along the cut. Den scrubbed at a bloodstain to provide a tactile distraction and held himself ready to block any reaction if the distraction failed. The channel concentrated, using selyn currents to seal the edges of the gash and encourage healthy cells to divide and replace their damaged neighbors.

"Yes, a coming-of-age party," the Donor confirmed. "It's traditional in Sime Territory, when a child changes over or Establishes."

After a moment, Buchan said slowly, "What a strange idea, to celebrate no matter what your child becomes. I don't see any reason to be happy, myself. I'm glad Jainy will live, but I've still lost her. I'm too old to start another family, so I'll never have grandchildren."

"Why not?" Den asked, with genuine surprise. "People get married and raise families on our side of the border too, you know."

"Well..." the principal began, then fell silent as he realized the possibilities.

The cut had closed to a thin red line that would disappear entirely in a few days. The channel withdrew his laterals. Den used a fresh towel to wipe off the last few bloodstains, giving his cousin time to retreat to the other end of the room. "All done," he announced.

Buchan opened his eyes, scanned the room for Rital, then relaxed when he located the channel at a psychologically safe distance. His fear allayed, his practical side asserted itself.

"I'm a mess," he observed, looking down at his stained and tattered shirt.

"That shirt isn't even fit for rags," Ref agreed. "Try this instead." He offered the short-sleeved chef's jacket he wore over his shirt.

In the process of changing shirts, Buchan noticed that his forehead didn't hurt. He lifted a hand to the injury and his face twisted in confusion when his fingers found only smooth, if tender, skin.

"It's mostly healed," Den said, with a combination of reassurance and matter-of-fact acceptance. "In a few days, it won't even be tender." Rital tensed.

"But..." The principal stared at them in disbelief, unable to decide whether to be afraid, indignant, or relieved. He squinted at his reflection in the small mirror over the table, tracing the thin red line on his forehead. "That's amazing!"

The Donor gave a casual shrug. "Channels come in handy."

"I guess so," Buchan agreed. He looked at his reflection again, then turned to more important matters. "If Jainy must live in Sime Territory," he announced, "I should honor the customs of her new home. I'd like to attend this coming-of-age party."

"You'll be welcome," Rital agreed. "Jain will appreciate your support. However, for your safety and hers, you must donate selyn first, so you'll be low field."

"Donate selyn!" The man's eyes widened in alarm.

Den blocked most of the surge in the ambient, but the channel still flinched. *He took some real damage when I didn't block that first panic attack,* the Donor realized, placing a protective hand on his cousin's arm.

At the channel's reaction, the principal apologized. "Still," he finished with honest belligerence, "it's not right to blackmail a man who just wants to say good-bye to his own daughter."

"Principal Buchan, if you don't want to donate selyn, you can communicate with Jain by letter or telephone," the Donor clarified. "Your flare of fear just now hurt Rital right through my blocking it. Jain doesn't have a channel's defenses. You could really injure her."

"My feelings wouldn't change just because I donated selyn," Buchan warned.

"The strength with which you project them would," Rital explained. "It works like this: Gens have six storage levels for selyn, like a series of dams along a river. Those 'dams' form your selyn reservoirs. Without them, the selyn you produce would dissipate as fast as it was made."

Buchan nodded slowly, provisionally accepting the comparison.

"The three inner, TN storage levels, that hold the most selyn, are protected by strong barriers," Den took up the story. "They never relax unless the Gen releases them. Learning to do that is part of the training of a technical-class Donor like me."

"The three shallower, GN levels," Rital continued, "will release selyn if the Gen is simply relaxed. The outermost, GN-3 barrier can't ever be closed fully."

Den offered, "Healthy Gens produce selyn continuously. The outer storage level dissipates enough selyn to prevent it from backing up and making you sick. It's like a weir—when the 'water' reaches the top, it flows over whether or not the floodgates are open."

"Forming the river beneath the dam?" Buchan asked.

"That's right!" Den smiled. "That discharge is your field—what a Sime zlins—and like the water in a river, it reflects the condition of the reservoir; that is, how you're feeling physically and emotionally."

"Right now, your river is running high enough to injure a new Sime like Jain," Rital explained. "What channels do, that renSimes can't, is to lower the level of the weir without, er, damaging the infrastructure. That reduces leakage from behind the barrier to a trickle."

"So, Jain can wade, but won't drown?" Buchan followed.

"Exactly!"

Buchan nodded slowly. "If I have to donate selyn before I can see Jainy, it might as well be now." His voice quavered. "It won't get easier later."

"True," the Donor agreed. "The Collectorium is right around the corner." Turning to the chef, he asked, "Ref, would you show Principal Buchan the way and ask Seena to help him with the paperwork? We'll be there after we've checked on Jain."

"Certainly," Ref agreed. "If you're ready, Principal Buchan?"

"All right." Buchan rose and started for the door, then turned to face Rital. "Take good care of my daughter, Hajene," he begged. "She's the only family I've got."

Rital responded with a channel's formal commitment: "I will see her through until she's out of danger, on my honor as a First."

* * * *

"Are you sure you want to handle Jain's changeover personally?" Den asked, eyeing his cousin's face with concern. "You're as pale as a ghost. How badly did Buchan's panic attacks hurt you, anyway?" *Particularly the first one I failed to block.* The Donor acknowledged his guilt and then set it aside, where it wouldn't interfere with his ability to deal with the consequences of his mistake.

"I've got a headache, that's all," the channel replied, massaging the back of his neck with all eight handling tentacles. "It'll be gone long before Jain can zlin." He frowned at the Donor's skepticism. "Really, Den, I've worked Dispensary shifts with worse. Though not recently."

The unspoken criticism was clear. *It's been a long time since you messed up this badly.*

Perhaps realizing that his last statement had been tactless, the channel hastened to reassure Den. "I'll be fine, and it will comfort Principal Buchan to know his daughter is in familiar hands."

"Rital, I'm not asking you to break your word," Den argued. "However, Jain's changeover is progressing normally, or Zir would have called for us. At least let me take care of that headache."

The Donor was totally unprepared when the channel meekly turned back into the infirmary. *Shen, he's hurting more than he admits, if he isn't putting up even a token fight!*

In the treatment alcove, Rital sat and buried his face in his hands with a groan. The nager of a trained Gen could treat many Sime ailments, but even the best Donors sometimes resorted to stronger measures. Den poured a stiff dose of fosebine.

The channel peered at the opalescent liquid suspiciously. "That's way too strong," he objected.

"Drink it."

"Sadist," Rital grumbled. Holding his nose with two tentacles, he gulped the medicine, then put the glass on the wetbench with a shudder.

Den moved behind the chair, placed both hands on the channel's neck, and set to work.

It took him almost fifteen minutes to unravel the disruption that Buchan's panic attack—and his own failure to block it—had caused in Rital's systems. It was more difficult than it should have been, as if the channel was resisting.

Is he having trouble trusting me, because I let him get hurt?

He removed his hands and stepped back, inspecting his cousin carefully.

"Thanks." Rital sat back with a sigh of relief. "This will be easier now." There was color in his face again, although he still looked tired.

"Are you *sure* you wouldn't rather let Tyvi handle Buchan?" Den asked. Tyvi ambrov Frihill was the Sime Center's other First Order channel. "She's more than competent, and if you're going to look after Jain, she'll have to take your Collectorium shift."

"Principal Buchan has never met her," Rital pointed out. "It will be difficult enough for him to let *me* take his selyn. His support for our classes in his school is invaluable. I can handle a First Donation and still keep my commitment to Jain."

Den inspected the channel carefully. "You look less like a sheet of paper," he admitted. "I should probably take you off duty for a few hours, just out of principle, but I won't...on one condition."

"What?" Rital asked, with instant suspicion.

"Let me do as much of the work with Jain as possible. Then you'll be in condition to help her at the end."

"You're overreacting."

" A lot depends on Jain having an easy time, so those are my terms. You can accept them, or you can go lie down for a while. Frankly, as the one responsible for keeping you in top form, I'd prefer the second option."

"The staff channels would never support your taking me off duty for a little thing like this."

Den raised an eyebrow. "You mean our work-starved staff channels itching for an excuse to get their tentacles on a patient?"

"That's blackmail!" Rital protested.

"Do we have a deal?"

The channel considered his options. He didn't have any. "All right."

* * * *

In the changeover ward, Zir puttered with medications at the wet-bench while Hammil sat by Jain's bedside, taking an informal lesson in English. The Third Order Donor understood most of what Jain said, but could not yet construct proper English sentences. When his instructor broke into giggles, he gave her a good-natured wink.

"You think I talk funny?" he asked. "You be also bad, when you learn Simelan. At least Simelan make sense."

"English makes sense!" Jain protested.

"Too many words," Hammil explained. "You have different word for say-happy, say-mad, say-loud, say-confused... Too hard learn them all. Simelan have one word for say, use nager add how the feeling."

"Use nager?" Jain asked. "How can a Gen *use* nager, and what does it have to do with meanings?"

"Wait a few hours," Hammil told her, "and I show you."

"But you're Gen," she insisted.

"Already you think like Sime!" the Gen told her. "You think Gens can't think or talk just because they don't have testicles!"

The proper sheltered girl in Jain warred with her adolescence as she blushed rosily and tried to cover a burst of laughter at the same time.

"You think Gens be funny?" Hammil asked, confused and offended. "Already you make fun of us?"

"No! No!" Jain protested. "W-wrong word! It's tentacles, not—" hotter blush, "—what you said!"

Hammil frowned. "What I said? What means testicles?"

Den could see that Jain was rapidly descending from laughter to the verge of tears as the hormones of changeover magnified every feeling. "Hammil," he said gently, "testicles are something men have and women don't."

It was Hammil's turn to blush as he got it, and realized that Jain was mocking his command of English, not his larity.

Jain turned to Den and Rital. "How's my Daddy?"

"He's fine," Rital said, crossing to the bed with Den at his heels as Hammil retreated to his own channel's side. "I healed the cut on his forehead, the way we talked about in class. Do you remember?"

"I thought that was just a story," she said.

Den laughed. "It's real enough. Your father will have a mark on his forehead but only for a few days. He's fine."

"Now let's see how *you* are doing," Rital suggested.

Jain's eyes darted to the channel's arms and she stared at his partially extended handling tentacles. Her face paled and she shrank back against her pillow. Rital retreated a step and Den moved between them, projecting calm.

"Hajene Madz won't hurt you, Jain," he said, giving her thin hands a reassuring squeeze. "He just wants to zlin your progress. Will you let him do that?"

The young Sime considered the request, then gave a jerky nod, gritting her teeth as she braced for the ordeal.

Rital smiled reassuringly, then casually touched Jain's wrists, with fingers only. Den held her hands as she reflexively tried to pull away, then stilled.

"You're doing fine," the channel said when he finished. "You're nearing the end of Stage Two, so your breathing will ease soon and you'll feel stronger."

"My arms *itch*," Jain complained. She looked down at the red streaks from elbow to wrist and her face twisted in disgust. "This looks worse than poison ivy."

Den chuckled at her adolescent vanity. "Don't worry," he told her. "You'll heal in no time. My word as a Donor." He gave her hands a last squeeze, then followed his cousin over to consult with Zir.

"Has she been this uncooperative all along?" Rital asked.

Zir nodded. "I'm afraid so, Controller Madz," he admitted. "She's all right with the breathing and relaxation exercises, but she tenses every time a tentacle comes near. Hammil was trying to distract her."

Den sighed. "I should have expected it," he said. "Rital, if we can't teach changeover classes at the school, we've *got* to find a room we can post as Sime Territory. Our students have to get used to the sight—and feel—of tentacles. Training won't help if they still fight the channel trying to treat them."

"I know," Rital agreed, taking his Donor's cue. "For now, you coach Jain, Den, and I'll check her progress when necessary."

"I'd be happy to take care of that, Controller Madz," Zir offered, in a respectful tone that didn't hide his eagerness.

"You're on duty at the Collectorium this afternoon," his senior reminded him.

"Reyna can cover for me," the younger channel argued. "I've been looking after Jain all morning. She knows me now. Besides," Zir's voice oozed concern, "you don't zlin at all well. What happened to you, anyway?"

"Jain's known me a lot longer than you. I'm fine…just had some difficulty with her father, and the answer is no," Rital said firmly.

Den was shocked by Zir's lack of discipline when the young channel opened his mouth to protest his Controller's decision.

"No more argument," Rital added before Zir could speak. "I'll have Seena send Temmin over here. We may require an extra set of hands and tentacles."

Zir's shoulders slumped. "Yes, Hajene," he conceded.

* * * *

When Den and Rital reached the Collectorium, Seena had Buchan's donation paperwork ready. She handed Rital the newly-assembled file, saying, "I don't envy you this one, Hajene. He's as skittish as a flock of doves with a hawk circling overhead."

"The good principal is a Simephobe," Den explained as he scanned the file over Rital's shoulder.

"He has good reason for wanting to be low field, though," Rital added. "So, we'll have to manage."

"I gave him pamphlets to read while he waits," Seena told them. "Perhaps they will help."

When the cousins entered the waiting room, however, Buchan was reading a pamphlet on selyn-powered technology, rather than the one describing selyn donation.

Is he so afraid of donating that he can't even read about it? For a moment, Den reconsidered forbidding his cousin this donation. However, though easier on Rital, it might be harder on Jain's father.

"How's Jain?" Buchan asked as they entered the waiting room.

"She's fine," Rital assured him. "Everything's progressing normally. That gives us time to take care of you."

The out-Territory Gen's shoulders tensed. "Now?" he quavered.

"Yes, now," the channel assured. "If you'll come with us?"

Rital led the way down a well-lit corridor decorated in bright, welcoming colors. Buchan followed like a condemned man on the way to execution. Den tried to shield Rital from the principal's apprehension.

Rital paused at the door of his usual workroom. "This is one of our collecting rooms," he told Buchan quietly. "If you choose to follow me inside, I will get you through a selyn donation. You probably won't enjoy it, but neither of us will suffer any lasting harm. Later, you can see Jain."

Buchan's already-pale face assumed a greenish tint and Den once again cursed his cousin's insistence on complete honesty.

"It's your choice," Rital reminded him. Then channel and Donor stepped through the door, leaving Buchan in the corridor. It took the principal almost a minute, but he followed them inside.

Like the hallway, the collecting room was decorated in cheerful colors. It smelled of furniture polish and ink, with a whiff of lavender from the slipcover on the comfortable transfer lounge. Soft music played, a tune familiar on both sides of the border. It was all designed to feel ordinary and non-threatening: a place where it was safe to relax.

"Have a seat, Principal Buchan," Rital invited, taking the desk chair. While Buchan settled on the very edge of the visitor's chair, Den switched on the 'In Use' light and perched on a stool, supporting Rital without blocking his cousin's ability to judge Buchan's nageric responses.

Rital began by asking routine questions about Buchan's medical history, less for information than to pry the man's mind out of its frozen panic. Soon Buchan sat back properly in his chair and his face regained some color.

Shen, you're good, cousin, the Donor thought, letting his admiration show in his nager.

Judging that the principal was ready to listen, the channel asked, "Did you read through the pamphlet on selyn donation?"

"Err, no," Buchan admitted.

"It's a very simple process," Rital explained, leaning back in his chair. "You lie down on the couch over there and I sit beside you. I make a transfer contact, coax open the floodgates Den was talking about to release selyn from behind that shallowest barrier, and leave you low field so you can't injure Jain." The channel appeared quiet and relaxed, but Den saw his cousin's lateral tentacles peeking out of their sheaths, tracking Buchan's responses. "It doesn't take long and you won't feel anything happening. Do you have any questions?"

"It does sound simple," the principal observed skeptically.

"It is," Rital assured him, nodding at the transfer lounge. "If you're ready to try it, lie down over there."

Buchan walked to the lounge with determination. When he had settled, Rital sat beside him and held out steady hands, tentacles retracted. "Put your hands in mine," he directed softly.

Den placed a hand on the channel's neck, lending strength against the other Gen's fear.

Buchan put his hands into Rital's, but turned his face away, squeezing his eyes shut.

Rital murmured, "What you're imagining is far worse than the reality. Would so many of your neighbors donate selyn every month if it were terrifying or painful?"

"I suppose not," Buchan admitted with an attempt at a smile.

"Listen to the music," Den suggested, as a velvet baritone began crooning a popular ballad. "Before the song is over, you'll be low field."

"I'll try," Buchan whispered.

Rital shifted his grip to the Principal's wrists and extended his handling tentacles to grasp Buchan's arms firmly, immobilizing them as the Gen flinched. The small, nerve-rich lateral tentacles emerged, sliding across the Gen's arms in search of the selyn-rich forearm nerves. The channel bent to make the lip-to-lip contact necessary to draw selyn.

The principal's nerve faltered and he twisted his head away. Rital followed the movement and easily completed the full contact, pressing his lips impersonally against the Gen's. Buchan emitted a muffled squawk. The channel's eyes unfocused as he shifted his attention to zlinning Buchan's selyn field.

"Relax, Principal Buchan," Den murmured, hoping to curb the incipient panic attack. "Rital isn't hurting you."

In full lateral contact, a channel experienced the full onslaught of a Gen's emotions and there was little a Donor could do to change that, since interfering with the channel's perceptions would prevent him from taking the donation safely.

"Listen to the music," Den advised Buchan again, hoping against hope that the crooner lovingly detailing the attractions of his lost lady would provide sufficient distraction.

For a moment, it seemed to be working, but as the singer swung into the chorus, Buchan's nerve broke. He strained against Rital's tentacles.

CHAPTER 5

CHANGEOVER

Like any Sime, Rital could augment his strength by consuming extra selyn. Protecting his vulnerable laterals from the shock of mid-draw disruption provided a strong incentive. It wasn't until the crooner began the next verse, confessing how his lady's charms had not, after all, prevented him from dallying with another, that Rital broke lip contact.

"Principal Buchan, hold still," he ordered, his calm voice cutting through Buchan's panic. "It's over. You aren't hurt, but you are low field. You can see Jain when she's ready for visitors."

Buchan froze and the channel quickly retracted his laterals, sheathing the delicate organs before his handling tentacles released the out-Territory Gen. The principal's eyes rested on the purple-red marks they had left behind, then met Rital's in silent accusation.

"You fought me hard enough to bruise yourself," Rital explained, without apology. He had, after all, been acting in accordance with the Gen's express wishes. "Those marks will fade in a day or two."

The channel retreated behind the desk, putting Den's nager between himself and Buchan. "Do you want a voucher, or would you prefer to assign the selyn credit directly to Jain?"

The principal rubbed his face with his hands. "Selyn credit?"

"Simes pay the Tecton for the selyn they consume," Den explained. "It covers the Tecton's expense in collecting it and compensation to the Gen who donates it."

Buchan sighed. "I did this for Jain. She might as well benefit from it. Let's do the credit."

"As you wish," Rital agreed, reaching for the proper form.

So, it was left to Den to suggest, "You can do this for Jain every month, if you wish. Think about it. It would never again be as difficult as today and Jain will feel warm and loved, because her father is thinking about her and sending her the gift of life."

* * * *

As they neared the changeover ward, Rital turned to Principal Buchan. "A few ground-rules. Jain's having a normal changeover and I want to keep it that way. If we ask you to step out, do it immediately and without arguing, so we can provide her the care she requires."

"That's reasonable," Buchan agreed. "I won't interfere."

Rital nodded, zlinning his agreement. "Jain's arms are sore where her tentacles are developing and she's experiencing uncomfortable new sensations. If she doesn't want to hold hands or hug you, it doesn't mean she doesn't love you. Right now, those things hurt."

"One last thing," Den added. "Jain is starting to respond to selyn fields. If you are angry, upset, or fearful, she'll pick up on it."

"Even if all goes well," Buchan said, "my little girl's leaving me to live far away where I can't protect her. It's hard not to be upset."

The Donor suggested, "Concentrate on your love for her and how that's not going to change. She'll feel that…and be stronger for it."

Rital paused in the doorway to Jain's treatment room, zlinning. "Stage Three," he told Den. Switching to the Gen language, he continued, "You're breathing much better, Jain."

"I ache from head to toes," their patient complained.

"Your body's making a lot of changes," Den told her. "You're living in a construction zone, but it'll be complete in a day or two."

"And then I'll be a Sime." Jain made it sound like the death sentence it would have been without the Sime Center.

"Yes, you'll be Sime," Rital repeated crisply. "A new adult, ready to start a new life in a new Territory. It'll be a challenge, but not an impossible one."

Jain looked skeptical, so Den changed the subject. "You have a visitor," he told her, stepping aside so that she could see her father.

"Daddy!" Jain looked shocked to see him. "Go away. I don't want to hurt you." She turned her back and curled into a protective ball around her vulnerable forearms.

"You won't hurt anyone," Buchan reassured her. "That's why we came here. Remember?"

"I don't want you to see me like this," she muttered into her pillow.

"Jain, you're my daughter," Buchan said with the patience of a man used to dealing with adolescents. "I love you and I'll always want to see you."

Some of the tension left Jain's shoulders, but she didn't turn to look at her father. "I love you too, Daddy. Now go. Please? I'm so tired." Her voice trailed off and her body went limp. Alarmed, her father dodged around Den, only to find his path blocked by Hammil.

"She's entering Stage Four, right on schedule," Rital announced. "She'll sleep for most of the next day, as her tentacles finish developing and her body switches from burning calories to burning selyn."

"I want to sit with her," Buchan said.

"That would not be wise," Rital explained. "Even low field, your anxiety would cause her to burn through her selyn reserves faster. She can't afford that."

"You can stay here at the Sime Center," Den told the disappointed father. "Nothing exciting will happen for hours. Rital and I will take over here. Hammil, Zir, would you show Principal Buchan where he can get something to eat and get him settled?"

* * * *

"Don't scratch your arms, Jain," a frustrated Den warned his patient the following afternoon.

"They itch," she complained.

The Donor had assumed that this changeover would be easy for Rital, since Jain knew him. However, although she had sought their help for fear of killing, she was almost as tentacle-shy as her father.

Still, Jain was their first patient with any training at all. As long as someone—a *Gen* someone—coached her, she could use the techniques she'd learned to keep her selyn consumption down. Den had napped for a few hours, but he was not at his best and he knew it.

As her tentacles matured and her body chemistry began to stabilize, Jain became increasingly restless. She plucked at the bedspread nervously, until Den captured her hands. "Not yet," he told her. "Just relax."

"I can't," she complained fretfully.

"Of course you can," the Donor said, projecting calm confidence. "Try the breathing exercises. You remember." He demonstrated, taking a deep breath and letting it out slowly.

Jain tried to follow his example, then gasped in sudden fear. "I'm falling," she wailed. "Daddy!" Her hands tightened on Den's with Sime strength and she panted, too upset to remember the breathing pattern that would have helped.

Rital came over to the bed. Jain submitted to his examination meekly, closing her eyes until it was over. When she opened them again, he smiled at her.

"It's transition to Stage Six," Rital explained, running a gentle finger along her cheek. "You're right on schedule. It won't be much longer before you're a full-grown Sime."

Jain gagged at the close-up view of the channel's sheathed tentacles. When the transition ended, she curled into a fetal ball again. "Why doesn't it *stop?*" she demanded when she caught her breath. "I'm dying, aren't I? Daddy should've let Reverend Sinth's people have me. At least that would have been quick."

"You'll be fine," Rital assured her. "What you feel is the beginning of Need. It's frightening, I know, but it'll be a lot less uncomfortable if you stop fighting it."

"Let me help," Den offered. He rubbed Jain's back soothingly, focusing his attention to control her Need. The young Sime's laterals were mature enough to make her vulnerable to this most seductive weapon in a Donor's arsenal. Soon she uncurled from her tight ball, as close to rational as any new Sime approaching breakout.

With their patient stabilized, Den prepared to relinquish control to Rital, to prevent Jain from becoming fixed on a Donor she couldn't have. Determined not to hurt another Sime in his care, Den focused with a single-minded intensity that he hadn't used since he finished training. He was aware of every field that influenced his selyn production, from Jain's growing Need to Rital's strong, steady presence. He could even pick up a faint hint of Temmin, the renSime attendant in the doorway.

Rital placed a hand on the back of Den's neck to begin relinquishment, blending the Donor's projection with the channel's Gen-like showfield. The technique allowed a Donor to surrender control of the fields to a channel with no loss of support to their patient.

Den usually remained passive and let Rital assume control of his selyn field. This time, he took a more active role. By deliberately modifying his own projection in synch with Rital's manipulation, he could protect both Rital and Jain from any fluctuation in the fields. They had never managed the tricky maneuver so smoothly before, without the slightest disorienting waver in the steady ambient they projected.

Unfortunately, despite her growing sensitivity to selyn fields, Jain followed the out-Territory habit of relying on her eyes. When she saw Rital moving closer and Den getting out of the way, she lost control of her breathing, choked, then gasped for breath.

Den picked up Rital's cue to abort the relinquishment almost before it was given and resumed control of the ambient with a smooth shift of focus that astonished him, not least because it was so effortless.

Den readjusted Jain's blanket as if that had been his intention all along, then sat again. His patient decided that he was not, after all, abandoning her to a Sime's mercy. She whimpered in relief, her breathing improved, and Den saw trouble ahead.

Jain's grudging cooperation with the channel disappeared as Need ate away at her rationality. She wouldn't survive if she wasted her selyn reserves fighting Rital. However, the young Sime had reacted to the *sight* of the channel, not his nager. Relinquishment could be done at any time during Stage Six...and at the very end of that stage, just before breakout,

Need would force Jain hyperconscious, unable to perceive the channel as anything but a Gen-like nager.

Den looked up and met Rital's eyes, so closely attuned that the Donor could almost read his cousin's thoughts. *We'll delay until the last moment.*

Across the room, Temmin's eyes widened as she realized the chance they were taking.

With Den's coaching, Jain stayed calm enough to conserve her limited supply of selyn as long as Rital stayed back. Still, by the time her tentacle sheaths filled with fluid, primed for breakout, Jain was close to Attrition and frantic with Need. Den handed her a rolled towel to grip.

Only a perfect relinquishment would allow the young Sime to accept Rital in Den's place. The Donor surrendered awareness of anything but the reflection of the ambient nager in his own body. There would be no third chance. He felt Jain's terror as the first breakout contraction gathered, an imperative that could not be denied. He steadied the fields, wrapping her in a nageric cocoon of support.

At Rital's signal, he let his cousin take control of the ambient *through* him. They had never worked with such precision. Despite his exhaustion, Den was exhilarated by the challenge of providing the pattern for Rital's Gen projection.

Hyperconscious and distracted by the gathering breakout contraction, Jain never noticed the switch. She screamed as the first spasm hit and squeezed her towel. The second followed almost instantly and she choked as she tried to breathe against the convulsions.

Den and Rital switched places as a third contraction wracked their patient's slender body. Den focused on keeping his own moving nager from interfering with the channel's support. Just for an instant, he thought he saw Jain *look* at him, with the blind panic of a trapped animal. He stepped back and formed his field into uninviting neutrality, no competition for Rital's Gen projection.

Jain was hyperconscious again when the fourth convulsion hit. As it crested, her hands opened wide and her tentacles broke free, spattering all three of them with blood and fluids. She panted in confusion, trying to comprehend the information bombarding her, then snarled as First Need overcame her.

But Jain had seen Den move away and wasn't willing to accept Rital as a substitute. As the last hint of the Donor's nager faded, instinct took over and the new Sime attacked, lunging toward the escaping selyn source.

Rital intervened, entwining her tentacles with his own. At the offer of immediate relief, she forgot Den and greedily reached for lip contact with the channel. It took only a moment to slake her Need.

"Congratulations!" Rital said warmly as she let him go. "You're all grown up now."

Den smiled indulgently as Jain looked around in confusion, disoriented by the disappearance of her new Sime senses. He added his own congratulations, but she didn't display the pride of a new in-Territory Sime.

"At least I didn't kill anyone," she said dispassionately, glancing down at her retracted tentacles. One bloody dorsal emerged clumsily from its sheath and she grimaced in disgust. "What a mess."

Den laughed and beckoned Temmin over. "Let's wash that mess off," he suggested. "You'll want to look your best at your party."

"It's time to celebrate," Rital confirmed. "You've become an adult today."

Den escorted the young Sime to the washroom and helped her clean her arms, impeded by her uncertain control of her new tentacles and her reluctance to let them emerge from their sheaths. Temmin brought a party frock to exchange for Jain's stained gown and the Donor left the girl to assistance that she tolerated as long as the other renSime's tentacles remained sheathed.

Den found Rital in the office, updating Jain's chart. He looked much more tired than he should. Still, Den's body respond normally to the channel's presence, without the vague unease that might indicate Rital's fields were disturbed.

Rital looked up as he zlinned his Donor's concern and smiled. "The headache hasn't come back, Den," he reassured his cousin. "I'm just tired, that's all. I'll be fine after a good night's rest."

Den nodded. "Just make sure that you *do* rest tonight."

"No more nageric stunts today." The channel smiled crookedly. "All right?"

Den rested his hand on his cousin's forearm. "All right," he agreed.

* * * *

When Den, Rital, and Jain entered the Sime Center's dining commons, the staff had already congregated. They greeted the guest of honor with smiles and congratulations as Den Escorted her into the room, keeping the fluctuations in the ambient nager from bothering her.

Seena and Ref had outdone themselves. A buffet table was covered with refreshments and the Gens were helping themselves to fruit, cheese, and other dainties. As Rital slipped away to consult with Tyvi, Den noticed with delight that Ref had made a batch of his famous banana-walnut ice cream. Most of the Simes contented themselves with the traditional glasses of amber-colored, spiced lantria.

The staff carried small wrapped packages of clothing, toiletries, books, and other items to ease the transition to life in-Territory. Most of the items came from a standard a travel kit, but at Rital's suggestion, the Clear Springs Sime Center presented the necessities as gifts from individuals to encourage the new Sime to perceive the staff as potential friends and the items less like charity. It was an important distinction for proud and vulnerable adolescents, most of whom had been rejected—sometimes violently—by family and friends.

Jain hadn't been rejected, however. Her father was there, holding a glass of lantria as he conversed with Tyvi's Donor, Siv Alson. The staff renSimes stayed on the other side of the room, but Buchan still inspected each person who approached him for tentacles.

Jain headed straight for her father. Den met Siv's glance and lifted an interrogative eyebrow. The other Donor nodded, so Den didn't try to stop Jain. The Donors positioned themselves to work the fields between their respective charges.

"Daddy! You're still here!" Jain blurted. She automatically reached out her arms to hug him, then snatched them behind her back.

Buchan bounced nervously on his toes, carefully looking only at her face. "Of course I'm still here, Jainy," he reassured her. "You're my daughter. How could I leave before I knew you were all right?"

Jain returned his smile tentatively, then frowned, blinking as if she couldn't quite focus her eyes properly. Finally, she turned to Den and asked, "How come Daddy glows so dimly? You and he," she nodded toward Siv, "are lots brighter."

Den managed not to laugh at the mess out-Territory language made of a simple concept like field strength. "Sosu Alson and I are carrying more selyn than your father," he explained patiently. "That's because we're technical-class Donors, but it's more obvious since your father's just donated selyn."

Jain's eyes widened in astonishment. "You did?" she asked Buchan. Her handling tentacles extended in surprise and one touched her wrist. She flinched and pulled them back into their sheaths.

Her father shrugged. "I had to, or they wouldn't let me see you."

Her eyes dropped to his arms, where red marks remained from the healed bruises. "You're hurt!"

"Just bruised a little," Buchan corrected. As she continued to stare, he added, "It's worth it, to see you. Besides, it wasn't *that* bad."

Den caught Siv's eye and rolled his eyes in exasperation. The other Donor glanced from the red marks on his charge's arms to Rital, who was clutching a glass of lantria as if hoping it would hold him up. Den held his hand out parallel to the floor and tilted it back and forth, then, with a nod toward Tyvi, gave the hand signal that channels used to ask their Donor to surrender control of the fields. Siv nodded agreement.

Good, Den thought. *He'll make sure that if some other crisis occurs tonight, Tyvi handles it.*

Jain was genuinely touched by her father's sacrifice and the two began to speak more comfortably with each other. The conversation faltered often, as they remembered that they no longer shared a future, but they could still share their past.

The two Donors held the fields steady and stayed quiet, giving father and daughter the illusion of privacy. Den's respect for Buchan increased. Even for a man whose profession involved dealing with adolescents, the principal excelled at guessing the meaning behind Jain's cryptic non-responses. In spite of his Simephobia, he showed his daughter that she had his love and respect, tentacles and all.

It was good therapy for them both. Buchan stopped scanning nearby guests for tentacles. Soon after, Jain brought her hands out from behind her back, although she kept her tentacles tightly sheathed.

Then grandmotherly Reyna Tast, the Sime Center's other Third Order channel, came bustling over. "Congratulations, my dear," she said, eyes twinkling merrily beneath snowy white hair as she offered Jain a neatly wrapped package.

Father and daughter moved in unison, shying away from the elderly Sime as if she were a raiding marauder.

So much for progress.

* * * *

That night, the Donor insisted on supervising his cousin's rest. When Rital finally fell asleep, Den rummaged through the carefully hoarded supply of chocolate he had bought on his last in-Territory rotation. He placed a bar of bittersweet on Rital's dresser in silent apology for the injury his mistake had caused.

Then he went to his office and wrote a letter to his friend Eddina, asking her not to come to Clear Springs. He described what had happened to Buchan and Jain to underscore his warning. A war zone was no place for an absent-minded civilian.

At breakfast the following morning, he saw Temmin in animated conversation with Alyce, the Sime Center's groundskeeper. From the glances the two renSimes threw in his direction, she was regaling her friend with an account of the fieldwork he and Rital had managed at Jain's changeover.

Gossiping renSimes, the Donor mused tolerantly, reaching for the jam. *Now they'll both want Rital for transfer next month, just to see if we really have improved. I'm glad only Ref was there when I messed up with Principal Buchan. He's discreet.*

Temmin caught his eye and gave him a flirtatious smile. *Oops. It's not only Rital's talents she wants to try.* Many renSimes enjoyed the vicarious thrill of seducing the Donors they couldn't have in transfer. Den was often happy to oblige this harmless whim. *Besides, she's cute.*

He nodded a discreet acceptance of her invitation, then opened the morning's *Clarion*. Reverend Sinth had placed a full-page advertisement in the front section, in the same font and style as a legitimate news article.

STUDENT TURNS SIME AFTER COMPLETING CHANGE-OVER CLASS, the "headline" read. The text assumed a cause-and-effect relationship between the two events and detailed the preacher's "prophecy" that Jain would change over, due to her association with the Sime Center and its staff. Annie Lifton's conflicting narrative was omitted.

The bad publicity upset Rital, particularly as several new demonstrators joined Save Our Kids, carrying "Don't turn *my* child into a **SIME**" signs. The channel suffered through a very rough Turnover, the point in his Need cycle at which he had used up half the selyn from his last transfer and began the descent into Need. Once Den got his cousin stabilized, the channel seemed normal enough. The Donor vowed to avoid another fumble, as the quality of his fieldwork at Jain's changeover made him as curious as the renSimes to see if he could do it again.

Den called Hank Fredricks to discuss damage control. Fredricks had already disciplined his advertising department for accepting Sinth's ad. It met legal standards for obscenity and slander, but Fredricks prohibited ad designs that might lead a casual reader to mistake them for a news article.

Fredricks promised to alter the ad's appearance in the rest of the week's editions. After some negotiation, he also agreed to print a feature article on Jain's changeover, to appear opposite Sinth's ad, emphasizing that changeover training had allowed her to recognize her symptoms and get to the Sime Center long before putting any Gen in danger. Den gave his expert opinion that changeover training did not affect whether a child would become Sime, which Fredricks agreed to quote in its entirety.

The article appeared the next day with an unexpected quote from Coach Farrow. "There's good reasons not to put such classes in the schools, but that's not one of them. The girl's looked Sime for over a year. I'm surprised it didn't happen long ago." A statement from Principal Buchan absolved the Sime Center of blame for his daughter's changeover and lauded Rital's expert treatment of her "unfortunate condition."

The article reduced Jain to tears. "How could Coach say that?" she wailed. "I thought he liked me!"

* * * *

The conflicting hypotheses regarding the cause of Jain's changeover threatened to eclipse discussion about the classes themselves. Den was concerned enough to attend the weekly meeting of OLD SOKS at the Sudworks Brewery, the students' favorite hangout.

Den found a seat between Tohm Seegrin and Branlee Arnborg, the graduate student with whom he wanted to share Eddina's letter. Branlee was unimposing, for a Gen, and his shock of unkempt brown hair, indoor pallor, and obsession with the mechanical properties of any material or machine, made him a living example of the literary scientific crackpot archetype. Since this was normal for a graduate student, the rest of the OLD SOKS membership tolerated him.

A server placed an empty glass in front of the Donor and exchanged two empty beer pitchers for full ones. Den poured a glass of the darker offering, wishing that the pub's selection included porstan, the favorite in-Territory beer.

Tohm was wrapping up the business portion of the meeting before the membership drank their second beers and lost interest. "So, Silva and Annie will check the thrift store in Berrysville, and Marcy the one in Oak Ridge. The goal is loose-fitting vests durable enough for our selyn donor escorts to wear in all weather. Don't worry about color, style, or incidental stains. We'll dye them all one color and then sew socks onto them so our people are clearly identifiable. All in favor?"

Half of the assembled students nodded or murmured "Aye."

"All in favor of ending the meeting and ordering sausage rolls?"

This time, the "Ayes" were loud, enthusiastic, and unanimous.

* * * *

"The fuss about Jain Buchan won't influence the school board's decision," Tohm reassured Den, pausing to sip his beer. "Not when Coach Farrow, himself, said Sinth's accusations are ridiculous. People respect a good coach and Farrow's one of the best."

"Tohm's right," Silva agreed from Tohm's other side, waving a sausage roll in emphasis. "The more Sinth rides his cause/effect theory, the more people will doubt his judgment, which is only good for us."

Den didn't understand why the coach's ability to win athletic competitions made him an authority on the causes of changeover, but he accepted the out-Territory quirk, relief settled in, and he was suddenly starving. Snagging a fried potato slice, he dipped it in the tomato chutney and popped it into his mouth.

With his primary mission resolved, his thoughts turned to pleasure: specifically, his dream of redeveloping the powered flying machines used by the Ancients, the pre-mutation humans who were neither Sime nor Gen. Turning to the graduate student on his other side, he said, "Branlee, I have news from Valzor for you."

This caught the young Gen's interest. "Did those replacement pieces of composite make it across the border without breaking?"

"They did, indeed." Den replied, taking Eddina's letter out of his shirt pocket and summarizing. "The shipment arrived unbroken in Valzor. Jannun and Eddina start building the wing assembly next week. They're confident they'll finish in time for this year's flying contest."

"Can they really build wings strong enough to fly out of that stuff?" The student's skepticism was clear.

"They're going to try." Den was grinning now. "Your rollerboard survived a spectacular accident with hardly a scratch, so I give it a more-than-decent chance. Once we have propulsion and a means of steering, there's far less chance of a flyer wing colliding with anything."

"I'm sorry the first batch turned out too thin and brittle. I shouldn't have substituted glass fibers for some of the carbon, even if it did make the sheets lighter."

The Donor nodded. "The Ancients built flying machines of metal. To some extent, weight stabilizes the whole thing. Or that's our current hypothesis. We'll see how it compares to other designs next summer."

The membership of the Valzor Model Flyer's Club, like many of their fellow hobbyists, were tired of building models and daydreaming about flying "someday." So, the annual East Nivet Territory Model Flyer's Convention had taken matters into their own hands and tentacles. Last year's gathering in Valzor City had featured a contest in which model wing assemblies were launched by a catapult, searching for a design that could fly, once they solved the propulsion issue.

Den and his friends had built the 'Spirit of Valzor,' a carefully crafted wooden framework with fabric stretched over it. It won second place behind the 'Right Flyer,' an entry that a pre-adolescent girl and her older brother had constructed out of bamboo, an old tarp, and a lot of string and tape. This year, the builders of the two winning entries had joined forces on a design using lightweight composites developed in Branlee's lab at Clear Springs University.

"The first sheets you sent aren't going to waste, even if they did break on the way to Valzor," the Donor assured Branlee. "Young Mandle's making small models from the pieces, finding what it takes to stabilize the whole structure in flight."

"I hope it works out," Branlee said glumly. "It would be nice to get something out the past two years of my life."

"What's wrong?" Den asked. "Is your research going badly?"

"My funding's been discontinued." Branlee emptied his glass in three swallows and set it back on the table. "The Products Committee decided that selyn power is the wave of the future and discontinued research on electrical motors. Professor Fibes is retiring early. I've got a job converting electrical equipment to selyn power at the Center for Technology, but that's only until the end of summer. How do I find a new research project, funding, and major professor at this time of year?"

The Donor felt some responsibility for Branlee's predicament. Opening the Sime Center had allowed Clear Springs University to build their new Center for Technology to use both electricity and selyn power. Selyn power didn't require stringing a network of expensive wiring through the walls. Selyn-conducting orgonics cables were much less expensive to maintain than the labyrinth of concrete conduits that Clear Springs University used to protect their copper-based infrastructure from thieves.

Unfortunately, the Sime Territory authorities saw no benefit to improving selyn batteries or orgonics cable, because the cheap solutions worked well enough. It was as short-sighted as the out-Territory obsession with unrealistic electrical systems. *If we put half of that effort into refining selyn power...*

A wild idea percolated up from the depths of Den's imagination, or perhaps those of his beer glass.

"Branlee," he said, pouring the graduate student a refill from the pitcher, "if your research on electrical systems is a lost cause, how about changing sides and researching selyn technology instead?"

CHAPTER 6

A MODIFIED CURRICULUM

"Selyn batteries are heavy," Den explained, helping himself to another fried potato. "They store selyn less efficiently, pound for pound, than a channel, and there's leakage as the gel spoils. It takes three batteries to power the Center for Technology for a week. While space isn't important in that context, about half the battery capacity on a *train* is used to move just the battery car, leaving only half to move the rest of the train."

Branlee blinked. "Why didn't someone invent a better battery long before the technology spread?"

The Donor shrugged. "Mostly because such research takes channels, preferably First Order ones. A First's primary responsibility is to ensure that renSimes have enough selyn that they don't have to kill Gens. Their secondary job is as healers for both Simes and Gens. Believe me, they don't have time to practice engineering as well!"

"So selyn technology becomes an afterthought?" Branlee shook his head. "They could expand industry with more efficient selyn use."

"To be fair, in applications where the batteries aren't moved, their size and weight doesn't matter," Den admitted. "Trains, cars and trucks are a spectacular exception, though. The sliderail network is expanding despite the lack of efficiency. However, from the perspective of flyer enthusiasts like me, we'll never ride in a powered flyer if the battery is so large and heavy there's no room for passengers."

"So, you want a smaller, more efficient selyn battery?" At Den's nod, Branlee frowned. "What makes you think I can develop one? I've never seen a selyn battery and I don't know how they work. Besides, you said only a channel could do it."

Den ticked off the graduate student's objections in order. "You know how to break down a complicated problem into answerable questions. I and my fellow flyer enthusiasts don't specialize in that, but I know enough about selyn batteries to get you started. You have expertise in materials, including some unknown in Sime Territory. Besides, if you knew what you were doing, it wouldn't be research, right? Finally, when you have something that requires a channel to test, I can talk Rital into helping out."

"What about funding?" Branlee wanted to know. "Materials are expensive and my landlady likes getting the rent on time."

"The Tecton pays me a very nice salary," Den assured him, "and I've been out here for two years with nowhere to spend it. I can cover your wages for, say, six months. That's enough time to determine whether a lighter battery is a solvable problem. We can scrounge most of your materials and I'll buy the rest. What do you say?"

Branlee held out a hand in the out-Territory fashion. "Sosu Milnan, you've got yourself a grad student."

As Den shook hands to seal the deal, he reflected that if they succeeded, perhaps the Economic Development Board would put some serious research money into developing powered flight.

Branlee chuckled into his beer. "I can't wait to see Professor Fibes's face when I tell him where I found funding."

* * * *

The next morning, Den made time to write a letter to Eddina and the rest of the flyer club in Valzor that explained the new project. "Branlee has materials that aren't found in-Territory, and approaches the problem from a completely different direction. Someone from an entirely different philosophical tradition just might find what the selyn battery experts in Householding Ohmand have missed for decades."

He frowned, then picked up his pen again. "It would be premature for you to visit Clear Springs, Eddina," he added. "Rital and I are trying to expand changeover classes into the school while the locals who dislike Simes are furious and looking for trouble. Branlee doesn't have a battery yet. You can wait until things are calmer."

* * * *

As she waited for her custom-made retainers to arrive from Valzor, Jain started to accept adulthood. Spurred by the insatiable curiosity of First Year, she talked with the Sime Center's Gen staff. Rital located a First Year Camp with expertise in handling tentacle-shy renSimes, run by Householding Tien. "Most of their members came from Gen Territory, so they know what she's going through," the channel told Den. "They can't take her for another month, though. We'll have to start teaching her how to be a Sime."

Den, Ref, and Reyna coaxed the girl into baking a batch of banana bread with them. As she shelled and chopped walnuts, Jain laughed for the first time since her changeover. She was learning Simelan and sometimes forgot her phobia and used her tentacles.

However, she refused to wear her new clothes, complaining that in-Territory fashions were "immodest" and "weird." Instead, she dressed in the clothes her father had delivered to the Sime Center, even those unsuited to her new anatomy. Den shook his head at Jain's teenaged defiance when she appeared for breakfast wearing a long-sleeved shirt. The puffed sleeves kept the fabric from squeezing her tentacle sheaths, but the cuffs were too narrow for a handling tentacle to emerge. Most Simes disliked having their tentacles confined, but Jain said, "I don't have to look at them this way."

Most in-Territory citizens, even channels, believed that a tentacled Simephobe was a contradiction in terms. Den had learned that an out-Territory child's instilled fear of Simes didn't disappear at changeover. So, the Donor took justifiable pride in his pupil's progress…and in her father's.

Principal Buchan visited his daughter regularly and no longer tensed when a Sime entered the room. He had tried to interest the Clear Springs police in arresting his attackers, but the District Attorney refused to prosecute the case.

"He can't prove how badly I was hurt in court, since the cut healed without a scar and only you folks saw it," the principal explained. "I should have had it documented by a medical expert."

Channel and Donor chose to ignore this slur on their professional standing and Buchan continued, "If I asked you folks to testify, Sinth would claim you made it up and Judge Lindsey on the criminal court would be inclined to believe Sinth. Maybe I can sue in civil court for the damage to the school's van. Judge Banklin is fair and that new windshield was expensive."

* * * *

Den arranged for Siv to cover his shift one morning so he could meet Branlee in Professor Fibes's laboratory, a large room on the second floor of the Center for Technology, to start the project. "A selyn battery, very simple," Den explained as he strained to lift a wooden box the size of his head from a dolly and place it carefully on a bench.

Branlee peered at the battery dubiously, then tested its mass. "It's heavy, but not that big," he said. "This would fit in a flyer."

"It would," Den agreed, "but while a battery this size is safe to experiment on, it doesn't provide much power. The ones in the basement here are half as big as a pickle barrel and the ones on the trains are the size of that cabinet." He pointed to an insulated storage cabinet for hazardous chemicals.

Branlee whistled. "Wouldn't that make them too heavy to move?"

"There's a modest savings in mass with larger size, because the surface-to-volume ratio changes," Den explained. Carefully avoiding the terminals, he popped the top off the battery. The box was lined with dull grey metal and filled with a semi-solid, green-brown substance. He let a few drops of oily liquid drip off the two leads that extended down from the lid, then set it aside.

The graduate student was already sketching a diagram. "Let's look at all the materials and see where we can save some weight," he suggested. "This outer box seems unnecessarily heavy. What is it made of, and can we use something else?"

"It's hardwood—usually oak or hickory—lined with lead," the Donor said. "It shields Simes from the field generated by the selyn inside the battery, which with large batteries is quite substantial. Otherwise, a train pulling into the station would incapacitate every Sime on the platform. The hardwood is dense enough to minimize the lead used and also contains it to prevent lead poisoning."

"So, the first question to ask is whether a lighter-weight material can perform the same function. Ideally, it should be less toxic than lead." Branlee looked speculatively around the lab. "What materials block zlinning?"

"Metals and stone, mostly," Den admitted. "Privacy curtains have red clay incorporated somehow, but I don't know the details."

"Can you get me a sample?"

"Yes."

"All right, then. We'll test different possibilities for a lighter box. In the meantime, let's look at what goes inside." He eyed the green-brown goop dubiously. "What the blazes is that stuff?"

"A proprietary gel developed and manufactured by Householding Ohmand, which is why they're richer than Keon and Zeor combined, despite being founded after Unity."

"Great. A box of mystery goop," Branlee said sourly. "Makes it difficult to improve on." He looked at a stray drip that had fallen onto the bench. "One thing it's got to have plenty of, is water. Water is heavy. We could start by seeing if the stuff still works when it's more concentrated. Then play with pH and temperature. After that, we'll see."

* * * *

While Branlee played with materials, Den focused on expanding his changeover training classes into the school. This was particularly urgent because the public library's auditorium they had been using was now booked solid for the coming school year.

"It's overflow classes from the remedial college-prep program," Miz Dilson explained. "Young men and women have little incentive to study when a third of them won't survive to adulthood, so the catch-up classes are always crowded."

After the last meeting had ended in a riot, Den worried the school board would either reject the changeover classes outright or delete all useful content. A week and a half after Jain's changeover, he was feeling a very unprofessional apprehension about the evening meeting of the curriculum committee to finalize their recommendations.

Den left early for the school, his cousin's stern admonition to "be honest" ringing in his ears. Rital's monthly progress report was late, as usual, so he let Den handle the committee.

It's just as well, the Donor thought. The *Clarion* had published many letters from parents outraged that their children might learn donating selyn was *possible,* and worse, profitable. *Although I'd expect parents to realize adolescents can read the letter columns, too!*

Committee members trickled into the meeting room. Den passed Ada Dilson a list of popular in-Territory children's books. Her delight was ample reward for time spent finding English translations.

Cessly Lornstadt was fifteen minutes late. Without apologizing for her tardiness, she claimed a seat as far from Den as possible.

Thaddus Webber called the meeting to order. "Last week I asked each of you for a list of concerns. Let's discuss each list in turn, if there are no objections."

Cessly stood up. "*I* have an objection." She pointed at Den. "What is that Sime-lover doing here? He's not a member of the committee."

Webber blinked. "It seemed efficient to have an authority present to answer any questions."

"Isn't it unethical to pick an 'authority' who will profit in salary and sales of materials if the classes are accepted?"

"Actually," Den interrupted, "both my salary and Controller Madz's are paid by the Tecton and will stay the same whether we teach the classes or not. The teaching materials would be provided by the Tecton, too. The only cost to the school district would be in providing us with a classroom... and our only profit would come from seeing more children survive changeover without killing."

Cessly frowned at the news that Den and Rital weren't money-grubbing opportunists. "If you must have a consultant who wants the classes," she tried again, "we should also have someone to represent the other side. I know someone who'd be willing to come tonight, despite the short notice."

A chorus of groans, shaking heads, and rolling eyes greeted this proposal. Webber held up his hand to silence them. "All in favor of inviting Reverend Sinth as a consultant?"

Cessly's proud "Aye" rang out alone.

"All opposed?"

"Nay," chorused everyone else.

"The Nays have it. Are there any *other* objections?"

Pressing her lips together, Cessly mutely shook her head.

"Then, I'll start by sharing my concerns," Webber said. "Sosu Milnan, you have eloquently described the value of changeover training for any child who turns Sime. But how would it benefit the majority who will become Gen? Could you include useful information for students who Establish selyn production?"

Den tried to imagine how Clear Springs parents would react to the material young in-Territory Gens were expected to master. *Especially things like how to help a channel take their donations, Donor potential... They'd be throwing bombs, not walnuts!*

"In Sime Territory, such classes *do* include as much information on Establishment as on changeover," the Donor admitted, choosing his words with care. "The in-Territory classes cover skills for Gens who live among Simes, particularly how to avoid provoking a Sime into an attack. But here, where the students are completely unfamiliar with the material, it isn't practical to cover more than I've listed."

"I see." Webber turned to the biology teacher. "Miz Ulman, would you outline your observations on the classes?"

"I think they'd be valuable," she said. "Too many parents don't teach their children about changeover, as if discussing it will make it happen. Those who want to prepare their children don't know how." The teacher laughed ruefully. "Reading Sosu Milnan's packet certainly showed me how little *I* know, and I'm supposed to be an expert in biology! The classes address a deficiency in our curriculum."

"Then you recommend the classes be adopted as proposed?" Webber asked.

"No," Ulman said. She looked around at the shocked faces. "Such an important course shouldn't be offered as an after-school activity. It should be offered during school hours, as a regular elective, so that children can take it without interfering with their athletics. The first hour of the school day is already reserved for three-week elective units, during which students try different skills like drawing or cooking. There's no reason not to include changeover classes."

"Sosu Milnan, are you willing to teach the classes during school hours?"

Den would gladly teach the classes at three in the morning, if it eliminated conflicts with the sacred athletic schedule. "I see no problem with that, if the school board agrees," he said, trying not to sound too eager. Attendance might improve, if the only competition was the academic curriculum. "Extra sessions would allow us to cover additional topics such as Establishment and how Gens can stay safe around Simes."

"Good," Webber said, with a satisfied nod. "I think we have some useful suggestions for the school board."

"Useful suggestions!" Cessly burst out, forgetting to smile in her horror. "You can't mean to let that Sime-lover and his slimy friend into the school when innocent children are around: children whose parents don't want them exposed to the filth he's proposing!"

"Miz Lornstadt!" Webber interrupted her tirade sharply. "I must ask you to hold your comments until you are recognized, or we'll be here all night. Miz Dilson, you've made your support for the classes clear. Would you expand on your reasons?"

The librarian nodded. "My job is to provide information," she said. "Parents often ask me to recommend books about changeover and Establishment. We try, but although the Sime Center has provided some materials, our librarians just don't know much about the subject. If genuine experts want to provide our children with accurate information, for free, we should accept their offer quickly, preferably in writing, before they change their minds."

"Let them teach in your library, then," Cessly protested. "It *would* complement the filth on your shelves. Why let Simes invade our school?"

Miz Dilson frowned, but refused the bait. "The class at the library was much less convenient for children than the school would be. Many families didn't know about it. Changeover classes save lives and should be available to *all* children."

Cessly opened her mouth to protest, then thought better of it as everyone glared at her.

"Thank you, Miz Dilson," Webber said. "Professor Ildun, have you anything to add?"

The bearded young academic nodded. "Research links low self-esteem, delinquency, and poor academic performance to uncertainty about the future, particularly the possibility of changeover. Psychologists agree that learning about an unpleasant subject reduces the psychological burden. These classes allow adolescents to plan for their future and concentrate on their studies, instead of on idle mischief."

Den made a mental note to ask Webber for clarification, as Ildun's last point might help win support. Still, it was odd to argue for giving future Simes life-saving information, because it might reduce juvenile delinquency in their to-be-Gen peers.

"However," Ildun continued, "we must respect the rights of parents who do *not* want their children to participate. If the classes are moved to regular school hours, I recommend that a description of class content be sent home with each child. Only children whose parents give written permission should be allowed to take the classes."

"That's a reasonable suggestion," Webber said. "Sosu Milnan, do you have any objections?"

Den wanted to shout with glee at the prospect of being allowed—no, *required*—to tell every Clear Springs adolescent and parent where to find accurate information on changeover. "Our original proposal limited enrollment to children whose parents gave written permission," he said. "We envisioned a simple permission slip, but we'd be happy to provide parents with a pamphlet describing the classes, so they can make an informed decision."

Den couldn't resist glancing at Cessly as he added, "Of course, such information will always be available to anyone who visits the Sime Center." The Donor had been hoping to slip that in. *That way, children with anti-Sime parents will know where to get changeover information. Not as effective as proper training, but a lot better than nothing.*

"Similar information is available at the library," Miz Dilson added with a touch of malice.

Cessly smiled sweetly at the librarian and announced, "No *decent* parent would allow a child to visit the Sime Center, or run free in any library *you* manage!"

"From you, that's a compliment," Miz Dilson retorted.

"Ladies, please," Webber scolded. "Miz Lornstadt, if you can refrain from insulting the other committee members, we would like to hear what you have to say about the proposed classes."

Cessly stood. "I don't want these so-called changeover classes in my school, in my town, or in my Territory. You are ignoring the clear teachings of Scripture regarding Simes, even though at least one of you should know better. Or *did* you ever read Scripture at that seminary that ordained you, *Reverend* Webber?"

"Don't call me 'Reverend,'" Webber objected mildly. "I'm not!"

"*That's* obvious," Cessly sneered. "However, even an *atheist* should refuse that Sime-lover's attempt to molest our children in our own schools. For instance, Jain Buchan turned Sime only weeks after she completed his class. That's how effective they are."

"Oh, come now, Miz Lornstadt," Nat Ulman objected. "I don't like speaking badly of any youngster, but as Coach Farrow said, Jain always looked like a changeover waiting to happen."

"So, you think her father was right to make *sure* his little girl was doomed?" Cessly asked. She pulled a stapled document from her purse by one corner, as if to avoid contamination. The printed text was liberally annotated in blood-red ink.

"I've read every word of this so-called curriculum proposal," she continued, shaking it disdainfully. "Changeover is described as a 'perfectly normal process,' with no reference to morality, sin, guilt, or divine retribution!"

When this revelation failed to produce shock in her audience, Cessly tried again. "There is no hint that true religions view Simes as inherently evil, unable to lead a moral life. In this section," she pointed to a paragraph circled three times with the red ink, "children in changeover are directed to seek help from the Sime Center, without even mentioning the moral option of seeking a humane death from their loving parents."

She slammed the proposal down on her desk, declaring, "Death is the only salvation for a child who is becoming Sime. This proposal is an invasion of family privacy, an affront to religious values, and a blatant assault on parental authority. Even the name 'changeover *class*' is an insult: it assumes that children should practice becoming Simes instead of praying to be Gen. Changeover is God's punishment for sin. A public school has no business teaching children otherwise!"

"Miz Lornstadt, it is the job of each denomination to teach its members' children church doctrine," Webber pointed out. "Sosu Milnan and Hajene Madz are not members of your congregation. You can hardly expect them to do your proselytizing for you."

"That may be true," Cessly admitted, "but my children's religious training shouldn't be undermined by their own, tax-supported school!"

Nat Ulman brought her fist down on the desk in disgust. "Once and for all, Miz Lornstadt, do you understand that participation in the changeover classes would be *optional*?"

"In a sense," Cessly admitted, "but…"

"Do you speak the language? Would it or wouldn't it?"

"My children will never set foot in a changeover class."

"That being so, Miz Lornstadt," Ulman continued relentlessly, "is it right for you to say, 'Not only will I forbid my child from taking the class, but I also want to forbid anyone else's child from taking it?"

"Of course it's right," Cessly said indignantly. "The laws in Scripture were given to *humankind*. They apply to everyone, not just believers. My children have classmates and teammates whose parents don't go to our church."

Den resolved to provide many extra copies of the handouts if the school board approved the classes, just in case Cessly was right. If even one child read a pamphlet and contacted the Sime Center for changeover assistance before a "loving" parent like Cessly could intervene, it would be worth the effort.

Nat Ulman sighed. "Miz Lornstadt, school exists to teach children to live in the world, not to hide the world from them. Our wars with the Sime Territories ended over a century ago. The Sime Center is here to stay. You can't prevent your children from learning it exists."

"Maybe not," Cessly allowed, "but I won't let my children be brain-washed into rejecting everything I and my husband believe!"

Den stifled the urge to defend the Sime Center. He wouldn't change Cessly's mind and the more paranoid she seemed, the less attention the committee—and the school board—would pay to her arguments.

"We won't settle these philosophical issues tonight," Webber said, "and it's getting late. Parental consent is adequate protection for those who don't want their children to participate, especially if parents are provided with full information on the content of the classes. Miz Lornstadt, assuming that some sort of changeover class will be taught, have you any specific criticisms of the course as outlined?"

Cessly looked at the hostile faces that surrounded her. "You've made up your minds already, haven't you?" she stated. "You're going to recommend the classes and never mind the consequences. Well, I can't stop you from submitting your report, but first I'm going to tell you exactly what's wrong with these so-called classes."

She picked up the textbook and flipped through it, holding up a page that diagrammed the Sime nervous system. "Look at this. The Sime-lover and his slimy friend want to teach our children what happens in changeover and how a Sime's innards are arranged. Teaching such obscene vocabulary detracts from childish innocence and leads to an unhealthy interest in Simes."

"Obscene vocabulary?!" Den yelped. "There are slang or gutter words, in Simelan and English both, but that textbook uses medical terminology. How can anyone prepare a child for physical maturity without using the words for the process?"

"*My* parents managed just fine," Cessly said, flashing her poisonously sweet smile at him, "and without fancy words for tentacle slime, either. Those of us who stayed human have no use for them, and the others didn't live long enough to feel the lack. I couldn't expect a Sime-lover like you to understand. Prostituting yourself to Simes…" She glared at the other committee members. "He may not know any better, raised in depravity as he was, but the rest of you ought to be ashamed of yourselves."

"Does anyone wish to modify their support for the classes in light of Miz Lornstadt's…edifying remarks?" Webber asked. When no one expressed such a desire, he continued, "Miz Lornstadt, you won't accept anything that contradicts Conservative Congregation doctrines, and the rest of us won't strip the course of useful content. I think we can write a majority report that all four of us will sign." The other committee members nodded. "If you wish to offer the school board a minority report, I'm sure they will consider your position."

"As carefully as you considered it?" Cessly sneered. "Ignore me if you want, but you can't ignore God's truth. The Simes are nothing but trouble. Stop by the Sime Center and see the bad manners, intolerance, and sheer bigotry that it inspires. You don't have to go in: just listen to the snakes' champions on the sidewalk. Do you want that in school? Because I guarantee, if that Sime-lover and his snake-armed friend seduce innocent children into perversion, conflict will follow!" With that, she swept dramatically from the room.

There was an audible sigh of relief as the door slammed. Webber shook his head, then returned to business. "If no one objects, I'll draft our majority report recommending acceptance of the proposal, with the alterations we discussed tonight. We'll meet next week to iron out the final version. Sosu Milnan, could you prepare an expanded curriculum, assuming the classes will be offered as a three-week elective? I'd also like to see the information pamphlet you would send home to parents."

"I'll send copies to each of you, and to the school board."

"Thank you. Then if nobody has anything *else* to discuss…" Webber smiled at their groans, "this meeting is adjourned at last."

Den was unexpectedly satisfied with how the evening had gone. He had underestimated Cessly Lornstadt's sheer venom, but in the end, she had undermined herself.

With enemies like that, who requires friends? As he walked through the parking lot, wishing Rital was there to share his triumph, a voice called, "Sosu Milnan, might I have a word with you?"

Den stopped and turned. "Of course, Professor Ildun."

"I was wondering if one of my graduate students and I could have an hour or so of your time to discuss a research project?"

"I don't see why not," he said, hiding his reluctance to take on another project, and settled on a time later that week.

Den watched the professor pedal off briskly on his bicycle, then made his way to the Sime Center's selyn-powered staff van, wondering how he was going to redesign the changeover class outline, in English, with such a short deadline. *Not to mention that propaganda pamphlet…*

It was going to be a busy week.

CHAPTER 7

OBJECT LESSONS

The next day, Den locked himself in his office and expanded his syllabus into the fifteen-hour course recommended by the committee. He skipped lunch and even neglected to check on Rital, telling himself that his cousin would call for help before a situation became critical.

Rital was in good shape, despite being close to Need, and his injury was long healed. Although they hadn't recreated the perfection of cooperation they'd achieved during Jain's breakout, the Donor hadn't dropped the fields since.

Den was exhausted by the time he started on the informed consent pamphlet. It was a delicate task. The text had to be accurate for Rital, bland for the school board, reassuring for fearful parents, convincing for parents who might let their children participate, informative for children whose parents refused to let them take the classes, and short enough that people would read it.

When Den finished at last, he was pleased with his efforts. The pamphlet began by explaining what changeover training was and why it was important. Next, it confronted Sinth's rumors in a question-and-answer format. After that was a list of topics to be covered, with a short explanation under each heading. Through creative euphemisms, Den had avoided controversial words such as "tentacle," "Need," or "donate," then ended with a section titled "**To Obtain More Information**" that directed readers to the Sime Center or the library. Telephone numbers were included.

* * * *

On the day before Den's scheduled transfer with Rital, nothing went right. It rained, not a brief summer storm, but the first cold, day-long drizzle of autumn. A clogged sewer flooded the basement, forcing Alyce to turn off the power while she made repairs. The Sime Center's staff were left with no trin tea, no hot showers, and a cold breakfast.

Perhaps that was why Rital was so critical of Den's pamphlet.

"How can you write so much and say so little?" the channel protested at breakfast. He sipped his fruit juice, made a face, and set the glass down. "There's nothing specific on what the classes teach."

"That's the whole point," Den explained patiently. "I did what the committee asked: informed parents why their children would benefit from the classes and provided an overview of the material."

"But look at this." Rital tapped one entry with a handling tentacle. "*How the Tecton functions* could mean anything from its bureaucratic structure to what we're actually teaching, which is how general-class donations provide selyn for renSimes. However, you describe that lecture as covering *how the Tecton prevents Simes from attacking Gens.*"

"It does!" Den pointed out. "That's what these folks care about."

The channel moved his tentacle up the list to another entry. "And here, you describe our sessions on changeover itself as covering *developmental processes associated with becoming Sime.* You don't say that we're teaching exercises to improve changeover survival rates."

The Donor shrugged. "Half the parents in this town find the idea of Simes surviving changeover unsettling at best. My descriptions provide enough information to make an informed decision, but won't raise complaints to the school board from anyone but Sinth's group. Any parent can get more information by calling us or the library; both numbers are listed on the last page."

"It's still dishonest," the channel grumbled.

"It's not dishonest; it's the way information is handled out-Territory," Den explained. "You present the positive side of your case, in the best possible light, without giving your opponents ammunition to use against you. Reverend Sinth will gnash his teeth when he reads this, but he won't find juicy quotes to exploit in his own pamphlets."

Rital zlinned his cousin. "You relish defying him, don't you?"

The Donor grinned. "After he's centered his career on making *our* lives miserable, the least I can do is to return the favor."

Rital wasn't amused. "You sink to his level."

"By engaging him, I can change the terms of debate," Den corrected. "Compare Sinth's current propaganda to his wild conspiracy theories when the Sime Center first opened. He's modified his arguments. He no longer accuses us of imprisoning general-class selyn donors for Kills, since it's obvious that no donors are missing."

"I don't want my Donor withholding information on our services from the people we're supposed to serve," the channel repeated stubbornly. "We have nothing to hide."

"The information is freely available for the asking," the Donor countered, pointing to the last page of the draft pamphlet. "I'm just not forcing details on people who don't want to know them."

"I don't see the difference."

"I know you don't." Den sighed, then started gathering his dishes. "Come on, we've got work to do."

The cold rain didn't prevent Save Our Kids and OLD SOKS from showing up when the Collectorium opened, but it did shorten their tempers...and those of selyn donors caught in the shoving matches between the two groups. Den refused to let Rital handle even experienced donors alone, ignoring his cousin's grumbling about overprotective, interfering Donors. By the time the Collectorium closed, neither wanted to face administrative chores. Still, they trudged dutifully—and silently—toward their respective offices.

As they passed the back door, Rital stopped, a conspiratorial smile on his face. "You know, cousin," he said with mock regret, "we've neglected our duties lately. As chief administrators of this insane asylum, we must write performance evaluations, but we haven't checked how Alyce is maintaining the grounds in weeks."

There was no mention of chocolate, so it wasn't an apology for scorning Den's pamphlet. Rather, it was an offer of truce so they could heal each other of the day's accumulated frustrations without prejudice. *The pamphlet can wait until after transfer, when he isn't thinking with his laterals. I'm not interested in discussing the stupid thing now, either.*

"Our inattention is shocking," the Donor agreed. "Why, the vegetable garden might be knee-deep in weeds. We must correct this oversight immediately."

"True." Rital winked. "Let's grab our capes before it gets dark."

Like two small boys contemplating mischief, the conspirators tiptoed up to their rooms. Thanks to Rital's Need-sharpened sensitivity, they avoided the other staff and escaped safely out the Sime Center's back door.

During the first months of negotiations to place a Sime Center in Clear Springs, Reverend Sinth had successfully blocked the Tecton from purchasing a suitable site. Eager to get selyn power for their new Center for Technology, the Regents of Clear Springs University had intervened by selling the Tecton a large estate left them in a bequest. The property was too far from campus for dorms or offices, and had become a liability for the University after the original mansion burned.

The Sime Center occupied only a portion of the property. Alyce had made great progress restoring the old gardens, which had suffered from a decade of neglect. The cousins spent a leisurely hour wandering through the expanse of lawn, woods, and flower beds. Even cold, drizzly, weedy and deserted, the grounds were beautiful.

I've missed this, Den thought, as he indulged in simple enjoyment of his cousin's growing Need. *Once our classes are approved, I can stop being a publicist and be a full-time Donor again.*

There were far worse channels than Rital with whom to work. *Maybe together, we can figure out what happened during Jain's changeover. We've never managed that kind of field control before. It could have been a fluke, but if it wasn't, we can do it again.* He grinned at the thought of recreating that perfection.

By the time the truants' heavy wool cloaks soaked through, prompting them to return to the Sime Center, they were in a much better mood. Just as well, because Ref pounced on them at the door.

"Hajene Madz," the portly chef held out a sheaf of papers. He had donned a heavy sweater against the day's chill. "Here's the list of food stores we'll require before winter, in case snow stops the trains. With Reverend Sinth out of jail, local suppliers will cancel our orders rather than face a boycott. Siv promised to deliver our shopping list personally when he escorts young Jain to Valzor."

Like any Sime so close to transfer, Rital had no interest in food. However, he dutifully fished a pen out of his shirt pocket with two tentacles and took the document. Unable to read it in the gloomy hallway and too lazy to zlin the impressions the typewriter had made on the paper, he led them around the corner to the library.

Rital opened the door and stopped short, coming to full alert. Passing the still-unsigned supply list back to Ref, the channel slipped the pen into his pocket and glided through the door. Den signaled Ref to stay back and followed, a half step behind to let his cousin handle the fields.

In the grey light coming through the windows, the Donor made out Jain's thin figure, glumly staring out at the rain. Her suicidal depression was palpable, even to Gen senses. She stiffened as she zlinned them, but didn't turn to look.

Rital's right hand and tentacles grasped Den's wrist briefly in a pattern that signaled the Donor to take charge. Trusting his cousin's professional judgment, the Donor drifted closer to the young Sime, assuming control of the fields with a deliberate precision that awakened a faint echo of the perfection he had felt at her changeover.

Maybe it wasn't a fluke, after all.

"What's the matter?" he asked Jain, feeling the answer in his increased response to her. Turnover, the point at which a Sime had used half the selyn from her last transfer and began the descent into Need, dampened any Sime's mood. In just two more days, Jain would leave the only home she knew for life in a strange Territory where she didn't understand the language or culture.

"I wonder if it's worth it," Jain said listlessly. She reached out a hand to pull the curtains closed. Two handling tentacles emerged reflexively to reinforce her grip, until she saw them and snatched them back into their sheaths.

Den hadn't expected the onset of Need to bring back Jain's aversion to tentacles, although it did explain why Rital had decided not to handle the girl himself. A Sime's first Turnover could be rough, but Jain's reaction was more typical of out-Territory Simes who had Killed someone they knew. Keeping his field neutral, the Donor gave her shoulder an encouraging squeeze and asked, "If *what's* worth it?"

Jain hadn't yet developed the habit of zlinning the moods of those around her. Responding to the Donor's physical reassurance, she gestured vaguely, tentacles sheathed. "All of this. I mean, your classes, the channels…it'll keep more Simes alive, but why? The best I can hope for is to not Kill…this month. I can't see my own father without an Escort to make sure I don't attack him. What kind of life can I have, as a danger to everyone around me?"

Following Den's lead, Rital also put his arm around the girl, working to dispel her Need-tension while the human contact offered comfort. "Jain," he explained with compassion, "part of being an adult—Sime or Gen—is having the ability to harm others just by carelessness. When you talked with your father, Sosu Den was there to protect *you*. With the best of intentions, your father might have hurt you, through simple ignorance."

"Hajene Rital's correct, Jain," the Donor confirmed. "In-Territory Gens know how to avoid hurting you, or provoking you into attacking them. Once you learn your limits, you won't have to worry about Killing someone by accident."

Jain stared at Den. "How can you say that?" she demanded incredulously. She nodded toward Rital. "If he hadn't stopped me two weeks ago, I would have attacked *you*!"

After a moment's thought, Den remembered that instant right after her breakout, when Jain had forced herself hypoconscious to avoid the solid field control he and Rital were imposing. She had been scared witless and had reached out to him for comfort before First Need had overtaken her. *She thinks she was attacking me,* the Donor realized. *Poor kid, no wonder she's so careful with the Gen staff!*

"Of course, you wanted Sosu Den to stay within reach," Rital said. "That's what Hard Need does to a Sime, particularly when a Donor's working to arouse it."

"I deliberately provoked you into attacking the nearest source of selyn…which was Hajene Rital, not me," the Donor explained. "You had to be fully committed, or you wouldn't have had a satisfying First Transfer. You might even have shenned yourself."

"Sosu Den was never in danger," the channel confirmed. "Even if you'd gotten past me, you don't have the speed or capacity to harm a Donor, much less kill one."

Jain zlinned the truth of their statements, but still wasn't convinced. She shrugged off Rital's arm and dropped onto the couch. "So, if I'm careful, and lucky, I won't actually Kill anybody. I'll still be living on selyn, though. For every month I live, someone will have to…" She shuddered. "What right have I to make someone do *that* every month, just to keep me from Killing?"

Den sat beside Jain, wishing they could have sent the young Sime in-Territory more quickly. It was futile to explain how Simes and Gens lived in peace there, when all she knew was life in Clear Springs.

"Many out-Territory Gens are afraid the first time they donate selyn," he admitted. "The unknown is frightening. Most get over it quickly, once they discover that it doesn't hurt."

"But it *does!*" Jain insisted. In her distress, her tentacles retracted so tightly that they formed visible lumps within their sheaths. "I saw the marks on Daddy's arms. He was hurt giving me a month's worth of selyn. Even if I don't kill anyone, people will suffer for me. I'm not worth it."

Jain's concern was genuine and deserved an honest answer. Besides, it was time she learned how much Sime overprotectiveness annoyed Gens.

"Your father is a capable adult and can decide for himself whether he wants to donate selyn," Den pointed out quietly. "If seeing you is worth it to him, do you have the right to tell him he can't? He wouldn't appreciate you 'protecting' him out of it, nor would any other Gen who wants to give someone a month of life."

Jain looked at him stubbornly. "If Gens have the 'right' to give selyn, then Simes can refuse to accept that gift. I *won't* live on other people's pain and terror."

"Jain," Rital said firmly, "I've taken donations from thousands of Gens, zlinning exactly what they feel. Mostly, that's nothing. Some selyn donors are frightened the first time. A few panic, like your father, and bruise themselves. But most Gens who come to the Collectorium aren't first timers. They know they won't be hurt, so they're not afraid."

Jain's skepticism was palpable.

A hearty chuckle came from the doorway. "You'll never get a stubborn youngster to just take your word on something so important to her," Ref observed. "Why should she?" He entered the room and tossed his shopping list onto a convenient chair. "Zlinning is believing, isn't it, young lady?" He gave her a winning smile.

Jain frowned, unsure which side of the argument he was taking, until the chef pushed up the short sleeves of his sweater, revealing his untentacled Gen forearms.

Den and Rital exchanged startled glances as they realized the demonstration Ref proposed.

Ref was a steady general-class selyn donor with decades of experience. He wouldn't give Rital any surprises, but collecting rooms were equipped with heavy insulation and warning lights for a reason. If someone walked in on a donation, the disruption in the ambient could precipitate an injury. On the other hand, moving the demonstration now, or even locking the door, would send exactly the wrong message.

Den watched Rital zlin the surroundings with Need-sharpened sensitivity, then signal "all clear," prompting Den for his opinion with an interrogative eyebrow.

He wants to do it, the Donor thought. *So do I. It's the right thing for Jain.*

"That's an excellent suggestion, Ref," Den approved. He adjusted his position to allow Jain to zlin the others clearly, while his field protected Rital from her agitation. The Donor took the precaution of grasping the girl's elbow, a token restraint to remind Jain not to interfere.

"No, you mustn't!" Jain warned Ref urgently. "He's in Need!"

"I know." Ref gave her a reassuring smile, letting her zlin that his lack of fear was genuine. "Need makes Hajene Rital lose his appetite for my cooking. It doesn't make him dangerous to me." He turned to Rital and held out his hands. "Will you take my gift of life, Hajene," he asked formally, "and pass it on to those who Need it?"

"It is my duty and my privilege," Rital answered with equal formality. He took the offered hands and wrapped handling tentacles around the Gen's wrists in the light, comfortable grip of a channel working with an experienced donor.

Jain's eyes widened as their lips met, then lost focus as she fumbled her way hyperconscious. Den felt a sudden increase in his attraction to Rital as the channel dropped his showfield, and Jain tensed as she unconsciously prepared to rescue Rital's "victim."

Den tightened his grip on Jain's elbow and she reluctantly settled back to observe. Ref didn't react to the nageric drama—a general-class donor's response to Sime Need was so small that he didn't perceive it consciously.

Rital let the inexperienced young Sime zlin to her satisfaction that he was, indeed, taking selyn from Ref while the Gen experienced no fear or discomfort, nor did Rital get any relief for his own Need.

When the channel released Ref, the chef murmured, "Thank you, Hajene." He chuckled at Jain's astonished expression and displayed his unbruised arms. "That really *is* all there is to donating. If you want an excuse to stop living, find another. Before you start looking, will you come to the kitchen and share a nice cup of trin tea with me? It's just the thing on such a gloomy day." Ref held out his hand.

After a moment, Jain hesitantly placed her small hand in the chef's larger one and let him pull her to her feet.

Ref smiled at her. "That's my girl," he said. "I'm making bread. Want to help me?"

"I helped my mother bake bread, before she died," Jain offered.

"Then you know how it's done. Did you know that tentacles are very useful for kneading?"

Jain extended a handling tentacle across the back of her free hand, flexing it experimentally. "I suppose they could be," she ventured. "What kind of bread are you making? My mother made the best sourdough…" The two cooks departed for the kitchen.

Rital shook his head with a smile, retrieved Ref's requisition, signed it decisively, and handed it to his Donor. "Den, will you see that this gets to Siv?"

"Sure," Den agreed, "if you'll do me a favor in return?"

"What?"

The Donor grinned wryly. "Next time I try to pass myself off as an expert on out-Territory psychology, will you remind me of today?"

* * * *

By noon the following day, Jesper Reft, the bilingual typist who was the newest addition to the Sime Center's staff, had transcribed Den's expanded changeover class curriculum. Den copyedited it, then scribbled a note asking Jesper to make clean copies for the curriculum committee, all school board members, Miz Dilson, and Hank Fredricks at the *Clear Springs Clarion*.

As an afterthought, he added Ed Buchan to the list.

There was enough time for Den to deliver the packet to Jesper before his transfer with Rital, but before he could get out the door the young renSime stopped him. "Sosu, you wrote some things I don't think you intended. Could you clarify for me?"

Ten minutes later, Den was ready to write a glowing performance review for Jesper's fluency in English. In his search for uncontroversial ways to describe the changeover classes, the Donor had unintentionally used phrases with idiomatic meanings in the Gen language.

"Shen! I thought my English was better than Hammil's!" he exclaimed—and then had to recount the story of the other Donor's gaffe.

When Jesper was through chuckling, Den agreed, "No, I definitely don't want to tell parents that the classroom's weather will be foggy, nor that we'll teach their children how to participate in orgies."

"Let me find alternative phrasing."

"Thanks." Den left the revision to the renSime and hurried to the suite used for channels' transfers.

Rital whirled toward Den with augmented speed as the door opened. The naked relief on his cousin's face awakened instant guilt.

"I'm sorry I'm late," Den apologized, closing the door.

"All Gens lose track of time," Rital said bravely. "Besides, there's almost fifteen minutes to go."

"I've neglected you lately," Den admitted. His cousin's calm competence made it easy to forget that the pulsing beat of Need felt like death to a Sime. Donors ensured that their channels didn't face it alone.

"You're here now," Rital pointed out, squirming uncomfortably at the Gen's self-condemnation.

Den set his guilt aside, so it wouldn't interfere with their transfer. "So I am," he agreed, turning his full attention on his cousin. Anxiety had roused the channel's intil, the psychological component of Need. The Donor felt himself responding as he guided Rital to the padded transfer lounge, eager anticipation driving out all other feelings.

When their transfer time came, Den was as ready as his cousin. Rital's handling tentacles gripped his arms as the channel desperately slaked his Need, the speed of his draw climbing perilously close to Den's limits. As the selyn flow peaked, their fields meshed in the perfect harmony they had achieved at Jain's changeover. Den didn't want the channel to back off. *We're so close right now, he knows what I can tolerate better than I do.*

Rital brought the transfer to his usual neat termination and Den was once more aware of external reality. He was pressed flat on the lounge, Rital almost on top of him, limp with relief. When the channel released his cousin's arms, Den stretched luxuriously and grinned.

"Well, *that* ought to be worth a few points the next time we go into proficiency testing!" he remarked with smug satisfaction. *Temmin won't be disappointed tonight, and from the looks of Rital, neither will Gati.* The Donor bounded to his feet to fetch tea—and crumpled as a sledgehammer hit the back of his head.

Rital caught him and deposited him back on the transfer lounge. "I'm sorry, Den," the channel apologized frantically. "I didn't mean to burn you. I'll never forgive you if you die on me, you idiot," he warned.

"I don't plan to die anytime soon," Den growled, "although I may change my mind if you keep yelling. Could you get me some fosebine?"

Bottles clinked as the channel rummaged through the medicines over the sink. He wrenched the stopper out of the fosebine bottle, flinging the hapless piece of glass to shatter against the wall. Den barely had time to wince before a glass was shoved under his nose. A splash of liquid flew over the rim.

Den looked down at the damp spot on the front of his shirt. "I'll be fine, Rital," he promised the channel. "You don't have to make extra laundry." He sat up slowly, careful not to jostle his aching head. "I'm just scorched a little. I had a lot worse in training." The Donor emptied the glass in three gulps, grimacing at the bitter taste.

The pounding in his head subsided. "It's not serious," he told the hovering channel. "Zlin for yourself."

Rital grasped the Gen's offered arms and made a full transfer contact, zlinning as deeply as he could so soon after transfer. Finally satisfied that his cousin wouldn't expire on the spot, he let Den go. "I should've been more careful," he said, radiating guilt.

"I should have signaled you to slow down. And you would have, long before I was in real danger. I wouldn't shen you."

With the immediate crisis ended, Rital could no longer hold off Post-syndrome. He sobbed uncontrollably, guilt over hurting his Donor magnifying petty failings and errors of the past two weeks which Need had prevented him from processing. Den hoped that the perfection they had achieved during transfer wasn't among Rital's regrets. *He's not going to be interested in anything but self-flagellation tonight. Gati will be furious with me.* The Donor patiently held his cousin and waited for the reaction to run its course, glad that the fosebine let him function.

When Rital recovered, he insisted that the Donor sleep. Well aware that even a mild transfer burn shouldn't be ignored, Den agreed. However, he refused to sleep in the infirmary, asserting that he required nothing but rest in his own bedroom.

* * * *

Rital sent Tyvi to examine his injured Donor before her own transfer with Siv blunted her sensitivity. Sometime after she left, Den was awakened by the sound of his door opening and closing. Hoping someone had brought him dinner, he sat up to greet his visitor.

Jain stood with her back against the door, staring. "Reverend Sinth is right. Even channels hurt Gens when they take transfer. Why did you lie to me?"

"We didn't, Jain," Den said. "I'm not seriously injured and I was never in danger." He groped for a way to explain. "Did you ever practice gymnastics so hard that you were sore the next morning?"

"Yes," she admitted cautiously.

"And didn't you improve the next time you tried the moves?"

Jain nodded.

"Well, being a Donor works the same way. Sometimes you get a little burn when you try to improve your abilities. But working at your limits extends them. Wasn't it worth a little soreness, to become the best gymnast you could be?"

Jain nodded again, very reluctantly.

"Well, I'd much rather suffer an occasional headache than live as half the Donor I could be."

The young renSime frowned. "Gymnastics doesn't hurt people so badly that they have to stay in bed."

Den laughed. "Hajene Rital would nag me to death if he caught me spreading my headache to other Simes. You feel it, don't you?"

"That's you?"

She was still learning to zlin. "It'll be gone tomorrow," Den assured, patting the coverlet beside him. "Come here." When she perched on the edge of the bed, he held out his arms. "Don't take my word for it. Zlin for yourself that it's nothing."

"I can't," Jain said, hugging herself. "I might hurt you."

"Jain, you're barely past Turnover and I'm low field. You'd have to be in Attrition to be tempted to attack me and even if you did, I know how to stop you without hurting you. Or me. This is safe."

After careful consideration, the young Sime took Den's hands and let her handling tentacles wrap timidly around his wrists. She hesitated, meeting the Donor's eyes doubtfully.

"Go on. You don't have to be a channel to zlin this."

Finally, Jain's laterals emerged from their sheaths to brush his skin. Her eyes lost their focus as she zlinned, then released the Gen.

"You see?" Den said. "I'm not hurt. Just a headache."

"True," Jain admitted, "but you're starving. I'm glad I'm not a channel. Gens are awfully easy to injure."

"So are Simes," the Donor pointed out. "Now, would you run down to the kitchen and ask Ref to bring me a tray?"

Jain nodded and tiptoed to the door, in deference to his invalid status. However, Den heard her skip down the hall to the stairs.

Maybe I'm not so bad at out-Territory psychology, after all.

CHAPTER 8

RESEARCH

The morning sun woke Den. His headache had subsided to a mild throb that disappeared after he drank the fosebine Rital had left on his bedside table. Beside the medicine was a chocolate turtle. He took a nibble to rid his mouth of the medicinal aftertaste.

Walnuts and caramel are a perfect combination, he thought with satisfaction, taking another, larger bite. Then he pulled on a fresh uniform and went down to breakfast.

As he settled at his usual table, he noticed Jain sharing a table with Seena, working her way through a bowl of porridge. Just past Turnover, that was probably more habit than appetite, but she seemed to be adjusting well to her first Need cycle.

Rital caught him as he finished and dragged him off to the infirmary for a checkup. "Light duty," the channel specified. "Leave the field management to Siv today, so you can take over when he leaves tomorrow."

* * * *

Professor Ildun arrived promptly at ten for his appointment with Den. Beside him was a tall, gangling young man with a startlingly prominent Adam's apple. "Sosu Milnan, this is my graduate student, Arth Tinkum. He's working on his doctorate and hopes that the study I wish to discuss with you will make a suitable subject for his dissertation."

"Pleased to meet you," Den said.

Arth extended a hand and the Donor shook it with practiced firmness. He wondered whether he would forget, the next time he was on leave in Valzor, and offer the out-Territory greeting instead of the cycle-dependent rituals used in-Territory. He understood the out-Territory handclasp now: it forced both parties to reveal their body temperature and offer a forearm for inspection. In the days of Sime Raids into Gen Territory, verification of larity had been a necessary precaution when dealing with strangers.

"Let's go up to my office," Den suggested. He led the way up the stairs. Arth lagged behind, peering into every open door they passed. Den couldn't tell if the young man was curious about his surroundings or trying to spot nearby Simes before they spotted him.

Den's office had enough insulation to insure the privacy of a First-Order Donor, so he didn't have to worry about his guests' emotions disturbing anyone outside. Den served trin and asked for details on Ildun's project.

"Have you heard about the proposed new sliderail route between Clear Springs and Sanger, over on the Tinusa River?"

Den nodded cautiously.

"Apparently the train can't carry enough selyn to run farther than fifty miles. Either the route has to detour into Sime Territory or they must put in a Sime Center. The Tecton charges so much for imported selyn—"

"No," Den interrupted. "The *batteries* are too heavy to haul both themselves and goods over longer distances, so you can't have selyn technology without a local source of selyn. We estimate three new Sime Centers between Sanger and Clear Springs, or four if they put in the detour around Guny Lake."

Ildun digested this information, then continued. "Sime Centers are… controversial, so far from the border. Politicians who invite the Tecton face strong opposition. Seven years ago, Sanger's mayor was ousted after his town was selected for a Sime Center that Tinusa rejected."

"New Washington wants the sliderail network expanded. They're looking for ways to persuade local governments to cooperate." The professor's chest expanded with academic pride. "I've received a grant from the Office of Transportation to study the impact of Sime Centers on the social dynamics of non-border towns. We've targeted several critical subpopulations, comparing interactions with and attitudes toward the Sime Center among certain demographic variables and—"

Lost in the sociobabble, Den held up a hand. "Please, Professor," he begged as his headache threatened to return, "English is not my native language and I know even less about your field of study than you do about mine. Could you please simplify?"

As Ildun groped for plain speech, Arth came to his rescue. "We want to know why people donate selyn at all and why some keep on doing it. If we learn what regular donors have in common and how they differ from occasional donors and nondonors, we can estimate the number of potential donors in a given community and how to recruit them. We can also determine who is most likely to oppose a Sime Center. The Office of Transportation can approach towns that might accept a Sime Center and not waste time with the others."

"There is some published data on Westfield," the professor added, "but that's a large border city with atypical demographics. At the changeover class meeting, Hajene Madz implied that the number of selyn donors in Clear Springs is increasing rapidly. There should be enough donors here, with a wide enough range of experience, for statistically significant results."

Shen you and your big mouth, Rital, Den thought. *How can I get us out of this diplomatically?*

At the expression on the Donor's face, the professor added, "We would, of course, give you appropriate credit when we publish."

"We'll run a two-staged investigation," Arth said. "First, we'll analyze your donation records."

"I'm afraid that isn't possible," Den said, glad to be handed an excuse to "regretfully" refuse. "Those records are confidential. Imagine what someone like Reverend Sinth would do with such information. Reading the files requires a written release from each selyn donor."

"For our purposes, the important data is gender, age, income, occupation, and education," Arth countered. "Could a member of your staff read us that information, redacting anything that could identify a specific individual?"

Den nodded reluctantly. "That could work. I'd have to consult a legal expert. You mentioned a second part to your project?"

"Yes," Ildun said. "We'll ask your selyn donors to fill out a brief questionnaire—voluntarily and anonymously—to learn whether subjective experience is a predictor of future donation history. Ideally, I'd prefer a longitudinal study, tracking a cohort over time, but we can make do with a cross section."

Den helplessly turned to Arth for a translation. "We'd like to know how each Gen reacted to his or her first donation," the young man obliged. "That will give us a pretty good idea how their first reactions correlate with how often they've donated since." Arth smiled wistfully. "It's too bad there's no way to measure emotions objectively. It would make our research much easier."

"Actually, there's a very good measure of a selyn donor's emotions," Den said, interested in spite of himself. "Our records show the…" he searched for a translation of the Simelan term, "the speed at which selyn is taken for each donation. Resistance is greater when a Gen is agitated, so the channel must slow the speed. There are other good indicators, too. For instance, a channel won't qualify a donor as a GN-2 or GN-1, tapping the deeper selyn storage levels, until he or she is comfortable enough to relax completely."

The Donor realized he'd made Rital's favorite mistake, volunteering too much information, when Ildun grinned in delight. "That's marvelous! If you'll give Arth the normal variation, he can do a statistical analysis. We'll still have to do the questionnaire, though. A number can't tell you how someone perceives an event. Often what people *think* they experienced is more important than what actually happened."

Den nodded in reluctant agreement, remembering how Jain had misinterpreted her own behavior during her breakout.

"Our data might even help you expand your roster of selyn donors," Ildun pointed out, "not to mention its potential to get your changeover classes approved." The professor paused for the Donor to absorb the implied threat, then added, "If you tailor your public relations efforts to the people most likely to respond positively, you'll get a much better return on your investment."

Den prided himself on his knowledge of out-Territory culture, but the philosophy behind Ildun's last argument was disturbingly foreign to everything the Tecton stood for. A Sime Center was supposed to serve *all* Simes and Gens. How could the Tecton work toward the dissolution of the Territory borders if it didn't communicate with everyone who required its assistance?

I'll never truly understand out-Territory culture, he admitted to himself. *And I'm not sure I really want to.*

What would happen if Den failed to cooperate was clear enough, though. The curriculum committee hadn't submitted its final report. If Ildun joined Cessly's minority report, the school board might decide that the classes were too controversial. Ildun's bland confidence made it clear that the professor knew the strength of his position.

The Donor considered the logistics. Besides the channels and Donors, two staff members handled the donation records: Seena ambrov Carre and Gati Forsin. They shared duty as Collectorium receptionists, greeting donors, maintaining files, and assigning less-experienced donors to the First Order channels. It was rarely busy enough to have both of them on duty, so maybe one or the other could translate for Arth. The records were in Simelan, so security wasn't an issue even if the out-Territory Gen saw the raw data. Den doubted Ildun's study would prove useful, but it seemed harmless and would apparently guarantee the professor's vote for the changeover classes.

"I don't have the power to authorize your study," Den temporized. "I'll put the matter before our legal counsel. If she approves, I'll discuss it with Controller Madz." *Who* won't *be happy about it.* Den wasn't happy, either. He resented being blackmailed into another time-consuming project. "But I will recommend that he insist on two conditions."

"Name them," Ildun said, settling down to negotiate.

"First, our selyn donors must not be pestered. Ask them to fill out your questionnaire once. If they refuse, leave them alone."

"Fair enough," Ildun agreed. "People won't give accurate responses if they feel coerced. What's your other condition?"

Den looked at Arth. "I can have *you* classified as volunteer staff. You can work in our library and eat in our cafeteria. However, you'll have to donate selyn every month and learn how to behave around Simes. Our ren-Simes are prepared for Gen emotional reactions in the Collectorium, but I won't ask them to stay on guard everywhere on the premises. We can't assign you a full-time Escort."

Arth blanched when Den mentioned donating selyn. "I wasn't envisioning a participant study…" His professor glared sternly and he added hastily, "…but I'll be happy to donate selyn if it's necessary." He smiled weakly. "It should be good for a chapter in my thesis."

After his guests had gone, Den placed a call to Plicera ambrov Shaeldor, the Tecton's legal advisor in Valzor. He outlined Ildun's project and asked about the legality of allowing access to the donation records for research purposes.

Plicera questioned him closely and finally said, "I'll have to look up statutes and case law to be sure, but I think it's possible with proper precautions. The Tecton compiles data for internal use and this isn't too different. Can I get back to you in a few days?"

"That would be fine," the Donor said, wishing she had just said no.

* * * *

The ability to perceive a nager didn't automatically mean that a Sime would interpret what he zlinned correctly. Later that day, hoping to ease Rital's guilt over burning him, Den offered a possible explanation for his erratic performance as a Donor over the past few weeks. The channel dismissed it out of hand.

"Den, I'd love to believe your capacity was growing. It's been too long since I've had a Donor with a Proficiency Rating higher than mine, but I'm afraid you're indulging in wishful thinking."

"But it all fits!" Den insisted. "One, it's a long time since I tested and I'm still young enough to grow. Two, growth happens most often when a Donor works frequently with a higher-rated channel. That's you, cousin. Three, my control has been getting worse, just as you'd expect when reflexes don't quite work for new parameters. On the other hand," he ticked off his fourth finger, "when I'm paying attention, not relying on habit, I work better than ever. Finally," he pointed to Rital's report of their transfer on the channel's desk, "if your estimate of your draw speed is accurate, I should have been burned a *lot* worse. So, my speed, sensitivity, *and* capacity have grown." He dared his cousin to argue.

Which of course Rital did. "It's hardly diagnostic that your control improves when you pay attention. Your control is off because you spend so much time outside the Sime Center, with no Simes to complain if you don't manage fields properly. As to our transfer," he ran a tentacle over the report, "nerve burn is tricky. The difference between draw speed and resistance won't always predict injury. I could be off on my estimate of the selyn flow, too. I'd love to believe your theory is true, but I don't think it is."

"There are ways to find out," Den said quietly.

"No!" the channel said, a little too quickly. "I won't…I *can't* risk pushing you to your limits again."

"It's my right to become the best Donor I can," Den pointed out.

"I know, but…" Rital looked for an excuse his cousin would accept. "It would mean sending you in-Territory for testing and I can't spare you. The only other way would be to push you beyond your documented limits. That's too risky. You've already been burned once." At the Donor's hurt look, he added, "You're the only First Order Donor we'll have until Monruss sends us a replacement for Siv. As local Controller, I can't risk having you unavailable."

"But after Siv's replacement arrives?" Den prodded.

A pause, then, "I'll think about it."

* * * *

That afternoon, the selyn batteries at the Center for Technology were scheduled for recharging. Rital took Den as Escort to the university campus. Although the weather was mild and the channel usually enjoyed the walk, he insisted on taking the staff van. "I don't want your legs giving out halfway," he said firmly.

Den was wise enough to pick his battles and let the channel coddle him. Besides, he enjoyed driving here, where the tables were turned and only Gens were allowed to drive.

The selyn battery bank at the Center for Technology was in an isolated basement room at the back of the building. Den unlocked the door with its diplomatic sign declaring the room Sime Territory—a legal fiction to allow channels to remove their retainers and fill the batteries—and let Rital lead the way down the stairs. The furnishings dated from the building's construction, when work crews had used the place as a break room. A safety grating shielded three selyn batteries that provided cheap power for the building.

Den helped Rital remove his retainers. He stretched out his tentacles while the Donor started water heating for tea, then the channel opened the grating and knelt before the barrel-like batteries. Carefully disconnecting the orgonics cables that carried selyn throughout the building, he extended his laterals to contact the battery terminals, touched his lips to the plate, and offloaded selyn.

Rital looked distinctly unwell by the time the third battery was charged. Den steered him to the couch and handed him a mug of tea. He was serving a portion for himself when there was a knock at the door and a voice called, "Sosu Milnan, are you in there?"

Den glanced at Rital, who shrugged helplessly. The concrete walls and surrounding earth prevented him from zlinning who was knocking, so the Donor climbed the stairs and opened the door.

"Branlee! What can I do for you?"

"I've got some materials to test for the battery box," the graduate student announced. "If any of them provide the right shielding, we'll have something a lot lighter. Since you and Hajene Madz are here already, you could save me hauling them across town."

"Let's ask Rital." Den led the way down the stairs and reminded his cousin, "Branlee provided me with that composite for testing as a flyer wing. The one Eddina wrote to me about?"

The channel nodded politely at the student, who was gawking at the batteries. Den continued. "He's got some prospects to test for a lightweight battery casing, if you'll zlin them for us?"

The project would let Rital postpone getting back into retainers. "I suppose the monthly report can wait."

Branlee had brought a utility cart piled high with various materials. Once they got them down the stairs, the graduate student pulled out a notebook. "Hajene, is there a standard measurement that indicates how well a material insulates against zlinning?"

"Yes, field attenuation."

Branlee nodded. "That sounds right. Can you give me the field attenuation of each of these samples?"

It took almost an hour to work through the samples of wood, plastic, ceramic, composites, fabrics, metals, and even a trio of orange, yellow and black shirts. Rital reported how clearly he could zlin Den's nager through each material. They tested each one three times in random order "to see how reproducible your numbers are," Branlee explained.

When they were done, the graduate student chortled over his notes. "You're amazingly consistent. There's almost no variation."

"There had better not be," Rital agreed dryly. "If I couldn't zlin selyn fields accurately, I'd have no business working as a channel."

Branlee was still studying his notebook. "I can definitely design a battery box lighter than hardwood-and-lead-foil," he decided. "Give me a week and we'll try again. That still leaves the mystery goop inside, but we've made a good beginning."

* * * *

As they returned to the Sime Center, Den dared indulge his dream that powered flight might become a reality before he was too old to enjoy it. What did a bird see when it soared through the sky? How much faster could one travel if one could proceed directly to one's destination "as the crow flies?"

The world was changing, improving. There was no better proof than Principal Buchan's arrival at the Sime Center late that afternoon. Den greeted him warmly, then sent Seena for Jain. The principal was increasingly at ease among Simes, but had a long way to go before he could be left unsupervised.

"I've come to have dinner with my daughter, before she leaves tomorrow," Buchan explained as he smoothed his suit, rumpled from his passage through the perpetual battle on the front sidewalk.

"She'll appreciate that," Den agreed. "Few Simes in her position have the security of a parent's support. Those who do usually adapt well to their new life."

Seena returned alone. "Sosu, Jain's not in the library or the cafeteria. If she's in her room, she's not answering. Nobody's seen her since lunch. She's been very depressed about leaving Clear Springs…"

In front of Jain's father, Seena was reluctant to say what she and Den both knew: suicides were common among out-Territory children who survived changeover. Jain didn't have the guilt of having killed someone, but she was a long way from accepting herself as a Sime.

"Is something wrong?" Buchan asked.

"Jain's unhappy about leaving," Den told him. "Seena, show Principal Buchan to the dining hall, while I roust Jain out of her sulk."

Den signaled at Jain's door five times, to show her that he wasn't going away, but got no response. That went beyond adolescent rudeness and into pathological depression, a medical issue. "Jain, your father's here. If you don't open this door in five seconds, I'm coming in."

The door remained closed. Surely teenaged dramatics would compel Jain to share her misery with her father before doing anything drastic?

Or, she could have done something stupid like eat strawberries, just because she never bothered to learn that they're deadly for Simes. He tried the door. It was unlocked, which argued against suicide, and he slipped inside.

The room was empty, but there was a note on the dresser. Its two sentences turned the situation on its head:

I've gone to the park to say good-bye to my teammates. Tell Daddy I'll be back soon.
Jain

Jain had made real progress recently, but she was still experiencing her first full Need cycle. Without an Escort, she might underestimate how strongly untrained Gen selyn fields could affect her.

The Donor froze as his glance fell on a trunk, packed full of Jain's belongings. On top rested her gleaming new retainers, carefully laid out for the morning, when she would join Siv on the long journey to Sime Territory. Den grabbed them and hurried out.

* * * *

"Jain is only two days past Turnover, but without retainers she's not only more vulnerable to selyn field fluctuations, she can be shot on sight, legally, by any Gen she meets," Den finished briefing the off-duty staff. In the presence of her father, he did not include that if a Gen spiked fear, it might overwhelm her uncertain control.

"Jain doesn't move like an adult Sime yet," Ref volunteered. "She was wearing an out-Territory shirt with long sleeves. If she keeps her tentacles sheathed, she might still pass as a child."

"Unless someone recognizes her," the girl's father pointed out. "She was the best gymnast on the team for the past two years and her changeover was…newsworthy."

Den nodded grim agreement. "We'd best find her fast. There are several parks close to the school and—"

"It's the one across the street from the school," the principal interjected. "There's a celebration today for the new year of competition. All Jain's friends will be there."

"Zir, you and Hammid take the ambulance," Rital decided. "Cover as much ground as you can between here and that park. Jain's trying to hide, so she may not use the main roads. Den, you and I will drive directly to the park with Principal Buchan."

* * * *

The park swarmed with people. Students were demonstrating a variety of athletic abilities. Parents cheered them on or staffed tables heaped with food. Coach Farrow barked orders with the authority of a drill sergeant.

"We'll circle the perimeter first," Rital decided. "Jain's most likely to hide in the bushes."

But as soon as Den parked the car, Buchan jumped out and headed straight across the trampled grass toward Farrow.

"Shen, I'd really hoped to do this quietly," Rital muttered as he and the Donor followed.

Den agreed. "I hope Buchan knows what he's doing."

"No, I haven't seen Jain," Farrow was telling his principal when they caught up. "Doesn't mean she isn't here. Her friends in gymnastics are doing the water-balloon toss against stickball on the north field." He set off, his bulk and status clearing a path through the swarm.

Den and Rital followed. If Jain was discovered, their Tecton uniforms and Rital's retainers might be sufficient to persuade the crowd to let them handle the situation, particularly if Farrow and Buchan backed them. Den kept his attention fixed firmly on his cousin.

"We met Jain behind the equipment shed," a stocky, athletic young woman confirmed, pointing across the field. "She promised to come say goodbye before she left for Sime-land."

The shed in question was away from the crowd, on the edge of the park. *At least Jain had enough sense not to walk through the crowd.*

Coach Farrow glowered. "Molly, if you wanted to tell Jain goodbye, you should have written her a letter. I can't believe a daughter of mine would endanger your teammates—"

"Jain isn't a danger," the girl objected. "She's our teammate."

Den wondered if he and Rital had done too good a job convincing the students that Simes were not inherently dangerous.

"She *was* your teammate," Farrow corrected his daughter sternly then demonstrated his priorities. "She quit the team for changeover classes. Combined with the deaths, the team fell apart and we lost."

"She took the classes on my orders," Buchan reminded the Coach. "It saved her life and possibly mine, as well."

"The gymnastics team won't fall apart this year," Molly assured the coach. "Jain said Jason, Vince and I are already Gen. If we plan the routines around the three of us, we won't have to redo them so drastically if we lose someone else. It's a big advantage, Daddy, and there's nothing in the rules against it!"

For once, the coach lost focus on adding more victories to his scoreboard. "You're a Gen?" he asked his daughter in sudden hope.

"She is," Rital confirmed.

"A channel teaching at the school could check the teams regularly for Establishments," Den pointed out.

Rital threw his cousin an annoyed look at this digression. "Is Jain still here?" he asked Molly.

"She left about ten minutes ago. She said she was meeting her father for dinner."

"Then we'll keep looking for her," Buchan said. "You've all been very helpful. Carry on, Coach Farrow."

* * * *

Unable to have a party of Simes zlin for Jain, their only choice was to head back to the Sime Center by the back streets she might choose. They were a block away when they heard the roar of a mob at the back of the Sime Center's grounds, followed by the sharp pop of a firearm.

"Jain!" Buchan wailed.

Heartsick, Den steered the car around the corner and saw what he'd feared: a mob of Save Our Kids activists surrounding an unmoving body, beating at it with their signs.

"Stay in the car!" Rital ordered urgently. "She's already gone, but that mob is only getting started."

But Jain's father had not been raised to defer to channels. He scrambled out of the car, pushing through the demonstrators. "Get away from her!" he commanded. Slowly, they parted. "What happened?" he demanded, kneeling to pick up the battered, bloody, lifeless body.

"We caught this Sime trying to climb the fence into the Sime Center," Police Chief Tains said casually, returning his service pistol to its holster. "It wasn't wearing those things on its arms, so we acted to preserve public safety."

"My daughter wasn't a danger to you or anyone else," Buchan argued. "You didn't have to murder her."

A few of the younger demonstrators looked vaguely guilty, but most looked indignant at the insult. The Gen language reserved the word "murder" to refer to death caused with criminal intent, while "kill" was used for other deaths, even if no selyn movement was involved.

"Now Principal Buchan," Chief Tains drawled. "I know you're upset, but that's no reason to accuse these good folks of wrongdoing."

"Yeah," the turmeric-haired man agreed. "It's no crime to exterminate Simes."

CHAPTER 9

SUBSTITUTIONS

A somber group of Sime Center staff gathered in the lobby the next morning to see Siv off to Valzor. There were no cheerful requests to pass on greetings to friends, or to bring back in-Territory delicacies. As Siv stowed the lunch Ref gave him in his duffle bag, the chef sniffed and wiped a tear from his cheek. Siv grasped Ref's shoulder a moment in an offer of comfort and made his solitary way out the door.

Jain Buchan's pastor reluctantly allowed her to be buried beside her mother in the church graveyard. He based his decision on the technicality that she had never killed, even though she was fully Sime. He made it very clear, however, that he was performing the service as a particular favor to her father and that under no circumstances were any Sime Center staff to attend.

Until Siv's replacement arrived, Den was responsible for both Rital and Tyvi. Fortunately, there were no changeover patients and neither channel required his assistance except with the most problematic donors.

Rital refused to reconsider Den's request to help him refine his new capacity and was meticulous not to exceed Den's official rating. His obsession with not hurting his cousin again overflowed into his dealings with staff Gens and out-Territory selyn donors, angering the former and frightening the latter. Den tried to convince his cousin to relax and trust their abilities, until Rital started avoiding him.

The stress between them became an open secret among the staff. People took sides, despite complete ignorance of the cause. Those who supported Rital hesitated to follow Den's instructions and the Donor's camp started to question Rital's judgment. The Sime Center's smooth teamwork was beginning to crack. It was only a matter of time before the out-Territory selyn donors sensed something wrong.

Den tried acting like a perfect Tecton Standard Donor. He followed Rital's instructions to the letter, but didn't offer help until the channel specifically requested it, as if Rital were a strange channel with unknown requirements and preferences. When he wasn't officially on duty, he ignored his cousin as thoroughly as he was being ignored.

Refusing to interact with one's channel was not a Tecton-approved strategy for handling a simple misunderstanding. Den would never do that with a stranger, but he and Rital had long since developed their own procedures for resolving arguments. Eventually, the channel's Need for a Donor's company would force him to settle with Den. Meanwhile, the Donor paid only enough attention to Rital to ensure his cousin didn't get into serious trouble.

While in pursuit of this strategy, Den accompanied Hajene Tyvi to refill the selyn batteries at the Center for Technology. Unlike Rital, Tyvi wasn't so fond of fresh air that she would hike through an out-Territory city in retainers. Den drove the staff car, carefully weaving through pedestrians, bicyclists, and delivery wagons. Even though the Sime Center had barely been open two years, there were more selyn-powered trucks and vans on the streets than before. Den had heard rumors of a plan to replace the horse-drawn trollies with a selyn-powered system, but so far, no official had asked the Sime Center about it.

Den was unlocking the door to the stairs when a boyish treble called, "Sosu Milnan! Wait a moment. I've got a message for you!"

With a sense of foreboding, he turned. "Raymond Ildun. What are you doing here?" Reflexively, he looked around for signs of the boy's latest prank.

Raymond grinned up at him, his freckles and carrot-colored hair projecting angelic innocence. "The new babysitter refused to watch my sisters if I was around, so I came to campus with my father. He told me to look around, but stay out of trouble. The labs up there are cool!"

"You're wandering around the labs unsupervised?" The Donor's reaction was horrified enough to win him an astonished look from Tyvi. However, the channel had never encountered the chaos and destruction that Raymond Ildun left in his wake as naturally as breathing.

"Labs are fun!" the boy declared. "Branlee won't let me play with the equipment, but he said if I took you his message, I could watch his experiment."

"What message is that?" Den asked grimly.

"He's got new materials to test and wants to know if Hajene Madz can look at them when you're done with the batteries." He looked at Tyvi. "But you didn't bring Hajene Madz."

"No, I didn't," Den agreed. "This is Hajene Tyvi ambrov Frihill."

On his best behavior for once, Raymond gave her a gap-toothed grin and said, "Pleased to meet you, Hajene Frihill."

Hit squarely in her maternal instinct, the tall channel smiled back. "It's Hajene Tyvi, actually," she corrected gently. "Frihill is my Householding."

"What's a Householding?" the boy asked.

"Think of it as a community, working together like a family."

Raymond made a face. "I already have two sisters and three cousins and my mother says I'll have another brother or sister in the fall. Too much family, if you ask me. Why do you want extra relatives?"

"It's nice to have friends and relatives everywhere you go," the channel answered.

Den didn't belong to one of the prestigious Householding "families" who still held most powerful positions in the Tecton. He hadn't had the advantage of the extra training, opportunities, and promotions high-ranking Householders provided to their fellow Householders, magnifying their power. What position Den had, he'd earned the hard way.

Resenting the way things are won't change them, he reminded himself. However, the technology of selyn batteries might prove easier to change than the century-old Householding stranglehold on Tecton politics.

"Tyvi, are you willing to zlin the efficacy of some new selyn-insulating materials?" Den asked. "It shouldn't take long."

The channel shrugged. "There's no emergency back at the Sime Center. Why not?"

Raymond gave a yip of glee and pelted off to tell Branlee. By the time the selyn batteries were refilled, the graduate student and his young assistant had returned with new materials. After Den explained the protocol they had been using to Tyvi, Branlee had the channel zlin some of the same materials he'd used with Rital to verify that she got the same results. Then he had her try some new composites.

One in particular caught her attention. "What is that?" she asked, as Branlee and Raymond held up a large sheet of hard, dull-red plastic between her and Den. "It blocks Sosu Den's field almost like a battery casing, but if it was that dense, you wouldn't be able to lift it."

The graduate student grinned. "I thought I might be on the right track! Try this one." He reached for a darker red sheet.

Tyvi extended her laterals, then blinked in astonishment. "Den, I can't zlin through it. It's like a sheet of granite–yet they can lift it."

"What is it, Branlee?" the Donor asked.

"Polycarbonate resin, mostly," the graduate student said. "It's good for industrial applications: affordable, durable, and moldable into multiple shapes. A half inch of the pure stuff insulates only a little less well than wood." He pointed out several sheets of dull white material of varying thickness among the "control" materials.

"So why does the red version insulate so much better?" Tyvi asked.

"Sosu Den said that battery casings are made of wood lined with lead, because metal blocks selyn fields most efficiently." Branlee explained. "Lead is very heavy, highly toxic, and expensive, so I looked for some other metal that was lighter, more common, and less toxic. The obvious candidate was iron."

"But iron is much more expensive than lead!" Den protested.

"Refined iron and steel, sure," Branlee agreed. "That's because refining is expensive and difficult. On the other hand, iron oxide is plentiful, cheap…and seems to insulate against selyn fields just fine."

"You dumped some rust into a batch of plastic?" Tyvi asked, examining the darker red sheet more closely.

"Yup," the graduate student admitted smugly. "The iron atoms provide the bulk of the insulation, the plastic holds them in any shape you want, and it's both lighter and cheaper than lead-lined hardwood."

"This will have applications far beyond lighter batteries," Tyvi observed.

"Lighter batteries are a good start, though," Den countered, imagining a powered flyer carrying passengers up into the sky.

"We don't have a battery yet," Branlee pointed out, bringing the Donor's daydream solidly back to earth. "A lighter casing won't help if the goop inside is still too bulky and heavy to be portable. You really don't know what it is?"

"Nobody knows except Householding Ohmand," Den said sourly.

Branlee shrugged. "Give me a couple weeks to experiment, and I'll have an idea what's in it. Then we can improve it."

* * * *

Den returned to the Sime Center feeling justified pride in their progress. Tyvi was right: a lightweight selyn field insulator more than justified his investment, even if they couldn't improve the battery gel. He wanted nothing more than to share his triumph with Rital…but the channel wasn't interested, just now.

Instead, Den shared the news with Eddina and the flyer club in Valzor. "If we develop a lightweight battery," he wrote, "the Economic Development Board will surely approve plans for a more efficient motor. We may yet use that Ancient pilot training manual I found!"

Den's resolve almost broke when Rital selected Third Order Donor Hammid as his Escort on his next trip to refill the selyn batteries, claiming that it was more important to have Den available for the Collectorium and emergencies. Den was unconvinced. Feelings still ran high after Jain's death and even at his highest field, Hammid couldn't shield a First from a mob. But there was nothing Den could do about it. Because of the Donor shortage, First Order channels were officially encouraged to work with lesser Donors to bring out latent potential.

Den wished his cousin was half as interested in Den's own latent potential. Still, the Donor couldn't deny that he was exhausted trying to keep up with two channels, especially after Thaddus Webber returned his draft curriculum, with a polite request to modify it according to the committee's suggestions, which were presented as a mass of academic jargon.

Den's euphemistic pamphlet, though, was accepted with only token editing. The Donor magnanimously refrained from mocking Rital with a well-deserved, "I told you so." It would be unprofessional to treat his Controller that way and besides, it was obvious to his experienced eyes that his cousin had gotten the message.

Five days after Siv's departure, Plicera called to confirm that Professor Ildun could be granted limited access to demographic information from the Sime Center's donation records.

Rital's response to Ildun's research proposal was immediate and predictable. "Let an out-Territory Gen wander around the Sime Center, poking his nose into our records? Out of the question," the channel fumed, tentacles lashing in irritation. "I don't know why you even bothered to call Valzor and get a legal opinion."

"I didn't have a choice," Den said unhappily. He explained the professor's thinly veiled threat to join Cessly Lornstadt's minority report, if his request for access to the records was refused.

"If Ildun turns against our classes, the school board will think that the opposition to them is broader than just Sinth and his crowd and they'll vote our classes out," the Donor finished. "If Ildun *really* felt vindictive, he could rouse the whole town against us."

"There's no reason to get melodramatic, Den," Rital said. "If Reverend Sinth hasn't turned the town against us in two years, there's no reason to think Ildun can do better."

"Yes, there is," the Donor contradicted. "Sinth's the leader of a small anti-Sime religious denomination. Ildun's a scientist, and scientific findings are useful to members of all religions. A few well-chosen remarks and we'd be right back where we were two years ago. Except this time, we'd have District Controller Monruss and the Office for Inter-Territorial Affairs breathing down our necks."

"That will happen anyway, if this graduate student gets himself hurt," the channel pointed out.

"It's less than a month until the school board makes its final decision," Den reminded him. "Once Ildun signs the majority report, he can't oppose us without labeling himself a hypocrite. We can prevent an accident that long. After the school board votes, we can cancel the project at the first sign of trouble."

The channel's mouth kept its unyielding expression.

"It's the only way to protect what we've accomplished here," the Donor pleaded, letting his conviction show in his nager. "You've often said I understand out-Territory politics better than you. Can't you trust my judgment on this?"

"Your political judgment isn't infallible, cousin," Rital said, gazing meaningfully at Den's left cheek.

The Donor squirmed, even though the walnut juice stain had long since disappeared.

"I zlin an accident waiting to happen," the channel said, in a tone that meant the topic was closed. He picked up a pen and reached for the next document in his "in" box.

Den was in no mood to let a stubborn channel destroy both their careers. Not caring for the moment how deeply the words would wound, he snapped, "You don't zlin *every* accident coming, Rital Madz!"

The pen snapped, spilling ink over the document. The channel stared at Den in disbelief.

He really does *feel guilty,* Den thought. *It's not ethical to use that against him when I've eaten his apology.* But for the sake of the children of Clear Springs, the Donor couldn't afford to yield.

Rital's shoulders slumped as he zlinned the Gen's determination. "All right," he conceded gracelessly. "Let this graduate student do his research, *after* I've taken his field down. Personally. However," he pointed a stern tentacle, "*you* are responsible for teaching him proper manners and the first time he causes the slightest trouble, he's out. Whether the school board has voted or not."

"Fair enough," the Donor agreed and left to inform the professor that he could begin his study.

Within the hour, a petrified Arth showed up at the Collectorium. Rital spent almost twenty minutes talking with the young man before taking his field down. This didn't prevent Arth from struggling in blind panic from the moment the first tentacle touched him. The channel nonetheless gently stripped as much selyn from the Gen as possible, knowing that each dynopter he took decreased the chance that Arth would provoke the staff renSimes to attack.

Fortunately, Arth didn't blame Rital for his fear. Afterward, Den showed the student which areas of the Sime Center he was allowed to enter. He also detailed the proper behavior for a non-Donor Gen around renSimes, using Jesper, who'd had transfer less than a week before, to demonstrate.

The Donor had Arth monitored closely during his first few sessions in the library. Then he sent the steadier staff renSimes to test him while Hammid idled over a book on the other side of the room and observed. Though

Arth was uneasy around Simes, Den's informant reported no immediate danger of the student provoking an attack.

At least, not while he's low field, the Donor thought grimly, cursing Ildun for forcing this on him when there was no time to deal with it. Fortunately, Arth didn't have a particularly strong nager and Den was prepared to order the student to donate early if necessary.

Den was very glad when Siv's replacement arrived a week after the other Donor's departure…until he saw the balding, dignified older gentleman with the quiet air of command.

Quess ambrov Shaeldor not only possessed a Proficiency Rating considerably higher than Den's was ever likely to be, he was also one of the Tecton's most noted diplomats. He had recently negotiated an end to the decades-long war between the Sime Territory of Cordona, on the Southern Continent, and its two neighboring Gen Territories, Amzon and Zillia. All three governments were now signatories to the First Contract.

Den might have welcomed the man's diplomatic perspective, except that last year, Quess had chaired an official inquiry into the conflict surrounding the Clear Springs Sime Center. Only after making his skepticism of Den and Rital's competence very clear had the senior Donor voted to allow them to stay in Clear Springs.

Den considered Quess a threat to the effort to spread changeover training to the local schools. *Not to mention my hopes of getting Rital to work with me, instead of at cross-purposes.*

It didn't help that Quess had a Householder's expectation of miracles produced on demand…or that he more than lived up to the unreasonable standards by which he measured others. Never less than courteous, Quess greeted Den cordially. "Sosu Milnan, it's good to see you again."

"Welcome to Clear Springs," Den replied, glad Quess was a Gen. He could never have concealed his hostility from a channel.

Rital shot his cousin a look that promised a private scold. "Sosu Quess will be staying with us for at least two months."

Rital's tone warned his cousin that they wouldn't settle their differences any time soon. *He won't admit I'm right about promoting the classes, much less help me work to my full capacity, so long as that interfering busybody offers him an alternative!* The illustrious Quess ambrov Shaeldor was too important to be assigned to an outpost like Clear Springs for long, however. *I could outwait him if my capacity was the only issue, but we have to get the classes approved before the next school term.*

Quess's enthusiasm appeared spontaneous as he told Den, "I read your reports for the last few months. You've made remarkable progress toward expanding changeover classes into the schools, and now Naztehr Plicera tells me that you've started a joint research project with an out-Territory professor?"

Shen renSimes and their endless gossip! Den thought savagely.

Oblivious to the younger Donor's rage, Quess continued, "I'm eager to learn how you've gotten such cooperation from the out-Territory community. Your approach could be valuable to the Tecton."

"You didn't think so last spring," Den pointed out. "You had 'grave doubts' as to whether my cousin and I should be allowed an out-Territory license."

The older Donor spread his hands and said simply, "I was wrong."

Life would be a lot less complicated if Rital were that willing to admit his mistakes, Den thought morosely, *and it would be much more satisfying to dislike Quess if he weren't so absolutely ethical.* Few people with a record like Quess's would admit a mistake in judgement to a hostile subordinate in front of Sime Center staff. By doing so, the Householder proved himself twice the professional that Den was. It was a very subtle rebuke… but effective.

"I'd be happy to discuss my current efforts," Den invited, although his voice sounded stiff and wooden.

"I look forward to it." Quess turned to Rital and asked, "Could someone show me to my room so that I can freshen up before dinner?"

"Of course," the channel said, signaling Seena to see to it.

As the receptionist escorted Quess up the stairs, Den noted that the diplomat's immaculate uniform still had regulation creases, even after the eight-hour train ride from Valzor. Den's own uniform was rumpled and, he noticed for the first time, he'd spilled soup on his shirt front during lunch. It was the final humiliation.

Unable to face the staff, Den fled to the library, hoping for a few minutes to recover his composure. A furious Rital burst into his sanctuary. "You insulted the man to his face. In front of the staff!" the channel charged, handling tentacles lashing in fury.

"Why not?" Den asked, absurdly driven to defend his indefensible behavior. "Inter-Territorial Affairs may maintain the fiction of a 'routine rotation of Donors,' but the illustrious Sosu Quess ambrov Shaeldor has too much seniority to be assigned where his particular talents aren't required. We're on trial again, Rital, this time without notice or a list of charges so we can defend ourselves."

"If you're right, all the more reason to be polite," Rital reminded his cousin. "I can't complain to Monruss about the assignment. He's the best Donor ever sent out here."

"And you can't wait to get your tentacles on him." Den couldn't stop a surge of pure Gen jealously at the thought of another Donor monopolizing *his* channel while Den was stuck with Tyvi, whose draw speed and selyn capacity were too low to satisfy him.

"That was uncalled for," Rital said coldly.

Den's shoulders slumped. "I'm sorry." He met the channel's eyes, not trying to hide his misery. "Are you really so mad at how I botched our last transfer that you'd get rid of me?"

Rital's expression softened and his hands and handling tentacles gripped the Donor's biceps with reassuring Sime strength. "Cousin, you're staying here as long as I can keep you, Quess or no Quess. But could you do me a favor and *try* to get along with him?"

After a moment's consideration, Den nodded. "If I have to," he agreed reluctantly. "Just don't ask me to like the man."

* * * *

Den kept his promise. He spent long sessions with Quess, explaining the local politics and going over the year's progress. The older Donor was skeptical at first of Den's claim that the situation was under control, particularly after seeing Save Our Kids and OLD SOKS in action, but the increase in selyn donations spoke for itself.

Quess took care not to undermine the younger Donor's position, even though his higher Proficiency Rating made him the final authority for matters requiring a Donor's arbitration. Instead, he managed to back *both* Den and Rital, demonstrating that the two were in agreement on most matters. Without clear sides to choose, the petty bickering among the staff subsided and morale improved.

To demonstrate his gratitude, Den took Quess to the Sudworks Brewery for the weekly OLD SOKS after-meeting festivities. There he introduced Branlee to the older Donor. "Branlee is working with me to develop a lighter, more efficient selyn battery," he explained with justifiable pride. The progress he'd made there was his one undeniable success. "We've found a new material that shields a selyn source better than wood and lead, at a quarter the weight. It's also cheaper and non-toxic!"

"Now, that's a useful discovery," Quess admitted. "I can think of a dozen applications offhand, aside from selyn batteries."

"I hope you've got it patented," a shamelessly eavesdropping Tohm remarked, leaning across the table.

Den and Branlee looked at him blankly.

"How will you convince a commercial supplier to make the stuff if you don't own the rights?" Tohm asked.

"We hadn't considered that," the Donor admitted sheepishly. "Is filing a patent complicated?"

"Nah," Tohm assured him, with a shark-like grin. "We lawyer types just pretend it is, so manufacturers will pay us to protect their interests. My father wants me to learn the practical side of the business. I'll get the forms, draw them up with Branlee, then talk Father into filing them for you."

"Thank you," Den said, relieved to have this unanticipated barrier removed so easily. "It'll be even more important if we develop a better gel for the inside of the battery."

"I do hope you're taking appropriate safety precautions," Quess warned. "Even regular selyn batteries can be dangerous and a new gel formula might behave in unpredictable ways."

Tohm and Silva plied Quess with questions about his diplomatic career. When they asked why he was in Clear Springs, the other Donor answered, "Light duty between missions." Den was relieved: the last thing the Sime Center could afford was a rumor that he and Rital were under investigation.

Quess never referred to his unofficial mission, or the influence of his expert opinion, but pursued his stated objective of learning Den's methods of handling out-Territory political controversy. He asked pointed questions about Den's newspaper column and the carefully crafted "information" pamphlet, listened to the younger Donor's answers, and didn't hesitate to offer praise as well as criticism.

Den decided to take advantage of the older Donor's interest. Rital might refuse to accept what he saw as half-truths from Den, but what if they were approved by a Donor with Quess's reputation? When the final draft of Den's information pamphlet came back from Rital's desk with a stiff note of approval, the Donor allowed himself a smug smile of victory—and sent it to the printer immediately.

Den thought he might even like Quess, if the man weren't so fiendishly talented. It was bad enough to see another Gen in Den's place at Rital's side. It was worse to see his cousin blossoming under the man's care.

It was just as well Den wouldn't have transfer with Rital for a month or two, even though the delay prevented him from testing his new capacity. When a Donor started feeling *that* possessive about a channel, it was all too easy to "accidentally" develop a transfer dependency.

But it's spending time with him that I miss most.

To keep his mind off Rital, Den focused on Tyvi. He made sure that she ate at least twice a day and scheduled time with her each evening to work on easing the day's accumulated tension, or sometimes just share a cup of trin tea. Although Den wasn't as talented as Quess, his Proficiency Rating was considerably higher than Siv's and Tyvi enjoyed the luxury of having a Donor she couldn't hurt. In the process, Den rediscovered the simple pleasure of using his talents as they were meant to be used.

With another Donor to share the workload, Den had time for other projects, so he often was available to translate donation records for Arth on workday afternoons. Den didn't see any pattern in the numbers, except the obvious one that experienced donors were less frightened than "virgins," as Seena referred to them, but Arth found his data sheets exciting. Professor Ildun was equally pleased and, being an honest blackmailer, he signed the Curriculum Committee's majority report and sent Hank Fredricks a statement promoting the changeover classes.

* * * *

They had never required support more, for Reverend Sinth was running a no-holds-barred campaign to scare Clear Springs parents into demanding the school board reject its committee's recommendation. The owner of the Clear Springs Graphic Design Shop, an outspoken supporter, helped the preacher produce four slick pamphlets guaranteed to give credibility to the most insubstantial rumor. Somehow, Sinth raised the money to print several thousand copies and Save Our Kids walked city neighborhoods, talking and distributing pamphlets. Others haunted the university campus, the shopping district, and the Farmer's Market. They even appeared outside the opening performance of the Clear Springs Comic Opera Company's fall season.

Den doubted any Clear Springs residents escaped Sinth's propaganda, and he had no resources to counter it. The Sime Center couldn't produce competing pamphlets and his personal funds were depleted by the battery research project. There weren't enough members of OLD SOKS to distribute copies to everyone in town even if classes weren't in session, nor would Rital approve the kind of hard-hitting attack that might counter Sinth's propaganda. However, Den found another way to reach the public.

Thanks to Sinth's efforts, the changeover classes were NEWS. Hank Fredricks, and thus his *Clear Springs Clarion,* supported the Sime Center. He sent a sympathetic reporter to interview Den for a feature on the classes, to be printed in the Weekend edition. Almost half of Clear Springs' residents would see it there, Den estimated, including three quarters of the long-term residents, who were the most reliable voters.

Den had been writing a Sime Center column for the midweek local news section for over six months. His next column addressed three of Sinth's claims that had inspired the most letters to the editor. A point-by-point refutation was much too long, but Den wrote one anyway. Sinth's complaints about the classes required factual rebuttals.

Two days before the reporter was to interview him, Den cleared an evening for writing. He found nothing new to rebut in the reissue of Cessly Lornstadt's minority report, **"Six Reasons to Stop the Classes."** Nor was he particularly concerned about the discussion of "obscenities" in **"What the pro-Sime lobby wants to put in YOUR child's textbooks,"** as it mostly featured drawings of Simes and Gens in transfer position and photographs of happy in-Territory, mixed-larity families, taken without attribution from Sime Center materials and therefore quite accurate. However, he had to counter the arrant nonsense in **"Are you one of the parents FOOLED by the Tecton?"** (**"Simes going through changeover in the halls, used as visual aids—no slides necessary!"**) He was starting on the conspiracy theory outlined in **"The SECRET TRUTH About the Tecton"** when Quess came to the door.

"What are you working on so late?" the other Donor asked.

"Just damage control," Den remarked absently. He set down his pen with a sigh, glad for the distraction. "According to this pamphlet, the Tecton assigned you to Clear Springs to prepare for Tecton forces to overthrow the city government in favor of a Sime dictatorship."

"Alas, they forgot to brief me on such a mission." Quess picked up the tract. His eyebrows rose as he read it, then exchanged it for another. "These are disgusting," he said.

"I know," Den agreed, "but a certain percentage of people will believe anything. Others won't know what to believe and don't have time to investigate. Such people may oppose changeover classes, just in case."

"So how do you counter this propaganda?" the older Donor asked with unfeigned curiosity.

Den explained, adding, "The paper won't publish the full rebuttal, of course, but if a credible source like the paper reveals that some claims in the pamphlets are false, people may doubt the rest."

"I see," Quess said. "What about people who don't read the newspaper?"

Den shrugged. "That's mostly students: temporary residents too young to have children and mostly ineligible to vote in Clear Springs elections. If our side gets fair coverage, the rest may hear the truth from friends. Otherwise, we'll hope they're too apathetic for Sinth to organize."

"It sounds rather haphazard."

"People who attend school board meetings likely subscribe to the local paper," Den pointed out. "Also, Hank Fredricks is trying to attract college students with the *Clarion's* back-to-school supplement. He lists the Sime Center under Community Resources, printed under a coupon for a half-priced lunch. And, much as it annoys Sinth's crowd, we pay donors."

Quess shook his head, "I wish you luck with your rebuttal."

"Thanks," Den said. "I have a sinking suspicion I'll require it."

CHAPTER 10

BAD TIMING

Tohm's older sister, Henna, interviewed Den for the *Clarion*. Although not a selyn donor, she was open-minded and proud of Tohm's role in OLD SOKS. Reverend Sinth had patronized her during his interview, she confided, and was openly hostile toward her brother.

Her article was so informative, accurate, and entertaining that Fredricks placed it facing the movie guide. Suddenly every club, civic association, and professional guild wanted speakers from the Sime Center. Den prodded the staff to volunteer, armed them with his course outline, and made sure they read Sinth's pamphlets and his own rebuttals. He couldn't risk sending speakers without a ready response to Sinth's outrageous theories.

Quess, his most effective speaker, won an endorsement for the change-over classes from the ultraconservative Downtown Businessmen's Association. The narrow alleys behind their stores were a favorite hiding place for changeovers. Quess suggested that placing a free telephone with a direct line to the Sime Center there could save both Sime and Gen lives, providing the merchants with lower costs for guards and insurance. To his amazement, enough "no" votes changed to "yes" for the idea to win approval.

"I fear I underestimated the Simephobia in this community," he confessed to Den. "An orange-haired man with appalling grammar who'd been heckling me all evening pounced on the idea." Den instantly recognized his turmeric-haired antagonist as Quess proved quite the impersonator: "'Put a police callbox down there, too,' he cried. 'But wait, we don't need no police. We got enough men with firearms permits, we can stake out the phone dusk to dawn!' And then he said to me, 'Make sure them kids are taught in them classes to come straight to the free telephone if they think they're turnin' Sime!'"

Quess dropped into a chair, shaking his head. "I've worked with Sime-haters before, but I have never seen them take such delight in—in murdering their own children. At least not once they knew they could live without harming anyone."

"It's not all of them," Den reminded him. "Only those in Sinth's clutches. If they want to stake out phones, though, we should offer to install a dozen. They'll either decide that's too many to guard and give up, or put so many people on it that they have to give up on some of their other projects."

Den emphasized public safety at a well-attended lecture at the library and gave a similar presentation at an informational meeting for Principal Buchan's faculty and staff. The principal had aged ten years since his daughter's death, but believed more than ever that changeover classes belonged in his school.

Many meetings featuring Sime Center speakers weren't open to the general public, which created problems for Save Our Kids. The consensus was that while Sime-loving selyn donors and pro-Sime activists like OLD SOKS might be fair game for harassment, it was unacceptable to attack the general public. As public feeling changed, the police cracked down on aggressive tactics, limiting Sinth's crowd to peaceful demonstrations. Den was not about to complain about anything that turned people against Sinth and instructed his speakers to begin by discrediting whichever pamphlet was being distributed on the sidewalk outside the meeting.

Arth gathered enough data for a preliminary analysis and began the second part of his research project, passing out questionnaires to every selyn donor who would consent to look at one. Den was surprised at how many people took the time to fill them out.

Den's own research project was also progressing. Branlee was preparing a selection of new battery gel mixtures for Rital to test, with the eager assistance of Raymond Ildun, who had become an unofficial lab assistant. The boy's father was pathetically grateful to find someone willing to supervise his trouble-prone offspring. Since uncharged battery gel was harmless, Den allowed it.

A week before Den's scheduled transfer with Tyvi, Rital dropped by his office. "I've got some good news for you," the channel said.

Noting the green transfer assignment card Rital carried, Den guessed facetiously, "Quess has been called to the southern continent over renewed hostilities in Cordona, so we're having transfer after all?"

Before their falling out, such a comment would have earned the Donor a laugh. Now, Rital's response was a raised eyebrow and a pained expression. "Not quite. Tyvi's son, Obis, has permission to spend a few weeks with her between assignments."

Family visits were a low priority for the Tecton, but Householders got most of them. It wasn't discrimination, exactly, but a disproportionate percentage of Householders held high office in the Tecton. Householding-affiliated Controllers were in a position to consider family and friendships of fellow Householders when making assignments.

"Obis was supposed to serve Controller Monruss this month, but when Monruss called just now, we decided to let the boy give his mother transfer," Rital continued. "I know you don't particularly like Tyvi."

"True, although she's a lot better than nothing," Den admitted. *If I can't have you, cousin, I'd rather not be around to see you enjoy Quess instead. Not to mention...* Temmin's interest had waned quickly and she had started to pursue Quess. So far, the senior Donor's lack of interest and decades-long marriage hadn't discouraged her.

"You'll go to Valzor this month, assigned to Controller Monruss," the channel continued.

"Monruss was my first assignment after I finished training," Den said. "I've got a soft spot for him. It'll be good to spend time in civilization, too."

The channel grinned. "You've been very good about it, cousin, but even though you missed building your next flyer contest entry, there's no reason to miss seeing it launch."

Den had forgotten the East Nivet Model Flyer's Convention. Eddina had sent a description of the entry she, Jannun, and young Mandle had constructed from Branlee's composite—now he would see it fly! Suddenly eager, he read the green card, and groaned.

"Den, what's the matter?" Rital asked.

Den pointed at the date of transfer. "It's two days early!"

"Don't worry," the channel said reassuringly. "Monruss is rated a bit lower than Tyvi. You'll have more than enough selyn for him."

"What?" Den asked in bewilderment, then flushed with outrage as he caught the channel's meaning. "Rital, I hate to deprive you of a guilt trip, but you'd have to burn me a lot deeper than *that* before I'd get transfer-shy."

"Then what's the problem?" Rital asked, genuinely bewildered.

"You and Monruss have scheduled me for a transfer in Valzor on the night the school board decides about our changeover classes!"

"Shen," Rital swore. "I forgot all about that."

"You're the only one in Clear Springs who's had that luxury," Den commented. "It's too late to change the schedule. I'll alert our supporters. Maybe someone will plead our case in my stead."

Quess would never allow Rital into a hostile ambient in Hard Need, particularly after the last meeting the channel had attended had ended in a hail of fermenting walnuts. *Rital doesn't talk back to* that *Donor,* Den thought enviously.

"Quess would go, if you asked him," Rital suggested. "Why have a noted diplomat on staff, if we can't use him?"

"You're right." Den forced a grin. "Although Quess may wish he was back in a nice, peaceful war zone!" *At least the Businessmen's Association showed him how vicious out-Territory Gens can be.*

Den passed the next two days frantically reorganizing to cover his absence. He went over his course outline, information pamphlet, and all the reports with Quess, then briefed him on school board members and other significant players. He even enlisted two OLD SOKS members, Silva Vornast and Annie Lifton, to accompany Quess and identify the important attendees.

"I think Quess is ready," an exhausted Den reported to Rital as they waited to greet Sosu Obis, due on the evening train. The young Donor would overlap with Den for a full day before Den left for Valzor, so the Sime Center's staff could respond to any messages the Donor carried.

"Quess is experienced at cleaning up political messes," Rital reassured Den as Seena led their anticipated guest inside.

But Obis had not traveled alone. Following him was a Sime, her arms clutched against her chest to protect her retainers from jolts. She looked so pale and woebegone it took Den a moment to recognize her.

"Eddina! What the shen are *you* doing here?" He pulled her aside, leaving Rital to greet Obis. "It's too dangerous for a renSime to visit here until the changeover class issue is settled."

"That was weeks ago," Eddina explained. "They must have settled it by now. I had some time off, I'm not in Need, and there was a Donor coming to Clear Springs willing to Escort me. I've wanted so much to visit you and see those books in the university library." She tried to smile, then admitted, "I didn't realize the train ride would be so long!"

"It's at the limit for a Sime wearing retainers." Den carefully worked the manacles off. Her tentacle sheaths showed angry red welts where the devices had pinched. "And that assumes the Sime is used to retainers. It takes practice."

By this time, Rital had welcomed Obis, received his packet of communications, and released him to greet his mother. Den beckoned the channel over to examine Eddina's injuries.

"No permanent damage," Rital concluded, "but Den should work on those welts before the swelling gets worse."

The Donor spent almost an hour healing and stabilizing Eddina. By the time he finished, she had regained her normal color and could use her handling tentacles again.

"I don't think I've zlinned you working as a Donor before," she observed over a celebratory pot of premium trin. "I knew you were First Order, of course, but… You're good, Den. Really good."

"Thank you," Den said, blushing. After weeks of being not-as-good-as-Quess, Eddina's compliment was balm for his self-esteem.

"Why did you come to Clear Springs, when I advised against it?" Den asked. "Gens here don't live with Simes. Some oppose the Sime Center. Feelings are particularly high about changeover classes."

"Den, I'm here to visit you and poke around the library," Eddina explained. "Not to get involved in local politics."

"The young renSime shot to death a few weeks ago wasn't involved in local politics, either. She just snuck out of the Sime Center to visit friends." At Eddina's downcast look, the Donor sighed. "Look, I'm off-duty tomorrow. I'll take you to the library in the morning, and then you can return to Valzor with me the next day."

Eddina grinned, her usual good humor restored. "Excellent! I want to know how the Ancients adjusted the wing shape of their flyers for landing. I think it had something to do with moveable flaps they put on the wings, but I haven't figured out how they worked."

* * * *

Several hours later, Den left Eddina in a guest room and told his plans to Rital. "Both you and Tyvi have other Donors, I'm mostly packed, and I haven't forgotten the monthly report, the supply list, the wish list, or that stack of letters."

"Relax and visit with your flyer-mad friend," Rital agreed. "You've earned it."

It was obvious that his cousin had intended the in-Territory rotation as a special treat and was dismayed that he'd timed it so poorly. But Den was not ready to forgive his cousin after Rital's stubborn refusal to consider Den's hypothesis regarding the cause of his injury. "You know, I'd like to show Eddina our progress on the selyn battery."

Rital's guilt increased, as the Donor had intended. "I'm sorry, Den. I know that Branlee wants to test some new mixtures, but even if I'd been able to get free, you haven't had time."

Den conceded that truth, then sprang his trap. "Tyvi's on duty tomorrow night. How about going over to campus after we've finished at the library? Branlee has been waiting for two weeks now. He won't mind working late, as long as he can make progress. Please?"

Den's kicked-puppy imitation wasn't quite as good as his cousin's, but he reinforced it with nageric pleading. Rital held out for two full seconds before yielding.

* * * *

After a night's rest, Eddina was eager for adventure. They left before the day's demonstrators arrived at the Sime Center.

Not even retainers could curb the renSime's enthusiasm. "The nageric distortion isn't so bad when I'm moving under my own power," she explained.

As they walked, they discussed the challenges of building flyer wings. "Our small-scale models either glide well or land well, but not both," Eddina complained.

"I'm not surprised," Den admitted. "The two tasks are very different." He shifted the picnic basket he carried to his other hand.

"A flat wing gives the longest glide." Eddina held out one hand with palm down, fingers straight. "However, the best wing shape to provide control at slow speeds necessary to land is slightly curved, like this." She cupped her palm, leaving her fingers straight, her thumb below the plane made by her fingers.

"I remember trying it with paper flyers," Den said. "Their flight path could be changed by altering wing shape."

"Exactly!" Eddina agreed. "A lot of Ancient aircraft had the back edges of the wings broken into several flaps that changed the wing shape to gain fine control, but I can't duplicate it."

At the library, Eddina could barely contain her excitement as she flipped through some of the offerings, looking at the drawings. Den stood back and let her absorb the wealth of new information.

When she was ready, Den pulled two books he remembered and they settled in an isolated nook to study them in detail. The first described a program the Gen military had started just before the Unity War, using hang gliders to spot Sime raiders in the western deserts, where dependable updrafts could keep them aloft. Most of the text examined the military aspects, but one chapter discussed the design of the gliders and another, how the pilots had been trained. Den translated as Eddina scribbled notes and sketches.

The second book was a real treasure: a translation of Ancient English instructions for training pilots to operate a small, powered flyer. Some illustrations were stylized diagrams of geometric shapes. The captions claimed these were blueprints of controls, but neither Den nor Eddina could see how they worked. Other illustrations, though, were more straightforward.

Of particular interest was a diagram of the parts of the flyer with detailed instructions for performing particular flying maneuvers. They still didn't understand how the various control buttons and levers altered how the craft flew. "But we don't have to understand," Den pointed out. "The technology differs for each power source."

Eddina looked confused.

"If you're sending messages using couriers on horseback," Den explained, "horseshoes and saddles are critical to the technology. It doesn't matter if your courier is illiterate, as long as she's good with horses and knows the route. If you're sending your messages by telegraph, then orgonics cable is the critical technology and your operators must be fully literate and able to transcribe messages. We want to fly and land a flyer, but we'll be using a very different power source. What we want from this manual is how the wing shape should change while taking off, turning, and landing. Then we figure how to do it with *our* technology."

"You're right," Eddina admitted, running a finger over one of the blurry, restored geometric diagrams, "but I still want to know what this means!"

With only a break in the selyn battery room for their picnic lunch, they spent the day studying. By late afternoon, they had sketched out several possible approaches to guiding a flyer to a controlled landing.

"Although," Eddina pointed out, "control would be easier if there were a pilot on board. "Like so…" She drew a quick diagram.

"One day, there will be flyers with living pilots," Den said, projecting confidence. "So, don't throw that sketch away."

That evening Den drove Eddina and Rital to the Center for Technology to meet Branlee. The graduate student was not alone.

"Shouldn't you be in bed by now?" Den asked, glaring down at Raymond Ildun.

"It's Mother's night out and the babysitter won't come if I'm there, so Father is stuck with me," the boy said, grinning broadly. "He's in his office, so he told me to stay in the building and out of trouble."

"See that you do," the Donor warned sternly, and had the satisfaction of seeing the boy's grin vanish. "We have work to do."

The lab bench held a row of large beakers. Above, shelves were filled with neatly labeled glass jars of chemicals. "I tried to analyze the battery gel you gave me," Branlee explained. "There's a few ingredients I'm sure of, but others I'm guessing at. We'll start with real battery gel as a control, then add things and see if any of them will hold a charge."

"Yeah!" Raymond chimed in. "I want to see Hajene Madz stick his tentacles in the goop!"

"I won't have to," Rital explained. "This building has orgonics connections to all the rooms. That's what powers the lights."

"Are you sure you can get good data with your tentacles covered?" the graduate student asked.

Rital shrugged. "The retainers distort, but I can zlin any differences in capacity large enough to be useful. If we find something interesting, we'll take it to the basement for a closer examination."

"I brought an outlet-to-battery charger," said Den, "so we'll just plug this end in and we're good to go." He opened one of the utility panels, revealing a shiny new outlet, and attached the cable.

"Is that what that's for? I was wondering." Branlee leaned over the bench to peer more closely at the outlet.

Den firmly pushed him back a step. "It's connected to the selyn batteries in the basement, so stay away from the terminal here. You could give yourself a nasty burn." He coiled the tubing, checked that the safety cap was still attached, and set it to one side where it wouldn't be in the way and, not incidentally, was out of Raymond's reach.

Branlee half-filled the first beaker with authentic battery gel. "This is our control," he announced.

"What does it control?" Eddina asked when Den translated.

"Our expectations," the graduate student explained. "It shows us that standard battery gel will charge under our test conditions. I'll fill these test beakers with half as much real gel, so they should hold at least some charge; then we'll start adding other things."

Raymond wiggled in excitement, reaching for some of the bottles at the back of the lab bench, and Den started to worry. "We test one at a time, Raymond. We'll measure how much of each test compound we put in and how much selyn the beaker will hold, then we'll write it down so we have a record. You can watch, but that's all. Selyn batteries are dangerous."

Raymond squirmed under Den's glare.

"I mean it, Raymond," the Donor snapped. "We've no time to waste preventing you from committing suicide. You follow my rules or you're out in the hall. Your choice."

When the boy's expression of hurt innocence won no support, he nodded reluctant agreement. Eddina beckoned to him and Den turned his attention to Branlee's briefing.

Letting Raymond stay, he realized later, was his first mistake.

"That battery gel is mostly oil, probably peanut oil from the smell, and a gelling agent," Branlee reported. "I couldn't get peanut oil, but the university cafeteria uses a mix of canola and corn oil for most things. That's our first test sample."

He topped off the first test beaker with cooking oil. Den turned on the charger and carefully immersed the terminals first in the real gel, then in the test beaker. Rital zlinned them with focused attention.

"It's twenty dynopters in the real gel and about nineteen in the test beaker. Your cooking oil works fine."

Branlee filled in the proper squares in a large chart he had drawn in his notebook. "That's good," he announced. "Cooking oil is cheaper and easier to get than battery gel. Let's use it to test the gelling agents."

Over the next hour, they tested ten different gelling agents, from starch to agar. None of them affected the amount of selyn the beakers could hold.

"Maybe gelling is its only purpose?" Rital suggested. "Liquid is more awkward and dangerous to move than equally heavy solid material, because liquid sloshes and leaks."

"That makes sense," Eddina agreed.

"This is boring," Raymond complained from the bench where he was making patterns with an assortment of screws, nuts, bolts, colored tape, and other random small hardware. "The same old number every time. Do something different!"

Den discharged the test beakers back into the building's orgonics system, while Rital and Eddina emptied the used gel into a washtub labeled "inert waste," and handed the beakers to Branlee for cleaning.

Not disposing of the waste gel immediately, Den realized later, was his second mistake, compounded by his restoring the charger to its original polarity in anticipation of further tests.

They took a short break before continuing. Den and Rital escorted Eddina to the basement to rest her tentacles without retainers. To celebrate the day's progress, they brewed a pot of the premium trin tea that Alyce had harvested from her trin patch.

"I think this hot plate is broken," Eddina complained when the tea was finally ready. "It shouldn't take this long to boil water. I'll stay here and try to fix it. I really don't feel like getting back into retainers."

Den filled an insulated bottle with tea for himself and Rital and they departed.

Leaving Eddina behind to tinker with the hot plate, he realized later, was the costliest error of all.

When channel and Donor returned to the lab, they found Raymond opening a food pail. "Branlee went for coffee," he reported, placing an apple next to a jar of homemade nut-butter with a layer of rich oil on top, some crackers, and three cookies. Childlike, he started his snack with the cookies. Den set the tea bottle on the lab bench and he and Rital set out to locate the departmental coffee pot.

Leaving Raymond unsupervised, Den realized later, was an open invitation for disaster.

Ten minutes later, Branlee accompanied Den back to the lab, clutching an oversized mug of the out-Territory comfort beverage. Rital lingered in the hall to read posters on recent research. The graduate student stopped in the doorway, stiffening in outrage. "Raymond Ildun, what did Sosu Milnan tell you about touching our experiments?"

Raymond looked up with a guilty start and his jar of nut-butter landed in the tub of waste gel with an oily plop. "You're finished with this stuff," he pointed out, logically enough.

"That's not an excuse and you know it," Branlee retorted, stalking toward the miscreant. "You promised hands off unless you had specific permission."

Raymond edged around the tub, keeping it between himself and the furious graduate student. The oily gel in the washtub had turned a light shade of green, Den noted, and then spotted his tea bottle lying on the floor, obviously empty.

"You dumped my good tea into the waste!" he barked, his outrage matching Branlee's as he started around the other side of the tub, cutting off the boy's escape.

"The goo looks more scientific when it's green like that," Raymond explained. The Donor was not appeased. The boy assessed the situation with expertise born of long practice and decided Branlee was the lesser threat. He faked toward Den, then shot through the space between the graduate student and the lab bench.

Branlee lunged to grab the boy and his foot came down on a dribble of oil. His arms windmilled, sending his coffee cup flying into the tub. He grabbed Raymond's shirt, but the boy slithered out of it and up onto the lab bench.

That was when Rital arrived.

With augmented Sime speed, the channel pulled Raymond off the lab bench, but not before one flailing foot tangled in the charging cable.

The safety cap popped off, the bare charger landed in the tub, there was a surge in the ambient nager that even Den could feel, and the room went dark. "Rital? You all right?"

"Good enough," the channel breathed.

Just barely, Den conceded, and doubled his effort to steady the fields. The ambient surge had to have been caused by dead selyn moving through shielded orgonics tubing, and Rital had been on guard and augmenting. *Maybe he is all right. Mostly.*

"All of you, stay where you are," Rital ordered in a stronger voice. "No one move! Branlee, be still!"

Den froze at his cousin's intense tone. Branlee moaned from the floor, then subsided. Rital demanded, "Is there an independent source of light in this lab?"

Branlee said, "The portable light in the corner runs off electrical batteries." Evidently, he pointed. "Ow! My ribs!"

"I said, be still. First things first," Rital directed. "Raymond, up!" Two sets of footsteps moved toward the indicated corner, one confident and one reluctant. "Walk," the channel ordered his captive. "I won't let you bump into anything."

"Let me go," Raymond whined.

"Not a chance," Rital told him. "That tub of waste drained all the selyn from the batteries in the basement. Touch it and the flash burn will Kill you." He used the word in the precise in-Territory sense: death by selyn movement. That was why—beyond the inconvenience of working with a blob of jelly—selyn batteries were encased in protective coverings

"All three batteries?" Den asked. "But Zir recharged them two days ago. That means they had what, two-thirds of a charge?"

"About that," Rital agreed. "And it's all sitting in an unprotected, open container!" A switch clicked and a floodlight threw blinding light and stark shadows that turned the tub of muddy-green gel into something sinister.

Mindful of stressing Rital with the Gen's pain, Den kept an eye on Rital while helping Branlee sit up. He followed Branlee's gaze to the tub of mixed waste, then estimated the volume in the tub. He ran a quick calculation, blinked in astonishment, and calculated the numbers twice more before he believed them.

"Rital, Branlee, don't you see?" he asked in growing excitement. "The volume of gel in that tub can't be more than a tenth of the volume in the batteries. We've proved it's possible to make a much more efficient selyn battery! Raymond, what did you throw into the washtub, besides my tea?"

"That's for me to know and you to find out," proclaimed the sulking boy.

"Oh, we will," the Donor promised.

"First, we have to restore power," Rital said. "We're not the only ones using this building."

Since Rital still had a firm grasp on Raymond, Den snagged the charging cable. "It's hot!" he exclaimed, pulling his hand back.

"I'm not surprised," Rital said. "It carried the whole charge, all at once."

Den wrapped a rag around his hand and tried again, letting the gel drip off the end of the charger before he flipped the switch that reversed the selyn flow and lowered it back into the washtub.

"It's not draining," Rital zlinned. "Is it disconnected at the wall?"

"Let me check," Den said, removing the charging terminal from the washtub again, just in case. The utility panel plug felt loose, so he tugged gently. With a squelching sound, the end of the charger pulled free, carrying with it the outlet and a melted mess. Blackened gel oozed out, emitting a foul odor.

"Shen!" Den swore. "It melted the orgonics tubing."

"Is it just the one outlet?" Rital asked.

Retainers! He can't zlin beyond this room. Which might have protected Rital from the worst of the field disruption. Den coiled the charger and its attached detritus onto the lab bench, went to the next orgonics hookup, and carefully unscrewed the outlet from the box. An arm's length of orgonics tubing came loose in his hand, dripping the same burned goo. There was an irregular line of metallic copper along one side, where the overheated orgonics system had melted the electrical wiring that ran through the same conduits.

"That's why the electrical power's out, too," Branlee observed. He gulped. "Chancellor Orzoff will *not* be amused."

"We should check the selyn batteries in the basement," Den said, placing the second damaged outlet on the bench.

"Not until that tub is secured," Rital objected. "We don't know if that gel mixture is charged to its full capacity."

"There's a temperature-controlled room over there," Branlee pointed at a doorway on the far side of the lab. "I use it to park my bicycle, because the door can be locked."

Rital surrendered Raymond to Branlee while Den improvised a cover for the tub. Donning insulated gloves, the two carried the tub gingerly into the controlled-temperature room and closed the door. Den fitted Branlee's bicycle lock through the hasp. The lock was a formidable creation that a team of horses couldn't have pulled open, so he was optimistic that it would keep Raymond out for a day or two.

"That will hold until we can move the gel safely to the Sime Center," Den told Branlee. "You can let Raymond go."

The boy rubbed his arm, scowling at the adults. Branlee located a second light and they set out through the dark building, Branlee to deliver Raymond back to his father and Den and Rital to see if the selyn batteries had survived.

Rital, less hampered by the uncertain lighting than a Gen, opened the door leading down to the selyn batteries, then cursed and charged down the stairs.

Alarmed, Den clattered down the stairs behind him. Rital crouched over a limp form, tearing at the latches to his left-arm retainer. "Eddina!" Den cried, dropping the light on the table and kneeling by Rital's side. He knocked his cousin's hand aside and removed the retainer, then started on the other. *She's alive.*

"That accident didn't just drain the batteries," the channel reported grimly. "It drained her, too."

"How the shen did that happen?"

Rital nodded toward the disassembled hot plate on the table and a burned-out length of orgonics tubing stretching to one of the batteries.

"It looks like she was testing the orgonics connection when the system drained." The channel's eyes went blank as he zlinned Eddina deeply.

Den's heart lurched even before his cousin said, "The nerve burn is too severe, Den, and there's no time for it to heal. She's entering Attrition."

Den's own field responded to Eddina's severe Need, producing selyn that her burned nerves couldn't accept. His desire to give it to her brought her back to consciousness.

"Den?" she asked in a weak voice. She tried to zlin him, but moaned.

"Don't zlin," he murmured, supporting her with arms and nager. Rital handed him a glass of fosebine and he held it for her as she sipped, made a face, then gulped it down. She closed her eyes and waited for the medicine to take effect, but the relief was more Den's nager.

Opening her eyes, she asked Den, "What happened? I bypassed the regulator and rigged a connection to one of the batteries to see if the hot plate would warm faster. Then…I don't know…"

"A direct connection?" Rital checked the tangle of burned tubing. "That explains it. The line around the regulator tangled with the plug-in for the plate. When the sudden demand hit from upstairs, the batteries flash-discharged."

"—from upstairs?" Eddina asked.

"An accident in the lab," Den told her. He summarized how the experimental waste, laced with unknown substances, had drained all three batteries, and Eddina as well. "You're not a channel," he finished. "Your system isn't supposed to run backwards."

She looked at Rital.

"I'm sorry, Eddina," the channel said. "I can't heal you fast enough for you to take a transfer." Though clearly, he was trying.

Her eyes widened as she absorbed the verdict, and Den felt his heart break. Rital flinched, then steadied focus on Eddina, signalling Den to shift support to her.

"I should never have started this project," he said savagely, following his channel's order. "From now on, I'll stick to being a Donor and leave battery development to the experts."

"Den, no!" Eddina protested. "You can't stop now that you've proved it can be done. The experts don't care about developing a flyer—but this new technology can't be lost!"

Den could not have cared less about new technology at that moment. "I shouldn't muck around with dangerous materials when I don't know what I'm doing."

Eddina snapped, "It's research! The whole point of doing it is that you don't know the answer ahead of time. You have to keep going. Every major advancement costs time, money and, yes, lives. I've already paid that price. It's up to you, Branlee, and the others to make it worthwhile."

Rital had linked Den's nager with Eddina's, as if Den were about to give her transfer. Their tight control kept her from realizing how little time she had left, but when Den took her hand, it was as cool as his own. Her body was shutting down.

She glared at him. "Promise me, by your Donor's oath, that you will find out what is in that tub of gel and use it to develop a lightweight battery. Lightweight means *fast,* Den. Fire trucks and ambulances that arrive in time more often. More trains going more places, bringing prosperity to small towns, not just the big cities. The Economic Development Board will have to see the value of that. And with the profits, you can build powered flyers to soar through the sky."

Den choked back tears, easing Eddina's pain with his field. She gathered a shuddering breath and weakly but clearly said, "Don't let me die for nothing. Create a battery that can run the world. And then...promise me that you'll develop a lightweight motor to go with it."

"That might not even be possible!"

"Flying is possible. The Ancients *did* it," Eddina assured him. "With the Gen's library, you can build a flyer. Call it...call it the *Spirit of Unity,* and when you fly it, I'll be there with you."

"The *Spirit of Unity,*" Den whispered, caught up in the old dream in spite of everything. "It would be that."

"Promise me!"

"I promise," he whispered.

Reassured, she relaxed against him. "I'm so cold."

He held her tighter, warming her with his body and nager.

And then she was gone.

CHAPTER 11

LEGACY

Chancellor Orzoff was not pleased that his Center for Technology would be without power until both electrical and orgonics systems were replaced. He was even less pleased to discover why.

"There will be no more unauthorized, unregulated experiments on my campus," he proclaimed when Rital explained the cause of the power failure. His face turned an alarming shade of purple. He paced back and forth, scattering the university officials who had accompanied him like startled sheep. "The Technology Center allows trained experts to advance knowledge," Orzoff continued. "It is *not* an after-hours playground for half-trained students and amateurs."

After spending the night grieving over Eddina, Den drew breath to object to being accused of playing. He knew more about selyn batteries than any of Orzoff's faculty, but it had still not been enough expertise to prevent Eddina's death. Rital signalled him to be silent. Den let out his breath and focused on Rital.

"Remove your experiment from my campus immediately," the Chancellor ordered. "There will be no more accidents to deprive our research community of the ability to do their work. Is that understood?"

"Yes, Chancellor Orzoff, we understand," Rital agreed with commendable humbleness. "We will remove all materials at once."

"See that you do." Orzoff's face faded to a normal color. Den hoped the worst was past, until the Chancellor continued, "Then there is the matter of damages. You not only burned out the selyn power system, but also melted the electrical wiring. Both must be replaced. We have in-house electrical experts, but they can't work with selyn technology."

He turned to nod at Vice-Chancellor Mathison. "You were right, Gillum. It was less than wise to invest in technology we can't repair. Of course, we thought the Sime Center would maintain the system, not destroy it."

"We will bring a team of orgonics experts to Clear Springs as quickly as possible," Rital promised.

"Good." The Chancellor nodded shortly. "You can pay them, too, and our electricians as well."

Den could not estimate the cost to clean the muck out of the narrow conduits and then string new orgonics tubing.

Vice-Chancellor Gillum Mathison was uneasy about his superior's decision. "Chancellor, we have funds for building repair and maintenance. If we tap those, repairs could be done sooner."

"We'll repair the building as fast as possible," Orzoff agreed. "And their Tecton can reimburse us." He glared at Den and Rital. "My mother was a potter and always told her customers, 'You break it, you buy it.'"

"I can't deny that our experiment was the cause of the damage," Rital agreed. "But you will have to apply directly to the Tecton for funding."

The Tecton was no more fond of spending large amounts of money fixing the blunders of its people than the University. They would put the blame—and the liability—squarely on the actual perpetrators. Den's First Order Donor salary was generous, but it would take years to pay off such a debt.

"I suggest you find a way to fund it." The Chancellor's lips twisted in a parody of a smile. "Until you do, don't expect our support for your other projects. Like those classes you want in our schools." He stormed out of the Sime Center, trailing his subordinates.

Den eyed Rital, his nager reflecting his sense of betrayal.

"Be sensible, Den," Rital scolded him. "There was nothing to gain by arguing. Your project *did* ruin both power supplies."

"But if I take personal financial responsibility for fixing their building, I'll have no resources to continue the battery research. Never mind that I will have no personal funds—I promised Eddina that her death wouldn't stop progress toward powered flight. I can't stop now, when we've proved it's possible to make a battery so much more efficient than the standard gel."

"You weren't listening," said Rital. "This way *we* fix as much as we can, and pay only the cost of technicians. And…having publicly both rejected and ejected it, the university has no claim on your project. I don't share your enthusiasm for flyers, but as Eddina said, there are many other applications for the work you and Branlee are doing. Those selyn-insulating panels would be priceless in a busy in-Territory Sime Center."

"He can't make more without space to work."

"We'll set up a workshop in the Sime Center's basement," Rital offered, "That way, you won't have to pay rent. We'll put in a dedicated selyn battery so another success can't burn out the Sime Center's orgonics, either. We'll build your more efficient battery, cousin—and it will pay for the repairs at the university and much more."

Den felt his shoulders straighten from their defeated slump. "It'll be more convenient to work here, so we'll make faster progress," he realized.

"I'll contact Branlee to move as much of his research materials and notes as he can before I have to catch the train." He paused. "Rital, the school board will likely follow Orzoff's lead if he tells them we can't be trusted. Is he angry enough to oppose the changeover classes?"

Rital stared at the front door. "If he is, could you blame him?"

* * * *

To Den's relief, Branlee was willing to move the selyn battery project to the Center's basement. "Professor Fibes is decommissioning his lab," he said. "I'd have to move anyway. The Sime Center is just as convenient for me as campus."

Rital saw that Branlee's equipment and the dangerously unsecured washtub of overcharged selyn battery gel were moved to their new lab, and Den arranged with Alyce to put a high-quality lock on the lab door. He wanted no more deaths on his conscience.

Den explained the confrontation to Quess in detail, but couldn't predict whether the withdrawal of University support plus his son's brush with a deadly experiment would inspire Professor Ildun to change his vote, or how it might affect the school board's verdict on the changeover classes.

We didn't tell Orzoff about Raymond's role in the disaster, Den worried. *Surely that's worth something to his father?* But would it be enough? Ildun might well blame them for exposing his son to danger.

Seena drove Den and the simple box holding Eddina's body to the train station. The Donor spent the long journey back to Valzor reading Eddina's notebook. Her engineering genius spoke to him through the pages of meticulous notes, and he promised her again that he would see their shared dream through.

After so long out-Territory, it was strange to see Simes moving freely at the Valzor station, unencumbered by retainers. It felt equally strange to be treated with deference as a respected professional. In Clear Springs, even their most loyal supporters thought that Gens who lived with Simes were crazy.

When he met Eddina's grieving family on the platform, they thanked him for bringing her home. Den doubted he deserved their deference and respect.

Controller Monruss was equally skeptical. When he joined Den in the heavily insulated transfer suite an hour before schedule, the balding, stocky channel accepted the cup of tea Den offered and looked him in the eye. "You're lucky there was only one death, you know."

It was a relief to have someone blame him as he blamed himself.

"I know," Den agreed.

"The District will cover the damages, of course," Monruss continued. "If we didn't, we'd never open another Sime Center in Gen Territory. I'm wondering, though, whether to shut down this experiment in Clear Springs and focus on towns closer to our border."

Den was hard put to keep his shock from hurting the Need-sensitized channel. "Look at the increasing number of selyn batteries we're shipping out," he argued, groping for a stronger argument. Most of the excess selyn from Clear Springs fueled out-Territory train routes; it was simply not cost-effective to ship it all the way to Sime Territory. Still, that freed up more industrial selyn for use in-Territory and every bit helped the Tecton's always-precarious selyn balance. "Clear Springs is a university town," he tried again. "Students are openminded and inclined to challenge traditions. You wouldn't have that in other towns."

"That's why I didn't shut you down last spring." The Controller rubbed a weary hand across his balding pate. "We can't let progress founder on bad feelings. Perhaps when you've paid the Tecton back and can afford hobbies again, you will keep your mind on our main mission of tapping the tremendous resource represented by an entire city of Gens."

There was nothing Den could say but, "Yes, Controller Monruss."

"What the blazing shen were you trying to accomplish, anyway?"

The Donor slowly drank his tea, working the fields for Monruss amid a highly edited account of his research goals, glad of his recent practice in using euphemisms and misdirection. While it was nearly impossible to get a lie past a First Order channel, a higher-rated Donor could finesse it with verbal deflection, while the work of raising the channel's intil provided a plausible excuse for maintaining nageric control. *It helps that Monruss isn't too familiar with how I usually zlin*, the Donor thought. *I'd never convince Rital that I wasn't hiding something.*

Monruss was sufficiently distracted by Need and the potential of Branlee's lightweight shielding that he didn't demand an exact account of Eddina's death. He had the authority to forbid Den from working on battery research, or even to turn Den's results over to Householding Ohmand, who had invented the selyn battery decades before…and not improved it since. Den forced negative thoughts out of his mind. After the turmoil of the last three days, he had to have this transfer as much as the channel did. All in all, Den considered himself fortunate to get away with just a stern warning and a debt that would take years to pay off.

The transfer disappointed Den. Nine years ago, Monruss had been a satisfying, if not challenging, assignment for a young Donor learning the difference between training exercises and the real world. In the years since, the channel's speed and capacity had stabilized while Den's had grown, leaving the Donor slightly depressed and not-quite-post. *I've grown a lot lately, but with Rital so stubborn, I'll never learn to use my new capacity.*

On the other hand, Tyvi wouldn't have been much better and she didn't have Monruss' ironic sense of humor. Den figured he'd come out ahead.

That didn't ease his worry about the situation in Clear Springs. While Monruss recovered from his first transfer in months with a higher-rated Donor, the school board was meeting to make their final decision. Quess would use his full diplomatic skill to argue for changeover classes. Could he convince the board to entrust their children to the man whose unauthorized experiment put a whole university department out of commission?

Worrying wouldn't change the outcome. If he couldn't do anything about the changeover classes, at least Den could tell Eddina's story to her friends. He changed clothes and set off for the Valzor Flyer's Club.

Jannun, the club's Gen carpenter, was preparing their contest entry to move to the convention's grounds with the help of Mandle, their newest member. She was thirteen natal years and still a child, but a welcome addition. Her "Right Flyer" had out-flown all the other contest entries last year.

The dilapidated workshop had changed since Den's assignment to Clear Springs. Pride of place was now reserved for blueprints of the "Spirit of Valzor," the full-sized wing assembly designed by Den and built by Jannun and Eddina. Last year it had flown the second longest distance before it hit the ground and shattered. Mandle and her brother had not worked from blueprints and their entry had not survived its crash landing, but the certificate awarding it first place hung, framed, over the battered tea table.

Jannun's enthusiastic greeting trailed off when he saw Den was alone. "Where's Eddina?"

There was no way to cushion the blow, so Den didn't try. "She won't be coming," he told his friend, fresh tears rolling down his cheeks. "She's dead."

Mandle's eyes widened. "Did the Wild Gens shoot her, like that girl?"

Den's letter warning Eddina to stay in-Territory had included the cautionary tale of Jain's death. If Eddina had allowed herself to be dissuaded, she would still be alive.

The Donor shook his head. "It was an accident during an experiment." He described what had happened. "Rital couldn't heal her burns in time to prevent Attrition."

Jannun's eyes grew wide. Simes lived by the Need cycle. Attrition nightmares stalked their collective consciousness, and those of the Gens who loved them.

Mandle, though, was young enough that Attrition was only theoretical for her. She focused on the other part of Den's news. "You made a single tub of battery gel absorb the selyn of three batteries?"

Den nodded. "It carried about sixty times the charge of normal gel, by volume. If we can figure out what was in that mixture and learn to handle it safely, we'll have our lightweight selyn battery."

"Then Eddina didn't die in vain," Mandle assured him. "Powered flight is possible with our technology. We have to figure out how to do it, but that's just a matter of hard work."

When Jannun nodded in agreement, Den stared in disbelief. They should be berating him for allowing a renSime to die under his protection, not focusing on the battery that had drained her.

On the other hand, "Eddina said the same." He swallowed a sob. "She made me promise to see it through, all the way to powered flight."

Jannun nodded solemnly and placed his hand on Den's. Mandle's hand settled on top. "All the way to powered flight," they vowed.

* * * *

The Valzor Club's entry for this year consisted of two wings, each longer than Den was tall, bolted to a packing crate of a realistic weight. "How did Branlee's rollerboard composite work out?" Den asked Jannun as they carried the first wing out to the wagon to transport it to the contest site.

They had settled on that material the previous summer, after Raymond Ildun stole Branlee's rollerboard and catapulted it through a chemistry demonstration. The flexible board had survived the crash undamaged, though the onlookers were less fortunate.

Why did I allow Raymond anywhere near the battery experiments? I know how disaster-prone that boy is.

"The composite is very different from wood," Jannun explained. "I ruined two sheets learning how to shape it. However, it's much less brittle, and that flexibility should help it survive wind gusts."

"The contest rules are different this year," Mandle reminded him. "Two thirds of the points come from distance flown, but there's another third for how well the assembly survives landing."

Den nodded. "We can't move past models until a pilot can survive the landing." He helped Jannun settle the wing onto the horse blankets that would insulate it from damage, then asked, "The crate hangs below the wings?"

"Like a dandelion seed, or like tying a stone in the corners of a handkerchief and throwing it," Mandle agreed. "The low-hanging weight keeps the wing assembly from tumbling."

"That will get us distance, but it's still got to land. Is that what those wheels you're carrying are for? To soften the landing?"

"Yes, three of them, because a tripod is most stable on a rough surface," Mandle told him. "It was hard to make the back two wheels land first, before the forward wheel. The models kept flipping over."

"Eddina reshaped the wings to tilt the nose up at landing," Jannun explained as he and Den carried the second wing out. "A weight deploys on launch and dangles on a string. When it touches the ground, the drag releases a latch that pulls these flaps at the leading edges of the wings down. The front end should tip up just as the wheels hit."

"It worked on the small-scale models," Mandle agreed, then corrected herself. "Well, on some of them."

"It's not just a matter of winning a contest," Den explained as the horses pulled the cart through the streets. "Powered flight may be ready for testing sooner than any of us imagined." He turned to their youngest member. "Which reminds me, Mandle. Does your school give lessons in the out-Territory language, English?"

The girl blinked. "Yes, I think so. Why?"

"You should take them. Study as hard as you can, as if your future depends on it. Because, if you want to be our test pilot, it does."

"The out-Territory Gens don't have powered flyers," Jannun objected. "They don't even make models of Ancient flying machines."

"No," Den agreed, "but the Gen Army used unpowered gliders to scout for Sime raiders in the western deserts before Unity. It was safer for untrained Gens than searching for junct Simes on foot. That program ended with Unity, but the library in Clear Springs has a description of it. There's also an English translation of an Ancient pilot training manual."

Mandle's eyes glowed with excitement.

By the time he made it back to his quarters, Den was too exhausted to wonder about the changeover classes. It was all he could do to find the right room and crawl into bed.

* * * *

Den woke later than planned. There was barely time to get dressed before heading for the annual East Nivet Model Flyer's Convention, and no time at all for the Sime Center's operator to place a telephone call to Clear Springs. Den told himself that if news of the meeting was good, it would keep. If not, there was nothing he could do about it from Valzor.

The convention again met at the dairy farm owned by the parents of committee member Kithra Borfin. They gathered in a machine shed with hay bales for seating. The pong of cow manure permeated the air and the outhouse buzzed with flies.

None of that mattered to the flyer enthusiasts, for beyond the shed was a pasture with a hay barn atop a steep hill. The winch that normally lifted hay bales up the precipice had been modified into a catapult to launch this year's entries. Everyone was eager to see what progress their fellow designers had made.

The contest took all day. Many entries launched well and flew a considerable distance, but entry after entry cartwheeled across the field or belly-flopped and shattered. The hastily-renamed *Spirit of Eddina* did not fly the farthest, but Eddina's improvement to the shape of the wing left the contraption mostly intact on landing, and it was judged the winner.

On the podium before the crowd of participants, Den accepted the framed certificate on behalf of the Valzor club, then took the next painful step. "Eddina's design worked under today's conditions. However, it must be made reliable under all conditions and put under the control of a human pilot." He scanned the audience, searching out those he knew were good mechanics. "That task will fall to you, because Eddina has died." A collective gasp of surprise and grief swept through those who hadn't heard. The renSime with the talent for tinkering had been loved by many.

"Her death occurred during experiments on selyn batteries," Den continued, "when we accidently created a gel that held a charge 60 times greater than standard." The gasps this time were of wonder. "Not enough to power a flyer, but proof that selyn batteries can be improved. If we can reproduce the results, efficient batteries will allow smaller, more efficient engines. Then, we'll be ready to try flying in earnest because with that technology, we can make powered flyers for human pilots."

Few of Den's fellow hobbyists had really believed they could build a working flyer. Dreamed about it, yes, and hoped for it, certainly, but they were resigned to futility. The news that human flight might be achievable within their lifetimes swept through the room like a firestorm. Spines straightened and eyes glowed with hope.

"It won't be easy," he cautioned. "Research is expensive. It cost us Eddina. The accident that Killed her," he used the Simelan word for death by selyn flow, not Attrition, "ruined orgonics tubing and electrical wiring for a large building. I'll have to pay for repairs before I can personally invest again. However, I believe the advances already made can be developed commercially and fund further research. If experts can be found—experts from both sides of the border, with different approaches to knowledge—we'll live to see flyers as human transportation.

"I pledged to Eddina as she died that I would see our dream fulfilled. I intend to keep my promise." He ended with the oath he had sworn with Jannun and Mandle. "All the way to powered flight."

The entire audience surged to their feet. "All the way to powered flight!" they repeated. Cheers threatened to bring down the cobwebs.

For a moment Den wondered if he'd inadvertently used his First Order nager to impose his emotions on helpless renSimes, an unforgivable lapse of professional ethics.

But he was low field and the Gens were cheering as loudly as the Simes. One of those Gens, a garment worker named Grittle, called out over the ruckus, "Now *that's* a scheme I'd gladly invest in!"

"Me, too!" said the man next to her, joined by several others.

Akedren, an elderly renSime bank clerk from Sommerin, joined Den and Kithra at the front. His club's entry, based on Mandle's winning bamboo-and-tarp design from the year before, had flown the farthest before it fell apart on landing. "Grittle's right," he said. "We can't expect Sosu Milnan to fund the redevelopment of powered flight out of his own pocket. Even a Donor's salary has limits and unlike young Mandle, I don't have decades to wait for results."

"My selyn battery research group consists of me, one out-Territory graduate student and my cousin Rital," Den pointed out. "Like the rest of you, we all have other jobs."

"So, what would it take to make the development go faster?" Grittle wanted to know.

"Funding, mostly. Branlee must have a full-time job when he graduates and I'd like to keep him and add other experts to the team as we develop a motor to go with the new battery. The only way to pay for that is to market the products we've got, starting with a lightweight, selyn-insulating material Branlee concocted. But, before we can sell it, we have to make it."

Den spread his hands. "I'll be paying off the repairs to their building for years. I can't fund a factory."

"Nor can any of us, as individuals," said Akedren. "But how about all of us? Let's found a company, funded by contributions from interested members and sales of products as soon as we start making them. Sosu Milnan, is this selyn-insulating material patented?"

"We've just applied for a Gen government patent."

"See me after the meeting," came from three different corners of the shed. The three lawyers who had spoken quickly huddled in the back of the shed, talking animatedly.

Satisfied that the patent issue was being addressed, Akedren returned to his own area of expertise. "Don't any of you invest money you can't afford to lose. It will be years before the company makes a profit. However, *I've* got a nice bit of cash I set aside for projects in my old age. I can't think of anything better than this!"

To Den's astonishment, a bidding war broke out, with people calling out pledges of financial contributions.

Two factory owners with practical experience in running a business led a brisk discussion on the structure of a new private company, named Flight Innovations by popular acclaim. It would file formal incorporation papers in both Valzor and Clear Springs, they decided, to have official standing on both sides of the border.

The patents must also be filed with both in- and out-Territory governments, the lawyers insisted. "The courts are supposed to enforce patents across borders, but that's difficult."

Legal ownership would rest with the investors, who would be limited to model flyer enthusiasts, with day-to-day operations under Den's control. Barring an outbreak of sanity among the investors, the pledged money would pay for Branlee's research. It was an awesome responsibility, since most of them made less than Den did and had much less job security. Yet they were willing to hand him money and trust him to make their shared dream a reality.

* * * *

Den slept poorly and woke later than he'd planned. He showered, dressed, grabbed breakfast, and with five minutes to spare before heading to the station, he stopped by the office to place a call to Clear Springs to discover how the school board had voted.

The switchboard operator was a young Gen, new to his post and *very* eager to please. "I'm terribly sorry, Sosu," he apologized. "Both out-Territory lines are busy with a conference call between Controller Monruss and New Washington Territory's Office of Transportation."

Den assured the young man it wasn't an emergency, he'd find a phone at the station. However, it took so long to win free of the young man that he had to sprint past the two public telephones in the sliderail station to catch his train. He consoled himself with the knowledge that the train made three stops along the way. He could reach someone at home soon enough. He settled back to endure the train ride, glad that his fellow passengers were all Gens. There were times when even Donors were hard-pressed to maintain control.

The long ride gave Den time to consider his responsibilities toward his new investors. Could he really sell enough of Branlee's selyn-insulating polycarbonate to fund the research program? He had no idea how the stuff was made or what it cost to produce.

If he couldn't make Flight Innovations profitable, the world might wait a long time for a better selyn battery, much less a working flyer. Or it might not happen at all, given Householding Ohmand's stranglehold on selyn battery technology and the Economic Development Council's chronic lack of funding. However, the Council would surely be interested in more efficient selyn batteries. *Don't talk flying machines to the Council,* he reminded himself. *Talk batteries!*

Of course, Flight Innovations would innovate nothing if Monruss closed the Clear Springs Sime Center. Den would become another bachelor Donor, rotating through the various Sime Centers in Valzor District. How many Controllers would let him experiment, especially after Eddina's death? His mind lurched between great hopes and darkest fears until he wished desperately that he *were* escorting a channel, so he could focus on something other than dreams and nightmares.

As the train approached Miltsharbor, the conductor announced, "Ladies and gentlemen, this train is behind schedule. Our stop in Miltsharbor will be only long enough to exchange batteries. Passengers leaving the train, gather your belongings and disembark promptly. Those continuing toward Clear Springs, stay aboard or risk being left behind."

Den gritted his teeth and remained seated, imagining worst-case scenarios. It was unfair for the future of powered flight to depend on a public relations miracle. Had Quess persuaded the school board? Or had Reverend Sinth's hatred of Simes combined with the disaster at the Center for Technology to make them reconsider?

Two hours later, the train approached Sheegan. The engineer must have milked the batteries for every dynopter, for they pulled in on schedule. Den leaped from the train and ran for the ticket window, where the motherly clerk was helping an excited young woman in a Clear Springs University T-shirt. The transaction included detailed advice on the habits of college men.

"Where's the public telephone?" Den demanded, when the aspiring student and her copious luggage had been entrusted to a porter.

"There's no reason to be rude." The clerk glared at him.

"I'm sorry," the Donor said obediently. "Please, I have an extremely important call to make before the train leaves."

She accepted the apology. "Our public telephone is in the restaurant, but the Kennys are at a funeral this afternoon, so it's closed."

"Could someone let me in, just to make my call?"

"The station manager's at the funeral, too. Old Miz Tilden taught school for nearly fifty years. Everyone in town learned reading and figuring from her. They learned proper, too, you can be sure. Why, I remember one time—"

The conductor's stentorian "All aboard!" rescued Den. Much as he approved of praise for a teacher, he was no closer to knowing whether he and Rital were about to join that profession. Too nervous to eat lunch, he agonized over whether Chancellor Orzoff had spoken against the changeover classes.

The Clear Springs Sime Center existed because Orzoff, wanting cheap selyn for his new building, had ordered the City Council to ask the Tecton for it. If he blocked the changeover classes now, the Tecton would at least question Den's judgment and perhaps Rital's, if an investigation revealed details that Den's cousin had omitted in his reports. *Like how a certain walnut riot got started.* If the vote was yes, well, no one questioned success. *But if Rital's next report describes a failure…*

The station manager at North Peak was loading freight cars. "Our public telephone's been out of order for two months. They promise to send a lineman, but give priority to towns without another public phone. There's one at Jerri's Market, only a ten-minute walk down Main Street."

The Donor's shoulder's slumped. "Thank you, but that would make me miss my train." He returned to his seat for another agonizing wait.

By the time the train reached Clear Springs, Den's mind had churned up so many possibilities that he half expected to be met at the station by the local police to take him into custody as a public menace, or by a telegram from the Tecton ordering him and his cousin back to Valzor to face charges of gross incompetence. Of course, the Tecton would want to ensure that he and Rital caused no more trouble. *We might never be allowed a transfer together again…*

Den found himself chewing a third fingernail down to the quick, a habit he hadn't indulged since childhood. Embarrassed, he sat on his hands and ran through a basic relaxation exercise. The world, he told himself firmly, had better things to do than drive one Donor crazy.

He grabbed his bag and jumped off the train before it fully stopped at the Clear Springs station. Old habit kept him from running inside the building, but he wove briskly through the crowd toward the public telephone. He dodged around boxes labeled **TRIANGLE WALNUT GROWERS— Perishable**, hoping that the telephone was working.

It was.

The booth was occupied by a young man arguing with his girlfriend. Den paced, hoping the hapless swain would give up. On his third lap, a newspaper vending machine caught his eye. It still displayed the previous day's edition.

"HUNDREDS TURN OUT FOR SCHOOL BOARD MEETING," the *Clarion's* headline screamed. A photo showed the Upper School's sacred gymnasium packed with people, many holding signs. Den made out **"Stop the Tecton Takeover,"** *"Cancel the Classes,"* half a dozen "Save Our Kids" placards, and one that read **"Education is MY Family Tradition."**

Underneath the picture, the text began:

An estimated 350 people turned out for the school board meeting last night, to debate whether changeover training should be offered as an elective in the Clear Springs schools. After a vigorous, three-hour debate, the school board voted three to two that the classes

The rest of the text was out of sight. Den fumbled coins out of his pocket, but none were local currency. Groping in his bag, he finally found the proper change. The first coin went in easily; the second fell through into the coin return three times before it was finally accepted. Den pulled the handle, then nearly screamed in outrage as the dispenser failed to open.

He jiggled the handle, banged on the side, and pulled the coin return lever in vain. The machine would neither give him a newspaper nor return his money. He regarded the fire ax in its glass cabinet and fantasized about demolishing the vending machine, but returned his attention to the young man as he pleaded, "But sweetheart—"

He broke off suddenly, pulling the receiver away from his ear to look at it in astonishment, then slam it back on its hook and stalk away.

Den hastily claimed the booth and fumbled in his bag for a coin.

He had used his only two out-Territory coins in his attempt to purchase the newspaper.

Rital's going to love this story, Den thought. He picked up his bag and headed briskly for the exit.

* * * *

The sun had just set and the summer night was pleasant. The rack outside the Sudsworks Brewery was full of bicycles with Clear Springs University decals. He saw an **O.L.D. S.O.K.S.** sign on the battered jalopy that was Tohm Seegrin's pride and joy. Unable to wait a moment more to find out how the school board had voted, Den went inside the pub.

OLD SOKS' table was easily identified by the creative costumes of its occupants. Silva wore a new button: white with large red letters spelling "Hatred *isn't* holy." Tohm spotted Den coming in the door and raised his stein in salute. "Hail the returning hero!" he intoned and sealed the toast with a huge gulp of beer.

The rest of the group responded with an enthusiastic "Hail!" and emptied their steins. "Come join us," Tohm invited, wiping the foam off his lips. "Hey, Knut, bring Sosu Milnan a mug of Yon's latest creation!"

Another chair was forced into the gap between Annie Lifton's older brother Rob and Branlee. Arth Tinkum sat on Rob's other side.

The Donor had hardly wedged himself into the offered chair when Knut reappeared, followed closely by Yon Keysvetter, the pub's master brewer.

Knut ceremoniously placed a mug in front of Den, who looked around at the expectant faces and asked, "What's the matter?"

"Just taste it," Silva urged.

Bewildered, the Donor raised the frosted glass and took a careful sip. "It's porstan!" he said in surprise.

"Did I get it right?" the brew master asked anxiously.

"Well, almost," Den said, taking another taste. "Take it out of the barrels a little sooner, especially if you want to sell it to Simes. Half a glass of this would get a Sime drunk, even without a shiltpron."

"I'll keep that in mind for the next batch," Yon said. "And this one is on the house."

"Thanks." Den turned to Tohm. "What happened at the meeting?"

"You haven't heard?" Silva asked in surprise.

Den shook his head.

"We won!" she told him with a grin. "The school board adopted the classes, as modified by the curriculum committee's majority report."

"That's fantastic!" *Now Rital and I won't face a major investigation. We won't be separated.*

Silva supplied details. "Ephriam Lornstadt voted against it, of course, but only old Purson went along with him. Purson thinks the curriculum should be nothing but sports, English, and math."

"It all happened courtesy of Reverend Sinth," Tohm gloated. "He insisted that he represented the majority of parents, so his supporters stayed home, thinking plenty of other people would be there to oppose your classes. Everyone who disagreed with Sinth came to the meeting."

"There were so many people that the school board only allowed comments from Clear Springs residents," Silva chimed in. "Sinth was furious. He'd bussed in anti-Sime fanatics from every town within fifty miles, who had to sit there while half of Clear Springs told the school board why they wanted changeover classes!"

"Sinth wasted his two minutes complaining that the meeting was rigged against him," Tohm went on. "That didn't go over well."

"After such a vote of confidence, Controller Madz and I had better teach a good class!" Den observed.

The conversation soon shifted and Branlee leaned over to say quietly, "I haven't had a chance to tell you I'm sorry about your friend Eddina. I liked her."

Den nodded in thanks. "Did you and Rital get that tub of battery gel safely to the Sime Center?"

"Yes, and my notes and equipment."

"I trust Chancellor Orzoff reserved the worst of his wrath for me and Rital?

The graduate student shrugged philosophically. "My committee already signed off on my thesis, so there isn't much he can do to me. Professor Fibes gave me a proper scolding about unauthorized visitors in his lab, but I think he meant Raymond Ildun more than you. Orzoff could cut off my stipend, but then he'd have to pay a crew to decommission the lab. I'm still taking inventory and placing equipment in other labs. If there aren't any takers, the stuff gets sold. There's a few items that might be useful for the battery project..."

"We'll have funding," Den told him, and explained Flight Innovations. "The idea is to fund research for powered flyers through sales of the products we develop along the way, like your rust-and-polycarbonate insulator."

"Can you patent that in Sime Territory?" Tohm asked.

"The lawyers will figure that out," Den said with a shrug.

"Patent your products on both sides of the border before you start selling them," the law student agreed. "Oh! Our patent has been granted! When my father learned you're trying to build a flying machine, he agreed to waive all but the filing fee. He's always loved reading about Ancient machines. So that's one side!"

"Thank you both," the Donor said, genuinely touched by how many people were eager to help. Turning back to Branlee, he said, "I don't know what our budget will be. For now, buy only essentials."

"Right," Branlee agreed. "Most of what I want is either so basic that the other labs already have it, or so specialized that nobody else will be interested."

"Make a list, with priorities and projected costs."

"Sure thing," the graduate student agreed, reaching for his beer.

With one of the Sime Center's research programs in hand, Den leaned around Rob to ask Arth Tinkum, "How's *your* research coming?"

The sociology student's face brightened. He extracted some smudged papers from a battered backpack. "Compared with Clear Springs as a whole, selyn donors are more accepting, politically and religiously. I also got statistical significance with age between sixteen and twenty-seven, low income, and some college education. That may be an artifact of Clear Springs being a college town. But here's the most interesting finding." He pointed at a line with three stars after it. "About half of the regular selyn donors–defined as someone who has donated at least four times–have a close friend or relative who also donates selyn."

"Well, a person's friends and family tend to have similar attitudes," Den pointed out.

"This stays significant even after I adjusted for that," Arth said. "Besides, what a person knows or experiences determines how they feel about new things. Hottios and Milner studied that ten years ago, comparing farmers who switched to tractors with those who stayed with horses. Where's that quote, anyway?" He produced a dog-eared page of notes. "Here: 'There is good evidence to show that beliefs have intellectual sources and psychological consequences. Thus, a person opposes modernity because of his lack of exposure to such ideas.'"

The student looked at Den expectantly. The first sentence of the quote was unintelligible to the Donor, but he thought he grasped the second. "People are more likely to donate selyn if they see other people doing it?"

"Context is important, too," Arth said. "After all, Sinth's followers see more people going in to donate selyn than practically anyone else in town. It's more a matter of deciding that donating selyn is 'something people like me do.'"

Den nodded, and munched his way through a basket of fried potato slices as Arth pulled out another set of tables.

"These are my other interesting results. I tried to predict which first-time selyn donors would donate again. About 30% come back the next month. According to these figures, how much a donor resists the first time correlates strongly with whether he or she tries again."

"That's not surprising," Den said. "Many frightened selyn donors don't come in because they want to, but because they are temporarily short of money or have to be low field for some reason. They have no principled commitment to donating selyn." The Donor tried a batter-fried cheese stick. It went well with the strange "porstan."

"But here's the interesting part," Arth said. "Each successive donation tends to be less frightening, with the largest drop between the first and second times." He shuddered briefly. "That's, um, reassuring."

A quick calculation confirmed that Arth was due for his second donation within the week, if he wanted to maintain access to the restricted regions of the Sime Center. *So far, he hasn't given us an excuse to kick him out.* After witnessing the student's previous donation, Den wasn't looking forward to it any more than Arth.

"The drop in fear correlated strongly with a change in reported reasons for donating selyn on the questionnaire," the graduate student continued. "First-time selyn donors felt pressured, and didn't feel that donating selyn was important in itself. This was reversed in experienced donors. The most frightened first-time donors were less likely to return, but those who *did* return, reported a similar change in motivation. Anyone who donates on four consecutive months is likely to keep doing so, no matter why they came in the first time, or even how frightened they were."

Den had a hard time believing that such personal feelings could be summed up in a table. Arth's conclusions also ran counter to the Tecton's theory of selyn donation, which held that some Gens *were* inherently transfer-shy and others could become so if mistreated. That difference might be important but Den was too tired to understand how.

"Arth, I'd love to discuss this," he said, finishing his porstan, "But I've been traveling all day and I'm exhausted." He fished a few bills out of his pocket. They were local currency, so he dropped them on the table to cover the cost of the food he'd eaten. With some effort, he located his travel bag and started for the Sime Center, tired but at peace with the world.

* * * *

Rital pounced as Den walked through the door. "Where have you been? The train got in an hour ago!"

"I stopped off at Sudworks for an update on last night's meeting."

Rital's face hardened into a stony mask. With an abrupt gesture of two tentacles to follow, the channel led the way to the insulated privacy of the infirmary, then flipped on the "in use" light. Turning to Den, he snarled, "Out drinking with OLD SOKS again. Couldn't you wait till tomorrow?"

The Donor shook his head in bewilderment. "What's gotten into you, Rital? I thought you liked Tohm, Silva and the others."

"Not when they're stealing my Donor. Ever since you met them, you've found excuses to leave this Center. You've neglected your duties and your control has gotten so erratic…" The channel's face twisted with abject misery and his voice cracked, "How long before you quit the Tecton entirely, so you can live out-Territory with your friends?"

Den's jaw dropped in utter astonishment. "You think I'm going native?" Suddenly, Rital's irrational accusations of dishonesty every time he played politics by out-Territory rules made sense. So did the channel's unreasonable criticism and his refusal to accept Den's growth in capacity.

There's nothing less reasonable than a channel who thinks he's losing his Donor—or more pessimistic. Rital must have hoarded these secret doubts for months: a channel's ultimate nightmare, to be stranded among hostile out-Territory Gens without a Donor's support. *Having Quess around finally gave him the courage to tell me.*

It was such a simple misunderstanding to have caused so much trouble. Den found himself chuckling, showing his relief nagerically. "You idiot," he scolded affectionately, "I have no intention to leave you, or the Tecton. Especially not to hang out with badly dressed lunatics who sing dirty ballads off key. Whatever gave you such an idea?"

"What was I supposed to think? For months you've ignored everything but your publicity campaign and the battery research."

Den sobered. "I've been worried sick ever since Inter-Territorial Affairs put us through that investigation. The Tecton doesn't like mavericks and we've ignored all their rules. If we fail, they'll pull us out of here so fast, we'll never know what happened. So I've worked hard to understand out-Territory politics. It's the only way to make the Tecton leave us in Clear Springs, *together*."

Den watched the channel's eyes blank as he zlinned. When Den finished, Rital slowly shook his head. "I wish I could believe that," he said sadly, "but cousin, I think you're kidding yourself."

An icy chill crept over Den as Rital slipped out the door, closing it silently behind him.

How long will it take to win back his confidence? the Donor wondered forlornly.

CHAPTER 12

THE SCIENTIFIC METHOD

"First," Den told Branlee, "we recreate the accident."

The two were in their new lab, a basement room in the Sime Center. It had been used for overflow storage, but once those crates had been moved to the supply room on the ground floor, there was ample work space. The door now sported a formidable lock. One death was enough.

The room was furnished with used chemistry equipment, including chemicals, a precision scale, a heating unit, and other surplus materials that Branlee had scavenged from Professor Fibes's lab.

A dedicated selyn battery prevented their tests from endangering the building's power supply. Branlee had already made a box from his selyn-insulating polycarbonate to enclose the tub of super-charged gel, which stood in one corner. A clear lid allowed inspection of the contents. He had also made a small battery box: a cube with sides about the length of a palm. As Den had explained, "If we can store a standard battery's selyn charge in this volume, it could power a flyer." Together, box and ungainly tub provided both warning and inspiration.

Branlee shook his head. "We don't start by recreating the whole accident; that's not how science works. We test each separate element to determine its contribution to the final result. Raymond thought testing gelling materials was boring, but it showed that they don't affect selyn capacity, just consistency. We don't have to waste time and resources on inert ingredients until we have a gel that works."

Den sighed. "That will make Tohm happy. He wants detailed, dated records of every experiment. Something about documenting for patents. It's going to take time. We should set up a series of trials, then ask Rital to test them. Let's brew our imagination-lubricating beverages of choice and plan our strategy." They had installed a dedicated table near the door with both a trin tea service and a battered coffee pot.

"Not a bad idea," Branlee agreed. "Our drinks *did* go into the tub." As Den put water on to heat, Branlee pulled out a notebook, wrote the date at the top of a clean page, and suggested, "Let's start by listing everything that went into that tub."

There was more than Den remembered, including real battery gel, cooking oil, various gelling agents, Den's tea, Branlee's coffee, and Raymond's nut butter. They even listed low-probability possibilities like the various containers used along the way.

Den added the burned orgonics tubing he had removed from the outlets in the lab, which had been dumped into the tub during the move. "The tubing wasn't a factor in the initial accident, but Rital says this stuff doesn't act like a normal battery. The tubing might affect that."

"How is it not normal?" Branlee asked.

"It's holding its charge better than a standard battery," Den explained. "Eventually we'll figure out why, but I'd like to address capacity first."

He pointed to the first few items on the list. "We already know the oil and gelling agents had minimal effect," he observed. "I'd say that makes the accidental additions more likely."

Branlee had reservations. "We can't be sure the gelling agents didn't interact with each other or the other ingredients. They do take up or release ions when they gel. Let's try tea and coffee first, though, since we've got them here. We know that our accidental super-battery holds a larger charge than a normal battery. We don't know whether it's the largest possible. By determining the individual contributions of each ingredient, we can optimize battery composition."

Den agreed. "Depending on what we find, we can move on to nut butter and gelling agents."

It was a good plan and, at first, a successful one. Over the next week they found that Branlee's coffee at optimum concentration increased the selyn-holding capacity of battery gel fourfold. Standard trin tea—a staple at Sime Centers across Nivet—doubled capacity, while the premium trin Den had brewed the night of the accident added another 50% increase. Coffee multiplied the effects of either trin fourfold, but the two kinds of tea did not act synergistically on each other.

The maximum increase in selyn capacity they obtained was tenfold: respectable, but significantly less than they had achieved by accident. Gelling agents did not magnify the effects of coffee or trin, nor did the ground peanuts they used to simulate Raymond's nut butter. They even tested the various containers and a simulated tub, to no avail.

"That tub of gel hasn't decomposed, even though it's open to the air," Den muttered after another unfruitful session. "I'd swear it's snickering at us." The lack of progress was particularly frustrating because the day's mail had brought in- and out-Territory incorporation papers for Flight Innovations from Akedron, in Simelan and English. Included were an in-Territory patent for the rust-impregnated polycarbonate to match the out-Territory one, papers appointing Den as the company's Chief Executive Officer and setting his salary at half the profits, and a substantial bank draft. Such trust and hope weighed Den down with responsibility to make the battery project succeed.

The company's profits might appear in some nebulous future, but Den's personal liability was current and growing. Technicians arrived from Valzor to make orgonics repairs to the Center for Technology. They stayed at the Sime Center, which at least saved on housing costs, but Den knew he'd have to generate income, and quickly.

"Our funds will run out before we can market an improved selyn battery," he complained to Branlee. "We have to find a product to sell now. Can you make sample sheets of that selyn-insulating polycarbonate?"

"Why not use the ones we already have?" Branlee pointed to a haphazard stack in one corner.

"Perfect," said Den. "Controller Monruss in Valzor wants to zlin its properties for himself. He might buy some for the District's Sime Centers."

* * * *

"Are you *sure* Raymond didn't add anything else to the tub?" Den asked, as the latest experiment stubbornly refused to cooperate.

"No, of course not," Branlee answered. "He hasn't talked to me since I told him he couldn't help us anymore. I've been over Fibes's lab six times, looking for chemicals that he might have moved, but I can't see anything obvious."

"Maybe we should just try anything within Raymond's reach?" Den suggested.

They did, and discovered six compounds that caused the gel to discharge selyn, but none that increased its holding capacity. Rital suggested they keep the best gel-discharger on hand in case of spills, but that was their only progress.

Their fundraising efforts were more successful. Monruss showed their insulating panels to other Tecton officials. Inquiries arrived about prices and availability, first one or two, then a stream, and suddenly a torrent.

"How fast can you make more rusty polycarbonate?" Den asked Branlee, waving a stack of letters. "These orders will give us income at last, but only if we can fill them."

Branlee thumbed through the inquiry letters. He had only started to learn Simelan, but numbers were the same on both sides of the border. "Making this many polycarbonate sheets will take a factory, not one person in a basement lab."

Den's shoulders slumped. "We can't afford to start a factory until we've already sold the product," he pointed out. "If the Tecton decides that the sheets are a 'critical, life-changing invention' and that we can't or won't meet the demand, they can revoke our patent and give it to somebody else. We would get nothing."

"It won't come to that, Sosu Milnan. Honestly." Branlee filled Den's mug from the ever-present pot of trin. "Lots of companies make polycarbonate. There's one in Berrysville that makes irrigation tubing out of it. It's their off season, so we can hire them to make a big batch—tinting it with our proprietary rust is easy. Not as much profit as if we made the sheets ourselves, but we'll still get a markup."

It was a good plan, making Den realize how much he depended on his out-Territory partner. While Branlee haggled with the factory in Berrysville, Den hired the Sime Center's bilingual typist, Jesper Reft, as Flight Innovations' office manager. When the sheets were delivered and Rital had checked them for quality, they were packed for shipping by whichever OLD SOKS members were temporarily short of cash.

* * * *

"Ref, could I borrow some cooking oil?" Den asked, nostrils flaring at the scent of baking bread. "We're out of Branlee's stuff."

"Still trying to build a better battery, are you?" the chef observed with half-concealed amusement. "Any success?"

"Not recently," the Donor answered shortly.

"Ah, that's too bad," Ref said, in a more sympathetic tone. "What sort of cooking oil fits your requirements?"

"Oil is oil, isn't it?" Den asked.

"Not at all. Some oils are solids at room temperature, like butter and coconut oil." The chef moved from refrigerator to shelves. "Some can be heated to high temperatures without smoking, like peanut and grapeseed oils. Corn, canola, and sunflower oils are good, cheap, general-purpose oils that keep food from sticking, but don't have much flavor. Expensive oils, like sesame and walnut, add flavors to foods."

The Donor blinked. "Maybe we should try several?" he suggested. "Say, corn, sunflower and some of the high-temperature oil?"

"Certainly." The chef decanted oil from a pair of smallish barrels. "These are corn and sunflower oils," he said, labeling the jars. "I don't have much peanut oil right now, but you can have some grapeseed."

"Thank you," Den said, with real gratitude.

The corn oil behaved much like the used cooking oil Branlee had pilfered from the university food service. The sunflower oil, however, gave them a fivefold gain over the standard gel.

"Let's try it with a shot of our multiplier," Branlee suggested, indicating their mixture of coffee and trin tea.

"That stuff looks evil," Rital complained, but after the oily, greenish-brown mixture was added to the sunflower oil, he obediently zlinned how much selyn the beaker drew from the standard battery. His eyes widened. "Now *that's* an improvement," he observed. "It holds almost forty times as much selyn as the normal gel—fully half as much as our accidental mix."

"Which is a great deal better than we've managed to date," Branlee agreed. "Let's try the grapeseed oil."

The grapeseed oil had half again the affinity for selyn as the sunflower oil, bringing the total capacity to about 80% of their accidental mixture's.

"Pretty close, given that we're recreating an accident," Rital pointed out.

"We've found the answer!" Den agreed.

"But we haven't, you know," Branlee argued. "The university cafeteria doesn't use expensive ingredients like grapeseed oil. Whatever makes the stuff in the tub hold so much selyn, it's not the oil. Whatever it is provides a bigger boost than coffee, trin, or grapeseed oil."

"I know." The Donor grinned ear to ear in triumph. "That means when we finally get Raymond to talk, we'll make a battery gel that holds even more selyn than the stuff in the tub. It might even be enough to power a flyer with a human pilot!"

* * * *

The next day, Quess asked Den to cover Rital's shift in the Collectorium so that he could take care of personal business in town. Den jumped at the chance to work with his cousin, even though the channel wouldn't require much help so soon after transfer. It had been an excellent one, judging by the proprietary satisfaction on Gati's face when she looked at Rital and the amount of time they were spending together.

Seeing his cousin so Post when Den was unlikely to have a decent transfer soon didn't endear Quess to the younger Donor. *If the interfering old lorsh hadn't gotten himself assigned here, my life would be simpler.*

Still, Den didn't have the heart to deprive Tyvi of her son, Obis, even if responsibility for a channel did technically pass to the next month's Donor after transfer. *Rital can't avoid working with me forever.*

The long separation would have made them awkward with each other even without their recent confrontations, but Rital wouldn't take full advantage of the support Den offered. *Is he afraid I'm going to leave him, or is he still afraid of hurting me? Shen Quess, anyway. You'd think the Wonder Donor would know better than to let a channel run away from that sort of problem.* If Quess hadn't taken Rital away from Den, the channel would have confronted his fears promptly. The longer he avoided Den, the harder it would be to rebuild the cousins' trust.

The Donor eventually seduced Rital into accepting his support, through force of habit more than anything else. The shift was uneventful, with no first-time donors and only a few who had some experience, but were still skittish. After his conversation with Arth, Den noticed that most of this second group were donating for the second or third time. *The out-Territory scientific method works, even if it is time-consuming.*

Late in the afternoon, Rital picked up the next file in their assignment stack, skimmed it, and handed the folder to Den. It was for Rob Lifton, Annie Lifton's older brother.

Den counted Rob among his personal successes. When he had first come to Clear Springs, the young Gen had been a devoted follower of Reverend Sinth, even attempting to vandalize the Sime Center. When Rob had been injured trying to escape over the Sime Center's fence, the channel and Donor treated the young man's concussion, but neither pressed charges nor told his mother. A week later, a conflicted Rob had come in to discover for himself the truth about selyn donation. He'd donated regularly ever since, except for a few months last winter, when he'd started dating Reverend Sinth's niece, Bethany, and was afraid she would reject him as a "Sime-lover."

It was nice of Gati to assign Rob to Rital, Den reflected, following Rital and Rob to the collecting room. With such a high percentage of nervous, inexperienced donors, the Thirds were usually assigned any Gen who could be trusted. It was an efficient use of the channels, but made it easy for the Firsts to lose touch with their strongest supporters.

While Rob described the fancy new bicycle he was saving to buy, Den skimmed the Gen's file. He was familiar with Rob's history, as was Rital, but had become more skeptical of assumptions since the selyn battery disaster.

An anomaly caught his eye immediately. He made sure he'd read the page correctly, but there was no mistake. After donating selyn regularly for over a year, Rob was still a GN-3, not yet cleared to work with the Thirds. His selyn flow resistance showed no decrease. Rob had remained skittish way too long.

So much for Arth's conclusions.

Tyvi, who had taken the young man's field down the previous month, had left a note speculating Rob might be a borderline Simephobe, perhaps due to some unknown trauma. Den knew Rob and his sister had absorbed a full dose of anti-Sime propaganda as children, but Rob had accepted Rital's friendship too easily for a Gen psychologically incapable of associating with Simes. Still, Rob tensed as Rital's handling tentacles gripped his arms. In a Gen with so many donations to his history, it was a clinical sign of Simephobia.

But what if Arth is right? Den thought. *Tyvi's diagnosis doesn't match what I know of Rob.* He put his hand on his cousin's neck and signaled the channel to stop. Puzzled but obedient, Rital did not complete the transfer contact.

"You know, Rob," Den remarked casually, "you've been through this quite a few times. You know exactly what's going to happen and how it'll feel. Don't you think it's time to stop being so nervous?"

Under his hand, Den felt Rital tense with shock. However, Rob just looked down at the tentacles wrapped around his arms for a long moment. "You're right," he admitted ruefully. "I *have* been making this difficult for myself, haven't I?" He chuckled and the tension seemed to flow out of him. "Go ahead, Hajene," he told Rital. "I'm fine."

Rital let his laterals emerge from their sheaths and slide into place. When Rob didn't twitch at the tingling sensation, the channel bent forward for the lip contact. He straightened a moment later with a broad smile and said, "Congratulations, Rob! You've just qualified as a GN-2."

"What does that mean?" Rob asked blankly.

"Among other things, you can buy that bicycle sooner than you thought," Den said. He explained that a channel could draw from the deeper levels only if a Gen was relaxed. "General-class selyn donors are paid by the dynopter, so as a GN-2 you'll earn more every month."

Rob's eyes lit up at the prospect. He was describing plans for a dinner date with Bethany as they left the collecting room. Den wondered what Reverend Sinth would think about his niece being courted with money earned by donating selyn.

Rob paused as they reentered the waiting room. "Darn," he said, looking at the empty space previously occupied by Arth's folding table. The graduate student had apparently left early. Rob pulled a questionnaire out of his shirt pocket. "Could you give this to Arth next time you see him, Sosu Milnan?" he asked Den. "I'm going to miss the OLD SOKS meeting tonight."

"Sure." The Donor absently put the papers in his shirt pocket, waved farewell, then turned back to Rital, who had just placed Rob's file in the basket. To his surprise, his cousin didn't pick up the next folder. Instead, Rital waved him into the unoccupied records room.

What's the matter? He wouldn't interrupt our shift to compliment me on handling Rob, would he? Has he finally accepted my improvement as a Donor?

With sudden optimism, Den obeyed the summons. However, as soon as the door closed behind them, the channel turned on him and snarled, "How *dare* you take such a chance!"

"What?"

"The only thing worse than dealing with a frightened selyn donor," the channel explained, as if lecturing to a particularly inept trainee, "is dealing with one who feels guilty and tries to suppress it. Were you *trying* to turn borderline Simephobia into the real thing?"

"Rob isn't a Simephobe, borderline or otherwise, and you know it, Rital," Den retorted. "A Simephobe wouldn't get curious enough to donate selyn after one brief meeting with a channel—and he sure wouldn't fight his mother to a standstill for the right to come back and donate again. And again, and again."

"When did you become an expert on Simephobia in out-Territory donors?" Rital asked sarcastically. "Did you zlin Rob thoroughly before you decided that he wasn't really afraid?"

Den was more than tired of having his professional judgment questioned. "Rital," the Donor said angrily, "sometimes I wonder how Simes ever managed to organize a Territory, the way you ignore anything you can't zlin and never think critically about what you can. Did it never occur to you that Rob was afraid simply because he thought that's how a Gen *should* feel when donating? Didn't you notice how he forgot to be afraid of your tentacles, though you practically waved them in his face when you two were comparing bicycles?"

"What's that got to do with anything?" Rital dismissed the observation with a wave of the tentacles in question. "Transfer-shy Gens aren't necessarily tentacle-shy, too."

"Maybe not in-Territory," Den argued, "but Rob's never seen an unsheathed tentacle except when he's donating selyn."

"But surely…" The channel thought for a moment, then conceded the point. "You're right. He was unconscious when I treated his concussion. But to risk frightening him on the basis of such a thin chain of reasoning…"

"It worked, didn't it?"

"You sound like a Householder."

"Don't be insulting," Den retorted. "I know Rob better than you do, that's all."

"That the young Gen's a drinking buddy of yours isn't a sufficient reason for taking that kind of chance," the channel snapped.

Den glared right back.

Rital made a visible effort to control his temper. "Den, this isn't the first time you've taken such chances," he said. "What if you'd misjudged Principal Buchan and he'd opened his eyes when I was healing his cut? Tecton policies on handling out-Territory Gens aren't bureaucratic whims. They codify the collective experience of thousands of channels and Donors, since the first Householdings. How can I trust you if you ignore procedure and go your own way? You don't even warn me, much less ask my opinion. Yes, you're good at out-Territory publicity. Since your information pamphlet went out, we've had over a dozen calls. However, knowing how to persuade Gens in general doesn't make you an expert on psychological anomalies in out-Territory clients. You are playing with people's lives."

Den shook his head. "Can you look me in the eye and say that what I did wasn't right *for Rob*? And for every channel and Donor who works with him in the future?"

Rital sighed. "A certain Donor once asked me to remind him of his fallibility on matters of out-Territory psychology. Your method worked…this time. Since it *did* work, I don't have to give you an official reprimand. Next time, consult me before experimenting. That's all I ask."

"Yes, Hajene," Den apologized dully. *Rital doesn't want my help or trust my judgment,* he thought in despair. *Did he accuse me of wanting to leave the Tecton because he wishes I would?* The easy partnership they'd once shared was gone as if it had never existed.

"Just don't do it again." Rital led the way out of the file room. "Now we've got work to do, unless you have another bright idea?"

Prudently, Den didn't answer. Technically, selyn donors were the channel's responsibility, not the Donor's. Interfering without invitation in the absence of an emergency *was* a breach of professional etiquette.

But it worked!

* * * *

Den got through the next hour without more than a dozen words to his cousin, then ate alone in the cafeteria, watching Rital and Quess chat comfortably at another table. *It's bad enough to lose my channel to another Donor,* he reflected as his cousin laughed at something the older Donor said, *but does Rital have to be so shenned happy about it?*

Unable to watch any longer, he left for the Sudworks Brewery to drown his sorrows in Yon's porstan. The latest batch showed remarkable improvement. *At least here they respect my expertise.*

He stayed late. *What does it matter if there's an emergency? Quess can handle it better than I could ever hope to.*

It wasn't until his shirt pocket crinkled as he got undressed that Den remembered Rob's questionnaire. He set the papers where he would see them in the morning, then fought a battle with his conscience.

Den had not expected his intervention during Rob's donation to work so well. He had intended to help Rob acknowledge suppressed fear as a first step to working through his nervousness, never expecting Rob to lose his fear so completely as to qualify GN-2.

Den had missed something important about Rob, although, given the happy outcome, he had no intention of admitting that to Rital. But if he understood *why* things had worked so well, maybe he could better handle other chronically nervous donors.

Technically, the questionnaire was a confidential communication between Rob and Arth, and thus no business of Den's. The information requested was personal.

But then, out-Territory Gens had a different concept of privacy. Most donors who filled out the questionnaires not only answered a long set of intrusive questions, but at the end checked the box that authorized Arth to quote their answers.

I'll look at the first page, Den decided. *It covers information duplicated in Rob's chart, which I'm cleared to read. I already know his political leanings and that he hasn't been to church since Bethany Sinth decided that she liked him even if he donated. If Rob asked Arth to keep his answers confidential, I'll stop there. But if he didn't...*

The Donor unfolded the crumpled papers and nearly cheered when he saw Rob's full name and address boldly inscribed at the top and a firm checkmark in the authorization box. He flipped to the second page, then froze in shock as he skimmed the first paragraph.

Under Arth's neatly typed **Question 1. Why did you decide to donate selyn the first time?** Rob had scribbled, "It was a mistake. Reverend Sinth said the Sime Center had a secret Pen in the basement. I was trying to trick Hajene Madz into putting me there so I could expose it. When he didn't, I had to donate selyn so that he couldn't tell my mother I'd been to the Sime Center."

One of Reverend Sinth's pet peeves was that in-Territory law defined all Established Gens as adults. Thus, parents of Gens under sixteen were not informed when their "children" donated selyn.

Dazed, Den went on to **Question 2. If you have donated selyn more than once, why have you continued to donate?** Rob answered, "I stood up to my mother, when she discovered I'd been to the Sime Center against her orders. I have to keep donating selyn or she'll think I've given in and she can run my life. Besides, most of my friends in OLD SOKS donate. I can stand doing something unpleasant once a month and the money sure comes in handy!"

The answer to **Question 3. What advice would you give a friend who was donating selyn for the first time?** was even worse: "Don't think about what the channel's doing. Listen to the music, recite the multiplication tables...whatever it takes."

But it was **Question 4. If you donate selyn regularly, how have your perceptions of donation changed over time?** that dispelled the Donor's remaining illusions. "They haven't changed much," Rob had written. "It's still pretty scary if I let myself think about it. I mean, there's this Sime and he's going to take selyn from me and if he makes a mistake, I'm history. Nobody likes to be that helpless."

Shaking with reaction, Den sat down on his bed. *How could I have misjudged Rob so completely?* he wondered. Rital and Tyvi had been right all along. Rob *had* stayed GN-3 for over a year because of fear. He had never donated selyn except under duress. His answers offered no hint of compassion for renSimes who depended on his selyn to survive, or even interest in selyn-powered technology.

Den knew a handful of Gens in Valzor who'd struggled with their monthly donations for years, but those Gens had Sime friends and family. Also, in Sime Territory, a Gen who *could* donate selyn, but refused to do so, was regarded with contempt by Simes and Gens alike. There were very few incurable Simephobes and the ostracism of in-Territory non-donors, combined with legal penalties if their high fields caused accidents, convinced most to emigrate out-Territory.

For genuinely transfer-shy selyn donors, the worst mistake was to disparage their fear. As Rital had pointed out, pressure added to the guilt and embarrassment of being considered irrational and selfish. Careful handling and uncritical sympathy were appropriate means to help such donors stop fighting the channels.

As Den considered how much damage he could have caused, to Rob and Rital both, by acting on the out-Territory mass-statistics approach to knowledge rather than on the individual, he began to shake. *I owe Rital another apology,* he realized. *And this time, with chocolate!* He was glad of the excellent insulation surrounding his quarters.

Nevertheless, his experiment had worked, false assumptions notwithstanding. I wonder why?

He shuddered as he reread the answer to the first question. *One thing's sure. I'm not curious enough to let* this *get published.* If it became public knowledge that Rob had felt coerced into his first selyn donation, Reverend Sinth would have a field day. Even worse, Rital would blame himself for "attacking" an unwilling Gen. *And my cousin doesn't deserve that, even if he's an insufferable prig upon occasion.*

Den picked up the incriminating papers, shredded them into confetti, and flushed them down the toilet.

CHAPTER 13

A CHOCOLATE APOLOGY

The next morning, Den was at the door when Clear Springs' best confectioner opened. He purchased a half-dozen assorted truffles, avoiding the strawberry creams. When he returned to the Sime Center, the daily demonstration was in full swing, with conflicting chants of "Sime-lovers don't know God's grace, you betray the human race!" and "Save Our Kids, you're a disgrace, should be ashamed to show your face!"

To avoid the mob, Den used the unofficial entrance, scaling the back fence with the ease of long practice. He found the head groundskeeper, Alyce, raking leaves out of the vegetable garden and covering the bare ground with compost from the previous year.

The Donor's curiosity got the better of him. "Wouldn't it be easier just to leave the stuff that's already on the ground?"

Alyce shook her head and pointed at two trees bordering the garden. "Those are walnut trees," she explained. "Their leaves have a chemical that stunts the growth of vegetables."

"But you're putting the walnut leaves in with the rest of this year's compost," Den protested. "Won't you use that as mulch next year?"

"After proper composting, the chemical decomposes. Your tomatoes and corn are safe."

"That's a relief," the Donor said. "But how about the melons? Seedlings are tender and compost is full of mold."

Alyce laughed. "I spray the seedlings with Bordo mix. It's based on copper, so you shouldn't overuse it, but it gives seedlings a boost until they can fend for themselves."

"I see the garden—and my stomach—will prosper." Den patted the latter in anticipation, then continued inside.

He found his cousin preparing his monthly progress report. Unlike Den, Quess didn't view this chore as an excuse to hang out in Rital's office, drink trin, and make "helpful" suggestions.

The channel looked up as Den sidled through the half-open door, peace offering in hand. As he zlinned his cousin's true contrition, an incredulous smile lit Rital's face and he looked five years younger.

"You were right," Den said, setting the decorated box before Rital. "I shouldn't have interfered with Rob without consulting you."

The channel opened the box and looked up appreciatively. "What changed your mind?"

"Something I saw last night convinced me that I misjudged the situation," the Donor replied. "I don't know why it didn't end in disaster."

"Dumb luck?" Rital suggested with a crooked smile. He filled the "Good to the last dynopter" mug he'd given Den for Faith Day, topped off his own mug, then reached into a drawer for napkins.

"You aren't the only one who exercises bad judgment," Rital observed, placing two truffles on the napkins. "I left you to get our changeover classes approved, when it's my responsibility to handle out-Territory relations." He held up a tentacle against Den's objection. "I know you don't mind, and you're better at it, but I added insult to injury by not respecting your decisions."

Rital handed one truffle to Den, who took a bite. *Cherry cordial filling, not the vanilla cream! He really means it,* the Donor concluded with delight.

Rital nibbled his own confection and rolled his eyes in pleasure, then continued. "I don't have your luck, either. During our transfer… Den, I *knew* your limits and it never occurred to me to be careful!"

"You had other things on your mind. So did I, for that matter." Den winked suggestively. "But cousin, one thing you're not is careless with people's lives. That it *didn't* occur to you should tell you something." Den held his breath as, instead of rejecting the suggestion out of hand, Rital actually considered it objectively.

"You may be right about your capacity growing," he admitted. "If it really *isn't* that you're getting careless and losing your reflexes…"

"I'm not, I'm not!" the Donor reassured him.

"…then I'm willing to help you learn to handle it."

"I'll hold you to that," Den warned, with a grin of sheer delight.

Rital enjoyed his cousin's happiness for a moment, then sobered. "We've worked too closely for too long. We're not in anything the Tecton would recognize as a dependency, but I hadn't realized how far we've drifted from Tecton standard until I started working with Quess."

"I feel the same working with Tyvi," Den agreed. "I keep expecting her to deviate when you would, but she doesn't."

"Our ability to improvise…it makes us a good team, but it can get dangerous if we don't get our signals straight." Rital grimaced in remembered pain. "I shouldn't have waited for you to signal that I was drawing too fast. I'd never have been so careless with a strange Donor. And since you'd been dealing with the curriculum committee, I should have let you decide how to handle them at the meeting."

"I didn't have perfect judgment that evening, either," Den said wryly, putting a hand to his cheek. The walnut stain was long gone, but the lesson lingered. "It's no better if I jump in when you don't expect it. When I think what could have happened with Rob…" He was glad the incriminating questionnaire was dissolving into sludge at the Clear Springs sewage treatment plant.

"It's like dancing," Den observed, after a moment's consideration. "If both partners try to lead, or neither, you trip over each other's feet. But things go smoothly if one partner leads and the other follows, and it doesn't matter who's in charge. They can even switch back and forth."

"Is that how it works?" Rital asked wistfully.

"Well, for most people," Den said, smothering a snicker. His cousin was that rare commodity on the dance floor, a Sime with two left feet. "I'll tell you what," the Donor offered. "I won't interfere with your patients or donors without consulting you first, if you don't take unnecessary chances. All right?"

Rital nodded. "Fine. And I'll let you make the calls on out-Territory politics, unless I zlin something you don't know about. If I'm stumped, you take the lead. Just warn me before you start one of your schemes, all right?"

Den laughed, feeling more comfortable with his cousin than he had in weeks, and popped the last of his cherry truffle into his mouth. "You've got a deal!"

"Good. But Den?"

Rital shifted uncomfortably and the Donor raised an encouraging eyebrow.

"Why didn't you telephone me from Valzor, if you wanted to know whether the school board had approved our classes?"

"It wasn't for lack of trying," Den answered. "Let me tell you about my quest for a modern communications device…"

He had to pause halfway through the story when the giggling channel choked on his tea, then stayed when the tale was done, offering creative suggestions for Rital's report. "No, Den, the Tecton won't pick up OLD SOKS' beer tab as a security expense, even if that *would* double the number of counterdemonstrators."

Den almost danced down the hall to his own office. *I've got my cousin back!* The Tecton's policy of rotating Donors assured that Den would get his channel back soon, too, and with him, the promise of using his new capacity. *Now that I know it's not forever, I can wait.*

That evening, Den and Rital shared a table for the first time since Quess had arrived, ignoring the whispers and indulgent smiles of the other diners.

Den didn't even mind when Quess, uncharacteristically late, carried his tray over to their table and asked, "May I join you?"

"Certainly." Rital waved the diplomat to a seat on his other side and Den let the older Gen assume responsibility for his assigned channel. Quess ate his stew with single-minded enthusiasm and Den controlled a smile as Rital took another bite of his half-finished casserole. *Nothing like a hungry Donor to get a channel to eat!*

When Quess had taken the edge off of his hunger, he paused for a sip of tea. "I'm glad you two have settled your differences," he observed. "Your private lives are your own business, as long as they remain private. Your lack of communication could have halted your progress with the community, or even endangered your clients."

"Umm, yes," Den agreed, cursing the man's too-acute perception. "Isn't the bread delicious?" he commented, trying to distract the other Donor's attention. "Ref is experimenting with out-Territory recipes."

* * * *

A week before the first changeover class, Reverend Sinth distributed two new pamphlets. "**Moral Standards in Education**" argued that because the Teachers' Association had endorsed changeover training, they were morally bankrupt. As an example of depravity, Sinth cited the time Principal Buchan allowed Den to intervene after a young Sime took his Gen half-sister hostage. It made no difference to the preacher that the hostage was his own niece, Bethany, nor that Den had saved her life, if not her brother's.

Since Rital was Sime, the pamphlet didn't waste words citing his unworthiness, but a third of the space was devoted to proving Den unfit because of his status as a Donor, his lack of an out-Territory educational credential, and his willingness to discuss changeover in public.

I'll have to consult Tohm about libel laws. It's not worth a lawsuit, but pointing out that Sinth is breaking the law might make some people see his hypocrisy.

The other pamphlet was more problematic. Titled "**How the Tecton plans to STEAL your Child,**" its cover was graced with an adorable urchin far too young for changeover. The conspiracy theory inside might scare out-Territory parents from entrusting a child to the Tecton, even after the adjectives were deleted. There wasn't enough substance for Den to construct a rebuttal and reading through the Tecton briefings filed in the Sime Center's library turned up no clues.

In desperation, Den sought out Quess. The senior Donor was in his office, staring sadly at something in his hand. When Den cleared his throat, Quess looked up, then placed the object on his desk. "Come in."

The younger Donor took a chair, glancing curiously at the trinket on the desktop. It was a model of a sailing ship, crudely made as if by a very young child. The hull was half a walnut shell filled with wax. A toothpick was embedded in the wax for a mast and a tattered scrap of faded cloth made a sail.

"My daughter made that for me, long ago," Quess explained. "Is there some way I can assist you?"

Recalled to business, the younger Donor passed him the pamphlet. "This is Sinth's latest," he explained. "It claims the Sanger Sime Center kidnapped the mayor's son. I recall some gossip about Sanger when I was in Valzor, but I can't remember the details. No mention of the channel involved. It's tough to write a rebuttal, if I can't find out what really happened. Do you know?"

Quess skimmed the pamphlet, raising a well-bred eyebrow at its crude tone. "I know of the incident," he admitted, setting the pamphlet down with distaste. "Hajene Timothy ambrov Tien, the Controller of the Sanger Sime Center, is a young hothead. He grew up in Sanger and thinks he can run around town as freely as he did as a child. He crashed a party at the virulently anti-Sime Mayor Cappa's house, while in Hard Need, no less."

The older Donor shook his head in disapproval at such foolishness, but Den understood the frustration motivating Hajene Timothy to force his former neighbors to see him as a *person*, not just an ambulatory collection of tentacles.

"During the party," Quess continued, "one of the guests went into changeover. Mayor Cappa grabbed his gun, but his son, Mark, stepped between them and got a bullet through the shoulder for his trouble. There was no time to call an ambulance, so Timothy offered his services and the boy's mother agreed. Unfortunately, Mark had just begun to Establish and with Hajene Timothy in Need, that…"

"Induced a Donor's instinctive response to Simes in him," Den finished. "How long before the boy ran away and joined the Tecton?"

"About three months," Quess replied dryly. "Of course, he spent most of that first month recovering from his injury."

"Maybe I shouldn't answer this pamphlet," Den said. "If anything about a Sime Center scares out-Territory parents, it's knowing they can't control their offspring's reaction to Simes. They already resent that their Gen 'children' can donate selyn without their parents' knowledge. If they learn there are circumstances under which the Tecton *will* encourage their offspring to run away… Can you imagine how they would react?"

Quess shuddered. "After watching the mob on your sidewalk, I'd rather not."

"Maybe the immigration laws should be changed," Den suggested. "It might make life easier for out-Territory Sime Centers."

"Would it really?" the older Donor asked. "You're a First, Den, and a pretty talented one. Mark Cappa has the potential to be as good. Could you have told him that he couldn't start training for two more years? Could you have let such talent be crippled by the delay?"

Den thought back to his own Establishment and the obsessive *need* it had brought to be with channels, to soothe their distress, to share the joy of transfer. "No," he admitted softly, "I don't think I could."

* * * *

Despite Sinth's efforts, the first changeover class at the Southside Upper School had full enrollment, with ten additional children on the waiting list. Den and Rital worked hard to prepare the day's lesson. Den was confident his cousin would be discreet, or at least pay attention to his Donor's "shut up quick" signal if necessary. Den had invited Hank Fredricks to send a reporter to the first class, but the *Clarion's* owner showed up in person, looking over the stacks of pamphlets and handouts near the door, which sported a sign declaring the classroom Sime Territory.

Seating the students and taking roll took time, because the students were distracted by Rital's tentacles. Their initial apprehension faded, though, when the channel handed Establishment certificates to the four Gens in the group. Four children on the waiting list were located and brought to class, while the four who could have left decided to stay and watch.

Since Reverend Sinth claimed that Den and Rital wouldn't cover Establishment, they started there, describing Gen selyn storage, how selyn production began, and the physical and psychological changes that accompanied it. They did not cover Establishment in Gens with Donor potential. It wouldn't do to advertise that a Gen's own body could make any career but that of a technical-class Donor inconceivable.

They completed the first lesson ten minutes early, so Den invited questions.

After almost a minute of dead silence, one girl raised a tentative hand to ask, "How do Gens who live in Sime Territory keep Simes from killing them?"

"That's a very good question, Kora," Den congratulated her. "We'll cover safety more thoroughly later. The short answer is that in-Territory Gens donate selyn regularly. After donating, a Gen doesn't have the field strength to accidentally provoke a Sime to attack. Even a berserker will avoid a low field Gen if there's any alternative—like a channel."

Another hand shot up. A tall boy asked, "What is it like to donate selyn?"

Rital briefly described a routine donation, not mentioning that inexperienced donors were often nervous or afraid. Den let his nager reflect his approval and then blinked as three new hands were raised. The questions came quickly after that.

"How much selyn does a channel take during a donation?"

"How long does it take?"

"How much money can you get for a selyn donation?" posed by the proud recipient of a brand-new Establishment certificate.

"If fear makes a Sime attack, how do channels keep from hurting donors who are afraid?"

"What's the difference between a regular selyn donor and a technical-class Donor?"

"What does transfer feel like?"

"Why did you decide to become a technical-class Donor?"

There were actual groans of disappointment when the bell rang. Den assured the students that questions were always welcome and dismissed the class.

The students hurried out to their next classes, some snatching extra pamphlets and handouts. Hank Fredricks stood slowly, stretching cramped muscles. "That was a very informative hour," he remarked, casting a wary glance in Rital's direction. When the newsman had interacted with Rital before, the channel had worn retainers. But as Rital started packing up the handouts, the out-Territory Gen relaxed and closed his notebook, putting his pencil in his shirt pocket. "It's good there's a place that offers children honest answers to difficult questions."

"That's a major reason the Sime Center exists," Den pointed out.

"I know. Too bad the parents aren't taking the class, too." Fredricks gave a thoughtful frown. "Could I audit the entire course? I can't do justice to the material in one article. Perhaps a series…"

It took all Den's self-discipline to keep from jumping up and down and cheering. As it was, the sudden glee in his nager earned him a smile from Rital.

"Come as often as you'd like," the Donor invited. "We have nothing to hide."

* * * *

Den could hardly wait to see the next morning's *Clarion*.

NEW CLASSES PROVIDE ANSWERS FOR FUTURE GENS the headline read. Underneath, the text began, "From how selyn production begins to how a Gen can keep Simes from attacking, Clear Springs students found answers to their questions yesterday at the first session of the newly approved Adolescent Maturity classes." The article was reasonably accurate—no dangerous errors, only odd wordings of things tenuously understood. As a token gesture toward reporting both sides of the issue, Fredricks quoted from Sinth's pamphlets and press releases. Unfortunately for the preacher, the quotes selected were of Sinth insisting that Establishment would not be covered at all.

Den chortled over his eggs when he read the last paragraph: "How can a Gen keep Simes from attacking? According to Sosu Milnan, even berserk Simes won't attack a Gen who has little selyn in him. The best protection, it seems, is to donate selyn safely to a channel every month."

Den could have wished for a less dramatic ending, but drama sold papers. Fredricks didn't mention Rital's tentacles, or the students' fascination with donating. Overall, the Donor was very pleased.

The community's reaction to the *Clarion's* coverage was mixed. Three children were withdrawn by their parents, including the curious Kora. They were replaced promptly from the waiting list, which now had nearly thirty names. The *Clarion* ran letters on the subject each day. At first, most opposed the classes, but then Sinth's attacks shifted target, from Den and Rital to the school in general, and public opinion began to shift.

The turning point came when the *Clarion* quoted "a loyal Save Our Kids member, name withheld by request" saying that since the classes began, the Southside Upper School had become a "hotbed of adolescent rebellion, disrespect for authority, disregard for teammates, and every other parental nightmare." Within hours, a petition was circulated demanding an apology from Save Our Kids for this affront to the Cougars. Over five hundred students, teachers, and parents signed. Hank Fredricks published the full text a few days later, complete with two pages of signatories in small print. Den recognized the names of several children of Save Our Kids members among them.

Fliers appeared around town. "WANTED DEAD OR ALIVE for Gen-running, Den 'Sime-lover' Milnan," the headline shrieked, over a photograph of Den with his Tecton uniform altered to resemble prison garb and mock "prisoner identification numbers" in the margin to enhance resemblance to a prison record.

Below the picture, the text continued: "Personally responsible for delivering thousands of Gens into the tentacles of Simes! Raised to believe Simes are human, Milnan has delivered hundreds of victims to his Sime masters, causing untold physical and spiritual harm. If you see this man, call the police and report his whereabouts!"

Upset, Rital warned his cousin to be careful when he left the protection of the Sime Center.

Den laughed off the warning. Obis' departure the previous day had left him with Tyvi. It felt so good to be working with a channel again that the Donor found it hard to take Save Our Kids seriously.

Sales of the selyn-insulating polycarbonate sheets were brisk and Flight Innovations ordered a second batch of polycarbonate sheets from the factory in Berrysville. This success compensated, in part, for the lack of progress on the selyn battery gel. Test mixtures with the expensive grape-seed and sunflower oils spoiled just as quickly as the standard gel, while the cheap cooking oil in the tub remained uncorrupted.

It felt to Den as if the evidence from the battery accident was in stasis, waiting for him to figure it out. Then the orgonics repair team reported oddities.

"We'll be done sooner than expected," the team leader, a renSime named Hald Beggit, commented when he stopped by Den's office to give him an update. "The damage was localized. The outlets and the first few feet of orgonics tubing and electrical wiring are melted to slag, but both systems are intact beyond that. One of the electricians from the university is working with Vespin to adapt the outlets to create an even more localized point of failure"

"Why would you design an outlet specifically to fail?" Den asked. "Job security?"

Hald's husband Vespin chuckled. "When you design a system likely to be stressed to failure, you put the point of first failure somewhere that's easy to get to. It saves time and effort getting the repairs done, makes the clients happy, and saves our knees and backs."

"If the outlet melts before the tubing and wiring behind it, then all you have to replace is the outlet," Hald continued. "Much easier. Like most repair experts, we're lazy."

Den thought about the outsized charges of his experimental batteries and the pitfalls of adapting them to systems designed for a conventional battery. "Your new outlets should be installed in buildings from the start."

Vespin predicted glumly, "That would make too much sense. We'll pass the word along, but Householding Ohmand manufactures most orgonics supplies. We're just repair techs, not Householders. They aren't interested in our improvements to their products."

"My company, Flight Innovations, could market your design," Den said. "We're developing a selyn battery with a much bigger charge, so safeguards will be critical. When and how we could manufacture your new outlets would depend on the final design, but if you're willing to stay a couple of days after you've finished the repairs…" He broke off in confusion at the repair tech's reaction. "Is something wrong?"

Vespin blotted tears from his face. "I never thought my tinkering would interest anybody. That you want to produce and sell it... I've always dreamed of improving orgonics products, not just cleaning up the messes left by construction techs."

"I don't know what you're complaining about," Hald retorted. "It's not like the last job we were on, bundled up in the heat to protect ourselves from the mold. The melted tubing here has hardly spoiled at all. We've never had an easier cleanup."

"Have you any idea why the burned gel isn't spoiling?" Den asked eagerly.

"The crew chief thinks the spoilage bugs can't grow because of the melted copper wiring mixed in," Hald explained. "I hope he's wrong. Copper wire is expensive."

Den remembered Alyce's copper-based fungicide. "Perhaps there's a cheaper solution. I've got one idea to test, anyway. In the meantime, Hald, if you and your crew want to stay and commercialize Vespin's outlet design, talk to Jesper Reft. He's handling our accounts."

* * * *

Den didn't tell Rital about the mail he was receiving. His cousin would become more paranoid if he learned of the flood of death threats or the bill for a bogus insurance policy covering "Sime-luver Milnan" for "death and dismemberment," described in gruesome and explicit detail.

The *Clarion* denounced Sinth's "wanted" posters in a scathing editorial. The reaction of the community at large was more nuanced. A few new faces joined Save Our Kids in front of the Sime Center, along with nearly a dozen new counterdemonstrators. Despite the obstacle course, the number of selyn donations rose to almost Faith Day levels.

One of the new donors was Thaddus Webber. When Tyvi finished taking his field down, the white-haired theologian sank back on the lounge with a sigh of relief. Then he turned to Den and said, "I was hoping to see you during this visit, Sosu Milnan. My congregation has followed the controversies surrounding the Sime Center. It's hard to know what to believe. Would you or one of your colleagues speak to us about the goals of your Center and the programs and services you offer?"

"Certainly," Den agreed cautiously. There was so much blind opposition from out-Territory religious institutions that it was difficult to trust a religious leader. However, Webber had supported the changeover classes. If his congregation was similarly open-minded, they could be valuable allies.

"Marvelous," said Webber. "Our next meeting day is tomorrow—too soon—so how about the next week? We have a regular lecture series..."

The two arranged the details and the clergyman departed to collect his payment.

Over the next few days, Den worked on the presentation. The Sime Center's two books on out-Territory religions had no information on Webber's Rational Deists and there wasn't time to visit Miz Dilson at the public library. The best Den could do was to assume that their beliefs were similar to those of the larger sects and design his talk accordingly. The result was a lecture full of bland generalities that avoided offending anyone's sensibilities by having no recognizable content.

Of course, I'm assuming that any of Webber's congregation attend my lecture, when they find out who's speaking.

CHAPTER 14

THE RATIONAL DEISTS

When Den arrived at the Rational Deist Meeting Hall, he was surprised by the number of people about. *They must be here for the weekly service.* He followed the traffic toward the main entrance, which featured imposing double doors with an inscription carved into the lintel: "The World is my Territory, and to do Good is my Religion"—T. Paine.

Pondering the secular-sounding quote, the Donor entered the building. He had come early, hoping to learn more about Rational Deist beliefs, so he set off in search of Thaddus Webber. Looking for a building directory, he stopped to read the announcement board and discovered that his lecture was listed as a "special guest sermon" in conjunction with the regular service.

"There you are," Webber's cheerful voice rang out as he hastened toward Den. The theologian was dressed formally, but not in the flowing robes that Reverend Sinth favored. "We look forward to learning more about your Sime Center."

"You didn't say anything about giving a sermon."

Webber shrugged. "It was easier to have you speak at our service, than to find another time when everyone could come."

"But I don't even believe in your god," the Donor protested.

"You'll fit right in, then," Webber reassured him. "We're about evenly divided between those who believe in a god, those who don't, and those who feel that speculating about the whole god issue is a waste of time."

Den blinked in puzzlement. "If you can't agree on whether or not a god exists, how can you call yourselves a religion?"

"Our atheist members *don't* call Rational Deism a religion and quite a few religions agree." Webber shrugged. "It's just semantics, anyway. Whether or not there is a god, the world and its various peoples certainly exist. If we are to avoid destroying ourselves as the Ancients did, we must learn to live together."

Den couldn't argue with that.

The theologian led the Donor deeper into the building. "Many religions view non-members as objects of proselytization or pity. Some, like Reverend Sinth's Conservative Congregation, deny other faiths' right to exist. As proponents of reason, we seek an ethical code, independent of any creed, that works for people of all faiths and none."

"So, you want to replace the ethical codes of other religions, in the name of religious diversity?" Den asked. "Isn't that inconsistent?"

"Human beings have never been known for consistency," Webber pointed out good-naturedly, "and we're very human!"

Den trailed after him, wondering whether the Rational Deists were a religious congregation or a philosophical debating society.

Webber led the way to the basement. "Our weekly school is in session. We have a volunteer staff and I'm very proud of their efforts."

Den followed without objection. He was already confused. Seeing what they taught their children might help him avoid offending his hosts.

The basement was carpeted in cheery yellow, with rainbows painted on the walls. Children's drawings documented a field trip to a nearby wildlife refuge. Many showed birds and flowers, but several featured a bearded man up to his neck in a muddy pond. Den deduced that the expedition had produced some unanticipated excitement.

In the first classroom, four- and five-year-olds were listening to a story. The young heroine was investigating her friend's claim that his house was haunted, and had just discovered that the nocturnal noises were caused by a family of opossums in the attic.

"We teach children not to believe everything they're told," Webber explained. "They learn to look for alternative explanations for why things happen. Later we'll teach them that extraordinary claims, such as supernatural entities, magic, or miracles, require a higher standard of proof than claims consistent with natural laws."

In the next room, seven- to nine-year-olds were earnestly discussing a proposed flood control project on the Tinusa River. Each child had been assigned one aspect of the question to research: cost, habitat destruction, flooding, potential failure rates, current use of the land, and alternative solutions. Led by their teacher, they took turns reporting their findings and discussing their importance.

"Once children learn to ask useful questions, we teach them how to research answers," Webber continued. "They also learn how the same facts can lead to opposite conclusions, depending on points of view and personal values. We discuss how to make decisions with insufficient data, or when both options are right or both wrong, but a choice must still be made. Also, to respect other people's right to make different choices."

Like Raymond Ildun, Den thought, as the carrot-haired boy argued eloquently against the flood control project on the grounds that floods spread destruction in a delightful variety of ways, which he proceeded to enumerate. In detail, with examples.

"Very good, Raymond," his teacher praised. "You've done a thorough job of informing us what floods can do."

Raymond beamed at the praise, then as the teacher's attention moved on, he removed the cap from the inkwell on his desk. Stealthily, he reached for the long braid of hair dangling temptingly from the head of the girl in front of him.

Although the girl was following the debate, she was obviously aware of who sat behind her. The instant Raymond touched her hair she spun in her chair, slapped his hand away, recapped his inkwell, and removed it to her own desk for safekeeping. Raymond opened his mouth to protest, but noticed the teacher watching and thought better of it.

In the next room, ten- to twelve-year-olds were bent over glossy fliers featuring prominent, smiling photos of well-known faces. "This is our rhetoric class," the teacher told Den.

"Rhetoric? At this age?"

"People are already trying to manipulate them. Last week, we discovered how selective truth can deceive. Today, we're finding examples from political campaigns." One of her students waved a hand, bouncing up and down with excitement. "Did you find one, Jasmine?"

The girl held up a lavishly illustrated pamphlet. "Senator Norris takes credit for reduced shipping rates that have improved the Clear Springs economy. But actually," she showed a rate table, "the rates are lower because Clear Springs has a Sime Center. In his fundraising letter from two years ago," she waved another document, "Norris ran against the Sime Center, so he opposed lower freight rates."

"Very good, Jasmine," the teacher praised, and the little girl beamed.

Only the teenagers were discussing topics traditionally related to religion.

"Who remembers the First Cause Argument?" the elderly pedagogue leading the class asked. His beard was white and very bushy, as if to make up for his bald pate.

An awkward young man, just beginning his adolescent growth spurt, volunteered, "Isn't that the one about, uh, everything must have a cause, except for the First, Uncaused Cause defined as god?"

"Very good, Paul. Your homework was to look for logical fallacies in this argument. Who found one?"

There was a pause as the students traded glances to see who was willing to venture an answer, then the boy sitting next to Paul spoke up. Den recognized Jerree Bolin, the young man who had learned he was Gen at the curriculum committee's hearing. "The argument offers no support for its initial premise, that everything must have a cause," he offered. "If that's false, the whole argument is nonsense."

A blond, precociously developed girl smiled approvingly at Jerree, trying to catch his attention.

"Right," the teacher agreed. "There's another, even more basic error, though. Did you find it, Sandie?" So, the old man had not missed the girl's flirtation, even if Jerree had.

To Den's amazement, the girl blinked at her teacher and responded, "It's self-contradictory, of course. If *everything* must have a cause, then god requires one, too, and you have to assume an infinite series of gods, each the Cause of the one before. If god *doesn't* require a Cause, then the initial premise is false and, like Jerree said," a smile to the boy, who blushed, "the whole argument fails. The principle of parsimony requires us to prefer an uncaused universe to a universe caused by an uncaused god, because the first assumes one less thing than the second." *So much for stereotyping flirtatious girls as stupid!*

"Very *good*, Sandie," the teacher said. "You'll become a philosopher yet. Class, Sandie just cited the principle of parsimony. Can anyone tell me why it should be used with caution? Paul?"

The young man, who had been glaring jealously at Jerree for attracting Sandie's attention, started guiltily. "Uh…" His classmates giggled and Paul pulled himself together. "The probability thing?"

"Exactly," the elderly teacher agreed. "Parsimony says that the simplest explanation is only *most likely* to be true. Plenty of times the true explanation is *not* the simplest one. Parsimony allows a tentative decision in the absence of evidence, but it's no substitute for hard data."

Webber took Den back out into the hall. "We're lucky to have Professor Perrinstein teaching philosophy," the theologian said as they started back to the stairs. "By the time students leave his class, they know exactly what they believe and why. That gets them through their confirmation ceremony with confidence."

"Confirmation ceremony?" the Donor asked, suspecting it would bear little resemblance to the professions of faith described in his texts. *And I have to address this group in a few minutes.*

"The candidates prepare a ten-minute presentation," the theologian explained. "It can be a philosophical argument, a discussion of an ethical dilemma, or commentary on some topic of current interest. Some artistically inclined candidates present their argument in the form of dance, or poetry, or artwork, which is permitted as long as it makes a clear statement. At the first weekly service after their sixteenth birthday, the candidates present their work to the congregation, who then engage them in discussion. At the end of the ceremony, the youngsters register to vote, to show their adult intent to work toward improving their community, the Territory, and the world."

"Oh." Den rather liked the idea. It was certainly consistent with the Rational Deists' obsession with educating their children to think independently.

Back on the ground floor, Webber ushered the Donor into a crowded meeting room where several hundred Gens gathered in small groups, talking enthusiastically. There were familiar faces: the parents of four students from the changeover classes at the library, Professor Ildun with a woman who must be his wife, Vice Chancellor Gillum Mathison, and quite a few of the Sime Center's regular non-student selyn donors. The feisty Mr. Duncan, Annie and Rob Lifton's grandfather, waved at Den from across the room.

As he followed Webber through the crowd, Den caught scraps of conversation on a variety of topics: the prognosis for an arthritic knee, the impact of a new clothing factory on the Clear Springs' economy, a recipe for pasta topped with tomatoes, artichoke hearts, chopped walnuts, and fresh basil that sounded delicious, a comparison of two historians' accounts of the Battle of Shen, and the qualifications of the candidates running for positions on the town council in the upcoming election.

Webber offered Den a chair in the first row, then stepped behind the podium as the children filed in and joined their families. The theologian rang a small bell vigorously until the hum of conversation quieted and the audience settled into the chairs. Sandie and Paul had apparently settled their differences: they sat at the very back, where nobody would see them holding hands.

Webber called for reports on a variety of projects, including a poetry reading, a charity dinner, transportation to events on campus, an adult literacy class, a literary discussion group for its graduates, a support group for drug and alcohol addicts, and an upcoming "retreat" to the mountains. Only the last of these activities seemed to have anything to do with religion but if so, why was Webber emphasizing the expertise of the retreat's leaders in botany, ecology and wildlife management? *I suppose it's no crazier than asking me to give a sermon.*

When the project leaders had finished, Webber began his presentation. "As you know, I am researching Ancient moral and ethical codes for a book I plan to write. Much Ancient philosophy seems bizarre to modern eyes, but for today's reading, I'll share some quotes from a man whose ideas strike me as particularly sensible.

"Robert Ingersoll lived on this continent. His best work criticized the practices of religions of his day." He looked down at his notes. "This is from a fragment that seems to have been a lecture on blasphemy. 'If god is infinite, you cannot injure him. You cannot commit a crime against any being that you cannot injure.' Later we have, 'It is far more important that we should love our spouses than that we should love god, and I will tell you why: you cannot help god, you *can* help your spouse.' Ingersoll recommends that people care for their children and build a strong, supportive community, rather than expanding their churches."

Around the sanctuary, heads nodded thoughtfully, even skeptically.

Den knew he was in trouble. The carefully inoffensive treatment he'd prepared would offend a congregation whose classes taught critical thinking and logic and whose sermons were educational lectures. With a sigh for the wasted effort, Den abandoned his carefully crafted euphemisms. Unfortunately, he was out of time to find a replacement.

Webber had put his glasses back into his pocket and smiled at the Donor, then turned to the congregation. "Our congregation has a long history of inviting speakers from outside our community to share their experiences and knowledge with us. Today's speaker comes from farther away than most: from the Sime town of Valzor, in Nivet Territory. His profession as a Donor is highly respected there, but I doubt any of us has a clear idea of what he actually does.

"When the University proposed bringing a Sime Center to Clear Springs, the Rational Deists supported it. We welcomed the prospect of a new power source, new technology, and the improved economy they would bring. Since the Sime Center opened, we have discovered additional advantages, most recently the prospect of having our children educated in how to identify changeover and seek help before they Kill us. They even tell us when our children become Gen.

"It has become apparent that a Sime Center provides more than cheap power and beer money for college students, which is why I suggested to the Programming Committee that we invite a speaker from the Sime Center to explain the full range of services it offers, the philosophy behind them, and what additional benefits our community might be provided.

"So, without further ado," the theologian concluded, "let me present today's speaker, Sosu Den Milnan!"

Applause broke out as Den approached the podium slowly, clutching his useless notes and hoping desperately for inspiration to strike. He was very glad that Rital wasn't there to zlin him. If the channel could zlin his nervousness, he might decide that Den's control really *was* eroding from spending too much time among out-Territory Gens. However, the thought of his cousin gave Den an idea.

If my euphemisms won't work for this group, perhaps Rital's tell-them-everything approach will.

It wasn't much, as ideas went, but by the time he had carefully arranged his useless notes on the podium, he hadn't thought of anything better. *And with several hundred pairs of eyes focused on me, I doubt I will.*

Cautiously, Den began to improvise. "The purpose of the Tecton is actually quite simple: to allow Simes and Gens to co-exist in peace and safety. Like most simple ideas, it's a great deal more complicated than you'd expect. To succeed, we must supply every Sime with selyn every month, selyn that our channels must first collect from Gens. That's quite a logistical challenge all by itself, because channels and Donors get tired and sick, and natural disasters like floods and fires make it difficult for people to travel, but nothing—nothing at all—can be allowed to interfere with the selyn delivery system. It was a collapse of the selyn distribution system in Norwest Territory that started the Unity War, sending its entire Sime population raiding across the continent simply to survive."

A shudder passed around the large room, but Den had definitely gotten their attention. The story was not told in that way in Gen Territory.

His audience seemed interested, so he told them the story of Faith Day and the founding of the modern Tecton as it was known in-Territory. It was clear from their reactions that even the selyn donors among them hadn't given much thought to what happened to their selyn after their vouchers were cashed.

He took a deep breath and scanned the sea of upturned faces. "Everything the Tecton does is related to one single purpose: the preservation of human life."

People nodded and with that encouragement, Den launched into an explanation of how that purpose was applied in practice. He explained the less well-known services the Tecton provided and how they related to its primary mission: providing medical care, educating children to prepare them for adulthood as Simes or Gens, the First Year camps that turned out-Territory Simes into productive in-Territory citizens, and charging the selyn batteries that ran the trains and powered in-Territory cities. He even touched on the Sime Center's sponsorship of the research being done by Branlee and Arth.

With ten minutes to go, he was down to the Sime Center function most likely to upset even open-minded out-Territory Gens: collecting selyn from Gen donors. There were too many selyn donors in the audience to chance soft-pedaling it. However, his frank description of donation didn't upset the non-donors in the audience as much as he expected. The first question told him why.

"There's something I've always wondered, nosey amateur historian that I am," Webber said, claiming the official host's prerogative to ask the first question. "The Nivet Army that fought alongside our soldiers during the Unity Wars—they were mostly Simes who Killed every month, if I understand correctly?"

"You do."

"In that case, how did they avoid turning on their allies?"

"There were channels among the troops," Den explained, knowing that almost all out-Territory accounts ignored the critical reason why the improbable alliance had worked. "Before the battle, the Gens donated selyn to the channels and the channels transferred it to the Simes. The Gens weren't carrying enough selyn to tempt Simes who weren't in Need, so they fought safely side by side."

It was Professor Perrinstein who asked the dangerous follow-up question. "If the Simes who usually Killed were able to take their selyn from the channels during the siege and battle, why were they killing at all? It seems wasteful, if nothing else."

Den was oh, so tempted to answer that question fully. Some, maybe even the majority of this audience might be able to accept the answer: that killing was instantly addictive to Simes and that junct Simes could only survive breaking that addiction if they started the long, painful process within a few months of changeover. Older junct Simes could manage channel's transfer for a few months, but then they had to Kill or die.

However, he dared not encourage such rabid researchers to examine that particular issue too closely, because it led directly to the Tecton's darkest hour. Despite the pledge on which the First Contract was based, the brand-new Tecton could not allow all the non-Householding adult Simes in Nivet to die within the year, leaving their children orphaned. Nor did they have the personnel to care for the thousands of Gens still in the Pen system, kept docile all their lives with drugs that severely stunted mental development. So, they had let the two problems solve each other…and hadn't told their Gen allies, lest it discourage the selyn donations on which Nivet depended.

The Secret Pens had lasted less than a decade, but that was long enough to teach a generation of non-junct Simes the skills to carry on civilization. Years later, when the notorious Oliver Teague had written an expose on them and published it out-Territory, the only thing that had prevented Unity from collapsing was that the majority of out-Territory authorities simply refused to believe a mere entertainer.

So, instead of providing a full answer, Den turned Professor Perrinstein's question back on him. "Simes aren't any faster to accept change than Gens. Think about it. The Sime Center has been open for two years now, but many Clear Springs parents here still choose to shoot any child they suspect might be in changeover."

"Not Rational Deist parents," Perrinstein argued. "We have supported the Sime Center and the technology it brings from the start."

"Really?" Den asked, scanning the audience and trying to judge their reactions. "And yet, fewer than a third of your congregation has ever donated selyn to support those changeovers, or the selyn-based technology you want to use."

The non-donors in the audience shifted uncomfortably in their seats, unwilling to meet his eyes.

Den let them think about it for a moment, then asked, "Do any of you non-historians have questions about how the Tecton and its Sime Centers operate today?" At least that was likely to produce questions he could answer without equivocation.

It did. No one called him a Sime-lover or accused him of collaborating with "dangerous" Simes. However, Flora Mills, the grey-haired woman from Berrysville who had scolded the parents of Clear Springs for being ungrateful for the changeover classes, gave Den an equally harsh scold.

"How come your Tecton will only place Sime Centers in large cities with sliderail train stations?" she demanded. "Small towns have children, too, who turn Sime and Kill somebody if no one shoots them first. Why only try to save people in Clear Springs? Is it because you make a larger profit where there are more people to donate selyn?"

"It's not about profit, it's about the health of our channels," Den explained, startled by her vehemence. "Small out-Territory towns don't provide enough work to keep channels healthy."

"Don't small towns in Simeland have Sime Centers?" she asked.

"Well, yes," Den admitted. "But in those towns, every Gen donates selyn and all Simes Need transfer, every month. In-Territory Sime Centers also provide medical care. A small-town Sime Center on this side of the border would be much less busy."

"You could manage, if you *wanted* to," she muttered.

Den could not resist. "Miz Mills," he said, "if the people of Berrysville *wanted* to, they could come here to Clear Springs once a month and donate selyn, declaring each time that they are doing so to persuade the Tecton to put a Sime Center in Berrysville. If you can average ninety Berrysville citizens donating selyn every month for six months, I can guarantee that the Tecton will take your application for a Berrysville Sime Center very seriously, indeed."

"But…that's almost one sixth of our adult population!" she protested.

"Yes," Den agreed. "Looked at another way, it's just three donations a day. Almost enough to keep a Third Order channel healthy, if we rotate personnel back to Clear Springs every few weeks."

The woman blinked. "Well, uh…I will let our town council know the Tecton's terms and we'll see what happens." She started to sit down, but popped back up again. "Hey, Fredricks—you be sure to put that in the paper, so my townsfolk will believe me!"

"And Miz Mills," Den added, "if a child goes into changeover in Berrysville, or if you *think* it may be changeover, you are welcome to bring that child to our Sime Center for a diagnosis. If it is changeover, our channels can offer proper care and arrange for the assistance the new Sime will require to start life in Nivet Territory."

"I'm supposed to transport a Sime myself?" the woman asked.

"Changeover takes time. Let me be specific: if you see streaks on the child's arms, but they are not yet swollen above the skin, you have at a minimum *eight hours* to get that incipient Sime to a channel. So yes, you can transport a child in changeover safely in any available vehicle, as long as you do it before the tentacles form in their sheaths. If you ever think a child *might* be in changeover, *bring that child to us.* We *don't* mind false alarms. It's far better than letting an adolescent be murdered for contracting common flu with fever and vomiting."

"That's another thing," a new questioner asked, "if channels provide the medical care in Simeland, why doesn't the Clear Springs Sime Center provide such care?"

"Channels follow an ethical code much like that of your doctors," the Donor answered dryly. "Among other things, it requires the patient's consent for treatment."

That brought a volley of questions about what ailments channels could treat and how. Den answered a few, then begged off, saying "We'd be here all night. If you have a health problem your doctor cannot treat, you are welcome to have a channel examine you. The main advantage channels have over Gen doctors is in diagnosis. Once the problem is identified, you can decide where to go for treatment."

The most difficult question came from Professor Fibes, Branlee's former major professor. "Sosu Milnan, the recent power failure at the Center for Technology, triggered by your experiment, was unusually severe. What failed during your experiment? Was it predictable, or unanticipated?"

There was nothing Den wanted less than to discuss that disaster with an out-Territory audience. On the other hand, these trained logical thinkers might understand the importance of improving selyn batteries.

"It wasn't an unanticipated failure that burned out the orgonics," Den explained. "It was an unanticipated success."

People leaned forward eagerly. Encouraged, Den continued. "We were attempting to design a lightweight selyn battery. We anticipated small improvements, but instead created one with a capacity so large that it burned out the orgonics and melted the electrical wiring, too."

"Of what use is such a battery?" asked a tall woman at the back.

"It would make any process that requires moving batteries more efficient, and therefore less expensive," Den said. "That includes selyn-powered vehicles and the sliderail train network, which could expand if its cost in selyn could be brought down. Eventually…"

He hesitated. Would this audience understand his dream, the dream Eddina had shared and tasked him with completing?

"…eventually, I hope to design a battery small enough to power a flying machine, like the Ancients used. Even if we use trains for routine transportation, flyers would save lives in disaster situations. Small rescue parties can make a huge difference in outcome, but only if they arrive quickly."

"This enterprise is obviously important to you, on a personal level," Professor Ildun remarked. "Would you mind sharing why?"

Does Ildun want to know whether I'll reveal his disaster-prone son's role in the accident? The professor no longer had a hold over Den to ensure his silence and, while Chancellor Orzoff hadn't found it cost-effective to punish Branlee, Ildun had tenure and academic feuds could be vicious.

"My aunt and uncle died when a damaged trestle collapsed and spilled their train into a flooding river," Den explained. "Everyone knew the bridge was unsafe, but the people on the other side were desperate for help. Flying the would-be rescuers across would have saved countless lives."

Ildun looked relieved.

Webber called off the interrogation after half an hour, but when Den joined the line for refreshments, he was cornered by a man who introduced himself as, "Dr. Lennard. I run the medical clinic in Berrysville." The young physician consumed three cups of strong coffee as he interrogated Den on how the in-Territory medical profession handled various conditions. The Donor hadn't faced such an inquisition since his oral proficiency exams, and those had been in Simelan.

Still, it was refreshing not to face accusations that the Sime Center harmed the vaguely defined "spiritual welfare" of those who used its services. The Rational Deists might have a strange definition of theology, but they judged the Sime Center by the real-world consequences of its actions.

Besides, the Donor thought, *Rital will be glad to know there's one group of out-Territory Gens who would appreciate his inability to keep his big mouth shut.*

* * * *

The Rational Deists were one out-Territory denomination among many. Den lost track of them as more immediate concerns took his attention. His transfer with Tyvi satisfied the channel, but not Den. He soothed his frustration by telling himself Rital was due for a rotation. Monruss was unlikely to send another First Order Donor to Clear Springs when Quess left because Den was already present.

Sure enough, the green transfer assignment card Den received a few days later had his cousin's name on it. He put it on his desk, next to the growing waiting list for changeover classes. He paused at intervals to gloat over both documents. When his thoughts turned to the lab, where beakers blue-tinted with Alyce's fungicide remained free of spoilage, he would gloat some more.

Two transfers with Quess had left Rital in excellent shape, so Den didn't have to provide the therapy his cousin had required after Siv Alson. Instead, Den held Rital to his promise to help the Donor learn to use the new capacity in which the channel still didn't really believe.

They spent an hour each day on training drills meant to make Tecton-standard field handling a reflex for new Donors. It was like growing up all over again—his new sensitivity threw his perceptions slightly *off*, the way throwing a ball was slightly different every week during a growth spurt. The drills were frustrating, because Den had to unlearn reflexes born of years of experience in the field.

As his performance improved, Rital started throwing unexpected field gradients, forcing him to be aware of the fields every moment. Gradually, the channel became less selective about times for these drills, until Den might be required to pick up the fields instantly, even when his cousin was doing something that made improper control risky.

The selyn battery improvement project, in contrast, seemed content to let the Bordo fungicide preserve the status quo. Branlee and Den tested every chemical that might have been misplaced onto shelves that Raymond could reach, plus every substance in the closet and even various plastics and metals. Nothing provided further improvement in selyn-holding capacity. The small, empty battery box taunted Den.

Branlee continued de-commissioning Professor Fibes's lab. Boxes unrelated to the battery project appeared in the basement lab, as the graduate student salvaged materials that he couldn't bear to simply throw away. Raymond helped, but even Branlee's bribes of three magnets, a vial of iron filings and six different colors of tape hadn't gotten any useful information out of him.

Tohm, now working part time at his father's law firm, filed patents for selyn battery gel containing sunflower or grapeseed oil, coffee, or trin tea. "They may not power an aircraft," he admitted, "but they're a reproducible improvement to the existing technology." Tohm also helped Hald's orgonics repair team patent their new connectors.

The *Clarion's* coverage of the changeover class continued. Reverend Sinth ran a demonstration in front of the school each morning, before heading to the Sime Center for regular donor harassment. This was no mean sacrifice, since the weather had turned cold and nasty.

The protesters' inability to isolate the changeover class students didn't endear them to parents whose kids were screamed at every morning. Sinth's claim that the classes endangered student health and morals was unpersuasive, when each lesson was accurately described in the next day's newspaper.

Some parents decided that changeover classes were acceptable, since only raving fanatics opposed them. The waiting list continued to grow, Principal Buchan reported at the opening of their second session.

"Good," Den said, "because five of our new students have already Established."

"I'll have the secretary notify the next five on the waiting list," the principal offered. "We could add a second section, if you have teachers for it."

"We'll see what we can do," Rital promised.

"If you can commit within two weeks, we could start two sections with the next activity cycle. I want every child, whose parents allow it, to learn about changeover. If my Jainy hadn't taken your class…" His voice caught. "I want her life to be remembered."

"I understand," Den said, "and we appreciate your support."

If Buchan could make the changeover classes Jain's legacy, why couldn't Den honor Eddina's memory? If Buchan could stand against Sinth, surely Den could figure out what had landed in a tub of gel? The tub was not sentient. Despite appearances, it had no malevolent intent.

* * * *

The following morning, the Sime Center got a call to pick up a child in changeover. The youngster wasn't one of their students, but she had met Rital in the halls of her school. Her acceptance didn't extend to the other channels, though, which left Rital with a dilemma.

"I can't leave her, Den," he said softly, so as not to wake their patient. "Not for the two hours it would take to teach our class and get back here. Tyvi and Reyna are on Collectorium duty and Zir doesn't know anything about teaching. I could send Gati with you, I suppose…"

"I can teach the class by myself," Den said. "I'll just substitute tomorrow's lecture on Gen anatomy for today's lesson on Gen safety around Simes. I don't like leaving you without a Donor when you're managing a changeover, though."

Rital zlinned his patient. "You'll be back long before she hits Stage Four. If there's an emergency, Quess can cover. Tyvi only requires a Donor for the borderline Simephobes and they can wait, if necessary."

It's Rital's call as Controller, the Donor realized, *and if I want him to respect my judgment as a Donor, I'll have to return the favor.*

Rital grinned reassuringly. "Give my regrets to our students," he said. "And tell the five new ones that tomorrow I'll let them know if they've Established."

Before he left, Den privately asked Seena to call him at the school if Rital requested Quess's aid. *Even a Farris Donor couldn't provide support to two channels working in two separate departments.*

The students were curious when he explained why Rital wasn't present. *At least they seem to find it reassuring,* the Donor reflected as he began his lecture, noting the absence of their *Clarion* reporter.

It wasn't only the children who had noticed the channel's absence. Den was explaining the differences between GN and TN selyn storage levels when the classroom door burst open.

"This obscenity stops now!" Cessly Lornstadt screamed. Close behind her came more Save Our Kids demonstrators. The turmeric-haired man and an equally husky friend grabbed Den while Cessly and Len Dusam, who had run for mayor last year on an anti-Sime platform, descended on the supply table.

They dumped the undistributed handouts on the floor, kicked them into a pile, then ripped down the posters of Sime and Gen nervous systems and deposited them on top. Florence Grieves, whose younger daughter had Killed her older sister, took a large bottle of blue ink from her purse and emptied it over the pile.

Den struggled, but, like most in-Territory Gens, he hadn't settled an argument with his fists since his Establishment. In-Territory, every Sime within zlinning distance converged immediately to prevent a Gen from being harmed. With no Simes to object, Den longed to plant a fist in the turmeric-haired man's smug face, but there were his students to consider. *Besides, Rital would have a fit.*

The students' voices added to the confusion as the vandals let go of Den, whipped out handcuffs, and chained themselves to the most immovable objects they could find.

"You'll not teach filth today, Sime-lover, so go back to your slimy friends," Cessly announced as she tested the bracelet imprisoning her right wrist. She had opened two windows and secured herself to the frame between them. Den hoped the cold draft chilled her thoroughly.

A chant of "Sime-lover go home!" arose as Den herded his students into the hall and closed the door, leaving the protestors self-imprisoned within. He sent the most level-headed girl to fetch Principal Buchan and concentrated on calming the other students.

"Sosu Milnan, what's the problem?" Buchan asked. Ten eager voices, none of them Den's, started to answer. The principal held up a hand. "Quiet down," he admonished.

The Donor explained, "Some members of Save Our Kids decided to end the changeover class." He gestured to the closed door, through which the strains of a hymn could be heard.

Buchan opened the door, glanced in, and chuckled. The vandals broke off singing to yell insults. The principal calmly shut the door again. "Your teaching materials are beyond salvage."

"We have plenty more at the Sime Center."

"That's the spirit." Buchan clapped the Donor on the shoulder. "Never hand your opponent the victory. I'll call the police. Handy, how our troublemakers detained themselves."

The police were accompanied by the reporter from the *Clarion*. While they waited for a locksmith to unfasten the handcuffs, the police photographer documented the damage. The officer in charge asked to take Den's statement, "so an officer doesn't have to make a trip out to the Sime Center." A quick telephone call to Seena assured him that Rital wasn't in trouble, so the Donor agreed to stay.

He paced the school's lobby, too angry to sit. His students were dismissed to a study hall, but other classes continued as usual.

"I'll see that this doesn't happen again," Buchan promised later, as the shivering vandals were led away. "And they *will* be prosecuted. Demonstrating on the sidewalk is one thing; disrupting a class on school grounds is a different matter. Not to mention damaging the floor."

"Actually," Den said, signing his statement, "on *my* side of the border, their treatment of selyn donors in front of the Sime Center would be the more serious crime."

"Really?" Buchan asked curiously. "Why is that?"

The Donor shrugged. "Simes are averse to any physical threat to a Gen, particularly one who donates selyn. One learns to tolerate a bit of over-protectiveness."

CHAPTER 15

MOBILE SERVICES

Den was relieved to find Rital and his patient unharmed by his prolonged absence. He was less pleased with the *Clarion's* front-page coverage of the incident. **VANDALS INVADE SCHOOL, INTERRUPT CHANGE-OVER CLASS** the headline announced over the photo of a grinning Cessly Lornstadt. Thirteen students had been distracted by the commotion and arrived late for gym class, the article claimed. Den could almost feel Sinth gloating that his destructive prank had banished the reopening of the Center for Technology to an interior page.

Den wished the bill for the repair work could disappear as easily. His share of profits from the polycarbonate sheet sales, combined with the portion of his income that wasn't supporting himself and Branlee, was enough to mollify Controller Monruss for a while, but it would be years before he could begin the monumental task of designing a motor powerful enough to pull a flyer through the air.

It would also be a long time before the out-Territory courts would curb Reverend Sinth. The charge was disturbing the peace, with a token fine. Since the teaching materials were provided free, Judge Lindsey ruled their market value could not be determined. Cessly and her friends owed no compensation.

"We'll do what is necessary to stop Sime takeover of our community," Reverend Sinth proclaimed in the *Clarion.* "We gladly break earthly laws in God's service, for we follow His laws first."

"That's easy for *him* to say," Annie Lifton scoffed when she dropped by for her monthly selyn donation. "*He* didn't pay the lawyers and fines. He'll do a mass mailing within the week anyway, begging for contributions to offset expenses he didn't cover."

Even Coach Farrow was displeased with Cessly and her partners in crime. "How can children prepare for serious competition when hoodlums bombard them with political rhetoric?" his letter to the editor demanded. "It is time to restore order in our schools."

There was an emerging consensus that Sinth and his followers were not reasonable people. The school increased security, although Den thought

privately that Rital's unshielded tentacles were a far stronger deterrent…
and the waiting list for changeover classes grew to four pages, then five.

"We misjudged the parents of Clear Springs, Rital," an amused Den
observed over breakfast. "They may be obsessed with athletics, but they
want an orderly, if not rigorous, academic curriculum. According to their
letters, ripping up posters is a major crime, but assaulting donors is legitimate political expression." He grinned. "Maybe you should refuse to refill
the batteries at their Center for Technology until they clear Save Our Kids
off our sidewalk. It worked that time they passed an ordinance forbidding
us to leave the Sime Center."

"They're starting to see changeover classes as part of a child's education," Rital said, appropriating the front page.

"The Sime Center as part of an education," Den murmured, gazing off
into space. "Of course!"

"Of course what?" Rital asked, zlinning his cousin suspiciously.
"You've found a new way to make trouble, haven't you?"

"Me?" Den asked innocently. Then, "Seriously, I don't think it'll cause
much trouble. Many parents *do* want the Sime Center. The waiting list for
changeover classes speaks for itself. Ever since Miz Dilson asked about
books for children, I've been thinking: if parents and children are *both*
comfortable with the Sime Center before the children reach changeover
age, we'll win."

"You have a way to do that?"

"Yes," Den leaned forward eagerly. "A Children's Day. We give tours
of the Sime Center and hand out pamphlets and balloons. Any parents who
wish can donate selyn, letting their children watch."

"A brilliant idea," Rital drawled.

Stung by the channel's sarcasm, the Donor pointed out, "It worked for
Jain."

"It would work for the children of experienced donors," Rital conceded, "but what if an inexperienced parent panics?" His voice assumed a
syrupy tone. "Look, children, see the nice channel terrify your mommy and
daddy. Doesn't that make you want to donate selyn when you grow up?"

"At least they'll know donating isn't fatal!" Den snapped, annoyed.
"Even that's progress. If we show an unsheathed tentacle or two when they
arrive, Simephobes won't volunteer to donate."

Since the channels were careful to sheathe their tentacles in the Collectorium's waiting room for exactly that reason, the channel went on to a
new objection. "Our collecting rooms aren't set up for observers."

Den shrugged. "A child's nager won't cause problems. With a Donor
present, you'll hardly zlin them."

"It might work," Rital admitted, "but Monruss won't approve."

"Shen Monruss," Den said, snapping his nager rudely. "He sent us here to do an impossible job and tied future advancement to our success. His last directive recommended more community outreach, so that's exactly what we'll do."

The channel shook his head in mock despair. "Why do I let you talk me into these things."

"Look at it this way," said Den said. "When those children start donating, they'll be easier to handle than their parents."

* * * *

Den advertised his Children's Day in the *Clarion* and asked Principal Buchan and the principal at the elementary school to send a notice to parents. OLD SOKS distributed fliers at the Farmer's Market.

Reverend Sinth covered walls, trees, and bulletin boards with angry denunciations of this "**PLOT to seduce your children into EVIL!**"

The fliers spread to nearby towns, with an unexpected result. Den was translating for Arth one afternoon, fighting sleep after spending the night seeing Rital through an unexpectedly difficult Turnover, when Seena poked her head in. "Sosu Milnan, a selyn donor wants to talk to you about Children's Day."

"I'll be right there." Den finished the current file, then excused himself. When he entered the waiting room, a half-dozen Gens looked up, saw he wasn't a channel, and all but one went back to reading. The exception, a familiar, silver-haired woman, rose to greet Den.

"Sosu Milnan, it's good of you to see me so promptly," Flora Mills said cordially, extending a hand.

Den shook it smoothly.

She went straight to the point. "I still hold that small communities like Berrysville are shortchanged by your policy of placing Sime Centers only in large cities."

"Miz Mills," the Donor said patiently, "You can only persuade the Tecton to open a Sime Center by proving there are enough selyn donors in the community to keep a channel healthy. Cities like Clear Springs meet that specification, but small towns just don't."

"Yet. Check your records. Berrysville had thirty-five donors last month and twenty-two the month before. They were mostly different people, too." She looked at him sternly. "The primary difficulty is that you're only getting those who have other business they can't manage closer to home, which is hardly a fair measure of local interest."

Den sighed. "I realize the injustice—and the urgency you feel—but there simply isn't any other way to measure how many people would actually donate selyn."

The satisfied look on Flora Mills' face should have warned Den. "Perhaps not," she argued. "We agree that your current measure of interest in a permanent Sime Center for Berrysville is flawed. So, how about getting a better measure of the number of local selyn donors with a temporary Center?"

"What?" Den asked, wishing he were more clear-headed.

"Quite frankly, it's a nuisance to travel to Clear Springs to donate selyn. If my daughter and her family didn't live here, I probably wouldn't bother. Many Berrysville folks *don't* bother, though they'd be glad to donate locally. Others want to know whether their children are out of danger for changeover. That's enough people to keep a channel busy for, say, one day each month?" She held his eye, daring him to contradict her.

"Definitely," the Donor said. "Still, I doubt the Berrysville officials would let us use city property for such a controversial purpose."

"True," Flora agreed, with a ladylike contempt for cowardice. "I should know: my boy Jon is our Mayor. Fortunately, the rest of us Rational Deists aren't concerned with public opinion or reelection. We've already voted to host a temporary Sime Center once a month, if the Tecton will send us a channel. How about next week?"

"Umm," Den stammered, trying to catch up with Flora's enthusiasm. "That decision rests with the Controller…"

"Fine. Let's go talk to him."

The discussion was attracting attention. To avoid a public scene, the Donor escorted Flora to his cousin's office. She didn't know how skeptically Rital viewed stunts so far outside standard procedure.

But Den had overlooked the fact that, most of the time, he had convinced Rital to allow his "stunts." The channel was past the instability of Turnover, but still no match for such a determined Gen. To Den's surprise, his cousin didn't even try to resist. Before she left, Flora Mills had extracted a firm commitment for at least one channel and Donor to visit Berrysville the following week.

* * * *

The more Den considered Flora's scheme, the more he regretted it. Berrysville was eight miles away and its citizens were much less cosmopolitan. In a small community that viewed outsiders with suspicion, there could be real trouble when a Sime came to visit.

Even worse, Rital was enthusiastic about the chance to reach so many untapped selyn donors. His only concession to common sense was to go to Berrysville personally, rather than ask another channel to risk it. Saving the most dangerous and difficult work for the best channel was a tradition as old as channeling, but that didn't make Den any happier. His cousin was growing unstable as he approached Need and Den's help was less effective than the Donor liked. There was an underlying core of resistance in Rital that he couldn't overcome. *I thought we'd settled our differences.*

* * * *

On the appointed morning, Den was in the staff car's back seat, trying to protect Rital from the nausea induced by traveling in retainers. It was a bitterly cold day and sudden gusts of wind swayed the car unpredictably. Seena drove, with Ref in the passenger seat. Both were steady GN-1s above midfield, calm role models for any inexperienced Gens donating today.

The Berrysville Rational Deist Meeting Hall was smaller than the one in Clear Springs, but built of selyn-insulating stone. *There's not much soundproofing, though.* Den could hear a hymn echoing from the back of the building. Sinth's demonstrators had made Den a reluctant expert on out-Territory religious music. This song didn't follow the usual themes:

> *"My thoughts, they are free, no one can betray them.*
> *They're secret to me, unless I should say them.*
> *They never will cower before mortal power.*
> *This truth I decree: my thoughts they are free!"*

That song's composer never lived in-Territory, the Donor concluded. While Simes couldn't read minds, zlinning emotions could be more useful, since most people acted based on their feelings, not their thoughts.

They had arrived early to let Rital recover from the journey. Flora Mills was directing volunteers setting up chairs in the sanctuary. Den recognized a few selyn donors among them, but most were strangers.

Flora bustled over. "I'm glad you're early," she said. "We'll use the sanctuary as a waiting area. That horrible moaning is the coffee urn. It'll quiet down once the water's hot. We're mulling cider for the children. On a day like this, everyone wants a warming drink." She cast a sharp eye on the box that Ref carried. "What's that?" she asked.

"Pamphlets on changeover and Sime Center services," Den said. "Where would you like them placed?"

"Berl, Cadey," Flora flagged down two of her helpers. "Put out another table, would you?" She turned back to Rital. "Hajene Madz, you'll work in our library." She took them to a room directly off the sanctuary.

"This will do nicely," the channel said.

The cheerful little room featured floor-to-ceiling bookcases filled with an eclectic variety of well-thumbed volumes. The mantel over the fireplace held pottery vases with imaginative design flaws and unusual choices of color that suggested children's work. A fire warmed the room.

The library held a small desk, several upholstered chairs, and a large couch. It wasn't a transfer lounge, but lying down comfortably might help nervous selyn donors relax. Best of all, the book-lined stone walls provided insulation from the ambient nager–and noise–in the main room.

Hald's team had constructed portable selyn-insulating screens from Branlee's rust-impregnated polycarbonate. They blocked the ambient nager well, but provided no soundproofing. Out-Territory Gens associated privacy with freedom from eavesdroppers, not from nageric clutter. Any loud sound from behind such a screen might startle nervous Gens waiting to donate, wondering what was being hidden from them. Assuming there were any waiting to donate.

Den left Rital in the library and went to post the "Sime Territory" signs. The sooner he got his cousin out of retainers, the better.

More volunteers had arrived, including Dr. Lennard, the young physician who had questioned Den about in-Territory healing techniques. Seena and Ref were laying out pamphlets and forms.

Den sorted through Establishment certificates, donation consent slips, and medical history forms until he found the signs. As he went to retrieve hangers from the car, he spotted a familiar bus parked just down the road. Cessly Lornstadt's face peered out the window and Den recognized other Save Our Kids members inside, too.

Den posted the signs that allowed Rital to remove his retainers, then warned Flora Mills about the demonstrators outside.

"We're expecting them," she said calmly.

The choir rehearsal ended just as the demonstrators started their first chant. The singers, including the choir director, raided Flora's refreshment table, then reassembled on the sidewalk out front.

Cessly Lornstadt had brought her two young children. The shivering and reluctant youngsters held up a banner reading "**Protect the Children.**" *Any parent who makes her children picket on such a cold, windy day is guilty of abuse.* The choir members, unlike OLD SOKS, avoided obscene drinking ballads. They resumed work on their hymn:

> *"I think what I wish; it's all part of knowing*
> *The world as it is, and where it is going.*
> *My thoughts give me traction to take proper action.*
> *It's simple, you see: my thoughts they are free!"*

* * * *

Den's fears that no one would donate selyn proved unfounded. The first volunteer was Dr. Lennard, who provided Rital with an unexpected challenge. He wasn't upset or repelled by his first sight of tentacles—quite the opposite. He wanted to examine them to determine how they worked. The channel quieted him by demonstrating.

Despite Save Our Kids and the bad weather, by the end of the afternoon most of the pamphlets had been taken. Dr. Lennard appropriated the rest for his waiting room. All the Establishment certificates had been presented to relieved youngsters and Den had names and addresses for three more young Gens who would receive theirs by mail. Seventeen Gens had donated selyn, including one couple who asked that their four children be allowed to watch. Two of the children responded to Rital's patient coaxing and touched his handling tentacles. Most interesting of all, one woman wanted Rital to zlin whether her recent surgery had removed all of a malignant breast tumor.

"Dr. Lennard said you could tell us, Hajene," her husband said, eying the channel's tentacles nervously.

"I'm *not* going through more treatment unless it's absolutely necessary," his wife concluded firmly.

Once he got over his horror at the way she had been mutilated, Rital was able to give her good news.

They stayed an hour later than planned and were all exhausted. Rital was more stressed by the day's work than a First Order channel should be, even working in makeshift facilities and approaching Need.

* * * *

Den wondered if his fieldwork was still off, but Rital swore he had progressed amazingly. Still, as their transfer date approached, Rital suppressed his Need more than required to protect his clients. *Which is just as problematic as his carelessness with his speech.*

Den scoured Rital's records of the past two months for traumas, but found nothing. He was worried enough to consult Quess, but the older Donor didn't know what the problem might be. All Den could do was free extra time to work with his cousin, possible because Hald's team had taken over the packing and shipping of polycarbonate sheets.

On their transfer day, Den took Rital to the transfer suite an hour early. He worked to raise the channel's intil, the psychological component of Need, with only moderate success.

His cousin patted his hand in comfort. "Don't be nervous, Den," the channel said in the soothing tone reserved for skittish new donors. "I won't burn you again, but if you like, we'll ask Tyvi to monitor."

"So *that's* why you've been fighting me!" Den laughed. "I thought we settled that weeks ago. I'm not afraid you'll hurt me! I've been worried sick you'll hold back and spoil this. It's been three months since I was really Post. I'm not willing to settle for less."

Zlinning his cousin's sincerity, Rital finally relaxed and let the Donor coax his Need to the surface. Still, he refused to let the transfer set its own pace, keeping the speed below even their usual.

Den wanted to howl with frustration as the flow peaked and ebbed without tapping his new capacity. *I earned it the hard way and now he's too timid to let us enjoy it!* The Donor did retain the presence of mind not to grab control and force Rital's draw.

After being stuck giving transfer to lower-rated channels for so many months, it was genuine shen to go unfulfilled yet again, without even the vicarious pleasure of knowing his partner was fully satisfied. *Gati won't speak to me for a week.*

Settling our misunderstandings was only the first step, Den realized as he helped his cousin through the inadequate Postsyndrome. *I've got to re-build Rital's confidence–in himself, as well as in me.* That would be a long, slow process that no amount of chocolate could hasten.

* * * *

To Den's disappointment, his next transfer assignment was with Tyvi, while Quess would once again have Rital. Den was starting to wonder about the older Donor's continued presence. Neither Rital nor Tyvi required a Donor of Quess's ability and the diplomat had had ample time to evaluate the situation in Clear Springs.

Added to the mystery was Quess's "personal business." *What sort of personal business does a high-ranking Householding Donor like Quess have in an obscure out-Territory town?* he wondered when Quess left him in charge for the second time in a week. Householding business seemed unlikely. Shaeldor specialized in ships and shipping. There was no navigable river closer to Clear Springs than Oxbow, although there was a sliderail line from there to Sanger. The surveyors had only started mapping a direct route between Sanger and Clear Springs. It would be at least a year before the first train.

To ease his frustration, Den focused on Children's Day. He ordered pamphlets and balloons from Valzor, placed a full-page ad in the *Clarion,* and consulted Ref about refreshments. He even recruited Arth Tinkum's girlfriend, an art student, to paint decorations on the younger children's faces.

The staff pitched in to help, scrubbing the Sime Center until it sparkled. Jesper Reft replaced the slipcovers on the transfer lounges. Den also had one of the spare collecting rooms set up, knowing some parents would not let children watch their donations. With an empty collecting room in the tour, Den could describe donating selyn to everyone.

The big day dawned cold but clear. Save Our Kids arrived half an hour early, Reverend Sinth's tall, forbidding figure much in evidence. OLD SOKS was reinforced by volunteers from the Rational Deists. For once, the counterdemonstrators could maintain a clear path into the Sime Center.

The first three families arrived at opening time and helped themselves to refreshments. One little girl wanted her face painted immediately with "a biiiiig flower, red like my pants." While Arth's girlfriend worked, the girl's mother joined a couple with three children at the pamphlet display. A man who had brought his two sons wanted them to see him donate "at once, we've got to be at Grandma's for lunch," so Den sent them off with Rital and Quess. When the little girl's forehead was adorned, the Donor began his first tour.

By mid-morning, the lobby was filled. There were enough families waiting in the Collectorium to keep all the channels busy.

Looking out the window, the Donor noticed nearly half the Save Our Kids demonstrators were missing—*including Cessly Lornstadt and her kids. I guess she has some sense, after all,* Den observed. Reverend Sinth tirelessly screamed threats of damnation at the passing parents. The turmeric-haired man at his side called a fervent "Amen!" on the rare occasions when the preacher paused for breath. With so few demonstrators to block, OLD SOKS and the Rational Deists started rotating a portion of their group inside to warm up.

Den's latest tour reached the empty collecting room and he was patiently explaining once more that donating selyn *didn't* hurt Gens, when there was a commotion out in the hall. He stepped out to investigate.

Shouts echoed from the waiting room, but a more immediate problem headed down the hall toward him: Cessly Lornstadt, dragging her children behind her. She saw Den and immediately dodged through the nearest door, ignoring the flashing "in use" light.

It was the collecting room Reyna Tast preferred. The elderly Third Order channel only handled experienced Gens and she was pre-Turnover. However, she was working alone today because her Donor, Hammil, was confined to his room with a cold.

Reyna insisted on doing her Collectorium duty; her only concession was agreeing to leave families with Established "children" to Zir or Rital. A child's nager, she said firmly, wouldn't disturb her in the least, so there was no reason to expect any problems.

But since when do problems arrive when you expect them?

Den slipped through the door after Cessly and her children, using his selyn field to grasp control of the ambient.

To his relief, the transfer lounge was unoccupied, so Reyna had not been disturbed during the vulnerable moment of selyn flow. However, the intruders had shoved her elderly client, Mr. Duncan, to the floor. As Reyna zlinned him for injuries, Den glared at Cessly.

She smiled back at him, jiggling her left wrist, securely handcuffed to one of the cabinets behind the desk. Her children were secured to the legs of the heavy oak desk. They looked up at him, eyes enormous.

Mr. Duncan glared. "What idiotic prank are you playing, Cessly?"

"Those Sime-loving collaborators on the sidewalk won't let us near the deluded victims lured here today," she said, smiling sweetly, "but your friends, the snakes, can't eject us from here! If they want to stop us from telling the truth about them, they'll have to close down for days, until the in-Territory police get here."

She's right, the Donor thought grimly.

"However," Cessly looked at Den slyly, "Clear Springs Police Chief Tains happens to have duplicate keys to our handcuffs. If you ask him nicely, he might let you post the Sime Center as Gen Territory long enough for him to free us. He'll even arrest us for trespassing. Of course, he's a busy man. He can't respond to your call before the press gets here, so I'm afraid the whole town will learn the truth about donating selyn…"

"The truth about donating?" Mr. Duncan scoffed. "It's time *you* learned it, Cessly!" Ignoring Reyna's protests, he struggled to his feet, then stalked stiffly over to sit on the transfer lounge. "If you would oblige, lovely lady?" he asked Reyna politely, rolling up his sleeves.

Reyna hesitated, weighing the advisability of taking a selyn donation from an angry Gen with a high-field Simephobe in the room. Then she zlinned Mr. Duncan and turned to Den, her eyes twinkling with suppressed glee. "Of course," she replied with equal courtesy, signaling the Donor to attend her with a graceful gesture of two handling tentacles. She joined Mr. Duncan on the lounge with the dignity of a Tigue matriarch in a corporate boardroom. *He's dispelled his anger.*

"Not in front of the children!" Cessly squealed, horror in her wide eyes.

"Why not?" Den asked. "It *is* Children's Day." He drifted across the small room, to the spot from which he could best control the ambient nager. Mr. Duncan was an experienced selyn donor, so Den's primary concern was to keep Cessly's nager from interfering: an easy task, since the Donor carried more selyn than anyone else in the room.

He perched on the desk, where he could block Cessly's nager while giving her—and her wide-eyed children—a good view of the proceedings.

"Zeke, Clarinda, you are not to watch," Cessly ordered as Reyna took Mr. Duncan's offered hands. "This is a grownup thing." She couldn't have said anything better calculated to pique childish curiosity.

"I'm big now, Mommy," Zeke proclaimed, with the full authority of his five years.

"So am I," his three-year-old sister chimed in.

"You are not!" scoffed her brother.

"Am, too!"

"No more backtalk," Cessly snapped. "Remember, bad children turn into Sime monsters. Cover your faces at once."

The two children cringed at this threat and covered their faces with their hands, peeking avidly through their fingers. Cessly gasped in horror when Reyna made the transfer contact, but her children…giggled.

"They're kissing!" Clarinda squealed, with a child's delight in catching an adult being naughty.

"Yuck!" Zeke said. "Mushy stuff!"

"Give yourself time, son," Mr. Duncan said, sitting up as Reyna released him. "In ten years, you'll be surprised how much fun it is to kiss a pretty lady."

The little boy considered this claim for a moment. "Naww," he denied skeptically. Losing interest in "mushy stuff," he returned to more important matters. "Mommy, I hafta go to the bathroom."

"Me, too," Clarinda said.

"I told you to take care of that before we left the house!" Cessly reminded them.

"That was hours ago," Zeke complained. "I hafta go again."

"So do I," Clarinda agreed.

"You'll have to wait," their mother said helplessly.

"Nonsense," Reyna said as she stood stiffly. Den moved to her side. "There's a bathroom right down the hall."

"But I can't," the boy protested, pulling on the handcuff that chained him to the desk's leg.

"Me, neither," Clarinda chimed in, jingling her own.

"Here." Reyna knelt next to the children. "I'll lift the desk and you two can slip those bracelets right off the ends of the legs."

"Get away from my children, snake!" Cessly demanded.

Ignoring the belated display of parental concern, the channel got a good hold on the edge of the desk and tilted it, augmenting to manage the weight. Den helped the children free themselves, then made sure no small feet or fingers got in the way when she lowered the heavy piece of furniture back to the floor.

"There you are," she said kindly. "Let's find that bathroom now, shall we?"

"Zeke, Clarinda, you sit back down and behave yourselves!" Cessly ordered.

"But, Mommy, I gotta go to the bathroom," her son explained with childish logic.

"Me, too," his sister lisped indignantly.

"Come along, then, and I'll show you where it is." Reyna held out a hand to each, tentacles retracted. Turning their backs on their mother, the children took the channel's hands and let her lead them out the door.

Den looked from the outraged Cessly, who wailed, "My babies!" to the chuckling Mr. Duncan. The elderly donor shook an admonitory finger at Den, who shrugged innocently. Leaving Cessly chained to the cabinet, the two Gens left the collecting room, ignoring her startled squawk as the Donor turned out the light.

Den escorted Mr. Duncan to the waiting room and discovered six additional Save Our Kids members chained to furniture. Cessly's husband, Ephriam, led the group in a hymn from his seat by the reception desk, keeping time by clanking his handcuff against the wastebasket.

The Reverend Jermiah Sinth was conspicuous by his absence. *He'll risk anything to close us down,* Den thought cynically, *except running out of melic weed.* The preacher had undergone forced withdrawal from the drug during his incarceration in-Territory, where even the contraband brokers refused to trade with him. *Why should Sinth risk jail, when he has followers eager to accept the penalty? I doubt they'll see any of the contributions he collects for their defense, either.*

The Gens waiting to donate milled about, exchanging remarks with Den's tour group, who had come to see what the uproar was about. Rital and Quess tried to calm them and the excited children.

The channel looked up when he zlinned Den. "I don't suppose your Children's Day plan included this, did it, cousin?"

"Not exactly," the Donor admitted.

"Seena called Valzor. The police might arrive tomorrow, soonest."

"The lorshes are counting on that," Den said. He explained about the duplicate keys in Chief Tain's possession. "They've already called the *Clarion.*"

"We can't allow them to use us for publicity," Rital declared.

"Then we'll deal with the situation ourselves." Den looked around thoughtfully. "Move everyone to the main lobby, then leave the press to me. I'll give them a story about Children's Day, not Save Our Kids."

"It might work," Rital admitted. "What about the demonstrators?"

The Donor shrugged. "They aren't going anywhere," he said in Simelan.

But Ephriam Lornstadt paused his singing to sneer, "Call Chief Tains, Sime-lover. You can do nothing to us!"

"Exactly," Den switched languages, smiling maliciously. "I promise, we will do nothing to you."

When the room was emptied of out-Territory visitors–the invited ones, anyway–Den asked Ephriam Lornstadt, "Have you and your wife made provisions for your children?"

"Our neighbor, Miz Terlin, will look after them for a few hours," he answered indifferently.

"I meant for the next three years or so," Den clarified, "while you and your wife are in jail."

"WHAT!" Lornstadt tried to jump to his feet, but the handcuff prevented him from standing. "Chief Tains will arrest us for trespassing. That's punishable by a fine, not jail time."

The Donor shook his head. "Your leader forgot to clear his plan with us," he pointed out. "The Valzor Police have jurisdiction here, not Chief Tains. When they get here, in-Territory police will arrest you for disrupting a Sime Center. It's a second offense for you, and your wife barged into an occupied collecting room. You'll both be in jail for years. So, who's going to look after your kids?"

"My sister might take them," Lornstadt suggested hesitantly. "We've never been on the best of terms, though."

Den sighed. "How can we contact her?"

CHAPTER 16

A MYSTERY SOLVED

Despite the interruption, Children's Day was a success. Over a hundred families attended and an astonishing forty parents let their children watch their selyn donations. Most had donated before but, under the watchful eyes of their offspring, even the new donors sought to be calm, reducing stress on the channels.

A reporter and photographer arrived to cover Save Our Kids' occupation of the Collectorium. Den told them, "No one was harmed and we've dealt with the situation," gave them pamphlets, and invited them to take the tour, directing Gati to omit the Collectorium waiting room with its unwanted occupants. Fortunately, the witnesses to the occupation had gone. The news team left with a story about Children's Day, complete with smiling children with painted faces.

When the lobby was back in order, Den sought a well-earned supper. Ref had prepared a savory vegetable stew flavored with pomegranate juice and thickened with chopped walnuts, with a slice of sourdough bread made from Jain's mother's recipe.

In the dining room, Reyna and Quess were sharing a table with the Lornstadt children. "Do you mind if I join you?" he asked.

"Not at all," Reyna said cheerfully. "Children, finish your dinners quickly—there's pie for dessert."

Zeke glared at his bowl of stew. "It's all *vegetables!*"

"Why, so it is," Quess agreed amiably. "Delicious, aren't they?" He took a bite and patted his stomach in appreciation, saying, "Yumm."

Clarinda giggled. "Yumm, yumm!" she said, banging her spoon.

"No, you have to do it like this," Quess said. Taking another bite of stew, he demonstrated, "Yummmm!"

Giggling, the children began eating, punctuating each mouthful with an enthusiastic "Yumm!"

"Did you contact their aunt?" Den asked Reyna softly in Simelan.

The channel frowned. "Yes, but she won't take them. Their only surviving grandparent is too frail to care for herself, much less two active youngsters. I don't know what will become of them. They can't stay here."

Clear Springs was a hardship post, so the permanent staff were without young children. There was no provision for child care.

Quess leaned back in his chair and sighed. "I suppose they'll become wards of the New Washington Territory Court."

"Which will turn them over to Reverend Sinth," said Den. "His so-called church runs a horror house of an orphanage, where ill-fed children do forced labor for his profit. I'm not exaggerating," he protested at Quess's scandalized expression. "I can't tell you the worst of it while we're eating."

Quess studied Den's face for a moment, then offered, "If there is no appropriate place for them here, we can send them to Valzor with their parents. Shaeldor has a Children's Home in the city, to foster the children of our members when their parents must travel. If the elder Lornstadts agree, I'll arrange for the children to stay there, so they can visit their parents."

"The Lornstadts won't be pleased to have their children fostered by a Householding," Den predicted.

"I'm sure they are good enough parents to want their children nearby and able to visit. Is there a better solution?" the older Donor asked.

"Anything is better than Sinth's hellhole."

Quess frowned, but before he could question Den further, Zeke and Clarinda displayed their empty bowls and demanded pie. Reyna had finished her Sime-sized portion, so she and the children left the Gens to their conversation and went to explore the dessert table.

Quess looked after them. "Clarinda reminds me of my daughter," he said wistfully.

"The one who made the model ship on your desk?" Den asked.

"Yes. She died years ago." His voice had the flat tone of a Donor controlling strong emotion lest it disturb nearby Simes.

"If you'd rather not talk about it…" Den began.

"Thank you." Den recognized the older Donor's long stare into his bowl as a calming exercise. When Quess recovered his composure, he asked, "Would you cover Hajene Madz's Collectorium shift the day after tomorrow? I have personal business in town."

Den wondered again what mysterious "business" required the attention of a noted diplomat. However, if completing it meant the senior Donor would stop monopolizing Den's channel, Den was happy to facilitate. *And work on my stubborn cousin's foolish overprotectiveness.* "Sure," he agreed. "Things have been quiet lately. Mostly."

"Your friends Tohm and Silva are worried about Reverend Sinth's latest fundraising effort."

"For the farm he wants to buy out by Clearston? He plans to build a church and retreat center."

"I don't understand his motives," said Quess. "If he and his followers move to Clearston, they'll no longer be on your doorstep."

"We're concerned that he may move his reform school outside Clear Springs jurisdiction and much farther from the Sime Center."

"Ah," said Quess, folding his hands before him. "We've finished eating. What did you hesitate to tell me?"

Den saw that Reyna was keeping the children busy. She knew what he was about to reveal.

"Sinth runs a 'school' for orphans and children of his parishioners who are deemed 'out of control.'"

"Wait," said Quess. "Orphans not of his faith are put in his school?"

"It saves Clear Springs from having to develop a fostering system—they pay Sinth to take the kids in," Den explained.

"Hence it is a *reform* school," Quess said flatly. "Sinth would require every child to convert to his religion."

"It's worse than that," said Den. "Not long after we opened, a child went into changeover, but escaped to the Sime Center. If Sinth had caught him, he would have been…shot in the gut and thrown into a cage to bleed out as the other children were forced to watch. Sometimes the gut shots aren't severe enough, or the changeover is relatively advanced and…the child is allowed to die of Attrition, as an object lesson to the other children about what it means to become a Sime."

Quess's folded hands now gripped so tightly Den feared he might break a bone. The blood drained from his face and he swallowed, hard. Reyna turned, startled—but then immediately distracted the children toward ice cream and sprinkles for their pie.

Finally, Quess spoke again, his voice empty of emotion. "He calls it a church. But a church is a place of peace and comfort, contemplation and meditation."

Den shook his head. "A church is just a meeting hall, and it's only as peaceful as the person who runs it. Sinth will want the money the city would pay him to keep the Lornstadt children, so he will tell his congregation that what happened to their parents is our fault. He'll lead prayers for our destruction and tell his followers that they must honor the vows he made in their names."

"Independent adults aren't bound to honor a pledge someone else makes in their names," Quess objected. "That's ridiculous."

"Really?" Den raised a skeptical eyebrow. "Do you feel bound by decisions made by Householding Shaeldor, even if you personally oppose them?"

"Of course, and you and I are both bound by decisions of Tecton Controllers—but those are rules, not vows. We chose to take the vows we made when we joined the Tecton—and if we don't like their rules, we can campaign to change them."

"But didn't your parents vow their children to Shaeldor?" Den persisted.

"Yes, and the Householding in turn vowed to care for us if our parents could not. It's a custom left over from before Unity, when the junct government would incite riots against Householdings, appropriate the orphaned children and sell those with at least one Gen parent to Genfarms. We preserve that custom because it ensures that no matter what, decisions about our children's future won't be made by strangers who don't know them. If the Conservative Congregation church had that kind of vow, the Lornstadt children would be placed with a family known to them and remain among their friends."

Den nodded, remembering the confusion after Rital's parents had died. It had taken weeks for the overworked officials at the disaster site to figure out how to contact his family, because he couldn't remember his uncle's full name or what city he'd most recently been reassigned to. It was one more example of the privilege that Householders enjoyed, and which even the best of them didn't seem to notice.

"Den, I will require your backing and Rital's to make this work," Quess said. "The first step is to move the Lornstadt children in-Territory, before Sinth convinces the city to assume custody."

"Isn't that kidnapping, at least technically?" Den asked. "After all, the children aren't being charged, so they aren't under arrest like their parents."

"Ah, but their parents can't be charged officially until they go before a judge in Valzor," Quess argued. "Until then, they retain legal custody of their children and can choose where to place them. That opens a critical window of opportunity, if we can convince them to take advantage of it. That's where you come in. They've had enough experience with you to believe in your honesty, at some level. Convince them that Shaeldor is a better guardian than Sinth, and the courts on both sides of the border will go along with it."

Reyna returned with the children, carrying bowls of pie and ice cream. As Den and Quess helped her seat them, Reyna said to Quess in Simelan, "Did you know that for a moment you completely disappeared from the ambient?"

"I didn't want to disturb you with my revulsion."

"I've heard about Donors who could do that, but never zlinned it before. It's...unsettling."

"The Tecton does not approve of the technique, but there are times..."

"I was not offended," the elderly channel assured him. "I know what Den had to tell you."

* * * *

As Den had promised Ephriam Lornstadt, "nothing" was done to the seven protesters chained in the Collectorium. As a result, they were too hungry, thirsty, and exhausted to resist when the Valzor police arrived the following evening. Once freed, they were given a meal to keep them from broadcasting their hunger and thirst to Simes, then the elder Lornstadts were escorted to the room where their children waited with Den and Quess.

"Oh, my babies!" Cessly sobbed, as she and her husband hugged them. "What have the Simes been doing to you?"

Clarinda lisped, "Simes are nice, Mommy. Hajene Reyna's a Sime. She put us to bed last night and told us stories."

"And she gave us pie for dessert," Zeke chimed in, with the priority of a boy undergoing a growth spurt. "With ice cream and sprinkles."

"You have a choice to make," Den told the elder Lornstadts. "Neither of your relatives is in a position to care for Zeke and Clarinda for an extended time. If we turn them over to the Clear Springs authorities, they would become wards of the court and enter foster care. I think you know where they are most likely to be placed."

"No!" Cessly gasped. "They're good children, too young to be dangerous to anyone. They deserve a real home, not..." Ephriam grasped her shoulder, his expression as agonized as her own.

"There is an alternative," Quess told her quietly. "My Householding, Shaeldor, runs a foster home in Valzor to provide the children of our members a stable home when their parents must travel. If you make Shaeldor their guardian, I can place your children there for the duration of your sentence. They would be well cared for and could visit you every week."

"This foster home," Cessly asked. "Is it run by...Simes?"

"It's run by families," Quess said. "Families made up of both Simes and Gens. And their children, who would be the playmates of your own."

"I know this is difficult for you," Den added, "but you must decide quickly. Unless the children go to Valzor with you, Reverend Sinth will sue us for custody in the Clear Springs courts...and win."

Cessly closed her eyes with a sob, clutching her daughter tightly.

"They would be safe in your foster home?" Ephriam demanded.

"I give you my word, unto Shaeldor," Quess vowed formally.

The two out-Territory Gens did not understand that when a senior Householding Companion sealed a formal promise with that particular oath, Shaeldor would see it fulfilled if Quess could not do so personally. However, Quess hadn't become a senior diplomat without learning to project sincerity. The Lornstadts looked at each other for a long moment, then Cessly gave a small nod.

"We accept your offer," Ephriam told Quess.

"Excellent," the senior Donor agreed. "I will have Shaeldor's Valzor law office draw up the guardianship papers. They will meet you at the precinct house so you can sign them before you are charged formally, while your right to assign custody is still clear. Then you can meet your children's new foster parents and see them off."

For once, Den sensed complete sincerity in Cessly's words as she looked at Quess and whispered, "Thank you! You don't know what this means to my family. But why? Why are you doing all this?"

"Because, Madame," Quess stated formally, "it is the right thing to do."

"That was well done," he added to Den after the Lornstadts and their children had been loaded on the bus for the long journey back to Valzor.

"Sinth will still sue for custody, you know," Den predicted. "The children are out-Territory citizens, after all."

"I expect so," the diplomat agreed. "However, if Shaeldor already has legal and physical custody and the children adjust well, the court will likely agree to leave things as they are. Children require stability, and the fact that this arrangement allows them to see their parents regularly will weigh heavily in our favor."

* * * *

When Den and Rital started their shift in the Collectorium the next morning, the only sign of Save Our Kids' occupation was a few scratches on the reception desk from Ephriam Lornstadt's handcuff. Fewer Gens donated than usual, but Den wasn't sure whether Save Our Kids was responsible, or if the Gens who would have come that day had donated at Children's Day instead.

The short winter day was drawing to a close when they escorted their latest client back to an empty waiting room. A glance out the window showed snow falling and a layer of powder on the ground.

Rital told Seena, Reyna, and Hammil to quit early. "We'll stay in case someone decides to donate on their way home from work."

The cousins poured mugs of tea, then settled on the couch before the window, watching the snow and talking quietly of nothing in particular, something Den had missed. *I've got to stop letting differences of opinion come between us,* Den decided. *What's the point of being here with Rital if I never spend time with him?*

The snow thickened. Save Our Kids and OLD SOKS left early.

A few minutes later, Rital sat up with a start. "We've got business," he said, just as the door opened and a shivering, snow-covered figure stumbled inside. Their visitor dropped a heavy knapsack on the floor, then fumbled at the buttons on a heavy winter coat.

"Bethany Sinth, what are *you* doing here?" Den demanded as the coat's hood fell back, revealing Reverend Sinth's niece. There were purple bruises on her face and she moved stiffly.

"I'm here to donate selyn, of course," she answered. "Why else would I come to a place like this?"

On Bethany's last visit to the Sime Center, she had sat in the waiting room trying to scare off the selyn donors with horror stories. The Donor pointed out the obvious. "Your uncle won't approve."

"If I'm lucky, he'll never get the chance." She shivered; whether from fear or cold, Den couldn't tell.

Rital could, though, and fetched a mug of tea. "Here," he said, urging Bethany to sit on the couch. "This will warm you."

She sipped, made a face at the taste, then gulped it down.

When she was no longer shivering, the channel spoke in a no-nonsense tone. "Tell us what happened. Start with who beat you so badly. Your back is one huge bruise."

Bethany's eyes widened and she shrank away from the channel. "How did you know that?"

"I can zlin the ache," Rital answered as Den moved closer to block Bethany's projection. "What happened to you?"

"There's no *time*." Bethany wrung her hands in distress. "I've got to catch the evening train or be sent to reform school. This is my only way to get money for the ticket without Uncle Jermiah's permission."

"Now you've *really* got me curious," Rital said. "I won't lay a tentacle on you until you tell me the whole story."

Bethany's shoulders slumped. "My uncle found out I'm still dating Rob Lifton," she admitted reluctantly. "He ordered me not to see 'that traitor Sime-lover' again. I told him it's my life and I can choose my friends, and he went berserk. He beat me with his belt, saying that I belonged in his reform school." Her voice rose to a shout. "I won't go there, I won't!"

"Where will you go instead?" Rital asked briskly, cutting through the girl's incipient hysteria. "And how will you survive when you get there?"

"A border city, maybe one with a university like Westfield. Someplace big enough that a stranger isn't news and without a Conservative Congregation church. I can work, if I can find a boss who won't ask for proof of age, and I can donate selyn. Once I turn sixteen, Uncle Jermiah can't touch me." She dug in the pocket of her dress. "If I have to, I can sell my mother's ring. I don't think she'd mind, if she knew. There are scratches inside the band, but the carving's pretty and it's got a diamond. It should be worth something, don't you think?"

The ring she pulled out had an exquisitely detailed ship carved into the face, a diamond glittering on the hull. The Donor inspected it closely.

Interwoven with the ship design was another crest with which Den was intimately familiar, since it was carved into the ring on his own hand. The "scratches" were a worn but still legible Simelan inscription: "Lissabee ambrov Shaeldor" and the date, eighteen years before, when she had Qualified and pledged.

More trouble, Den thought. He handed the ring to Rital. "I think we should ask Quess to join us."

* * * *

Quess read the name carved inside the ring. "Oh, yes, I recognize it," he said softly. "It belonged to my daughter Liss." He looked at Bethany with a hungry, wistful expression.

Bethany was outraged at the suggestion that she was related to a Donor. "You're wrong," she protested hotly. "My mother's name was Lizzie and she was an orphan when she married my father."

"Is that what they told you?" Quess asked sadly.

"It's true," Bethany insisted.

"I assure you," the older Donor said with some asperity, "the last time I checked, I was very much alive. So is your Grandmother, Nerina." Then he smiled. "You look like her, you know. You also have a pair of uncles and some assorted cousins who'll be glad to meet you. Shaeldor has been searching for you for thirteen years."

When Bethany pursed her lips skeptically, Rital intervened. "Let's hear the whole story. Den, would you make fresh tea?"

"Liss was our oldest child," Quess explained while Den served tea and chocolate-walnut cookies. "She was beautiful, headstrong, and as talented as her mother. She qualified as a First Order Donor a month after she Established. We were so proud of her…" He took a hasty swallow of tea.

"A Donor?" Bethany interrupted. "My mother prostituted herself with *Simes*?" Her face twisted with disgust.

Quess looked at her sadly. "Your mother was a talented Donor," he confirmed. "We were all astonished when she married an out-Territory Gen named Gerryn Sindle, even though he refused to pledge her House."

"Your House doesn't approve of marrying outsiders?" Den asked.

"It's unusual for a Companion, though it happens. But we only began worrying when her husband refused to donate selyn. They could only live together when she was assigned to a border Sime Center. We wondered what kind of life Liss could build with a man who rejected so much of what she was, but she seemed happy and a year later she had a daughter of her own." He smiled at the memory, and at Bethany. "You were our first grandchild. Nerina adored you. She said it made her feel young, to have a baby teething on her tentacles again."

"Tentacles!" Bethany shrieked.

"Why, yes." Quess lifted an eyebrow. "Your grandmother's a channel. So is your Uncle Lijin, for that matter."

Den hastily sipped tea to avoid laughing at Bethany's expression.

"Gerryn's family were no happier about the marriage than we were," Quess continued, "but when Liss was pregnant with her second child, a channel, her in-laws invited her and her husband to visit. Liss's first pregnancy had been easy and there were no signs of trouble with the second. She decided to risk the trip so her husband could reconcile with his parents."

Quess absently stirred his tea. "Her brother-in-law, Jermiah, was violently opposed to having a Companion in the family. The two brothers got into a fight and Liss tried to stop them. Jermiah kicked her in the stomach and she miscarried. Out-Territory doctors couldn't help at all, and there wasn't a channel in fifty miles. She...died."

"Uncle Jermiah murdered my mother?" Bethany asked.

Quess shrugged. "I doubt it was deliberate. No one bothered to tell the Tecton what had happened. Nerina and I were out west, helping survivors of an earthquake. It was weeks before we even learned Liss was gone. I tried to find her husband and daughter, but Gerryn's brother had convinced him that Shaeldor would take you away from him. We wouldn't have, although we'd have stayed in touch with you—and we *would* have sued for custody when your father died, rather than have you go to the man who murdered your mother. However, we didn't get the chance. Gerryn had changed his name and moved, no one knew where."

"How terrible," Rital murmured.

"You never found where they'd gone?" Den asked.

"Not until last year," Quess said quietly. "Liss had provided for her daughter through an out-Territory bank, mostly stock in Shaeldor-owned businesses. She wasn't sure her children would choose to pledge, when their father had refused. The account went untouched for twelve years and I assumed Liss's husband didn't know about it."

"He died in a mining accident, not long after my half-brother Zakry was born," Bethany explained.

Quess continued, "About a year ago, someone started withdrawing funds from the account, selling off the stock."

"Right after my stepmother died and Zakry and I came to live with Uncle Jermiah." Bethany nervously crumbled the cookie she held.

At least she's listening...and believing, Den observed.

"I knew you couldn't be managing the account," Quess told Bethany, "because you're still legally a child out-Territory. The money could only have been withdrawn by your parent or legal guardian. The checks went to a post office box in Clear Springs. I called in every favor I could to get permission to spend a few months trying to find my granddaughter."

"So *that's* why you kept going downtown," Den said, fighting conflicting emotions. It was a relief to know that he and Rital weren't under investigation, but... *Why didn't he tell us? We could have helped.*

"Indeed," the older Donor agreed. "Technically, there was no crime I could report, so Shaeldor's lawyers could not find out who owned the post office box. The best I could do was hang around the post office, watching who picked up the mail." He winked at Bethany. "It's an inefficient way to find someone and I'm very glad you showed up here instead."

Bethany looked less sure than ever that she wanted a Donor for her grandfather. Still, she was a practical young woman. "I can't stay with Uncle Jermiah anymore," she said. "I suppose I'd better stay with you."

An overjoyed Quess promised, "I'll get Shaeldor's lawyers to work on the papers right away. We have documents proving your mother's intent."

The agreement almost ended five minutes later, when Quess asked Bethany to let Rital heal her back. "I'll donate selyn if I have to," she grumbled, "but why should I let a snake touch me any other time? I'll heal fast enough on my own if I'm not beaten again."

Rital had to threaten to expel her from the Sime Center as a nuisance to the staff renSimes. When she realized that he meant every word, she reluctantly agreed to let the channel treat her, rather than return to her paternal uncle's not-so-tender care. And once she had agreed to that, she permitted them to call the police to document her bruises first, to bolster the case against Sinth.

Den thought Quess showed remarkable patience. The older Donor knew what sort of beliefs Bethany's out-Territory relatives held. Still, it must be a shock to see his beloved daughter's child cringing from a channel's touch.

Shaeldor had an excellent legal staff, like most Householdings. Within a week, the Clear Springs juvenile court awarded custody of Bethany to her grandfather, largely on the basis of how severely the young woman had been beaten. "I won't leave a child with someone who abuses her," Judge Banklin said. "Even if the alternative guardian's profession is..." she searched for the least offensive way to phrase it, "...questionable."

Quess raised a dignified eyebrow at this description of his distinguished diplomatic career, but wisely held his peace. Reverend Sinth's outrage was spectacular, even for him. Right there in the courtroom, the preacher launched into a diatribe about "snake-loving seducers who steal the children of the righteous," and had to be ejected by the bailiff.

"Of course he's furious," Bethany explained after the hearing. "My inheritance has been paying for his melic weed and all those pamphlets that

Save Our Kids hands out. He probably used it as collateral for the loan to buy his farm over by Clearston, too."

"I hadn't realized that he spent your money on drugs and political activities," the older Donor said. "That will make recovery even easier. He can't claim those things were for your care."

The preacher suffered a second legal loss a few days later. He had filed suit in the Valzor courts to contest Shaeldor's guardianship of the Lornstadt children. However, the renSime judge was not convinced by Sinth's argument that the children must be raised in the Conservative Congregation, despite the arrangements their parents had agreed to under duress. When lawyer Plicera ambrov Shaeldor showed her Rital's report on healing Bethany's bruises, the judge promptly awarded custody of the Lornstadt children to Shaeldor.

Rob Lifton visited Bethany almost every day. She enjoyed seeing him openly and was warming to her grandfather as well. She even picked up a few words of Simelan, although she wouldn't study it. "Plain English is good enough for me."

She was not pleased three weeks later, when Quess told her during dinner that they were moving in-Territory. "I want to stay here!" she objected. "This is where my friends are. Why would I want to live in a city full of snakes?"

Quess's lips narrowed at the epithet, but his voice remained calm. "Bethany, you know I am a Donor. There's nothing in Clear Springs that requires my particular skills, so it's fortunate I could stay this long. Your grandmother and the rest of the family are very eager to meet you."

"But I don't even speak their language!"

"You'll learn," her grandfather assured her. "Besides, most in Shaeldor speak at least a little English."

Bethany's mulish pout didn't soften.

"You may be an adult by in-Territory standards," Quess pointed out, "but you can't live out-Territory without a guardian. Would you prefer to return to your uncle?"

Her shoulders slumped. "All right, I'll go to Valzor." She glared at him. "I won't be fifteen forever. When I turn sixteen, I can live where I please."

Rital set his tray next to Den's. "Why is Quess so upset?"

"Bethany told him she doesn't want to live in Sime Territory."

"No wonder he's disturbed," the channel said, eating his soup with the appetite a Sime displayed only right after a good transfer.

Rital may not like *Quess, particularly,* Den realized, *but my dear cousin does* trust *him enough to draw at a decent speed. If I could only convince him to trust me like that...*

"Quess hopes Bethany will pledge Shaeldor, so he won't lose her," Rital continued.

"He's a fool, then," Den observed, "but what can you expect from a Householder? If you don't pledge to their House, you're not family, no matter the blood relationship." He shook his head in disgust. "If Quess had reached out to his son-in-law and earned the man's trust, he wouldn't have lost Bethany in the first place. If he keeps trying to turn her into a Householder, he'll lose her again. As if she'd be any less his granddaughter if she settles down out-Territory!"

* * * *

Den was too happy at having his cousin back to dwell on Householders. As winter faded into early spring, he and Rital taught three changeover classes daily at Buchan's school.

Flight Innovations ordered a third, larger batch of selyn-insulating polycarbonate in anticipation of planting season, when the Berrysville factory would return to making irrigation pipes. Orders from Sime Territory slowed as the first wave of interest ebbed. With another payment looming, Den considered marketing a lightweight selyn battery made with sunflower or grapeseed oil. But who would buy it? They had sold only a few dozen of Vespin's custom outlets, mostly to friends of Held's crew in the construction business. His hopes that building contractors would make them a standard safety feature were fading.

Den was busy enough that he almost didn't miss being Post. *With Quess gone, Rital won't be able to hold back much longer. He's going to break soon, whether he wants to or not...and I'll be ready!*

The Berrysville Monthly Mobile Sime Center attracted a fair number of selyn donors, many well on their way to being "regular donors," by Arth's classification. The program was so popular that the Oak Ridge congregation of Rational Deists sponsored a similar event at their own Meeting Hall. At Reverend Sinth's insistence, the Clearston City Council passed an ordinance banning such "perverse activities."

Reverend Sinth's anti-Sime message was now largely ignored in Clear Springs, so the preacher took to the road. He became a popular speaker, telling how the "sinful, slimy snakes" had stolen his beloved niece. Without Bethany's funds, he issued fewer new pamphlets, but by combining speaker's fees and contributions to Save Our Kids, he didn't lose his farm or his drug addiction. Melic weed made him forget to eat, and his increasingly gaunt appearance gave him the otherworldly air of a mystic.

One day, Flora Mills' son, Jon, the Mayor of Berrysville, announced that, since their Mobile Clinic had reached a reliable 50 donors per month, the Town Council had authorized him to ask the Tecton for a Sime Center. "It's nice that the Rational Deists host a channel in Berrysville once a month, but that's not convenient for everyone. Besides, the chance that a changeover will happen to occur when a channel is available is too small. If we can't get a full-time Sime Center, maybe they'll give us a part-time one."

Controller Monruss was intrigued by the idea of a part-time Sime Center. Since there was no precedent, he referred the matter to the Office for Inter-Territorial Affairs. A group of diplomats and staff arrived in Clear Springs to conduct the negotiations.

It didn't surprise Den that Quess was part of the delegation, although he'd brought his own channel this time: his wife, Hajene Nerina. She had the same long, thick, wavy hair as her granddaughter, but hers was silver. Bethany accompanied them, more comfortable around Simes than she'd been a few months before and able to manage a simple conversation in Simelan. However, she was overjoyed to be out-Territory again.

"Do you think she'll stay with you after she turns sixteen?" Den asked Quess.

"I hope so," the older Donor replied. "Nerina was devastated when we lost Liss and it's made her so happy to have Liss's daughter."

To Tyvi's delight, her son, Obis, came as Escort to one of the delegation channels. He happily took charge of his mother, who was due for a rotation.

The overabundance of channels dangerously lightened their workload. Scheduling each for enough work hours to avoid entran was complicated by the negotiations schedule. On some days, the Collectorium was closed by the time the weary diplomats returned from Berrysville.

The regular donors were used to their four channels. Apprehensions resurfaced when they faced a stranger, making the channel's task more difficult. And one young Second Order channel, Hajene Sumulo ambrov Ohmand, proved a special trial.

"Look at this file!" Rital groaned, passing it to Den. "How can I turn a channel with this record loose on our donors?"

Den skimmed the report on Hajene Sumulo's last out-Territory assignment in disbelief. "A tenth of the out-Territory donors he handled in Sanger never returned, and another twenty percent requested any other channel. He almost scared off an induced Gen with First Order potential–twice! –and they sent *him* to help negotiate a new out-Territory Sime Center? Has Inter-Territorial Affairs lost what little sense they ever had?"

"Hajene Sumulo was supposed to spend three months retraining at Tien's school for out-Territory immigrants," Rital said, pointing out the relevant entry with a tentacle. "Looks like he talked his uncle, Sectuib Cyril, into handling the matter within Ohmand."

"Trust Householders to sweep a problem channel under the rug," Den commented sourly, flipping through the rest of the file. "There isn't even an official reprimand!"

"Hajene Sumulo spent two weeks in-House, 'training' with his uncle, who then got him assigned to Inter-Territorial Affairs. He probably sees himself as Quess's successor."

"He's got the connections for it."

"Now, Den," Rital scolded. "Householder or not, Quess's reputation is well-earned."

"So it is," the Donor conceded gracelessly. "What can you do about Sumulo?"

"I can't bar him from the Collectorium until he makes a mistake. His assigned Donor, Kamrin, is a member of his House. He'd never report his Sectuib's nephew, particularly not to a Tecton Controller who might take it seriously." Rital looked at his cousin hopefully. "Kamrin's an auxiliary translator in Berrysville tomorrow. If I assign Sumulo a morning shift at the Collectorium, would you make sure he behaves?"

Den sighed and nodded. "I suppose our changeover class students can wait another day to get their tests back."

"Good. And Den?"

The Donor raised an inquiring eyebrow.

"If Sumulo does misbehave, take whatever action you think appropriate and I'll back you. Maybe our combined authority can curb that walking menace before he tears down everything we've built here."

CHAPTER 17

A BACKHANDED COMPLIMENT

Hajene Sumulo ambrov Ohmand was waiting for Den in the lobby after breakfast. He was of average height, with dark brown hair and eyes a few shades lighter. A spattering of freckles and an arrogant expression made him appear even younger than he was. His freshly pressed Tecton uniform was custom-made. Den wondered sourly whether he'd ironed it himself, or ordered his Donor to do it.

The Second Order channel zlinned ostentatiously, as if inspecting Den's nager for acceptability. "So, you're the Houseless nobody who created such a mess by experimenting with selyn batteries," he drawled in a thick Gulf Territory accent. "You really should leave that to the professionals in Ohmand."

He's exactly the arrogant, privileged brat his file describes. Den raised a pained eyebrow at the display of rudeness and drawled back, "The same professionals who haven't managed an increase in selyn battery capacity in decades?"

"Nonsense," Sumulo scoffed. "Ohmand improves our batteries all the time. I'm something of a prodigy in Ohmand for creating high-capacity batteries, you know."

"You are?"

The young channel puffed out his narrow chest. "My selyn battery holds twice the charge of a standard one. The process is proprietary, but I have the expertise to evaluate what you've done."

"I see." Den's response was deliberately noncommittal.

Sumulo continued with the confidence of his status as a Householding prince. "Sectuib in Ohmand, my uncle Cyril, sent me to examine your prototype. If I decide it is potentially useful, I'm authorized to compensate you for your discovery. I'm prepared to be quite generous. Perhaps up to half of the debt I understand you owe for…what was it? Destroying the orgonics system of an entire university research facility?" He tsked, shaking his head, clearly expecting the Donor to squirm with embarrassment.

Den didn't oblige.

When he zlinned that his tactic had failed, Sumulo continued. "I'm told you also make those selyn-insulating sheets that Controller Monruss likes so much? My uncle thinks they're quite clever."

"Yes, that's a product developed by my research program."

"The material has some potential," the young channel observed. "Without a House behind you, though, you can't realize it. Ohmand has the manufacturing capacity you lack. We can make the sheets in quantity and find additional uses for them. We'll share the profits with you, of course. Say, ten percent after expenses? That will make your debt shrink nicely. If your improved selyn battery also goes into production, you might die a wealthy man."

Sumulo beamed at the Donor in what even a Gen could see was feigned civility. "What do you say, Sosu Milnan? You won't get a better offer from another House, you know."

Den did not allow the Second Order channel to zlin his fury. Ohmand's offer was stingy to the point of insult. Their stranglehold on battery technology produced an income rivaling that of a small Territory. Retiring his entire debt wouldn't dent their discretionary income.

The offer was also condescending, which suggested Sectuib Cyril was less interested in improving Ohmand's batteries than in keeping anyone else from making a better one.

"Hajene Sumulo, I'm…impressed…by your Sectuib's offer," he began.

"Excellent," the young channel interrupted, one tentacle flicking lint from his shirt. "I'll inspect your inventions after our shift and then you can sign the papers. I'll ask Sosu Quess to release me from his diplomatic staff and take the morning train to Valzor to deliver them. I've no wish to remain here among the Wild Gens longer than necessary."

"I regret to say that you won't be returning to Valzor that quickly," Den said, meaning every word.

"You want more time to study the papers?" Sumulo gave a bored sigh. "Well, if you must. I will endure the primitive conditions."

"You misunderstand me, Hajene," Den told him coldly. "I'm not going to sign my superior selyn battery over to your House for a fraction of its worth, so that Ohmand can maybe do something with it someday. I'm not going to give you the right to make my selyn-insulating material, either. There will be no papers for you to carry back to Valzor."

Sumulo bristled. "You're making a mistake, Milnan," he warned. "The Tecton has no place for rogue troublemakers. You've gotten off lightly so far, but that can change. My uncle has influence."

"Influence? Perhaps with those who approve of how he and his representatives conduct Ohmand's business." Den was rewarded when Sumulo flushed. Satisfied he'd made his point, the Donor held open the door to the Collectorium. "I believe our shift is beginning. Shall we?"

A flurry of shouts from outside signaled the arrival of the day's first donors.

"Hi, Sosu Milnan!" Rob Lifton greeted Den cheerfully. He shrugged out of his jacket, then turned to help his grandfather remove a worn sheepskin greatcoat. The young Gen danced over to hang the garments on the coatrack, humming a happy tune all the while.

Mr. Duncan's eyes gleamed with suppressed laughter. "Young love," he explained. "Bethany Sinth is coming to visit this afternoon."

"I see." Den wondered if Quess knew of his granddaughter's continuing out-Territory involvement.

Seena brought the two donors' files from the records room. Due to the flexibility of youth, Rob was donating more selyn than his grandfather since his qualification as a GN-2. On paper, he was steadier and should be assigned to the Second Order channel.

It would be a disaster if Sumulo reawakened Rob's apprehensions. Before Seena could place Rob's file in Sumulo's basket, the Donor smoothly relieved her of the other one. "Mr. Duncan, you come with me and Hajene Sumulo," he suggested, passing the elderly man's file on to Sumulo.

The young channel zlinned Den suspiciously, but Seena smoothly handed Rob's file to Tyvi. Unable to verify a violation of normal procedure, Sumulo led the way to their assigned donation room.

The channel went directly to the desk and sat. Without saying a word to either Gen, he opened the file and began to read.

Mr. Duncan raised an eyebrow at this discourteous behavior, then lowered himself carefully into the visitor's chair. Turning to Den, who had perched on a stool beside Sumulo, he asked, "When do you think Berrysville will get its Sime Center?"

"The Tecton may decide that such a small town can't support even a part-time facility," the Donor warned.

Mr. Duncan chuckled. "Not much chance of that, son," he said confidently. "The honorable Mayor of Berrysville is a brave man, but he's got a healthy respect for his mother. I've known Flora Mills all my life. Negotiations won't end until she's satisfied!"

"If you are quite finished gossiping," Sumulo complained irritably, "perhaps we could get to work?"

"No reason to be rude, youngster," Mr. Duncan scolded. Ignoring the channel's glare, he rose, steadying himself on the desk, then walked stiffly over to the transfer lounge and lay down. His gnarled hands fumbled at the buttons on his shirt cuffs.

Sumulo waited with growing impatience for the man to roll up the sleeves of his worn flannel shirt. As soon as Mr. Duncan's arms were legally offered, the channel grabbed them and unceremoniously pinned his client to the transfer lounge.

Mr. Duncan had never resisted during a donation, not even his first one. However, Den saw the wrinkled hands twitch in protest at the rough handling, then flinch as handling tentacles clamped down tightly. The Donor watched closely, prepared to halt the donation if necessary, but after that first instinctive retreat, the elderly Gen relaxed. *At least Sumulo's got enough sense to keep the selyn flow imperceptible.*

When the young channel released Mr. Duncan, the elderly donor sat up. "No reason to be so rough, boy," he complained, rubbing red marks the handling tentacles had left on his arms.

Sumulo, who had already returned to the desk, ignored the criticism and scribbled numbers on the chart…along with a complaint of his own that Mr. Duncan had failed to cooperate.

"Hajene Sumulo has much to learn," Den apologized as he helped the elderly Gen stand.

"Let the brat learn it on somebody else," Mr. Duncan muttered.

"Here," the channel said, thrusting a voucher into the donor's hands. "Take this to the waiting room and they'll settle your account."

The out-Territory Gen took the offered paper and made his slow way to the door. He paused in the doorway and looked back at Sumulo. "I don't know what's bothering you, youngster," he declared, "but you'll never be a professional until you learn some manners. There's no excuse for taking your bad temper out on the people whose selyn supports you."

"Insolent Gen," Sumulo sneered as the door closed behind Mr. Duncan. Then the channel turned on Den. "Milnan, I know the Houseless are often sorely lacking in discipline, but I expect any Donor who works with me to behave in a professional manner. You are to remain silent and leave the donors for me to handle. You will not question my competence again. Do you understand?"

Den had agreed not to interfere with Rital's treatment of donors because his cousin's ability to soothe nervous out-Territory Gens was far superior to Den's. It was quite another matter to hear the same complaint from a channel half his age who violated proper etiquette, Tecton regulations, and common sense.

Den controlled his temper, the better to focus it. "*Hajene* Sumulo," he answered, emphasizing the title, "I'll stop questioning your competence when you show some. The way you handled Mr. Duncan was a disgrace."

Sumulo flushed and his tentacles knotted with anger. "I don't think you understand your position, Milnan," he snapped. "I am ambrov Ohmand.

My House invented the selyn battery and we own the patents on the central technology of civilization. We are important and powerful in the Tecton."

"Oh, I think my position is clear," Den said softly, relaxing control for Sumulo to zlin the depth of his fury. "I'm no Householder—" His voice oozed contempt. "—but I can make a selyn battery gel that holds a charge over three times that of Ohmand's mix. That your own small improvement hasn't replaced the original shows your House's lack of interest in technological innovation. I could be refining my selyn battery right now, but because of your well-documented incompetence I'm babysitting a spoiled brat of a Second Order channel who can't be trusted to take a donation from a cooperative Gen. A Gen, I might add, whom our Thirds handle easily. This isn't the first time you've mistreated out-Territory Gens, but it's the last. You are hereby barred from the Clear Springs Collectorium."

A normal Second Order channel would have cowered before an angry First Order Donor, but Sumulo's arrogance exceeded his sense. "Don't you threaten *me*," he snarled. "Sectuib Ohmand won't stand aside while his nephew is slandered by an anti-Householding bigot!"

"Ah, yes, your uncle," Den said. "He got you out of retraining at Tien's school by promising to handle your re-education in-House. Then he sent you out here instead."

Sumulo shrugged negligently. "Your unauthorized battery must be examined by an expert to assess whether it's worth acquiring. That's far more important than whether some Wild Gen has his feelings hurt."

"Mr. Duncan might have different priorities," Den pointed out. "In either case, your Sectuib can't get you out of the consequences for today's misbehavior."

The young channel's sneer never wavered. "Do you think Controller Madz would accept the word of a Houseless nobody over that of a Sectuib's nephew?"

"You may be Sectuib Cyril's nephew," Den pointed out bluntly, "but Controller Madz is my cousin. He won't take the word of a Second Order channel over mine," Den tried to match Sumulo's contemptuous tone. "Particularly after he guessed your retraining might be…inadequate… and delegated me to deal with you as I see fit."

Sumulo's sneer faded. Den took advantage of the momentary breach in the brat's defenses to lay down the law.

"Since you don't believe out-Territory selyn donors should be treated with respect and courtesy, I won't ask you to compromise your principles. There are enough *competent* channels here to handle double our current roster. That won't leave much for you to do, but since you're an *expert*," his voice oozed sarcasm, "Controller Madz might let you charge selyn batteries…if you ask him politely. When you're not doing that, you can translate records for Arth Tinkum's research project. Is all of this quite clear, or should I explain it again?"

"I know my rights," Sumulo whined. "Controller Madz can bar me from the out-Territory Collectorium while he's investigating your ridiculous charge. That won't be long, once my uncle hears about this. But your precious, Houseless cousin *can't* bar me from the in-Territory Collectorium." The sneer returned. "So, don't think I'll go crawling to the Controller begging for battery work."

"You're quite the little lawyer." Den's smile turned feral. "There are only a dozen or so in-Territory donors in Clear Springs, including the diplomatic delegation. We don't have an in-Territory Collectorium like the border Centers." He paused to enjoy Sumulo's appalled expression. "On the other hand, while entran isn't life-threatening for a Second Order channel, it *can* be a nuisance for a Donor to handle. Sosu Kamrin isn't responsible for your boorishness, so if any of the Gens on the Sime Center staff request to donate *to you*, I'll allow it. *If* you treat Arth with respect and courtesy. Is that perfectly clear?"

Sumulo glared his hatred.

"You will follow my rules, because I will be watching you closely." Den matched the young channel glare for glare. "If I'm not satisfied with your behavior, I will bring formal charges against you, the kind even your uncle can't keep off your record. Understand me?"

As Sumulo finally grasped that Den had the authority to impose such a draconian penalty, his defiance began to wilt. "I understand you, Milnan," he muttered.

Den scowled at the channel and barked, "You understand, *what?*"

"I understand, *Sosu* Milnan," Sumulo rephrased with bad grace.

"I hope you do," the Donor said. "Arth will arrive in an hour. I suggest you use the time to review basic professional etiquette. Our library has an excellent selection of texts."

The young channel crept out the door, swearing under his breath…but not too loudly.

Den sighed, hoping the brat's uncle wouldn't cause trouble. Sectuib Cyril would not be happy that Den refused to sell Ohmand his patents. He would be even less happy with a superior battery in direct competition with Ohmand's monopoly. Getting Den into trouble with the Tecton would be an easy way to retaliate. *Too easy.*

He relaxed deliberately, letting the anger drain out of him, then paged Zir, who was overjoyed to cover the rest of Sumulo's shift. Branlee and Hald's crew all knew not to talk to the diplomatic delegation about Flight Innovations work or allow them into its facilities. So, when Den passed through the basement to double-check the lab, he caught Sumulo lurking in the hall, glaring in frustration at the padlock on the door.

"You were misdirected," he greeted the young channel blandly. "Arth does his research in our library. Let me show you the way."

When Den told Arth that Sumulo was now his official translator, he eyed the glowering young channel apprehensively and started when Sumulo's tentacles carelessly emerged. However, help on his project was enough to win his agreement.

* * * *

That evening, as Den lingered over trin tea, Sumulo entered the dining hall. He strolled toward the table where the weary diplomatic delegation was eating a late dinner, detouring close to Den's table.

"I hope you enjoyed this morning," he murmured to Den with a smug smile, "because you're not going to enjoy what happens to you and your Houseless cousin now."

The Donor watched the young channel swagger over to the diplomats. Quess was leading an analysis of the day's work. Sumulo assumed a distressed expression, interrupted the senior diplomat, and engaged him in an animated conversation. The subject was obvious from the glances sent in Den's direction.

The Donor leaned back in his chair and pretended to listen to the local folk tale Gati was relating to enthralled listeners.

"…and when Memoria cracked open the shell of the first walnut the little woman had given her, a splendid dress fell out, made of a shimmering gold fabric as fine as woven cobwebs…"

Den lost interest in the tale as Quess got to his feet, picked up his tea mug, and started for Den's table. The other Householder trailed behind, smirking at Den.

Oh, shen, Den thought, working hard to avoid giving Sumulo the satisfaction of zlinning his concern. He had expected consequences. *But they could have waited until the entitled brat was safely out of town.*

"May we join you for a moment, Sosu Milnan?" Quess asked.

Den invited them to sit with a polite wave.

"Sumulo tells me you have barred him from the Collectorium," the older Donor said, in such a neutral tone that it was impossible for a Gen to guess his feelings.

Den nodded agreement. "So I did." He met Quess's gaze levelly. "I've spent time and effort building this city's roster of selyn donors. I won't let that work be ruined because one spoiled young channel won't mind his manners around out-Territory Gens." He met Sumulo's eyes. "No matter which Householding his uncle runs."

"You see, Naztehr Quess?" the young channel complained. "He doesn't like Householders, so he picks on me."

The diplomat turned to Sumulo with an admonitory look. "I am well aware of Sosu Milnan's dislike of Householders," he said quietly. "I warned you to watch your step around him."

Sumulo lost his smirk at Quess's forbidding frown.

"If you remembered my warning," the diplomat asked, "why did you immediately prove his misgivings about you were correct?"

"But I didn't *do* anything!" the channel complained.

"Just as you 'didn't do anything' in Sanger?" Quess asked. "Alex ambrov Slader told me how you treated out-Territory Gens there."

Sumulo squirmed. "They were only stupid out-Territory Gens," he mumbled, "and I've done nothing to deserve being banned *here*."

"You call spooking one of our steadiest selyn donors 'nothing'?" Den demanded, bristling with outrage.

"He just wants an excuse to push around a Householder," the channel whined. "He won't even let me see his experimental battery so I can go home."

Quess silenced them both with a look. "Sumulo, I agree that Sosu Milnan has an unfortunate prejudice against Householders." He held up a hand to forestall the young channel's agreement. "However, he doesn't let it interfere with his professional judgment or his duties. A lesson you might learn from him, incidentally."

Den was so astonished at this backhanded compliment that he couldn't frame a response. Sumulo recovered faster. "But my uncle—"

"Your *Sectuib*," Quess corrected, "asked me to look after you. I believe your interests are best served by Sosu Milnan's discipline."

Den, like Sumulo, had assumed that Quess would side with a fellow Householder. He barely managed to keep his jaw from dropping as he admonished himself, *Don't blow the fields!*

"But Naztehr Quess…" Sumulo whined.

"Don't 'But Naztehr' me, young man," the object of his plea said sternly. "You hide behind your uncle far too often. It's time you took responsibility for your own actions."

"But if I can't work in the Collectorium, I'll have entran by the end of the week!" the young channel protested.

"Entran isn't life-threatening in Second Order channels. Swallow your pride and ask Controller Madz for battery work. I suggest you also be helpful to Arth Tinkum and the Gen staff. Now, I must get back to the discussion." He nodded to Den and returned to diplomatic discussion.

Sumulo flounced off to drown his frustrations in porstan, but Den lingered over cold tea, wondering if he had misjudged at least one influential Householder.

* * * *

Sumulo sent a thick express letter to his Sectuib the next morning. That afternoon, Den caught him informing Seena that she and all Gen staff members would be donating to him. Faced with open rebellion, Den and Rital served Sumulo with a Controller's Injunction that made the terms of the channel's discipline both public and legally binding.

Sumulo endured a week of enforced inactivity before he received an answer from his uncle. From the young channel's furious reaction, Sectuib Cyril's influence (or perhaps his patience) was not as strong as his nephew had assumed. There was no accompanying order overruling Rital's Injunction, or reassigning Sumulo in-Territory.

Abandoned by his uncle, the young channel finally asked permission to charge the selyn batteries whose export justified such a remote out-Territory Sime Center. Since this was the most unpleasant duty assignment for channels, there was little competition. But when Den went to the Sime Center's basement one morning, to tell the young channel that Arth had arrived early, he surprised him outside the locked door to Branlee's laboratory, carrying a prybar.

Sumulo claimed he intended to use the prybar to help move the heavy batteries, but the look in his eyes made the Donor uneasy.

The young channel's attempts at the entran out-function had not been successful, nor was his wooing of the Gen staff. His desperation grew with every Gen who donated to someone else. Den was human enough to enjoy the brat's dilemma–at least when he wasn't close enough to respond to the chronic discomfort of improperly managed entran.

Even Ref, who could forgive a youngster almost anything, let Sumulo suffer after the young channel made unflattering comments about the out-Territory dishes on the Sime Center's menus. Jain Buchan's sourdough bread recipe was well received by everyone else.

Sumulo looked for ways around both the Injunction and Den's refusal to sell Ohmand the battery improvement. When Branlee refused to speak with him, he started cultivating Raymond Ildun. While Den was pretty sure Raymond didn't remember much about the experiments, a friendship with Sumulo would not convince the boy to help Den reproduce their spectacular result.

Sumulo was carefully polite to Arth, making Den hope that the channel was getting along with at least one out-Territory Gen. The negotiations were also going well, giving hope that Sumulo ambrov Ohmand would soon be some other Sime Center's problem.

When the Berrysville weekly newspaper predicted their part-time Sime Center would open by mid-summer, Reverend Sinth moved to correct the situation…and profit from it. The preacher's financial situation had become desperate when Judge Banklin ruled that he must repay the money he had embezzled from Bethany.

"The record is clear: Lissabee ambrov Shaeldor intended to provide for the welfare and education of her daughter, Bethany Sindle, now known as Bethany Sinth. The Reverend's defense that his vendetta against the Sime Center promotes his niece's welfare is certainly unique. However," said the justice, "I doubt Lissabee would agree."

Shaeldor's excellent legal team had cataloged the preacher's financial assets before the trial, including the secret "consulting fees" he paid himself out of Save Our Kids donations. Sinth's accounts were emptied before it occurred to him to protect that money by moving it back to the Save Our Kids account.

"It's time to take action against the Sime-lovers destroying our community!" he thundered in a guest sermon at the Berrysville Church of the Purity. He announced a date when "I ask every God-fearing citizen who opposes the Sime menace to gather at dawn for a prayer rally at the Clear Springs Conservative Congregation Church. Afterward, we will form a Caravan of Decency and pay personal calls on the offenders!"

He named a long list of possible targets, including the Sime Center, Rational Deist Meeting Halls, the City Halls of Clear Springs and Berrysville, Principal Buchan's Southside Upper School, the Center for Technology, and the homes and businesses of selyn donors. "I won't announce the order of targets," he continued, "so the Sime-lovers' defenses will be spread too thin to stop us. Besides, I want *all* of them to sweat over the consequences of their treachery!"

Over two hundred people paid the pledge fee to join the "Caravan of Decency." Since most weren't from Clear Springs, the local anti-Sime activists were hard-pressed to find accommodations for them. Sinth refused to spend the pledge money on hotel rooms when there were more worthy causes, like mortgage payments and melic weed.

OLD SOKS and the Rational Deists tried to cobble together a defense plan. However, as Sinth's exact targets were unknown, there was no way to get ahead of the attackers. On the day, pro-Sime activists gathered at the most vulnerable sites, hoping that a small group of determined people could hold off the Caravan until reinforcements, or the police, arrived.

To ensure that reinforcements reached Sinth's target quickly, each group of defenders selected one person to remain by a telephone to call for help or relay messages. Den and Tohm would follow the Caravan to direct the defense, wherever the final target might be.

Den had hoped for an early spring rain, but at dawn on the appointed morning there was only a light mist. Still, the moist chill was uncomfortable as he sat next to Tohm in an unmarked car borrowed from the diplomatic staff.

In anticipation of a long day, Den had replaced the gel in the selyn battery that powered the vehicle with his best grapeseed oil blend. The motor, designed for use with a standard battery, was protected by one of the new combination surge-protector-and-selyn-flow-regulators designed by Vespin and his out-Territory electrician friends. Under test conditions, the device prevented the surges that had burned out the orgonics in the Center for Technology.

The OLD SOKS members assigned to protect the Sime Center were in place, as were the teachers shielding the Southside Upper School. From the grim look on Principal Buchan's face and Coach Farrow's matching scowl, Reverend Sinth's people would not cause trouble at their school again. Although the Center for Technology was on Sinth's list, OLD SOKS had decided splitting their force would weaken them too much. If the University's flagship department was attacked, the campus police would have to defend it.

"They don't have anything else to do on weekend mornings," Tohm told Den as they sat in the Center for Technology's deserted parking lot and watched Sinth's Church across the street. "All the undergraduates are fast asleep after last night's parties."

The lone campus police officer on patrol looked more bored than alert. The church parking lot overflowed with church busses and commercial delivery vans of all shapes and sizes. Many sported banners with "**THOU SHALT NOT SUFFER A SIME TO LIVE**" printed in blood-red letters, scriptural citation beneath. It was unlikely that Sinth would simply lead his followers across the street, for the university was empty on the weekend; the classrooms, offices and labs, locked.

Den would have liked to attend the rally, but Sinth would recognize him or Tohm, so Arth Tinkum was inside. Since the sociology student had conducted sympathetic interviews of Save Our Kids members, he wouldn't automatically be identified as an OLD SOKS spy.

That left Den in the car, watching mist condense on the windshield. The singing and chants grew more impassioned, until they morphed into the hungry, undisciplined roar of an angry mob.

Tohm muttered, "It won't be long now."

The Donor nodded and started the car's engine. It was a luxury model with tinted window glass. A few minutes later, the church side door cracked open and Arth slipped out. He sprinted across the street and scrambled into the back seat, locking the door behind him.

"Reverend Sinth has made a lynch mob. Look at them!"

People swarmed out of the church like angry hornets, piling into their vehicles. The hum of selyn-powered motors added to the uproar.

"Did Reverend Sinth let slip where they're going?" Tohm asked.

Arth shook his head. "He told the drivers to follow the lead car. There it is!"

The sober black vehicle to which he pointed had "Dusam Funeral Home" lettered on its side. Reverend Sinth's gaunt features were visible over the steering wheel, his wild gaze fueled with melic weed. The preacher leaned on the horn, waved, and the assorted vehicles moved into position behind him.

Although selyn-powered vehicles were seen regularly in big cities, this far out-Territory they had only recently ceased to stigmatize their owners as Sime-lovers. An expensive luxury before the Sime Center could refill the batteries locally, few vehicles were owned by private citizens.

Den had learned to drive as part of his out-Territory license requirements. Though Gens were not permitted to drive in Nivet, Den had been sent to Gulf Sime Territory, where any Gen who could pass the rigorous testing was granted a license. As a Donor First, he and his intentions were easily zlinned by renSimes, as long as he signaled properly. He had completed the intensive course designed to train drivers for emergency vehicles in disaster zones and earned his license in less than two weeks.

Den's training and reflexes were far superior to the average out-Territory Gen driver's and he used them to insert his vehicle into line directly behind Sinth's hearse. The rest of the Caravan of Decency fell in behind as Sinth headed out of town.

When the danger of getting cut off was past, Den dropped back. The mist was clearing and it wouldn't do for Sinth to recognize him. Sinth turned onto a narrow country road. Even if the Caravan's intended target was in Clear Springs, the preacher was not ready to signal his intentions.

The farmers were preparing their fields for spring planting. Scattered clumps of dirt adorned the pavement, along with noxious fertilizers contributed by local dairy herds. Den slowed to avoid skidding, but Sinth, high on melic weed and hate, did not. The distance between the hearse and Den's car widened until the Donor was tracking the preacher's vehicle by its dust cloud.

All went as planned until Den rounded a bend and found a team of draft horses hitched to a plow in the middle of the road. He braked hard and swerved onto the edge, threading the narrow gap between the team and the freshly worked soil of the field. Horns blared and brakes squealed as less skilled drivers sought to avoid a pileup. The horses spooked. The farmer gaped at the traffic jam on his peaceful road, then prudently moved his team. Den sped off after Sinth. The Caravan sorted itself out and followed.

The road split, but a dust cloud lingered over the unpaved branch. *Shen, what kind of shock absorbers does Sinth have on that hearse?* The dirt road rejoined a paved one and Den closed the distance to the vehicle in front of him. The winding road straightened and he and his passengers finally saw it.

"I hate to tell you," Arth remarked, "but we're following a manure truck."

"I *thought* the smell had improved," Tohm commented. "Sinth probably took the paved road. Maybe we can intersect him."

"Why bother?" Den asked. When the other stared, he shrugged. "Sinth can't do much by himself. All his people are following *us*."

The two out-Territory Gens broke into laughter. "Sosu Milnan, you're almost as devious as my Silva!" Tohm applauded, gasping for breath. "It's a beautiful day for a nice, long drive in the country."

Den drove up and down the country roads, making turns at random. He followed a creek for a while, then crossed it and headed out between fields and orchards. The Caravan followed blindly.

The selyn batteries on the older busses began to give out, forcing their drivers to turn around. Den's vehicle still had an adequate charge, but he decided that the game had gone on long enough. "How do we get home from here, anyway?"

His question was met with silence.

"Come on, now," the Donor urged with growing alarm. "Tohm, you grew up here and Arth's gone to school here for years. Surely you know your way around?"

"I'm a graduate student. I can't afford a car," Arth said quietly.

"My father lets me borrow his jalopy, but I don't drive it any further out of town than I'm willing to walk back." Tohm sighed. "Doesn't the Sime Center have a map?"

"Several," the Donor groaned, "in the Sime Center's ambulance. I didn't think to bring one."

"Maybe there's something useful in here," Tohm suggested, opening the glove compartment and pulling out a stack of maps. "They're in Simelan," he complained. "I don't recognize the geography, either."

Den waited for a straight stretch of road, then glanced at the maps. "Those are districts around Valzor," he confirmed.

"Would this be more useful?" Arth asked from the back seat, holding up a road atlas.

"Would it ever!" OLD SOKS's leader snatched the book from the sociology student. "There's a map that covers this area," he announced a few minutes later, "but it's pretty large scale and only shows the major highways. Where are we, anyway?"

"At the intersection of County Road 78 and an unnamed dirt track," the Donor said.

"If we keep going, we're bound to run into a town eventually," Arth said with more hope than conviction.

Tohm said darkly "It would be just like a farmer to build a road leading to a tomato field. What can you expect of people who decorate their orchards with confetti and ribbons, out in the middle of nowhere?"

Indeed, the row of trees on the right had ribbons tied around their trunks, in a variety of brilliant colors. Hunks of unspun cotton drifted on the ground below. About halfway down the row, the ribbons were replaced by large bags that encased the ends of the branches.

"Wait a minute," Arth said, pushing his nose against the window. "Are those walnut trees?"

"How should I know?" Tohm asked. "What does it matter?"

"It matters because if *they* are, I think I know where *we* are," Arth retorted. "My officemate made some cash last spring helping the professor who does walnut breeding make controlled crosses. They used bags to contain the pollen. The orchard was just south of Oak Ridge."

"Then if we head north, we'll hit civilization," Tohm whooped. "Although calling Oak Ridge 'civilization' might be stretching it a bit."

"All we require is a map," Den pointed out. "I'm sure they'll be happy to sell us one, if only to help us Sime-lovers leave as quickly as possible." Up ahead, Road 78 intersected with a similar paved thoroughfare. "Which way is north?"

Tohm looked around, then pointed. "There's a water tower."

Oak Ridge was a few streets of tumbledown houses, with thin, ragged children playing listlessly in bare dirt yards. Yet they passed five large churches, all freshly painted and well-maintained.

Den wondered how the parents in those faded houses could support churches with money that could have fed and clothed their children. *The conservative Gen denominations teach parents to hate and fear their children, who might reveal their secret sins by turning Sime. I wonder if there's a connection?*

Main Street had a dozen shops, selling groceries, hardware, or farm equipment. A group of schoolchildren crossed the street, following their teacher like a clutch of ducklings.

Oak Ridge City Hall was a three-story brick edifice, imposing next to the cheap wood construction of the privately-owned buildings. The sign in front directed visitors to the city government offices, the Chamber of Commerce, the Historical Society, and the Post Office.

"Let's see if the Chamber of Commerce will sell us a map," Den suggested. He steered the car over to the curb and parked.

"There it is!" someone yelled.

Before the Donor could open the door, the Caravan of Decency squealed to a halt behind him. City halls were on the list of targets. Participants had come to strike a blow against Sime-lovers, and knew neither the identity of the town nor its history of opposition to the Sime Center. They had started their morning with Reverend Sinth's rhetoric, and then spent hours driving aimlessly as their frustration grew.

The first wave of busses filled every parking space on the block. The rest of the Caravan abandoned their vehicles in the street. Sinth's followers jumped out, waving signs as they gathered on the front lawn and hesitated, waiting for directions from their absent leader.

Then the man with the turmeric-colored hair screamed, "Let's teach the Sime-loving traitors a lesson!"

The mob roared and surged forward, taking their foul mood out on the building and its innocent occupants. Windows shattered and screams echoed. Some employees escaped down the fire ladders; others were dragged outside. A filing cabinet crashed out a third-floor window and broke open, scattering papers over the lawn. Den decided it was time for a quick escape.

"Looks like the Chamber of Commerce is closed," he said, restarting the engine. "There's a bookstore down the street. Perhaps it carries maps."

CHAPTER 18

A DIFFERENT PERSPECTIVE

"What I don't understand," Den mused the next morning as he gave Arth a stack of records, "is why Save Our Kids has become so violent. They used to taunt donors and stage boycotts, but in Oak Ridge they put three city clerks and the postmaster in the hospital. With public opinion moving against them, you'd think they'd behave themselves."

"Actually, I'd expect the opposite," Arth said as Sumulo flounced in and appropriated the most comfortable chair, not greeting either of them. Arth pulled a partially-completed data sheet from his backpack, copied the number on the top folder onto it, then handed the folder to Sumulo.

Telltale brown stains on the channel's fingertips might explain his bad temper. *So, he did check the car to see whether we left the new battery in it. I'll tell Bors that his suggestion worked.* The electrical expert kept curious hands off his work by placing blobs of heavy grease and walnut juice where the unwary would touch them.

Den noticed that Arth didn't flinch when the Sumulo extended a handling tentacle to flip through the file. *Good. It's about time Arth got used to tentacles. Maybe he'll find it easier to donate.* The graduate student had spent the past few months disproving his own hypothesis about how quickly Gens became accustomed to donating.

"Social theory predicts that as norms change, groups that reject those changes become radicalized in proportion to the strength of their rejection," Arth explained. "Concurrently, previously radicalized groups become integrated into the mainstream."

He's been talking to Professor Ildun again, Den thought. "What?"

Arth turned the data sheet over and drew a horizontal line. "Say you want to know what the public thinks about something controversial, like the Sime Center. Ask a thousand random people and you'll get a wide range of answers. Some will think it's a great idea, some will want to run you out of town. Most will fall somewhere between." He wrote "anti-Sime" at one end of the line and "pro-Sime" at the other, then drew a vertical line at one end and labeled it "number of people."

"If you graph how many people hold each opinion, you'll get something like this." He drew a curve, close to the horizontal line at either end and rising toward the top of the page in the middle.

"How do you know it would look like that?" Den asked.

Arth shrugged. "It's called a 'normal distribution' for a reason. You get this same curve for any trait that varies over a population: political opinions, test scores, or even hair color. It just means that most people are pretty average. Sometimes the curve spreads out more, and there's always noise when you use real data, but if you get more than one hump, chances are you have more than one population."

"As far as their attitudes about the Sime Center are concerned, I'd say Sinth's people and the Rational Deists are two distinct groups," the Donor.

"Not really. They're on opposite sides of this curve, but they live in the same town, send their kids to the same schools, and shop in the same stores. More important, they have the same neighbors, mostly with opinions in between. As long as everyone on the chart gets along well enough to function in their daily lives, there's pressure to conform."

Sumulo yawned in an elaborate display of boredom, but Den was interested. "How do you know if you have two populations, or just, what did you call it, 'noise in the data'?"

"I can show you the math," Arth offered.

"I'll take your word for it," Den assured.

Arth poked his pencil at the middle of the hump. "As I said, on any controversial issue, most people's opinions are close to average—or the mean, as it's called." He drew a vertical line that cut the hump in half. "They represent the community's resistance to change. The people out on the fringes," he poked his pencil at the two tails on either side, "have to work hard to get majority's attention, much less agreement. They have nothing to lose by making trouble; it may be the only way they can start a discussion."

Den observed, "Reverend Sinth and Save Our Kids have the same opinions now as when we opened nearly two years ago. They aren't more radical. So why are they suddenly acting like criminals?"

"But they *are* more radical," Arth explained. "When the Sime Center opened, they were slightly more anti-Sime than average. Most people weren't upset enough to stake out your sidewalk, but they didn't trust you, either. Sinth and his people could pretend they represented most of the community. Today, a lot of people like the Sime Center. The mean has shifted."

The student sketched a new curve further toward the "pro-Sime" end of the scale. "Since Sinth and his followers didn't shift with the mean, their old, unchanged opinion is now radical. These days, their 'enemies' include just about everyone."

Den nodded slowly. "I think I understand. If you're right, Save Our Kids will create more trouble in the future, not less."

Arth shrugged. "Give it time. Sinth's followers grew up with community support for their beliefs. Their children's friends will take your change-over classes and may have parents who donate selyn. If Save Our Kids members want to live here, they'll have to moderate their position to be tolerable to their neighbors. Some day they may decide it's a religious duty to donate! Speaking of which," his Adam's apple convulsed, "I've got to donate tomorrow and I was wondering…"

Den raised an interrogative eyebrow.

"There are lots of new channels around," Arth continued. "I'm sure they're perfectly safe, but I'd rather donate to someone I know."

I hope you're paying attention, Sumulo, Den thought as he nodded. *You won't take another donation until you inspire the same confidence in a donor as Rital.*

Arth shuffled his feet, then blurted out, "So could I donate to Hajene Sumulo?"

"What??" Den yelped. Arth stared at Den. Den damped the fields.

Out of Arth's view, the young channel grinned in triumph at Den and made an obscene gesture with three tentacles.

"Why do you want to donate to Sumulo?" Den asked.

The student shrugged. "He reminds me of my kid brother."

"Hajene Sumulo isn't scheduled for a Collectorium shift tomorrow…" Den began.

"I can find time for your donation," Sumulo interrupted smoothly, with a remarkable imitation of a sincere smile. "Glad to help a friend."

"Hajene Sumulo is a Second Order channel, not a First like Controller Madz, Hajene Nerina, or Hajene Tyvi." Den warned. He couldn't say more without revealing things he dared not add to the Clear Springs rumor mill.

Arth shrugged. "I don't mind if he doesn't."

"No trouble at all," Sumulo murmured. "The Tecton tries to honor such requests, unless there's a good reason not to." He eyed Den smugly, daring the Donor to reveal the "good reason."

Den refused to take the bait. "The final decision rests with Controller Madz."

Sumulo stiffened.

"If you would come with me, Hajene Sumulo," the Donor continued, "we can consult him now." The young channel followed Den obediently enough…if one overlooked his confident swagger.

"Don't get your hopes up," Den advised. "Rital won't overturn his own injunction, even if you did con Arth into requesting you."

"Your Houseless lorsh of a cousin doesn't have a choice," Sumulo answered. "That injunction gives me the right to take donations from any staff member who requests me. You didn't specify that they had to be in-Territory citizens."

"That's understood," Den protested.

"Tell that to the regional oversight committee," the channel mocked. "That long-winded bore in the library is legally mine."

* * * *

"He's right, Den," Rital admitted reluctantly. "The injunction says staff, which technically includes Arth. However," he flipped open Arth's file. "Arth's always been handled by Firsts. I'm not sure he's ready to donate to a channel with less control."

"Don't try to intimidate me," Sumulo scoffed. "Your precious Arth Tinkum has the sensitivity of a brick wall. He'll never notice the difference working with a Second. Besides, last time he donated selyn, he only flinched from Tyvi, but didn't struggle the way he did with you a month before."

At Rital's surprised look, the young channel explained, "I looked at his file last week, after I discovered that he was officially 'volunteer staff'." His expression hardened. "You can't legally bar me from taking *this* donation and if you try, I'll charge you with abuse of authority."

Rital's shoulders slumped. Sumulo snickered triumphantly and said slyly, "Of course, if I was on my way back to Valzor tomorrow with papers for my Sectuib, then I wouldn't be able to take donations."

Den had never learned to submit gracefully to bullies, and OLD SOKS had taught him the value of communicating with an opponent in a language the opponent understood.

"Neither you nor your Sectuib will get your tentacles on my selyn battery improvements," he said firmly. "Now, consider this: if there's one thing the Tecton likes less than Controllers who abuse their power, it's channels who abuse donors. If you insist on your right to take Arth's donation, we *will* hold you accountable for how you do it."

Rital flinched from his Donor's nager, which—even though the channel was less than a week past transfer—must feel like an ice-water bath in midwinter. Den was sorry for his cousin's discomfort, but he gained Sumulo's undivided attention.

"You will treat Arth with respect and courtesy," he continued relentlessly. "Before you lay a tentacle tip on him, you will make sure he feels comfortable. And I want no just-healed bruise on his arms when you're done!"

"What if he just gets scared?" Sumulo whined. "Do you expect me to let myself get shenned?"

"Yes!" the Donor pointed out bluntly. "It's your job to make sure that he *doesn't* 'just get scared.' If you can't do that, let someone else take the donation. I will be watching. If I'm not satisfied with your behavior, you'll be relieved of all duties and confined to your quarters until District Controller Monruss can act on our recommendation that you be involuntarily retired."

The young channel blanched. Despite ongoing medical research, retirement for a channel often amounted to a death sentence…and a very unpleasant one, too. "That's blackmail!"

"You would know," Den pointed out.

"My uncle…"

"…is just another Second Order channel, to the Tecton. Monruss isn't a Householder and he's too honest to bribe. He won't let you accept House discipline again, so you'll be tried–and convicted–in the full glare of public scrutiny, to Ohmand's shame." Den gave a feral grin and asked, "Are you sure you really want to take Arth's donation?"

Sumulo wavered for a moment, then snarled, "Yes! I won't let you deprive me of my rights. If you think you can use this as an excuse for judicial murder, think again!"

The young channel stormed out, slamming the door. Rital flinched, then relaxed as Den let go of his anger to offer support. "I'm sorry," Den apologized. "You shouldn't have had to zlin that, but I didn't think anything less than the full treatment would get the brat's attention."

"Den, I said I'd leave Sumulo to you, and I will," the channel said, rubbing his eyes with all eight handling tentacles. "I'll even back you on his involuntary retirement, if I have to. Who knows, we might win despite the young hooligan's uncle. But if it comes to an official action, we'll be on trial every bit as much as Sumulo."

"I don't think it will come to that." Den said stepped behind his cousin's chair and began massaging the tension out of the channel's shoulders. "I just dared Sumulo to prove me wrong and do a good job with Arth. He's got the technical ability if he decides to use it. Arth trusts him, even if we don't. I'll bet you two mugs of Yon's best porstan that nothing happens."

"Done," Rital said, shaking off the Donor's hands as he reached for the next folder in his "in" basket. As Den left the channel to his paperwork, he thought he heard his cousin mutter, "If I lose, I'll buy a round for the whole table."

That evening the negotiators returned from Berrysville before dinner-time. Ref scrambled to produce their meals hours earlier than anticipated. They ate in their accustomed group, discussing the day's work. Tonight, though, there were shrugs and shaking heads.

Afterward, a frustrated Quess brought his tea over to the table Den and his cousin shared. "Would it be possible to enlist the Sime Center's aid to demonstrate a point to the Berrysville City Council?"

Rital raised a cautious eyebrow. "I don't see why not. Do you want to give them a tour, prove we're not hiding a Secret Pen?"

Den controlled his reaction tightly. Any mention of *that* particular ur-ban legend made him very nervous, ever since he'd learned that Rob Lif-ton's first, involuntary donation had taken place during an unsuccessful attempt to prove it true. *If Rital ever learns that...*

The channel looked at his Donor strangely, but was distracted as Quess explained, "Not exactly. I want to convince them that they should observe reasonable caution around Simes, even channels."

"What?" Den asked, unsure if he had heard correctly. "Isn't our pur-pose here to win acceptance from the out-Territory community?"

"Well, yes," the older Donor admitted. "But some limits must be ob-served, for safety's sake, just as we do in-Territory." He reached into the bowl of unshelled walnuts on the table for the nutcracker, positioned a nut between the jaws and explained, "The talks have stalled over the location for the part-time Sime Center. They want to put us in a wing of the Ber-rysville Community Clinic, but because it's their only medical facility, they refuse to close the clinic while we're there!"

"Didn't you explain that the nageric noise would drive the channel crazy, particularly if a serious injury came in?" Rital asked.

"Of course I did." Quess squeezed on the nutcracker, knuckles white with frustration, and the walnut shell shattered with a loud snap. "They said the most serious injuries are taken directly to the university hospital in Clear Springs. However, they've offered to install all the shielding we want, at their own expense."

"What does the clinic's doctor say about all this?" Rital asked.

"The idiot who suggested it claimed he *was* the doctor!" the diplomat said indignantly. He popped a piece of kernel into his mouth and bit down savagely.

"Was he young, enthusiastic, and addicted to strong coffee?" Den asked.

Quess nodded.

"Dr. Lennard!" Den and Rital chorused.

"He donates selyn each month at our mobile Sime Center," Den explained. "He always interrogates us about in-Territory approaches to healing. He's referred some of his patients to us for diagnostics, too. He's got some grand idea of developing a hybrid medical science, pulling techniques from both sides of the border."

"Shen, I didn't think it was that serious!" Quess said with obvious alarm. "The man's as daft as the Sectuib in Zeor!"

"You won't get him to understand the problems of mixing Simes and untrained out-Territory Gens," Rital warned.

"Fortunately, Dr. Lennard's not on the City Council, so he doesn't have a vote." Quess attacked another walnut. "However, Mayor Jon Mills and Councilor Jules Tansky are almost as bad. They think we can share space with a medical clinic as easily as with a church. In fact, Tansky claims putting the Sime Center at the Community Clinic will reduce potential trouble!"

"He's right," Den said, "if your definition of 'trouble' is political backlash. It's a pretty clever solution, actually."

At their blank stares, the Donor elaborated. "Most Sime Center-related incidents in Clear Springs result from Reverend Sinth's attempts to prevent people from accessing our services. The out-Territory community–and their courts–allow such behavior from anti-Sime activists, because anyone heading into a Sime Center is engaged in pro-Sime activity. But Quess, remember how angry people got last fall, when the demonstrators in front of the Upper School screamed abuse at all students, not just those taking the changeover class?"

The diplomat nodded slowly. "Now that you mention it, I do."

"No one enjoys bullying, especially if they're not doing whatever the bully wants to stop. It would be a public relations nightmare for Reverend Sinth to block access to medical care. Everyone in Berrysville would be threatened, so out-Territory law would stop Sinth."

"I see," Rital said slowly. "With the Sime Center in the same building as the clinic, we'd have the same protection from demonstrations that we enjoy in-Territory."

Den nodded. "Sinth's people can't distinguish our selyn donors from Dr. Lennard's patients. For that matter, all our Berrysville donors *are* his patients, and the right of access to medical care is the same on both sides of the border."

Rital looked thoughtful. "It might be worth putting up with the nageric static, if we didn't have to deal with donors being attacked on their way in."

"Putting the part-time Sime Center in the Community Clinic might limit problems *outside* the facility," Quess conceded, "but what about *inside?* Gens who are not comfortable around Simes can avoid our mobile

Sime Center in the church. They can't if we're in the Community Clinic. What if someone dies or is permanently harmed by delaying medical care to avoid us? That would harm our public image." He indicated Den with a nod. "To borrow a phrase from our expert on public relations."

"True enough," Rital said. "So. What do you propose?"

The diplomat shifted uneasily. "All Berrysville Council members like Dr. Lennard's proposal, but only Jules Tansky and Mayor Mills donate selyn. I doubt Eda Seebourgin, Mont Viller, or Silique Dramlin have ever seen a tentacle up close. They're practical folk. Experience might convince them to find us a more…isolated location."

"What sort of experience?" the channel asked dubiously.

Quess stacked his nutshells in a carefully balanced pile. "When diplomatic negotiations stall, it's customary to hold informal entertainments. The unofficial negotiations they allow are often quite productive. Informally, it's possible to explore compromises without losing face or threatening an official position."

"You want to throw a party?" Den asked. "Here at the Sime Center?"

The older Donor nodded. "Bethany reaches sixteen natal years next week. She'll be a legal adult on both sides of the border. It's plausible for me to throw a party for my granddaughter and invite the Berrysville City Councilors."

"A courtesy they can't afford to refuse," Rital observed, "but which will expose them to Simes not wearing retainers?"

"Yes. It should allow them to better grasp the reason behind our position."

"If it doesn't change their minds about having a Sime Center in their town at all," Den muttered.

"We have enough channels and Donors to keep things from getting out of hand," Rital calculated. "You have my permission to use Sime Center facilities. I expect Ref would welcome the challenge of pleasing a crowd from both sides of the border."

* * * *

Arth reported nervously to the Collectorium the following morning, to be greeted by a smiling Sumulo. Goaded by Den's projection of blatant skepticism, the channel put on an inspired "little brother" act. Arth's apprehension faded as they talked and he was less reluctant than usual when Sumulo suggested—politely—that it was time for him to lie down on the transfer lounge.

Despite Sumulo's nonthreatening attitude, the student shrank away when the channel's handling tentacles emerged from their sheaths to wrap around his forearms. *Oh, shen,* Den swore silently, projecting both alarm and malicious glee. The young channel stopped in his tracks.

Instead of clamping down to immobilize Arth, Sumulo moved with him, maintaining only enough grip to prevent the Gen from freeing his arms. It didn't take much effort, since the flinching was more reflex than a serious attempt to escape. A few murmured reassurances calmed the graduate student and he gave no more trouble as Sumulo sought full transfer contact—much more gently than he had with Mr. Duncan.

Den hid his relief under a simulated disappointment. Along with the physical relief of taking his first donation in weeks, that kept the young channel on his best behavior until Arth was safely on his way to the accounting window to pick up his donation payment.

"I told you he wouldn't give me any trouble," Sumulo gloated as the Donor escorted him out of the Collectorium. "You and your precious cousin can't bar me for incompetence now. Why, that long-winded fool of a would-be scholar actually thinks I like him! As if I'd make a friend of an out-Territory lorsh."

Den shrugged, dropping the control that had prevented the Second from zlinning his true emotions. "It doesn't matter whether you like out-Territory selyn donors or not," he pointed out, "as long as you convince *them* to like *you*. If you'd spooked Arth, it would have caused trouble for Rital and me."

Sumulo's glee faded as he realized he had been manipulated.

"You've now proved," Den continued, "that you have the ability to get along with out-Territory Gens…and that you didn't bother to use it for Mr. Duncan. The injunction stands for as long as you remain in Clear Springs." Den waved the young channel through the open library door with a flourish.

Sumulo gave a mutinous snarl as he saw the stack of donation records, then flounced over to his accustomed chair to wait for Arth. In an attempt to reclaim victory, he taunted, "Don't think you can bribe Raymond Ildun into telling you what you want to know by offering him that peanut brittle you had Ref bake."

Den raised an eyebrow, keeping his nager controlled so the Second Order channel wouldn't zlin his sudden interest. "What makes you so sure young Raymond will turn down such a delicacy?" he kept his tone completely disinterested.

With a superior sneer, Sumulo announced, "Because he breaks out in hives if he eats even one or two peanuts. His mother makes his nutbutter out of walnuts. Kid or not, he's too smart to risk peanut brittle."

Den shrugged. "I'll have to eat it myself, then." He nodded toward the stack of files. "Have fun translating. Now, if you'll excuse me, I have a bet to collect."

It wasn't collecting on his bet with Rital that had Den in his cousin's office a few minutes later. He could barely contain his excitement as he announced, "I've got it!"

"Is it contagious?" Rital asked.

Den rolled his eyes, then placed a jar of clear oil on the channel's desk. "Our missing ingredient!" The channel leaned forward to inspect the jar. "It was the jar of nutbutter all the time. It wasn't made from peanuts, though. Raymond's allergic to them. It was walnuts!"

Rital's eyes widened. "In this place? Of *course* it was walnuts! But are walnuts and peanuts that different?"

"They might be," Den said, shifting from foot to foot in nervous excitement. "We saw a lot of improvement using different oils. Walnut oil's the only thing left. Branlee will be here in half an hour. Do you have time to help us test it? I'd rather not ask Tyvi, in case it works."

No channel could resist something his Donor wanted so badly. "Of course," Rital agreed.

* * * *

"We're out of our coffee-and-trin tea mixture," Branlee reported, when they arrived at the basement lab. "I've started the coffee pot, but the trin box is empty."

"I'll get more," Den said, then paused as an idea struck. "You know, we never did test the different *kinds* of trin, except to find out that the cheap stuff doesn't work as well as a premium blend."

Branlee agreed. "We went with the cheaper one until we solved the rest of the puzzle."

"The primary difference between cheap and premium trin is the degree of peppery flavor," the Donor mused, remembering Arth's insistence that most measurable things came in a broad continuum arranged around a most-common mean value. "If the piperine concentration makes a difference…"

"Try the medicinal grade?" Rital finished, following his cousin's logic with the ease of long practice.

"There's a medicinal form of trin tea?" Branlee asked. "No surprise. It all tastes like medicine to me."

"This from the man who drinks coffee?" the Donor asked.

"Coffee is a hallowed balm that allows poor, overworked graduate students to function."

"Trin is a group of related species and hybrids," Den explained. "They have different flavors–you should taste the strange stuff they grow in Gulf

Territory–but they all have square stems and leaves that are covered with oil glands and grow in pairs on opposite sides of that stem. The medicinal species has a very harsh flavor, partly because it has a lot more piperine. We use it to cover up the taste of medicines."

"A battery won't care how it tastes," Branlee observed. "Let's test all three trin teas in sunflower oil first. Walnut oil's expensive and you don't have enough there to run more than a couple of trials."

"Why is that?" Den asked. "Here in the middle of walnut heaven, I can pick walnuts off the sidewalk for free."

"Leaving aside that the summer walnut drop happens before the nut-meats are mature enough to have oil," Branlee explained, "the process of getting oil out of the mature ones is difficult—and therefore expensive. You know how hard it is just to get the kernels out of the shells."

So, Den raided the pharmacy for medical-grade trin and the carefully horded stash in his office for the premium variety. Ref's pantry yielded a standard blend. On the shelf next to it was the Gulf trin that Sumulo drank as a matter of Territorial pride. With a malicious grin, Den helped himself to a sample.

By the time he rejoined the others in the lab, Branlee had decanted sun-flower oil into a series of beakers and Rital had the teakettle boiling. They prepared the teas, then Branlee carefully added a shot of coffee to each. The optimal dose of each mixture was added to four of the beakers, then Rital carefully lowered the charger into them, reading off how much selyn each drained from the standard battery.

"You were right about the medical trin," Branlee declared. "It's twice as effective as your premium blend."

"And Householding Ohmand uses the worst trin variety possible," Den observed, his attention fixed on the other side of the curve. "Why am I not surprised?"

Rital agreed. "Think of the selyn wasted on the sliderail alone, moving all that extra gel, packed in lead-lined barrels."

"Shall we see how the walnut oil does, since we have sunflower oil controls set up?" Branlee asked.

Den poured a measure of the walnut oil into a clean beaker. Branlee added coffee and standard Nivet trin, "because we have the best data on that combination," and Rital charged it.

The channel zlinned, blinked, and zlinned again. "No wonder we saw such a strong effect in the washtub, with only a finger's width of oil from Raymond's nutbutter jar. The battery is almost drained and we started the day with a full charge. That makes this combination…"

"… a hundred times more efficient than the standard gel," Branlee finished Rital's sentence, scribbling calculations. "And that was standard trin."

"Let's put all the pieces together, then, and see just how much charge a selyn battery can carry," Den suggested. "But let's do it right." He ceremoniously lifted the small battery box down from its shelf, blew the dust off, and placed it on the table. The graduate student poured a careful measure of walnut oil into the box, then added the coffee-and-medicinal-trin mixture.

"I'd better recharge the battery," Rital said. When he finished, he cautiously set the charger into the mixture.

Den shifted eagerly. "How far did the battery get drained?" he demanded, when his cousin didn't report quickly enough.

"Completely," the channel reported, his voice betraying his shock. "It drained the whole battery."

Branlee scribbled more calculations, frowned at the result, and tried again. When the same answer came up the third time, he said, "If our concoction drained a fully charged selyn battery, that means with the walnut oil we now have battery gel that holds about 270 times more selyn than the standard one. We should get Tohm to draw up another patent, first thing."

"Yes," Den agreed, as the importance of the afternoon's work hit home. He carefully removed the charger, sprinkled in some of Alyce's Bordo mix to prevent it from spoiling, and sealed the lid. Then he hefted it on one palm. "This weighs about as much as a dozen oranges. Maybe a bit less. A trivial weight, but a full battery's worth of power. Do you realize what this means?"

"That the train routes can expand to serve even more out-Territory communities?" Rital guessed.

The Donor shook his head.

"That we'll make a lot of money when we start mass production?" Branlee hazarded.

"It means," Den corrected, "that for the first time it's theoretically possible to build a selyn-powered flyer that isn't too heavy to get off the ground. We can soar like a hawk and eventually reach for the stars, as the Ancients did."

Eddina, we did it!

CHAPTER 19

A COMING OF AGE

Reverend Sinth was not held accountable for the destruction of the Oak Ridge Town Hall. Witnesses testified that the preacher had been eating a solitary late lunch at a diner in Clearston, ten miles away, when the riot started. Oak Ridge's only police officer had been locked in her office and could not identify the perpetrators.

Reverend Sinth refused to reveal the names of those who had participated in the Caravan of Decency. "When those good people committed to taking action against Sime tyranny, they made a vow to God through me, their pastor. Outrage at Sime atrocities drove their action against what they sincerely believed was a cesspool of pro-Sime sentiment."

Unable to punish those who had committed the crime, Judge Lindsey levied a substantial fine against Save Our Kids for inciting a riot. This hit Reverend Sinth hard, because he'd been using the Save Our Kids bank account for his personal finances since Householding Shaeldor had garnished his personal funds to replace the money stolen from Bethany.

The preacher was more irritable than usual. Den suspected that he was on the edge of melic withdrawal. His latest fundraising letter called for emergency donations to "allow our **Cause** to remain **Strong** in spite of the **Devil's** efforts to **Thwart** us with this **Unjust Fine**."

While waiting for his followers to pay his bills, Sinth started trying to win back his niece.

"He knows Bethany gets control of her money in another week," Quess remarked sourly.

* * * *

Rital was a gracious loser and accompanied Den to the next OLD SOKS meeting to pay his bet. The channels seldom left the Sime Center except for official business, so it caused a stir when the pub's patrons saw his retainers. However, nobody protested and Yon Keysvetter, who was tending bar, nodded in greeting.

Although the brew master didn't donate selyn, Den wasn't surprised. The more anti-Sime religious denominations also preached abstinence from alcoholic beverages, while hosting OLD SOKS meetings added significantly to the pub's profit margin. Also, Keysvetter's porstan sales would soar if a real Sime liked it, publicly.

The OLD SOKS activists greeted Rital enthusiastically. *They like showing everyone they're not afraid of the Sime,* Den thought with concealed amusement. *Even, or maybe especially, those who don't donate selyn.*

The business meeting was conducted in a lively, unstructured manner befitting college students with anarchistic leanings. Then Tohm shocked the group by asking them to use their less-obscene chants and songs on Wednesdays and Fridays. "That's when the Rational Deists will join us," he explained. "They're older and might not understand our fun."

"Let 'em stay home, if they haven't got a sense of humor," someone grumbled.

Tohm said crisply, "The Deists pledge twenty people on the sidewalk twice a week and more if we expect trouble." He glared at the heckler. "You know how thin we were stretched, guarding only two targets from Sinth's 'Caravan of Depravity.' If Sosu Milnan hadn't detoured them to Oak Ridge" –the phrasing made it seem deliberate– "they'd have done major damage to the Sime Center or the school. We can really use the Deists' help stopping the Holy Hypocrite. There's nothing gained by offending them."

Den was astonished. An aspiring lawyer, Thom had scoured the university's Law School Library for songs cited in obscenity cases. Then he had braved the Music Department's notoriously ill-managed Special Collection to locate a learned thesis with the grandiose title of "Bawdy Ballads, Lewd Lays, and Dirty Ditties: An Historical Commentary on Erotic Songs Through the Ages."

Despite their inability to master library cataloging, the Music Department's faculty held their students to a high standard of scholarship. The thesis had an appendix longer than the text, in which the score and lyrics of every song mentioned in the body of the work were reproduced. Tohm had devoted several meetings to teaching the worst of them to the rest of the group.

At least two women had stopped participating in Save Our Kids' demonstrations after hearing their rendition of the anatomically questionable, "We All Had Fun at the Orgy." Den understood why. OLD SOKS' sloppy diction and anarchistic approach to melody and key made it difficult to understand the words, although after reading the lyrics on Tohm's song sheets, Den doubted proper enunciation would help.

Still, Tohm was proud of his ballads and he'd never before worried that they might offend anybody. Den was puzzled by the abrupt change, until he saw Arth frantically making notes and recalled the graduate student's lecture on why Sinth's people were growing more radical.

It works both ways, he realized. *OLD SOKS used to be the radical fringe, so they misbehaved to prove their critics right. Public opinion has shifted and suddenly, they're almost mainstream.* Realizing that people might listen to them now, Tohm was moderating OLD SOKS' tactics.

The students asked about the proposed part-time Sime Center in Berrysville. Rital explained that he wasn't involved in the negotiations. Rob Lifton mentioned his concern that Quess would talk Bethany into living in-Territory with her new-found family. All Den could think of to say was, "Spend as much time as you can with her. You're right that she has a major life decision to make." *No way am I going to try to influence these kids. It's their life.*

As the evening continued, the consumption of his winnings had the predictable effect on Den. He shifted uncomfortably in his chair. Rital stood it for nearly five minutes, then broke off his conversation with Tohm's girlfriend Silva and turned to his cousin. "Go ahead," he advised softly, nodding toward the men's room. "Silva's low field and the crowd isn't hostile. I'm safe enough."

Den didn't like to leave his channel unattended out-Territory. However, Rital was pre-Turnover and many of the OLD SOKS crowd were regular selyn donors. No one else was talking loudly or looking in Rital's direction. In fact, the other patrons were ignoring the lone Sime.

Strictly speaking, Tecton regulations required that Den make his cousin accompany him to the bathroom. *But if Rital can trust my judgment on Sumulo, I can trust him to zlin for signs of trouble before sending me away.*

The Donor found his way to the men's room. A quick stop at the urinal took care of his most urgent problem, but the greasy onion rings were also making their presence known, so he headed for a stall.

Den was deciphering the graffiti on the stall's door, which was actually amusing, when he heard two people enter the bathroom.

"I'm sorry, Rob," Arth's uncertain voice echoed off the tile. "Let me help you rinse that out."

"It's only beer," Rob Lifton reassured him. "It won't stain."

"I know, but your mother might not understand if you came home smelling like you'd been swimming in your stein."

Cloth rustled. "Here, you take the shirt and I'll wash me."

Water splashed.

"Tohm is awfully concerned with keeping the Rational Deists happy, isn't he?" Arth asked.

"There are rumors that Sinth plans something truly spectacular if things don't go his way." Rob chuckled. "I'd like to see Berrysville get its part-time Sime Center, but I hope negotiations don't end on my donation day. I'd rather not be caught in Sinth's revenge."

The soap dispenser squeak was followed by muffled scrubbing sounds. "I envy you," Arth admitted. "I wish I was that casual about donating selyn. Every time I think about what Simes live on, my knees turn to jelly."

"Mine, too," Rob agreed. "I'm glad the channels put the selyn to good use, for the trains and all. I really like most of the Simes I've met, in spite of their…diet. But I'd rather not think about my friends having *me* for lunch, even indirectly!"

"So why doesn't donating selyn bother you?"

Den remained still, eavesdropping shamelessly.

"It's all in how you think about it," Rob explained. "It used to bother me a lot, until Sosu Milnan told me, 'You know what's going to happen and how it's going to feel.' Or something like that; I can't remember his exact words."

"I don't understand," Arth said. Wet cloth slapped against the porcelain basin as he rinsed soap out of Rob's shirt.

I don't understand, either.

"It's simple enough," Rob explained. "You don't feel the channel taking your selyn. Right?"

"I guess so," Arth agreed.

"In fact, you only have the channel's word that anything happens at all."

"They get selyn to run the trains from somewhere," Arth pointed out.

"Anyway," Rob continued, ignoring Arth's logic, "since I don't feel anything, I just tell myself that the channel is faking it. Much less scary."

"I don't know," Arth said dubiously. "It sounds strange to me."

That's an understatement, Den agreed silently. Rob was avoiding the problem, instead of facing and overcoming it. If the illusion crumbled, fear could return and trigger Sime aggression. *But as long as he stays out-Territory, it'll work.* Channels could handle an occasional flare of fear, the Sime Center's staff renSimes didn't take chances, and good manners wouldn't help Rob much against a changeover berserk with Need.

There was a sharp snap of wet fabric as Arth shook the wrinkles out of Rob's shirt. "Here, I think most of the beer came out."

"Thanks," Rob said. "Yeow, that's cold," he complained. A moment later he spoke again. "If pretending the channel is faking doesn't work for you, why not look at it like this?" he suggested. "Channels are just as strong as any Sime, aren't they?"

"Yeah."

"So, if a channel decided to kill you when you're donating selyn, there's nothing you could do to stop it, right?"

"Too true." Arth's voice quivered.

"Well then, why fight it? Either trust the channel or don't donate."

"If I want to keep my stipend, I have to do my research at the Sime Center," Arth objected. "I have to donate selyn, or I can't eat."

"Nonsense," Rob scoffed. "If you really believed channels were dangerous, you'd find a new research project. You've already decided that donating selyn is less risky than finding a new major professor."

After a moment, "You're right," Arth admitted. "It wasn't as frightening last time, with Hajene Sumulo."

"Hajene Sumulo? My grandfather didn't like him at all."

Shedoni! Den stifled a groan of despair. The thought of these two Gens comparing notes had been a recurring nightmare.

However, Rob just laughed. "Grandfather calls Sumulo an impudent brat with no manners." An affectionate note crept into the young Gen's voice. "But then, he says that about everyone our age. Grandfather's over seventy. He's earned the right to be a crotchety old man."

"He has, at that," Arth allowed. Shoes scuffled towards the door. "Thanks for the advice and for being a good sport about your shirt. Let me buy you a replacement for your beer?"

"Sure…"

As the door banged closed behind the two Gens, Den sagged in relief. *I'll never let anyone blackmail me into going against my professional judgment again,* he vowed. *There are good reasons for Arth and Rob to mistrust the Tecton, even if they don't know them.* If Rob had taken his grandfather's complaints seriously, there could have been major damage to the Sime Center's precarious position in Clear Springs.

I'll never object to cantankerous old grumblers again.

* * * *

The preparations for Bethany's coming-of-age party went smoothly, apart from minor details.

"Sosu Milnan, Grandfather hired a *string quartet* to play at my birthday party!" Bethany complained.

"The University Chamber Ensemble has an excellent reputation."

"Have *you* ever sat through one of their concerts?"

"Well, no," the Donor admitted.

"*I* have." The young woman sniffed. "They're *boring*. Why couldn't he hire a group that plays something *interesting*, instead of musty *old* stuff?"

"I'm sure your grandparents will enjoy the music. If your younger guests start falling asleep, we'll sneak off with OLD SOKS for a sing-along."

* * * *

"Den, do you know what my granddaughter's done?" Quess demanded. "She invited Reverend Sinth to the party and the lorsh accepted!"

"His latest fundraising letter must not have inspired many contributions," the younger Donor observed.

"It's not funny. That hate-filled, drug-addicted fanatic will view this as a Heaven-sent opportunity to make trouble."

"Of course he will," Den agreed. "But obnoxious or not, the man *is* Bethany's uncle."

"Whose side are you on?" the older Donor complained. "That's what she said. She threatened not to attend her own party, if her only living relative on her father's side couldn't come."

"Look at it this way: after his six months in the Valzor jail, the Reverend won't panic at the first glimpse of a tentacle. That's more than can be said for the guests *you* invited."

* * * *

"Sosu Milnan, could I have a moment of your time?" It was Ref. "It's about Sosu Quess's party." The portly chef was wringing his hands in distress. "I purchased a case of white table wine from the Walnut Crest Winery over by Oak Ridge. However, I don't know *what* to do about food. Sosu Quess wants both in- and out-Territory refreshments, but most out-Territory dishes are meat-based and Reverend Sinth's targeting the grocers again. They won't sell me enough fruits and vegetables. I could order from Valzor, but it wouldn't be fresh when it got here."

"Don't panic, Ref," the Donor advised. "I'll ask Miz Dilson to search for meat-free out-Territory recipes and OLD SOKS can buy what you require. Who knows, the grocers might forget to double the price!"

* * * *

"Hello, Den," Rital greeted him when the Donor sought refuge in his cousin's office. "About this party?"

"Yes?"

"With so many out-Territory Gens, I expect complications. We can't provide every problem Gen with an Escort, but we can cover the worst. Could you do me a favor?"

"What?" the Donor asked suspiciously.

"Would you keep Reverend Sinth out of trouble?"

"AARRRGHHHH!"

* * * *

Despite the difficulties, even Quess the Perfectionist admitted that professional event planners could not have done better. The cafeteria gleamed.

Serving tables groaned under an impressive variety of delicacies. The string quartet played softly, and even though Den agreed with Bethany about their repertoire, they added a touch of elegance.

Hajene Nerina had provided an evening gown for her granddaughter: a warm, orange creation with touches of brown. The guest of honor looked charming and blended perfectly with her grandparents' traditional brown and blue-green Householding livery.

Bethany had been encouraged to invite as many friends from Clear Springs as she pleased. However, since she had never been allowed to socialize outside her uncle's ministry, the majority of her invitations had been refused, with varying degrees of politeness.

She took the rejection philosophically. "I knew they would drop me when I left to live with Simes," she explained with surprising maturity.

Quess had recruited OLD SOKS to provide young faces. They jumped at the chance for free food and drink, even dressing up for the occasion. They were among the first guests to arrive and, after congratulating the guest of honor on reaching her majority, they headed straight for the refreshments.

Not all of Bethany's former friends deserted her. Rob Lifton came with his sister, mother, and grandfather. The young Gen looked handsome in a formal suit, but a stern look from Quess kept Bethany in the receiving line.

Older guests trickled in: the Berrysville City Council, some Clear Springs officials, and some of their steadier donors for additional nageric cushion.

"Our object," Quess explained to Den, "is a little healthy caution, not to run the Berrysville councilors off. Most Berrysville residents view this part-time Sime Center issue as another Rational Deist project, easily ignored by those not interested. It won't hurt to expose Mayor Mills and his colleagues to Reverend Sinth and OLD SOKS."

Den wasn't so sure. While most of the Berrysville guests steered clear of the Simes, the Gens from Clear Springs weren't sending the message Quess anticipated.

"Offering changeover classes in the schools isn't nearly as disruptive as I'd feared," Coach Farrow admitted to Silique Dramlin. "It doesn't interfere with practice and knowing which students are out of danger lets us build stronger teams. With a channel at the school, any child who develops...symptoms...can be handled without risk. I don't mind saying that's a relief."

"Didn't Miz Dramlin's son get his Establishment certificate at our last mobile clinic?" Den asked his cousin softly.

"Yes," the channel said, "but his twin sister's still a child."

"It's knowing what the public wants," Hank Fredricks confided to Mont Viller. "The *Clarion's* circulation boomed when I ran coverage of the changeover classes."

"Is it true that the series won a journalism award?" Mont asked.

"Sure is," the newsman confirmed proudly. "For 'excellence in covering of a timely issue.' We're thinking of doing the same for the mobile Sime Centers."

Den muttered to his cousin, "If there's one thing small town City Councils love, it's free publicity for their pet projects."

"Oh, they're a nuisance," Mr. Duncan answered a question from Eda Seebourgin. "But Reverend Sinth's a lot less influential than he thinks. Most people here like the changes the Sime Center has brought."

Quess is not going to be happy, the Donor thought. He guided his cousin toward the refreshments and fortified himself with the Walnut Crest white.

Tohm Seegrin, almost unrecognizable in a dark brown suit and tie, held forth over the vegetable platter. "—so Reverend Sinth is building a private school on his Clearston farm, where children won't be exposed to the 'contamination' of Simes."

Mayor Mills and Jules Tansky paused to listen. Den nagerically drew Rital's attention to them.

"There's precedent for such retreat from the world," Arth Tinkum commented, waving his wineglass. "The Householdings walled themselves off from Sime society for centuries. As a result, their ability to influence it was limited."

"I hope he doesn't say that in front of Quess," Rital chuckled softly in Simelan, nibbling on a grape.

"Especially since the comparison is valid," the Donor agreed.

The channel shrugged. "A private school won't help as much as Sinth thinks. Teenagers are rebellious. Only a true fanatic would *want* to be murdered for turning Sime, once they have an alternative."

"Let's hope so." Den shot a sly look at the channel. "In a strange way, Sinth is right. The Tecton *is* out to steal their children…and we're succeeding."

"What the shen do you mean by that?" Rital asked. "The only Clear Springs kids in Tecton custody are the young Lornstadts and Bethany, and both custody arrangements were approved by an out-Territory court."

"People have children to transmit their heritage to the next generation, cultural as well as genetic," Den pointed out. "The Conservative Congregation had a way of life here: traditions, community, a strong moral code—"

"Strong moral code!" the channel objected. "You call hunting children down like animals and murdering them a moral act?"

The Donor shrugged. "Before we opened here, all children in change-over had to be murdered or society would have collapsed. Believing Simes were possessed by demons let Sinth's followers do it without crippling guilt."

"Then we changed the rules on them?"

"Exactly." Den snagged a carrot stick and wave it in emphasis. "Almost overnight, their time-honored and necessary survival strategy was redefined as narrow-minded bigotry. Children are more flexible than adults, particularly when their lives are at stake. How many have defied their parents to read our pamphlets? How many who Establish will adopt their parents' extreme anti-Sime values? We're destroying a culture."

"You'll forgive me the feeling that this culture's loss is humanity's gain," Rital said. The channel stiffened, zlinning as he turned toward the cafeteria door. "Speaking of things I'd like to lose, there's Reverend Sinth. And he's not in a good mood."

Den groaned theatrically.

Rital briefly wrapped two handling tentacles around the Donor's wrist. "It could be worse. His nager doesn't have that impulsive edge. I don't think he's chewed melic today."

"So, he probably won't cause any more trouble than he actually intends," Den completed the thought. "Which will still be as much as he can." The Donor trudged toward the receiving line to greet his charge.

Sinth congratulated his niece with a cloying warmth that made Den want a shower. Bethany took it at face value, eagerly agreeing to her uncle's suggestion that they find time for a long chat, "to remove the unfortunate barrier that has grown between us."

From the worn spots on the preacher's clothing and the predatory gleam in his eyes, the Donor suspected that Sinth was most interested in removing the barrier between himself and his niece's money.

Quess discreetly elbowed Sinth aside to introduce honored guest, Mayor Ann Kroag, to his granddaughter.

The preacher huffed indignantly, then with poor grace accepted Nerina's offer of Den as an Escort and headed for the safety of the biggest group of Gens he could find.

He arrived just as Eda Seebourgin told Carla Lifton, "I expect we'll have our part-time Sime Center open by summer, maybe earlier. We'll be up and running within a week, once the agreement is signed."

Her colleagues Silique Dramlin and Mont Viller nodded.

Reverend Sinth flushed purple. "You should be ashamed of yourselves!" he admonished them. "You're not godless Rational Deists, but you're letting Sime rot into your community on their say-so, against the teachings of your own faiths. I'm surprised you sleep at night, with such sins on your conscience!"

Eda Seebourgin shrugged. "I'll not deny I prefer to keep distance between myself and Simes." She looked around the room and shuddered delicately. "But Reverend, I've got to face reality. Berrysville has a lot of Deists, they hold powerful positions, and they want a Sime Center. If I want to be reelected, I must ignore my personal feelings."

Mont Viller chimed in, "Every adult Deist will be at the polls on Election Day. When your Conservative Congregation can promise the same, Reverend, we'll consider your side."

"A part-time Sime Center in town might be a good thing," Silique Dramlin pointed out. "I'm not the kind of person who donates selyn," she wrinkled her pert nose in distaste, "but I like knowing my son is safely Gen. I didn't make him ask the channel," she added hastily. "He volunteered."

Den thought, *I bet that Quess didn't realize how out-Territory politicians fear losing their next election more than they fear Simes!*

The Berrysville City Council was united in their choice of location. "There just *isn't* anywhere else," Mayor Mills explained to Mayor Ann Kroag over stuffed mushrooms. "Not downtown, anyway. The Community Clinic is on the town square, across from the city offices."

"If the Tecton bought or rented a storefront, we'd lose sales tax revenue," Jules Tansky pointed out. "Also the property tax, if it's declared Sime Territory. We're not as wealthy as Clear Springs: we couldn't afford that. The library wants to expand and keeping up the playing fields at the high school costs a fortune. We're lucky Dr. Lennard wants to study channels so badly."

"It'll be convenient to have all the medical services in one place," Mayor Mills added. "Most parents ask the doctor first if they think their kid's in changeover. By the time they get an appointment, never mind a diagnosis, it's often too late to call in the Sime Center. Now, all they'll have to do is walk down the hall."

I really don't think Quess is going to scare them off, Den thought.

Reverend Sinth stalked to the window to glower down at the sidewalk he had patrolled for years, in his futile attempt to run the Tecton out of his city.

Flora Mills swept in just before the reception line broke up. After congratulating the guest of honor, she turned a gimlet eye on Bethany's grandfather. "So you're Sosu Quess," she said in a no-nonsense voice. "My son tells me you don't approve of our location for the part-time Sime Center. I realize that a city-bred man like yourself might not understand how we small-town folks decide these matters…"

Shen, Quess isn't going to win this one at all!

It was a harried diplomat who interrupted his guests' conversations an hour later. A hum of appreciation broke out as Ref proudly brought out the cake, decorated with roses of pink and green icing and candies that spelled out CONGRATULATIONS, BETHANY!

The string quartet started playing a tune Den didn't recognize and the out-Territory guests broke into song. *It must be an out-Territory tradition for natal day celebrations,* Den concluded from the lyrics.

Bethany blushed prettily as the song ended. "Thank you all for coming to help me celebrate my birthday," she said. "And special thanks to you, Grandfather, for putting so much effort into the arrangements."

Den wasn't quite sure how Bethany meant that last statement. Reverend Sinth had pushed his way to the front of the crowd so that his niece could see him singing in her honor. Now he smiled at her, but the expression didn't reach his cold eyes.

"I'm particularly glad that so much of my family is here," she glanced toward her uncle, then her grandparents. "I've been thinking about how I want to spend my future."

The preacher stiffened in sudden hope, echoed by Quess and Nerina.

"So, I'd like to take this opportunity to make a very special announcement," Bethany continued, holding out a hand to Rob, who took it proudly. She kissed him, then announced, "Rob Lifton and I have decided to get married.

Bethany's grandparents flinched at her quiet declaration, but said nothing. Her uncle had less control. "You can't do that!" he bellowed, all traces of affection gone. "I forbid you to marry that Sime-lover!"

Bethany blanched, but held firm. She pointed at the cake. "I'm of age now, Uncle Jermiah. On *both* sides of the border. You can't stop me from marrying whom I please."

"Oh, yes, I can!" Reverend Sinth snarled. "You can't get married without a proper ceremony and no Conservative Congregation minister will marry you to that boy against my decree."

Bethany looked at her uncle steadily. "There are other ministers, of other faiths, who would perform the ceremony."

"You would marry outside the church?"

"If necessary," Bethany warned.

"Do the promises I made in your name at your baptism, to be a good and obedient daughter of the faith, mean nothing to you?"

"Very little," she admitted, "compared with the promises I've made of my own free will."

"You realize that I can't attend such a travesty?"

Bethany gripped Rob's hand so tightly that her knuckles were white, but her voice remained steady. "Rob and I will miss you, if that's your decision. But it won't change our minds."

Sinth glared at his niece, his upper lip curled in contempt. "Then I have nothing more to say to you," he said coldly. "Now, or ever." He stalked for the exit, the crowd parting before him.

Den made sure that the preacher left the Sime Center, then returned to the party. The babble of conversation continued as the Donor made his way toward the couple at its center. Rob held his fiancée as she trembled with reaction. From his expression, he enjoyed hugging her tightly in front of everyone, after so many months of forced discretion. Quess and Nerina were pretending not to be hurt at learning the news in such an abrupt fashion. Den doubted they fooled anyone, not even the Gens.

Rob's mother, Carla Lifton, took charge of the situation. With a glance to make sure Nerina and her tentacles kept their distance, she ordered her son to let Bethany go. "Pull yourself together, girl," she scolded, giving a firm shake to her future daughter-in-law's shoulder. "You have guests to attend. Rob, give her your handkerchief. Annie, cut the cake. You there," she pointed at Quess and Nerina, "tell those musicians to play something. This is a celebration!"

As the cake was distributed, the guests returned to more normal behavior. Most didn't know Bethany very well. The OLD SOKS contingent teased Rob, but resisted the temptation to serenade the happy couple with a ballad's worth of raunchy marital advice. Den wondered how much of Tohm's consideration sprang from etiquette and how much from a desire to set a precedent for when he and Silva set a date.

The Berrysville City Council left after they finished their cake and the other out-Territory guests soon followed. The Liftons were the last, although Rob made it clear that his departure was strictly temporary.

When Bethany returned from seeing Rob off, her hair and the orange dress somewhat the worse for wear, Quess went to her. She didn't try to avoid him.

"Your grandmother and I hoped you'd choose to make your home with us," he said.

Alyce the groundskeeper, who was approaching Need, moved closer to Den, using his nager to block the older Donor's painful emotions. When Den concentrated on smoothing the ambient, she relaxed and went back to work cleaning up the table.

Despite Quess's gentle tone, Bethany flinched. "I'm not a child anymore, to live in someone else's home," she explained. "It's time for me to make my own home and I've chosen to do that with Rob." She met her grandfather's eyes defiantly.

He nodded slowly in resignation, and said, "I see you have. Be happy in your chosen future, then."

Bethany's jaw dropped in surprise, then she threw her arms around Quess. "Oh, Grandfather, I *do* love you!"

CHAPTER 20

A SHIFT OF MEANS

In the end, Quess allowed the part-time Sime Center to be placed in the Berrysville Community Clinic, to be staffed by a channel from Clear Springs twice a week, on Market Day.

The Berrysville Council wanted an armored room at the clinic, in which children in changeover could be confined until a channel was brought to rescue them. As a condition, Quess wanted a Third Order Donor present any time the Community Clinic was open. "If there isn't someone around who can give First Transfer," the diplomat explained, "Dr. Lennard will try to 'help' and get himself Killed."

Dr. Lennard was happy to get a permanent victim for his incessant questions. In return, he wanted relief from out-Territory property taxes on the Sime Center wing of his building. There was no precedent for only part of an out-Territory property becoming Sime Territory permanently, and the negotiations dragged on.

At the end of the second month, Den was assigned a rotation transfer with Nerina, although he worked mainly with Rital while Nerina and Quess went to Berrysville. It was years since Den had given transfer to a channel whose normal draw speed and capacity could Kill him and the experience was both exhilarating and humbling. Nerina pushed him to his limits and beyond, leaving him violently Post while her own Need was barely blunted.

And this was three days early for her!

"Thank you," she said dully when she released him. "That was better than I expected. Most Donors couldn't have trusted a relative stranger to work with such a small safety margin, particularly so soon after being burned."

Den fetched her a cup of trin tea. It *was* unusual for him to let go like that, particularly with a Householder. However, he had come to respect her husband over the winter and couldn't see Quess marrying someone untrustworthy. *Or has Rital been holding back on me so long that I'll risk anything to feel Post again? If so, that could get very dangerous.*

It wasn't reassuring when his cousin whirled to *look* at him when he was barely ten paces away with a startled, "Den, I can barely zlin you!"

Eventually, the tax question was settled, along with those addressing building maintenance, holiday hours, and emergency mutual assistance. In a joint press conference, both sides expressed satisfaction with the final result.

Dr. Lennard emptied the back wing of his building. "The rent will make up for the lost storage space," he confessed to Den, then went back to harassing the Tecton staff installing the shielding and equipment. Even with Branlee's lightweight polycarbonate, it was a big job.

The Grand Opening was set for Faith Day, one of two holidays celebrated on both sides of the border. Like most small towns, Berrysville took advantage of any excuse to celebrate. The City Council erected a stage in the town square for a formal document signing.

The stage would become a reviewing stand for the dignitaries to observe the annual Faith Day parade. The marchers included two day care centers, the Small Business Owner's Association, the winner of an elementary school spelling bee and her teacher, a dance studio, three fraternal organizations, a real estate agent, brand-new tractors pulling an array of farming equipment, assorted sports teams, and Mynga Tailor with her prize-winning milk cow. In addition, *both* the middle and upper school bands would march.

I can't wait to hear them slaughter the Nivet Territory anthem.

Den had hoped to attend the Clear Springs festivities instead; the university's marching band was excellent. However, since the Berrysville clinic would be staffed out of Clear Springs, Rital as local Controller had to co-sign the agreement. *With my luck, that prize-winning cow will deposit something smelly right in front of us.*

The Tecton dignitaries arrived in Berrysville on the appointed day: six channels and seven Donors, with five Gens and three renSimes as support staff. Clear Springs Mayor Kroag had sent Coach Farrow to represent Clear Springs at the event, so that the city's other officials could participate in the Clear Springs festivities.

Farrow was not the only representative from Clear Springs. Reverend Sinth and thirty-odd of his most loyal followers arrived early. Among them, Den recognized Nancy Resher, who still blamed the Tecton for the loss of her daughter at the tentacles of her teammate. They assembled on the lawn of City Hall, across from the Community Clinic and the temporary stage. Sinth was sweating freely and his eyes had a familiar manic gleam.

He's got money to buy melic weed again.

As Mayor Mills greeted his in-Territory guests, Sinth's followers unfurled a banner. "TREATY SIGNERS ARE GENRUNNING TRAITORS!"

it screamed in blood-red letters two feet high. Other signs read "**Stop the Tecton Takeover,**" "**Sime-lovers don't go to Heaven,**" and "**Tentacles are Trouble.**" Den spotted a familiar turmeric-colored head under a "**The Devvil Don't Honer Treetys**" sign.

Den nudged Rital and pointed out the man's heavy backpack. "What's he carrying?"

The channel studied the demonstrator and frowned. "Whatever's in there is too dense for food or water. Between the crowd and these retainers, I can't zlin it clearly, but it could be…a metal pipe?"

"Shen, I hope they don't plan another riot," Den muttered as the mayor shook hands with Quess.

"I doubt it. The others have nothing but signs." Rital zlinned the turmeric-haired man again. "I'll ask Seena to watch that odd-haired fellow when the demonstration breaks up. The situation here is too explosive not to take precautions."

Mayor Mills finished pumping Nerina's hand and reached for Rital's.

The demonstrators waved their signs and chanted in unison, "We'll make a note for when we vote!"

"It won't do them a bit of good to jot down a reminder," the mayor remarked cheerfully. "None of those folks live in Berrysville."

The local Faith Day celebrants were in a good mood, calling greetings as they jostled for position or chased after friends. Almost all of Berrysville's seven hundred residents had turned out to watch the signing and parade.

Mostly the latter, Den suspected. The scattered scraps of conversation he heard centered around crops and children, not Simes and Sime Centers.

So much for the historic importance of the agreement.

The front of the stage was draped in bunting that formed a canopy over the signing table. In-Territory guests shared the back of the stage with the City Council, their families, and local dignitaries. Later in the day, the shadow of the canopy would shade them, but in the cool morning they were warmed by the sun.

Den sat between Rital and a weathered farmer who introduced himself as Sam Kutchins, president of the Walnut Marketing Board. His blue cap had a decorative patch with "**Berrysville Walnuts**" embroidered over a cartoon of a grinning walnut in running shoes, sunshade, and hat.

Kutchins retrieved a knobby cloth bag from under his chair. It had the same logo, but printed underneath was "**Packed exclusively for the Walnut Marketing Board. Not for resale.**"

"I always bring samples when I attend these events," the farmer confided, picking apart the bag's stitching with his pocketknife. "It makes long-winded speeches more bearable. Want some?" He scooped a double handful of walnuts into the Donor's lap, put the bag in his own, and pulled a nutcracker from his coat pocket.

Den had rushed through breakfast and the snack was welcome. The two passed the nutcracker back and forth as Mayor Mills introduced the dignitaries. The crowd strained to hear, but the chants arguing "Who's it safer to believe? Scripture says all Simes deceive!" drowned out the ceremony.

The mayor glared at a woman in city worker coveralls. "Isobel!" he bellowed loud enough to be heard on the next block. "You said the sound system was working!"

"Turn on the microphone!" the woman shouted back.

Even Sinth's people stopped chanting to laugh. The mayor fumbled with the microphone, then his voice boomed out over the speakers. "Can you hear me now?"

"Yes!" chorused the crowd.

A voice added, "That's the problem, Jon."

Ignoring the heckler, Mayor Mills smiled broadly and started his speech again. "First, a warm welcome to friends and neighbors from Berrysville and Clear Springs, and our distinguished guests from across the border. Today Berrysville becomes be the smallest community in New Washington Territory to have its own Sime Center."

The cheers almost drowned out the boos from the demonstrators.

"I'd also like to welcome our other out-of-town visitors," the mayor said with a grin. "The Chamber of Commerce has asked the City Council to promote tourism. I'm glad our efforts have paid off." When the laughter subsided, he continued more seriously. "Friends, today Berrysville pioneers the most important step in inter-Territorial relations since the First Contract. Consider what our ancestors faced…"

As Mayor Mills began the Gen version of inter-Territorial history, Den noticed Rital's tension. He placed a discreet hand on his cousin's wrist, just below the retainer. *He shouldn't have to cope with this when he's in Need.*

The channel relaxed as Den anticipated their transfer, scheduled for afternoon. *Maybe after last month, he'll finally believe that I can keep up with him.*

Den set his frustration aside before it disturbed Rital.

"…This agreement expands on the alliance our ancestors made with the Tecton to halt the raiding parties of Killer Simes that ravaged our Territory. That historic alliance was formalized in the First Contract…"

The organizers had gone to great lengths to drive that comparison home. The table on which the document would be signed resembled the one pictured in Ordon's famous painting, *First Contract*: the one that graced children's history textbooks on both sides of the border. There were even an old-fashioned inkwell and quill pens. From his perspective, Den noted the "inkwell" was cardboard, the quill pens were moth-eaten, and the scrollwork on the table legs was painted, not carved. *Props from the school's Faith Day pageant?*

There were worse ways to spend a morning than sitting in the spring sunshine munching walnuts, Den decided, as Mayor Mills asked Quess to say a few words.

Over his immaculate Tecton uniform, the older Donor wore a formal, full-length Shaeldor cape, decorated with House rank symbols. The elegant display sparked an appreciative gleam in the eyes of middle-aged farm wives. The rest of the crowd was getting restless, however, so the diplomat limited himself to a few sentences.

Then it was Rital's turn. Den shoved the last walnut into his pocket, brushed shell fragments off his pants, and stood to Escort the channel, the image of a respectable Tecton Donor.

Rital's remarks were even briefer than Quess's. He introduced himself and Den, praised the City Council for their hard work, and expressed his eagerness to get to know the people of Berrysville.

Considering that most of those people have never donated selyn, the Donor reflected, *it's a good thing they don't know what a work-starved channel means by such an invitation!*

With great ceremony, Quess, Rital, Mayor Mills, and the rest of the Berrysville City Council signed the document. To Den's relief, they used modern pens—old-fashioned quills tended to splatter.

Mayor Mills invited his mother, Flora, "…whose efforts brought the Tecton to Berrysville,…" to hold up the document for everyone to see. As the applause died down, Sinth's voice shouted, "It's an abomination! Destroy it!"

With a roar, about half of his followers rushed the stage. However, they lacked the youth, athleticism, and specialized tactics OLD SOKS had developed for pushing through crowds. As Flora tucked the treaty into her blouse for safekeeping, the protestors lost momentum before breaking through, leaving them mingled with the crowd of onlookers in front of the stage.

Above the tumult, a man's voice screamed from the middle of the square. "You'll burn in Hell for this day's work, Sime-lovers! Tell the Devil I sent you!"

Everyone turned to stare at the turmeric-haired man. He had abandoned his sign and stepped up onto a crate. He balanced precariously, waving a cylindrical object.

"Is that a bomb?" the mayor yelped. Rital stiffened in alarm and the dignitaries sprang to their feet.

The crowd shrank from the heckler and Den saw the man grin with fanatical conviction. In his left hand was a lighted candle. The other held the thick pipe Rital had zlinned in his backpack. A short fuse dangled from it. His ginger mustache puffed as he laughed with manic delight.

"This *is* a bomb!" he confirmed. "A preview of where you Sime-kissers will spend eternity!"

"He isn't lying," Rital muttered in Den's ear.

"Calm down," the mayor ordered. "There's no reason to hurt anybody."

Nerina, the most sensitive channel present, was at the back of the in-Territory delegation, blocked from clear zlinning by their nageric haze. Rital, however, had a relatively clear perception of the terrorist over the heads of the milling crowd.

It's Rital's call how we respond, then.

A Tecton channel protected Gen lives at all costs. The obvious solution was for Rital to charge and overpower the turmeric-haired man before he could set off the bomb, but there were too many out-Territory Gens between their would-be rescuers and the danger: Gens who wouldn't know to get out of the way.

"The odds of reaching the fellow in time aren't good, Den," the channel murmured.

"Not to mention the reaction it would spark from the crowd," Den completed the thought.

Eda Seebourgin didn't wait for the channel's decision, but headed toward the steps at the side of the stage.

"Get back with your traitor friends, Seebourgin, or I'll light the fuse right now!" the turmeric-haired man screamed. He waved the candle close to the dangling fuse and the councilwoman returned to her place.

Nerina slipped off the back of the stage, but not even threat of an explosion could keep out-Territory Gens from shying away from a Sime right next to them. The turmeric-haired man spotted the disturbance immediately and threatened again to light his bomb. "Get back, ya slimy snake, or we all go right now!"

Prudently, Nerina returned to the stage.

Rital clenched his fists in frustration.

I don't want to die, Den thought, blocking the chaotic ambient for his cousin. *If he throws the bomb onto the stage, a channel might catch it before it exploded, but there's nowhere safe to throw it!*

Fear was fear. To avoid it, Den was trained to treat a frightening situation as an exercise in logistics. No one here could treat the channels, if any survived the nageric shock of the simultaneous death or injury of so many Gens. *Rital might die of Attrition before a replacement Donor could get here.* Nerina had a slightly better chance; she'd come up short after her inadequate transfer with Den and taken an early transfer from Quess two days ago.

A slim chance for survival was better than none. "Signal the channels to run if he lights the fuse," Den advised his cousin. "If you get away, you'll be healthy enough to heal the survivors."

The channel didn't dignify this suggestion with a response.

The terrorist grinned at the fear on the faces of his intended victims. Enjoying every moment, he cocked his muscular arm, preparing to throw the bomb onto the stage.

"Stop!" boomed Coach Farrow, pushing to the front of the stage. "Derk Scaval, have you forgotten everything I taught you? If you throw that bomb over here, your own teammates will be destroyed with the Simes." He pointed down at the mixed crowd of parade-watching locals and Save Our Kids demonstrators, packed against the front of the stage as they pressed away from the bomb.

Den saw the scowl on the coach's face and stepped to his left to put his own nager between Farrow and Rital.

"'The individual members of a team do not lose if the team achieves victory,'" the turmeric-haired man—whose name was Derk, apparently— quoted. "Save Our Kids is stopping this treaty, one way or another."

From the horrified looks on their faces, the Save Our Kids members in front of the stage hadn't agreed to be the designated casualties.

Farrow shook his head. "Your actions reflect on your team—and on the values for which they are fighting," he ruled, with the authority of many years' experience as a referee. "If you cheat by murdering innocent by-standers, you tell the world that your team can't compete honestly and must be banned from competition."

"He's right!" cried Florence Grieves, who had followed the charge al-most as far as the stage. "If you throw that bomb, you'll wipe out a lot of your teammates in Save Our Kids."

"We all agreed it's better to die than to sell out to the Tecton!" the turmeric-haired man pointed out.

It was obvious that the Save Our Kids members in front of the stage hadn't meant that vow literally.

"*Simes* kill anyone who gets in their way, Derk," Nancy Resher pro-tested from beside Florence Grieves. "We don't!"

"Shut yer mouth, woman!" the orange-haired man ordered. "God calls us to cleanse this place!"

As he slowly moved the candle toward the fuse, several Save Our Kids members who had not charged the stage, and who were therefore safely on the other side of the square, cheered and chanted, "Throw it! Throw it! Throw it!"

Sinth, Den observed, wasn't one of them. He appeared to be struggling with a decision.

Den felt his cousin's hands grip him and gently tried to remove them. He couldn't budge the Sime's hold and a quick glance showed that the other channels were just as stubborn. Even Sumulo had his arm around Kamrin's waist. Abandoning one's Gen to die ran counter to the most basic Sime instincts.

An authoritative voice rang out from the far side of the square. "Derk! I forbid you to do this!" Reverend Sinth decreed, stepping into the clear area around the bomber.

Rital looked at Den in astonishment. "I never thought *he* would try to save us," he whispered.

"He can't afford not to," the Donor realized. "Farrow's right. If he allows one of his followers–his teammates–to murder innocents, it taints the whole team's victory."

Rital zlinned the preacher. "Whatever his reason, he's sincere about stopping that terrorist."

The turmeric-haired man faced his leader. "You've said it many times, Reverend," he stated. "The Scriptures are plain. All Simes must die."

"God rewards those who destroy Simes," Sinth agreed, approaching his errant follower casually, "but there is a time and a place for that. A bomb can't be aimed and contained. If you set it off in this crowd, you will harm far more innocents than evildoers or Simes. Many of your own friends are close enough to be caught in the blast. Will you murder them, too?"

"They will die for a noble cause," the bomber insisted defiantly. "Executing traitors who sell their fellow Gens to the Simes." His glare fixed on the Berrysville city council members.

"The worst sinner may win God's grace through sincere repentance. Will you deny them a chance at salvation?"

"They'd better repent now, bunch of Sime-lovers." Derk spat in contempt, then turned back to the stage, swinging the bomb in clear warning to his chosen victims to remain in place.

"You can't limit the blast to the stage," Sinth argued, advancing a few steps closer behind the turmeric haired man's back. "Most people here just came for the parade."

The reply was a coolly indifferent shrug. "The parade celebrates the first traitorous treaty with the snakes. Then they cheered that abomination of an agreement. They're no innocents."

"What about the children?" the preacher demanded, taking three more careful steps.

"Stand back!" Derk screamed, and Sinth obeyed.

But he took only two steps back and they were small ones.

"It's Scripture, Reverend! 'The sins of the parents are revealed in the changeovers of their children.' The children are condemned by their parents' heresy. What difference if they die now or later?"

"The law…"

"I follow a higher law, God's law, as you claim to do!" the turmeric-haired man screamed. "You yourself called them Gen-runners." He pointed a finger at the banner. "May their deaths send a message to all Sime-loving scum!" He held up the candle to light the dangling fuse.

Den put his hands in his pockets to steady their shaking and discovered a round, hard object. "Distract the lorsh," he murmured to Rital, showing him the walnut.

Rital snatched the nut from his Donor's hand and threw it with a burst of augmentation. The missile sped to its target and, with poetic justice, caught the turmeric-haired man on the cheek as he turned to gloat over his intended victims. The walnut didn't have enough mass to injure, but the vigilante yelped at the sting and his attention shifted to the crowd as he searched for the source of the missile.

It provided Sinth with an opening. *"I forbid you!"* the preacher roared, closing his fist over the hand that held the bomb and pulling the man off the crate. "You'll not destroy *my* holy mission!"

The two men wrestled for possession of the device. During the struggle, they stumbled against the crate and as their arms windmilled, candle flame and fuse met. Sparks flew.

Men who had started forward to help Sinth retreated, shouting "Get down!" The turmeric-haired man tried desperately to throw the bomb before it exploded, but the preacher's melic-enhanced grip clamped his hand firmly to it. In his drug-induced single-mindedness, Sinth didn't seem to notice the sputtering fuse.

Den's own view was abruptly replaced with a close-up of a wooden plank. He grunted as his cousin's full weight landed on his back. Before he could draw breath, the pipe bomb exploded, launching the nails with which it had been packed outward with lethal force.

It wasn't a loud bang. The screams, as hot metal fragments hit living targets, were louder. Particularly the one in his ear.

"Are you hit, Rital?" Den asked anxiously as his cousin rolled off him, limp with shock. The Donor sat up carefully. It didn't hurt, so he focused on Rital.

"Thanks," the channel muttered. "Nothing hit me, but this ambient is hellish. Is any of that pain yours?"

"I'm fine," the Donor replied. "Just a scratch or two."

Reassured that his Donor was unharmed, Rital surveyed the casualties. Between the chaotic ambient and the retainers, he couldn't zlin with diagnostic precision, but he could see.

One glance at the half-charred red lumps on the blackened pavement at the explosion's epicenter told Den that Reverend Sinth and his turmeric-haired follower were beyond help. Indeed, it would take inspired guesswork to determine which pieces belonged to which corpse.

Fortunately, that's not my job. Den fought down nausea and turned away. He couldn't help Rital heal the survivors if he was losing his breakfast.

Sinth and the turmeric-haired man had held the bomb between them and thus absorbed much of the blast. Many people in front of the platform had crouched, placing children behind them for protection and shielding their heads with their arms. These had mostly light injuries. Those who had not responded in time were unconscious or groaning in pain.

With the magnitude of the emergency clear, Den checked his colleagues to determine their available resources. The other channels had also protected their Donors with their own bodies. The renSimes had done the same for their Gen colleagues. There were minor cuts or bruises, but Den saw nothing that would prevent them from working.

The only casualty among the in-Territory delegation was Quess. Not only had the senior Donor been in the more exposed front rank, but Nerina *had* stayed behind when he went forward to sign the agreement and thus could not shield her husband. The diplomat was seated on the absurd "First Contract" table as his wife examined a gash in his left thigh. She couldn't control the bleeding properly while in retainers, of course, but the older Donor wasn't in immediate danger.

Nerina can handle it, once she gets him inside, Den decided. *We equipped the changeover room to care for trauma cases.*

Rital had reached the same conclusion and was looking for a patient of his own.

Preferably one willing to be treated by a Sime, the Donor qualified.

Nearby, Flora Mills was bent over her left hand, from which blood spurted. The treaty she had rescued had fallen out of her blouse onto the stage, where it was collecting spatters of blood.

"Mother!" her son called. He caught her as she crumpled, then spluttered as a splash of blood caught him in the face.

Rital was at Flora's other side in a flash of augmentation, with Den a half second behind. They lowered the unconscious woman safely to the stage, then Mayor Mills called loudly for a medical team.

What does he think we are, a pair of plumbers?

First aid to save a life required no consent. The channel grabbed Flora's left wrist and applied pressure to the artery. The spurting blood slowed to a trickle, but much of the woman's hand was missing, along with three of her fingers. Den put his hand on his cousin's shoulder, knowing that between the ambient and his retainers, the channel couldn't apply a proper backfield to stop the bleeding.

"We could save her easily in-Territory," Rital muttered, "but I can't treat an out-Territory Gen without her consent or the permission of her kin, and certainly not out here." The channel was tensed against the shock of pain and death. He *needed* to heal some of it and if anyone in Berrysville had earned that healing, it was Flora Mills.

Fanned by the light breeze, a stack of smoldering hay bales on the other side of the square suddenly burst into active flames, which quickly spread to the decorative bunting draped over the nearby doorways. There were screams and shouts as the people still trying to push away from the stage ran into those fleeing the new threat. "They're turning into a mob," Rital reported.

"Jules, get everybody organized before somebody gets trampled," Mayor Mills ordered his fellow City Councilman, who reached for the microphone.

"The sound's dead," Tansky reported, tossing the useless microphone back onto the stage.

Mayor Mills scanned the crowded stage until he located the only other person whose voice was loud enough to carry through the noise. "Coach Farrow, will you do the honors?" he asked.

Farrow nodded, then pulled a whistle from his pocket and blew a shrill blast. To Den's surprise, the incipient mob stopped dead in its tracks and everybody turned to look at the stage.

"Now hear this!" Farrow barked. He pointed to various groups as he assigned tasks. "Get the injured over to the doctor's. Put out that fire. Check for anything else that's smoldering. Clean up the mess in the square. Collect any stray children and animals and hold them over there. Get all those things people were using for seats out of the way." As the rapid-fire orders continued, the crowd sorted itself into teams to tackle each task, just as they had in the gymnasium so many months before—and with the same complete disregard for political opinion. The surviving Save Our Kids demonstrators worked side by side with the Rational Deists and those Berrysville citizens who had simply come to see the parade.

Before Den could attract the Mayor's attention to ask permission to treat Flora, they were interrupted.

"Damn, that looks nasty!" an all-too-familiar voice swore in English. A black physician's bag landed on the stage with a solid *thunk* and Dr. Lennard knelt on Flora's other side. "She's going into shock," he observed. "I'm sure glad you channels are here; I can't take care of all these folks by myself."

Jon Mills stared at his mother's waxy-pale face, his fellow City Councilors gathered behind him, at a loss without obvious tasks to do. At the young physician's remark, the mayor straightened with a jerk. "Of course! That emergency assistance clause means we don't have to wait for help from Clear Springs."

"Point of order," Mont Viller objected, picking up the blood-spattered agreement and waving it. "Paragraph thirty-seven requires an official request from the City Council to invoke that clause."

"An official request?" the mayor repeated. "Nothing easier!" He waved his colleagues closer. "This meeting of the Berrysville City Council will now come to order," he said rapidly. "I move that we dispense with old business, and all that nonsense."

"Seconded!" Jules Tansky called.

"All in favor?"

"Aye!" the councilors chorused.

"Good," Mayor Mills said. "I move that the City Council request emergency medical assistance from the Tecton, in the person of Hajene Madz here and his friends."

"Seconded!" Tansky called again.

"All in favor?"

"Aye!" the others repeated.

"Passed unanimously," the mayor declared. "Meeting adjourned, and I wish they were all that short." He turned back to Rital. "There's your official request, Hajene. Now get your people organized and help my mother!"

Rital scooped up his patient and carried her toward the Community Clinic and its insulated Sime Center wing. Den directed the other channels and Donors to follow. Since Nerina had long since carried Quess inside for treatment, there was no one of sufficient rank to dispute his orders.

Not that the channels would object.

Den assigned the unpaired Donor, a TN-3 named Dontha, to organize the non-technical staff. Then he sprinted after his cousin. By the time he caught up, Rital had installed Flora on the changeover ward's treatment bed and was struggling with his retainers.

"Let me help," Den offered. With skill born of long practice, he freed his cousin's Need-swollen forearms from the manacles that had just compressed them under Flora Mills' weight. The channel grunted in relief and extended his laterals over Flora's ruined hand to apply a backfield.

The Donor slipped automatically into support mode. Then, remembering that he couldn't trust his habits, he brought his attention sharply back to his field control. To his surprise and joy, he discovered that he'd finally won his long struggle against his outdated reflexes. His automatic response had been the proper one.

For the first time in months, it wasn't taking all Den's attention just to keep his fieldwork from slipping. Freed from that burden, he turned his attention to Rital's work on the shredded hand. By anticipating the minute changes in the channel's field as he shifted his focused concentration from one patch of pulped tissue to the next, the Donor could respond as they occurred instead of half a beat behind.

"Keep that up and I'll save what's left of this hand before I have to bring Flora out of shock," Rital told him.

When the channel was satisfied that the blood clots sealing the damaged hand would hold, he moved his laterals to the back of Flora's neck and stabilized her blood pressure. Her clammy skin warmed as her circulation improved, but she remained unconscious.

"I was afraid of that," Rital said, tentacles knotting in frustration. "It isn't just shock keeping her unconscious. She's lost so much blood, her circulatory system is on the edge of collapse."

"If she dies under our care, there will be trouble."

"I know, Den. Only her response to my Need is keeping her alive. Don't worry, I won't tell the out-Territory Gens *that* part of it," he added sardonically.

"Good, because Dr. Lennard's making a fuss in the hall."

"Let him in," Rital said with a sigh. "He can bear witness that Flora's survived this long. Just block his nager and let me support her."

"Everything's more or less under control, so I thought I'd check on Miz Mills," the doctor explained. "The mayor's pacing holes in my nice new carpets." When Lennard saw the improvement in their patient's hand, his jaw dropped. "That's amazing!" he crowed, dancing a little jig.

"She's not out of danger," Den warned. "She'll require a channel's support until she's replaced some of the lost blood, or her circulation will collapse."

"Low blood volume?" Dr. Lennard asked. "Why, *that's* not a problem." He poked his head out the door and yelled incomprehensible orders. "I'd've suggested a transfusion outside," he told Den with a hurt puppy look, "but I didn't know you could stop the bleeding so neatly and there's no point pumping blood into a patient who's pumping it out again twice as fast."

When Den had mentally translated that, he swallowed, fighting to prevent his nausea from affecting Rital. He'd heard of the gruesome out-Territory practice of treating blood loss with infusions of selyn-dead blood dripped directly into the poor victim's veins. Such casual mention of the practice was horrifying.

Rital can't help Flora if his Donor is throwing up, he reminded himself. From his sudden pallor, the channel was having enough trouble overcoming his own reaction.

Dr. Lennard's nurse arrived with a collection of needles and tubes worthy of a torturer. She worked with professional dispatch, ignoring Den and even Rital. Watching the woman calmly stab her needle into a vein on their patient's uninjured arm was horrifying, but at least the unconscious Flora would not feel it, although   Rital would. After half the dead blood had dripped into her vein, he had to admit their patient looked better.

I don't think Quess and Nerina had this *in mind when they approved that "mutual aid" clause.*

With Flora out of immediate danger, Rital was free to help other victims. While they were occupied, Dontha had been managing triage. The other in-Territory staff were providing ice, sterile pads, and other stopgap measures to those waiting to be treated.

Dr. Lennard's staff was also doing triage, but they had different priorities. "They're obsessed with shock," Dontha complained, "but they want to just bandage wounds and send people home without healing them first."

The less severely injured would have to wait hours to see Dr. Lennard. A few were uncomfortable or bored enough to let a channel treat them. When the initial patients emerged unscathed and out of pain, others followed, particularly when they learned that the channels healed for free. Even Sumulo pitched in and, with weeks of inactivity to inspire proper behavior, treated his patients with exaggerated gentleness.

The groans and complaints of the casualties mixed with the bilingual babble of the staff, as the in-Territory personnel tried make sense of Dr. Lennard's patient evaluation forms and the equally strange devices the nurses used to measure—whatever it was they were measuring. The channels were running out of medications and supplies, but could still manage the fields.

Den and Rital commandeered an insulated collecting room and treated a parade of burns, cuts, and punctures, with an occasional sprain for variety. Most of the injuries were minor, but the out-Territory Gens found it difficult to relax so the channel could work.

It's just as well most don't know the purpose of that transfer lounge they're sitting on, the Donor concluded.

After an hour and a half of steady work, Den insisted that his cousin take a break. "The Seconds and Thirds have already had several," he pointed out.

The Donor escorted his cousin to the break room and found him a cup of tea. Unable to settle down, the channel sent Den for news of Quess's condition. "Nerina is treating the children, so he can't be in danger, but I'd like more details."

Den found Quess in Dr. Lennard's office, bandaged leg elevated with folded blankets. His ruined trousers had been replaced with wrinkled, pea-green sweatpants that clashed madly with the diplomat's usual sartorial choices.

"Sosu Den, come in," the older Donor invited. "Nerina says I'll limp for a while, but I can give her transfer next month as scheduled." He cocked his head. "I'm thinking of indulging in an elegant walking stick. Maybe black walnut, with a brass knob."

"Rital will be relieved," Den admitted. "Finding an emergency replacement for a high-rated First Order Donor isn't easy at any time. Just after the holidays, it's next to impossible."

From down the hall came a yelp of pain, soothed by professional reassurance.

"I'm told the mayor asked us for help?" Quess asked. When Den nodded, he continued, "You realize, I hope, that today's agreement isn't binding until ratified by both legislatures, so you're on shaky legal ground? Judging by the results, though, your cousin's decision was correct."

"After you threatened my out-Territory license for how I handled Save Our Kids, I'd expect you to follow the letter of the law."

"I suppose I deserve that," the older Donor admitted with a wry smile. "It may surprise you to hear this, Den, but I've done my share of questionable things. However, it takes sound judgment to know *when* to ignore the rules." He inspected the younger Donor closely. "Last year, you were taking crazy chances and not caring for the consequences. I think perhaps you've gained the maturity to know when to follow the rules and when to ignore them."

"Thanks," Den said. "I think," he muttered as he rejoined his cousin.

By evening, the waiting room was finally empty. Even the Save Our Kids members who insisted on waiting for Dr. Lennard had been treated. Thanks to the blood and Rital's Need-strengthened nageric support, Flora regained consciousness long enough to swallow a few sips of water. After that, Den insisted that his cousin let Nerina monitor those patients who could not be sent home.

He enticed his channel into their now-empty collection room and shut the door. Despite his Need, Rital relaxed as the polycarbonate-and-rust insulation extinguished all fields but his own and his Donor's. He sipped gratefully at the mug of tea Den handed him.

"Shen, what a day!" he groaned, extending his handling tentacles to relieve the pressure on his swollen ronaplin glands. He moaned with pleasure as Den massaged the tension from his shoulders, then stiffened as the

Donor began to work down his arms. "Don't, Den," he warned. "I'm raising intil already and it's a long way back to Clear Springs."

"Why wait?" the Donor asked, continuing his ministrations. "The insulation's good here and you're four hours overdue."

"I know that." Rital edged away, although to Den's practiced eye, he wasn't trying very hard to escape. "My projection of Hard Need let me save what's left of Flora's hand—"

"—but even if you were in Attrition, you couldn't heal her overnight," Den interrupted. "Nerina is monitoring Flora. The waiting room is clear and Quess is sleeping. You've fulfilled your responsibilities to others, Cousin. Now it's time to look after yourself. And me," he added, insinuating his hands between his cousin's tentacles.

"My control isn't very good, just now," Rital objected weakly, as his laterals extended, dripping with ronaplin.

"Good," the Donor said. "You don't require it. Didn't you read Nerina's report? If we went into test just now, I might rate a few points higher than you."

"Well…"

Den looked the channel in the eye. "Fair warning, cousin," he said. "If I catch you holding back this time, even a little, I'll grab control so fast it'll make your head spin. So, behave yourself!"

The day, and the month, had taken a heavy toll. The Donor found himself *feeling*, as never before, exactly what speed his cousin craved…and how much slower he was drawing.

Den decreased his resistance, speeding the selyn flow, and met his cousin's Need with his own long-frustrated desire, daring the channel to draw faster. He felt the moment Rital gave in to Sime instinct.

The flow jumped to the speed his cousin had used on that day, months before, when the channel had scorched him. This time, the Donor met his cousin's demand easily, sending waves of joy through them both.

When Rital couldn't accept one more dynopter, he dismantled the contact slowly, staring at Den in disbelief.

The Donor grinned. "Remind me to threaten you more often, cousin!"

EPILOG

On the first day of summer, Bethany Sinth and Rob Lifton were married in the main lobby of the Clear Springs Sime Center. Thaddus Webber presided with such aplomb, a casual onlooker would never guess that the entire wedding ceremony had been hastily reorganized after Sinth's replacement at the Conservative Congregation refused to let the bride's grandmother set foot in his church.

"Of course Thaddus got them through it," Professor Ildun assured Den and Rital at the reception, as he kept a nervous eye on his son, Raymond. "Strictly speaking, there's no such thing as *the* Rational Deist wedding ceremony. Rational Deists come from many backgrounds and like everyone else, we get married for all sorts of reasons. How could one ceremony or one set of vows fit everyone?"

I should have guessed, Den thought.

"Thaddus helps each couple design a ceremony that validates their personal decision to marry," Ildun continued. "They rework the vows until both parties feel they are binding. I've often thought the unusual stability of Rational Deist marriages is because we make each couple agree on their expectations of each other. The psychological implications…"

"Please excuse us," Rital apologized, edging away. "We haven't paid our respects to the groom's family." He grabbed his unresisting Donor's elbow and guided him through the crowd.

"You should know better than to get him started," the channel scolded affectionately.

The mother and grandfather of the groom were barely visible to Gen eyes, half hidden behind a potted plant too large to remove from the room. Carla Lifton wept into a handkerchief. "I can't help it," she told her father as he tried to comfort her. "I don't feel my boy is properly married after that ceremony, all about their duties and responsibilities to each other, but nothing about duty to God and Church. It's bad enough you joined the Deists, but for my little boy to leave the Church, forsaking God…" She choked on a sob.

"Give the boy some credit, Carla," Mr. Duncan advised. "Rob and Bethany got married here because your spineless new minister wouldn't perform the ceremony. They haven't changed their religious beliefs any more than I have."

Carla looked up at her father, reddened eyes wide with hope. "They haven't? *You* haven't?"

"Carla, my love," Mr. Duncan said with a smile, "the Rational Deists wouldn't dream of making me accept a particular concept of god as a condition for joining their congregation. After all, a good third of their membership doesn't believe in any god at all."

"Oh!" Overcome with joy, Carla hugged her father.

Mr. Duncan returned the hug, nodding a greeting to the channel and Donor over her shoulder. When she let him go, he patted her gently. "My faith is a strong as it ever was. Now, go wash your face. We should be circulating among the guests."

Carla nodded and hastened off. When she was out of sight, Mr. Duncan winked broadly at Den and Rital. "Of course, my faith never was strong enough that you'd notice," he commented. "I went to Conservative Congregation services because my late wife insisted."

"There are worse reasons for joining a church," Den assured him.

"I told myself that for forty-three years, whenever I listened to some fool like Reverend Sinth spout nonsense," Mr. Duncan said. "She's not around to object anymore, so now I can please myself." He fixed Rital with a stern glare. "So, tell me how Flora's *really* doing. She says she's fine, but she'd say that, no matter what."

"Flora's still weak," the channel admitted, "and it will take time to adjust to losing three fingers, but I expect a complete recovery. Fortunately, she has a good sense of humor."

Mr. Duncan chuckled. "That she does," he agreed. "The last time I visited her, she told me that when she agreed to give a hand with the signing, she didn't mean it so literally." He shook his head in disbelief. "She's quite a woman."

The admiring gleam in the old man's eyes hinted that his interest in the widowed Flora was more than casual, even if he didn't know it yet. *They'd make quite a pair,* the Donor thought. *Though I wouldn't want to get between them when they argue!*

Den and Rital next sought out Quess and Nerina. Bethany's grandparents were seated at an isolated table, where the channel's tentacles wouldn't disturb the more timid out-Territory guests.

"Things seem to be going smoothly, despite the last-minute changes," Rital complimented them, aware of how much work Bethany's grandparents had done to achieve that.

"I was expecting real trouble, frankly," Nerina admitted. "Many of the organizers and guests have spent the past several years fighting each other, after all. However, everybody worked smoothly together to accomplish their assigned tasks. I've never seen anything like it."

"I have," Den said. "At Berrysville, when Coach Farrow stopped a panicked mob in its tracks by assigning tasks."

"That's just human nature, isn't it?" Quess observed. "To save lives, you temporarily forget even large differences. That was the basis of the alliance that won the Unity War."

"Den and I also saw it happen when all there was to save was the floor of the school gymnasium!" Rital objected. He and his cousin took turns describing the aftermath of Raymond's unauthorized redecoration of the gymnasium scoreboard.

"It's teamwork," Den realized. "Out-Territory Gens spend years learning how to work together toward accomplishing a specific goal or task. Personal disagreements, preferences, or even aptitudes aren't allowed to get in the way, until the task is done. It stifles creativity and innovation, but if Coach Farrow is correct, it was a primary reason why Gen troops often held their own against raiding Simes."

"The Tecton could use some of that attitude," Quess admitted. "I've sat through far too many meetings watching my colleagues squabble about issues that weren't related to the task at hand."

"Speaking of Tecton politics, it's only three weeks since Rob and Bethany picked this date for their wedding," Den observed. "Who did you bribe, blackmail or threaten, to get time off on such short notice?"

Quess laughed. "Bethany's children are likely to be channels if they're Sime, or Donor material if they Establish. It's in the Tecton's best interest for us to maintain a close relationship with our granddaughter."

"Speaking of Bethany's children, Rital," Nerina said, "I had a long talk with her and Rob about the extra risk she'll have in childbirth. They plan to ask you or Tyvi to monitor any pregnancy. If it's a channel, Bethany has agreed to stay in-Territory until the baby's born." She smiled in relief. "We won't lose Bethany to out-Territory medical incompetence, the way we lost our Liss."

"And our great-grandchildren will grow up knowing they have a home with us, if they require one," Quess added with satisfaction. "We'll see Liss's descendants pledge Shaeldor yet."

The bride and groom were blissfully unaware of Shaeldor's agenda regarding their offspring. Den and Rital found Bethany showing her new sister-in-law the steps of Nivet Territory's newest dance craze, which was weird enough that even Den had hesitated to attempt it. Annie was doing a creditable job of imitating the complicated steps, although she came dangerously close to crossing her feet the wrong way and tripping.

No wonder Simes discourage Gens from learning it.

Rob was watching his sister and new wife with a look of infatuated pride. "Sosu Milnan, Hajene Madz," he greeted them. "Want to show us how those steps are supposed to go?"

Rital looked appalled and Den chuckled. "Maybe later. Have you two settled on a place to live?"

The young Gen nodded. "We found a nice house in Oak Ridge, much larger than anything we could afford in Clear Springs. Bethany's trust fund made a good down payment and if we both keep donating selyn, that will cover the mortgage and taxes. I've got enough saved to support us until we can find work, so we'll do well."

"Oak Ridge?" Rital asked. "That's pretty remote."

Rob shrugged. "It's about perfect, close enough that we can get to Clear Springs when we want and far enough away to discourage unwanted visitors. It's small, but we both want to get away from the hassles that come with a Sime Center, if you'll forgive my saying so. Two years living both sides of that fight is enough."

"You can escape in Oak Ridge for a while," Den agreed. "The Oak Ridge Rational Deists have lost interest in hosting a mobile Sime Center. Their efforts are going into a lawsuit against that chemical plant that tried to dump waste into their reservoir."

The young Gen grinned. "I bet that company fired the manager who scheduled the dump for the first day of trout season!"

* * * *

Social obligations fulfilled, Den slipped down to the Sime Center's basement. He found Branlee grinding yellow, green, and blue crystals to powder in a series of mortars.

"You're missing the party," he said, peering over the graduate student's shoulders. "What is that for?"

"Rust isn't the only available metallic compound," Branlee explained. "I thought I'd test a few others to see if they provide comparable insulation. To offer our customers a range of colors."

"Good thinking," Den approved. "Makes the customers happy while implying that the polycarbonate provides the insulation."

He drifted over to the shelf on which the walnut-oil battery sat, still unspoiled thanks to Alyce's Bordo mix. "It's more important than ever to boost sales, and our profits. Now that we have a battery light enough to mount on a flyer, we've got an even bigger challenge: designing a motor for it to power. It's got to be small," Den sketched out the desired dimensions, "light enough to carry, but strong enough to pull a flyer through the air. It could take years, but—"

Branlee abruptly left the bench and started rummaging through the pile of random junk he'd salvaged from Professor Fibes's lab.

"Aha!" The graduate student held up a mostly ceramic object. "We'd have to convert it to run on selyn instead of electricity, but do you mean something like this? It used to run a centrifuge."

* * * *

Back upstairs, the party was in full swing. Branlee filled a plate from the buffet while Den set off in search of his cousin. He found the channel in the garden, hiding from the commotion.

"What's got you so excited, cousin?" the channel asked, looking up from the rosebush he was admiring.

"Motors!" Den answered. "Because out-Territory cities use insanely expensive electrical power grids, they're far more concerned with efficiency than we are, with our cheap orgonics systems."

"That's nice," Rital said.

Den tried again. "Cousin, they make motors light enough for Branlee to lift easily, but powerful enough to operate heavy equipment."

"Good for them?" the clearly baffled channel guessed.

Den rolled his eyes at such cluelessness. "If we can convert such a motor to run off the walnut oil selyn battery—or better yet, use it as a starting point to design a purpose-made, patentable, selyn-powered motor—we will have a system lightweight and powerful enough for a piloted flyer. The rest is just tinkering with the design. Eddina's dream will be realized, Rital. In a few years, not decades!"

The channel's eyes widened. "That's a huge step toward rebuilding the technological civilization the Ancients had."

Den nodded. "And if that civilization is powered by selyn, not irreplaceable fossilized hydrocarbons, we can go even farther than the Ancients. They went to the moon; we'll go to the stars."

They settled on a bench under the mixed orchard of cherry, peach, and walnut trees, dreaming of the wonders the future would bring. Their silence was comfortable, with no unsettled differences festering between them.

It was definitely worth the time and effort to bring you around, cousin, Den thought smugly.

"You know," Rital remarked at last, "life in Clear Springs is very different without Reverend Sinth and his people. It's almost like being in-Territory."

"I know," the Donor agreed. "I was two minutes late for our Collectorium shift last week, because there's no more chanting to provide a ten-minute warning."

They paused to watch a fledgling blue jay make an awkward landing beneath a walnut tree. It scolded them impudently, then pecked at one of last year's nuts.

"I'd never have guessed Save Our Kids would just dissolve," the channel said, "after its members devoted so many years to opposing us."

"They lost in Clear Springs. When even a bomb didn't work in Berrysville…" Den shrugged.

"The surviving members of Save Our Kids claim that turmeric-haired fanatic wasn't a member and they had nothing to do with his criminal actions," Rital reminded his cousin.

"I know," the Donor said. "It might even be true. Reverend Sinth's attempt to stop him supports that. On the other hand, that wasn't the first time the fellow acted up at one of their demonstrations. When you issue an open invitation to violence, someone's going to take you up on it. It doesn't require a formal conspiracy."

Cocking its head for a closer inspection, the young blue jay decided that the walnut was acceptable. Snatching up its prize, the fledgling fluttered awkwardly into the bushes to eat it in safety.

"Whether or not Save Our Kids was involved, they've been judged guilty in the court of public opinion," Rital observed.

"I understand why. They let that unstable paranoid join their demonstrations and cheered every threat he made. They helped him attack Principal Buchan's truck and followed him to destroy the Oak Ridge City Hall. Some yelled encouragement when he threatened to throw his bomb." Den shook his head. "Of course people blame Save Our Kids, particularly when there was nothing left of the *real* culprit to prosecute. It'll be a long time before they're welcome in Berrysville, or Clear Springs, either."

A spectral rapping from the bushes presaged doom for the anti-Sime group, or perhaps only for the walnut.

"Still, moving the entire local membership to Clearston is a drastic solution."

"It's the only way they have a future," the Donor decided, remembering Arth's diagram. "The mean here has shifted too far away from them. The only way they can live as if the First Contract never happened, and transmit that culture to their children, is to move to a town where the Tecton has no presence or influence."

"I suppose that's true." Rital watched the blue jay emerge to snatch another walnut, then stood. "We've been gone long enough," he said, holding out his hand. "People will wonder where we are."

"You're right." Den put his hand in the channel's and let himself be pulled to his feet. "It should be an interesting evening. I understand that in- and out-Territory bands will play alternate sets so, as Bethany put it, 'everyone can make fools of themselves with unfamiliar dances.'"

As his cousin groaned, the Donor nimbly assayed a few steps of the dance Bethany and Annie had been practicing. The fledgling jay was startled into flight, pumping frantically to remain airborne on half-grown feathers.

"You're lucky," Rital complained peevishly. "People *expect* Gens to trip over their own feet but if Simes stumble, we're never allowed to live it down."

Den threw back his head and laughed. "Well, cousin, now that Clear Springs has accepted us, we'll have to put up with their strange customs, especially the ones that acknowledge our common past and affirm our future. They'll do the same for our customs and complain just as loudly. Once our efficient selyn batteries go into large-scale production, an expanded train system and powered flight will shorten travel distances. Maybe our kids and theirs will finally find a way to live together."

"Well, if you put it that way…" Rital mustered a sickly grin. "Let's join the dancing."

The blue jay squawked in triumph from a lofty perch on top of the walnut tree. The branch bent under the weight of the bird, the lush summer leaves, and the growing, healthy fruit. Cheerful scolding followed the cousins as they returned, side by side, to celebrate the future they had built with their neighbors.

ABOUT THE AUTHORS

MARY LOU MENDUM

Mary Lou Mendum moved to Davis, California, for graduate school and never got around to leaving. After several postdocs resulting in academic publications in subjects as diverse as grape genealogy, walnut tissue culture, and food poisoning bacteria, she found a niche editing plant science journal articles. She has been writing Sime~Gen science fiction for fun since the 1980s.

JEAN LORRAH

Jean Lorrah lives in Kentucky, with a small menagerie. Currently her furry family consists of cats Splotch (therapy cat) and Blue (feral cat turned lap cat), and dogs Bianca (therapy dog now doing scent training) and Fancy (diva and drama queen). All her pets are rescues, and all are wonderful.

Jean is now retired from teaching, but she has an extremely busy life of pet therapy, taking courses in subjects far from her own area of expertise, and of course writing.

JACQUELINE LICHTENBERG

An active science fiction fan since Seventh Grade, I created the Sime~Gen Universe when I was 10-15 years old. When I was 25 and a new mother, I sold the first story to be published written in this universe. It is *Operation High Time*, and was bought by Fred Pohl, who later also bought my first non-fiction book, *Star Trek Lives!* I was a *Star Trek* fan before there was a *Star Trek* fandom because *Star Trek* flung my own visions onto the TV Screen.

As I was learning to write, practicing the craft by writing *Star Trek* stories set in my Kraith Universe (now posted online for free reading at simegen.com/fandom/startrek/) I was also writing Sime~Gen novels for the traditional publishing market. *Star Trek* fans began writing stories in my Kraith Universe, and for a few years there was not an issue of a *Star Trek* fanzine that did not have a Kraith story or discussion in it. By managing the 50 or so creative contributors to Kraith, I learned how to integrate different visions into a master-plan. I used that practice to incorporate Jean Lorrah's vision of one of my characters, Rimon Farris, into the Sime~Gen Universe vision.

This was easy because Jean, too, is a *Star Trek* fan and fanzine writer whose *Night of the Twin Moons* is as famous as Kraith. Jean went on to sell a number of *Star Trek* novels for the paperback market, and as the Sime~Gen universe grew, we became partners and Incorporated to manage the Sime~Gen franchise.

We have always planned to add more writers to the professionally published series, and were delighted with the publisher's request for an anthology (Sime~Gen #13). We have many plans for the future, so keep in touch via Facebook.